THE WORLD OF THE TRAVELING CARNIVAL?

I t's a leftover of a bygone era, a curiosity lurking on the outskirts of town. It's a place of contradictions, where the bright lights mask the peeling paint and a carnie in greasy overalls slinks away while the barker enraptures rubes with his seductive call. Here, one must remain alert and learn the unwritten rules before it's too late. To beat the carnival, one had better have either a whole lot of luck or a whole lot of guns—or maybe some magic of one's own.

Featuring stories grotesque and comical, outrageous and action-packed, *Carniepunk* is the first anthology to channel the energy and attitude of urban fantasy into the carnival's bizarre world of creaking machinery, twisted myths, and vivid new magic.

CARNIEPUNK

A collection of riveting stories from

RACHEL CAINE   DELILAH S. DAWSON

JENNIFER ESTEP   KELLY GAY   KEVIN HEARNE   MARK HENRY

HILLARY JACQUES   JACKIE KESSLER   SEANAN McGUIRE

KELLY MEDING   ALLISON PANG   NICOLE D. PEELER

ROB THURMAN   JAYE WELLS

CARNIEPUNK

A collection of riveting stories from

**RACHEL CAINE   DELILAH S. DAWSON   JENNIFER ESTEP
KELLY GAY   KEVIN HEARNE   MARK HENRY
HILLARY JACQUES   JACKIE KESSLER   SEANAN McGUIRE
KELLY MEDING   ALLISON PANG   NICOLE D. PEELER
ROB THURMAN   JAYE WELLS**

Gallery Books

New York   London   Toronto   Sydney   New Delhi

G

Gallery Books
A Division of Simon & Schuster, Inc.
1230 Avenue of the Americas
New York, NY 10020

First Gallery Books trade paperback edition July 2013

GALLERY BOOKS and colophon are registered trademarks of Simon & Schuster, Inc.

For information about special discounts for bulk purchases,
please contact Simon & Schuster Special Sales at 1-866-506-1949
or business@simonandschuster.com.

The Simon & Schuster Speakers Bureau can bring authors to your live event. For more information or to book an event, contact the Simon & Schuster Speakers Bureau at 1-866-248-3049 or visit our website at www.simonspeakers.com.

Designed by Davina Mock-Maniscalco

Manufactured in the United States of America

10   9   8   7   6   5   4   3   2   1

ISBN 978-1-4767-1415-8
ISBN 978-1-4767-1433-2 (ebook)

CONTENTS

"Painted Love"

Rob Thurman

Love is a bitch.

There's no getting around it.

But I'll get to that later.

First . . . first came Bartholomew.

On any given day someone can be a hundred different people. I'm not talking Sybil here, and no voices in the head, but no one is singular within themselves. They're good . . . help a little old lady with her groceries. They're bad . . . steal a magazine from a newsstand. Sometimes they're smart, sometimes stupid. Sometimes loving as they give their child a kiss on the cheek and murderous in the next minute when they jack a car and kill a man in the process. People are people. Hateful and peaceful. Content and miserable. Honest and deceitful. With all of that inside fighting for control every minute of the day, it's a wonder everybody's not banging their heads against the wall. And those around you—even you yourself—aren't ever quite sure what they're going to get from moment to moment.

I knew that just like I knew from watching him that Bartholomew was nothing like that—the exception that proved the rule. Bartholomew wasn't at war with himself or his darker emotions. With Bartholomew it was all about Bartholomew. What he wanted and what he'd do to get it. Love wasn't a bitch to him, because he loved himself inside and out.

All the best sociopaths do.

It wasn't just my luck to hook up with one—it was an occupational hazard. I'd seen more of the world than most and it wasn't by drifting. I always had a plan. I'd long found that the best way to travel was to find someone who was going somewhere you wanted to be, stick with them, and keep your mouth shut. You'd be surprised how little they minded, mostly because if you picked the right ones, they were entirely self-centered. They were generally puzzled to one day realize they'd picked up a buddy, wonder how you'd slithered in under their radar and become a fixture in their lives. But that's another thing about people: they didn't want to ask too many questions. Some people didn't like to look stupid, some people didn't like to make waves, and some people—the smartest people—generally didn't *want* to know the answer.

And the ones like Bartholomew—they ultimately couldn't bring themselves to believe someone had put one over on them. After all, that's what *they* did, not what was done to them.

I was good at it, what I did. Maybe you could say I used people, but I did it out of harmless curiosity. My talent for hanging around by blending into the background was useful, but I didn't put it to the same use Bartholomew did his. He worked at a carnival, which was what had interested me in the beginning. I'd seen a lot of things as I made my way around the world, and a carnival was more or less next on my list. I came across Bart on a week away, whoring and drinking mostly, heard his glib stories about where he worked, and there found my opportunity.

His ego was my ticket to ride.

When he returned to the carnival with me tagging along, I saw his work. I don't mean him giving away stuffed prizes or running a few rides or ushering people into a mirrored maze, although he did do all those things. Nope, Bart's true occupation was hurting people. Sometimes for entertainment, sometimes for profit, but always with the zeal you find in those who truly love their jobs.

Bart . . . he couldn't get enough of his job.

Not that it was my problem. I wanted to see what the life in a carnival was like, and that's what I would do. If Bart liked to play mind games with gullible people, it was their fault that they weren't a little sharper, now, wasn't it? Or at the very least it wasn't *my* fault. I was just along for the ride. Speaking of . . .

His carnival was one helluva ride.

It had been settled for two weeks in one small scrubby field on long-bladed grass that cut like knives, and spectators' feet had stomped its grounds down into dry, pitted dirt. There was a Ferris wheel that made the most god-awful sound as it creaked up and around. It was the groan and rattle of a dragon's dying breath—the last dragon in the darkest of ages, its final breath heated by fire and coppery with sacrificial blood somehow caught and bottled to run some unimaginable, infernal machine. Only instead of all that, it ended up wheezing its way through a garishly lit wheel that, instead of grinding their bones to dust, spun screaming children along in paroxysms of delight. That dead dragon was probably embarrassed by it all.

I liked it.

Then there was the carousel. If you've ever read any book, seen any movie, heard any carnie tale, you know carousels are where the very best and worst things happen. Depending on which way you spin, depending on what animal you choose to ride, Fate either kisses you on the lips or slits your throat. I loved those stories, because they got it right. That's exactly how fate was: capricious as fuck. She would ignore the biggest decision in a person's life yet gleefully wipe your slate in a fatal do-over on something as innocent and simple as a merry-go-round.

Perched proudly upon it was one particularly shifty-looking red-and-black-striped tiger with faceted red glass eyes that glittered like bloody tears. I wondered where he'd take you if you climbed in his saddle. I doubted it was Disneyland.

The maze of mirrors: now, that was creepy, flat-out. If you looked just the right way, took the fastest glimpse over your shoulder, you could see your reflections turn to shadowed doppelgängers with sharp teeth, hungry smiles, shadowed holes for eyes, and taloned hands pushing against the glass that locked them away. Hardly anyone did, though, look just right. But I did, each time grinning and giving a friendly wave to my predatory images across a hundred gleaming surfaces. The clawed hands waved back and, blinking in curiosity, the eyes of soot and silver would give me a wink. *You caught us. Point to you.*

I wasn't superstitious and, no, not crazy. I'd traveled the world. I kept my eyes open and I'd seen things. Boring things, astounding ones, and everything in between. What I saw in the carnival was nothing unbelievable. It was more of a pitcher plant where careless flies were caught in the sticky nectar and slowly slid down to be devoured by digestive juices. If you weren't careless, you'd be fine. If you were careless . . . hey, carnivals weren't the only thing in the world that would eat you. In fact, after several days of following Bart through the maze of booths and rides, I'd come to the conclusion that carnivals weren't built. They grew. They accumulated, like a feast of flies on a hidden carcass. One day there was an empty field, the next the carnival bloomed like an ebony poppy. Eventually people—and things—came, populated it, and there you go.

A slow-moving predator came to life.

Some people were carnival people. They knew the carnival and the carnival knew them. They belonged. They were black poppies, too, only on a smaller scale.

Others were just people: good, bad, and indifferent, but all of them blind. They did the work, though, and the carnival needed them. They weren't the careless type, living the nomadic life, and they survived. I wondered what it was like to be blind like them. I'd seen a good deal of the world, but even with my first step, I'd always been able to see.

"Bart, do you have change for a fifty? Oh, look at your new friend. He's cute." The girl smiled at me. Becca? Yeah, Becca was her name. I'd heard it in passing the day before. She worked the psychic booth with her sister, and if she was older than fourteen, I'd need to see a birth certificate as proof.

I tried hard not to smirk back at her smile. Hey, I *was* cute. I worked on being cute. People, even self-centered, oblivious, or gullible people, didn't want someone with serial killer vibes following them around.

Bart smiled back at her, so friendly and affable that manufactured goodwill oozed out of his pores. "Doodle? He's all right. He hitched up with me on vacation. I thought I'd show him the sights."

It was a joke to him. Bart's kind didn't do anything for anybody, but Becca liked me, and Bart . . . Bart liked underage girls. And underage boys. Vulnerable women. People humiliated and naked, bound in chains. And that was only the top layer of porn stuffed in his footlocker. I didn't want to know what the second, third, or fourth layer showed.

"Change for a fifty, yeah? Anything for you, sweetheart."

Becca was young, with long waves of hair dyed cotton candy lavender, round blue eyes, small white teeth that showed when she laughed, and exactly five freckles spread across her nose like a spray of cinnamon chips on a Christmas cookie. Wearing a long, filmy green dress, all the better to look psychic and ethereal, she reminded me of a mermaid curled happily on a rock counting flying fish. She looked innocent and sweet and oh-so-gullible.

A combination Bart absolutely could not pass up.

Of course, sociopaths with questionable taste in porn weren't always as smart as they thought they were. There was a gleam in Becca's blue eyes that said she wasn't nearly as gullible as Bart thought. And if it hadn't been for me, his new pal, I doubt he'd have seen even a smile from her.

I hadn't run into the problem of being too cute before. Cute was harmless, cute was safe, and cute let me hang around as long as I liked. Unfortunately, this time it was helping out a predatory dick, and that annoyed me. As I'd thought before, whatever games Bart played weren't my problem. I was a traveler. I couldn't get bogged down by people's troubles. There were always going to be problems, and there were always going to be Barts in the world. I couldn't change that.

But I didn't like being used as bait in a trap. That's all. I just didn't like it.

Maybe Bart would behave himself and in a few weeks I'd be gone. Off to someplace new with someone hopefully somewhat less problematically evil than good old Bart.

"Good-bye, Doodle." Becca smiled at me again. The two front teeth were separated by a tiny gap and her smile was all the more perfect for it. She thought my name was funny, I could tell. But I didn't mind. I liked it. That was me. Humble Doodle, nothing less, nothing more.

"He's the quiet sort," Bart laughed. His laugh was perfect, too, but completely false. Becca's smile was a warm summer rain. Bart's laugh was a snow globe—cold glass and fake plastic whirling around, trying to fill the void beneath the hard shell. "Doesn't say a word. But come back and visit him anytime. I do enough talking for the both of us, Miss Becca."

Becca tilted her head. "Maybe." Then she smiled again, this time at Bart, and headed back to the psychic booth.

Just like that, I saw the gleam of good sense sputter and go out of her eyes. It wasn't her fault, not really. She was fourteen and Bart was a good-looking twenty-one-year-old in a carnival where her working age group was limited and dental hygiene was not the word of the day among most. Bart was blind, the most interesting parts of the carnival a mystery to him, but he was a black poppy, too—a different sort, but he'd eat you all the same.

I sighed. This had every sign of fucking up my good time here.

Bart frowned at me. "At least you're good for something."

That would be Bart, only noticing me when I did something for him—whether I'd meant to or not. The Bartholomews of the world . . . Bigger assholes could not be found.

While Bart continued to sucker people into trying to win teddy bears in a game so rigged Vegas would've been proud, I did my best to forget about little girls with lavender hair and concentrate on my sightseeing. I perked up as the Poodle Lady passed by us. She was a grandmotherly type with hair as short and curly as that of her dogs, pink cheeked and plump and with a thousand fake diamond rings, bracelets, necklaces, even a tiara. When the sun hit her, she glittered wildly, a star about to go supernova. She was a sight, but that wasn't what interested me.

It was the poodles.

I loved the poodles.

I whistled low and soft as they trotted by, bedecked in ruffled collars. All white, they were tiny dandelion drifts blowing across the ground, yipping and excited from their last round of acrobatic tricks. As one, each furry face turned my way at the whistle too soft for the Poodle Lady to hear. Each mouth opened and each pink tongue twisted to change into a tentacle with pulsing suckers and fully as long as each dog's entire body. Each eye turned the blind silver-white of fish that lived so deep underwater that sight wasn't necessary.

It tickled me. Cthulhu slept, but his goddamn *poodles* roamed the earth.

Then they were only ordinary poodles once again and they scampered on, one stopping to lift a leg on Bart's booth.

"Hey, you little shit!" he snapped, tossing a teddy bear at it with malicious force. In a fraction of a second the stuffed animal was nothing but shreds and stuffing and, after pissing on that as well, the poodle was gone.

A few minutes later five clowns wandered by, following the Poodle Lady to the lunch tent. I didn't bother with them. Clowns were the biggest disappointment in the carnival. They were supposed to be cannibalistic, murderous, child-stealing monsters with jagged metal teeth and makeup mixed of blood and ashes. But no. They weren't. They were just ordinary people who liked to make people laugh. Which, don't get me wrong, is nice in theory and all. Still . . .

Disappointing.

That's what happens when you buy into a stereotype. You think nightmares using intestines to make balloon animals and you get slightly dumpy, sort of sad, average people who had determined that if they couldn't laugh themselves, they would do their best to make others laugh. Noble, but a little bit boring. I wouldn't have minded seeing Bart, the porno-loving sociopath, end up as a balloon animal, as he seemed set on ruining my playing tourist.

Finally, Bart closed up the booth a few hours later to grab a meal himself. I went along, too, not that he would notice if I ate or not. Luckily, I could get by on little. Roaming the world will teach you that. Refrigerators and microwaves were rare in my life. I had eaten goat once in India. . . . I still felt rather bad about that.

Bart loaded up a paper plate with barbecue and long, slinky

fries dripping with grease. Sitting down at a picnic table, he dug in, and I rethought the goat issue. The food here looked as if that long-digested goat had vomited on a plate and then handed you a fork. Bart obviously didn't mind, as he plowed through the mess. I reflected on how he had a grin and a wave for everyone who walked by except the Poodle Lady, and I wasn't surprised. The clowns had their masks of greasepaint and Bart had this mask. The friendly guy who was enough of a flirt for the women and a bit of the roguish con man for the men—it was a good disguise. It said, "I'm good, but not *too* good." Too good can't be real, and Bart was smart enough to know that. He relied on the wink and the grin and the "I might cheat you at cards, but not for money."

He made you like him, and there weren't many masks better than that. Everyone here fell for it, even the black poppies, who I'd have thought would've known better. He really was that good.

But on that day, I learned I was wrong after all. One person did see through him.

Remember when I said love's a bitch?

Yeah. . . .

Now is when I come back to that.

Love *is* a bitch.

That's what people say. I hadn't come to the conclusion about how often people were right—I was a little naïve on the subject, I admit it—but in this case, with this one nugget of knowledge, the people were in the know. On the money.

Love is a bitch, and this being my first encounter with it, I wished the saying was longer. Love is a bitch . . . but here's how you deal with it. A nice list with bullet points would be appreciated. Some pictures, maybe? I'd take stick figures if that's all that was available. I wasn't proud. I traveled the world, but that didn't mean I was always wise in the ways of it. Any assistance I could get, I would happily take. I was stuck with Bartholomew, however, and helpful he was not. What he knew about love, he wasn't telling, which rather sucked for me, as I'd hooked up with him to learn more about the world I was traveling and life in general. I tried to learn from everyone I'd teamed up with. So far all I'd learned from Bartholomew about love was that he didn't much care for it. Correction: he didn't much care for it unless he could twist it to his benefit.

Like he was thinking about with Becca.

Becca, who was too young to know better.

"Bartholomew, I want you to stay the hell away from my little sister."

Her sister, though, she knew about the big bad wolves in the world. And where the huntsman would carry an axe, she would carry a shotgun.

Bart looked up from his plate with rage. Unadulterated fury that someone would dare tell him what to do. I looked up and . . . shit . . . I was head over heels. Love. There it was. There she was, and nothing in all my rambles had prepared me for it.

"Whatcha talking about, Starling my darling?" His hand white-knuckled around his plastic fork, but his voice was smooth as honey and slippery as butter. "Becca came over for change and to see my buddy, Doodle. She's a kid, for God's sake. What? You think I don't know that?" Bart was probably smirking on the inside about how very well he did know that . . . about how much he liked that.

I'd picked up on Becca having an older sister who played the psychic, but I hadn't seen her in my few days at the midway. Bart didn't cross her path . . . or maybe she didn't cross his. Didn't want to. As she sat down opposite him, I saw it in her eyes when she looked at him. . . . **Here There Be Monsters** reflected in onyx mirrors. It might as well have been painted on Bart, which was rather ironic, to her gaze at least. She knew. She knew about wolves and monsters and how a man could be all that and worse.

Starling's dark eyes passed over me. "Doodle?" There was scorn in her voice, but it was for Bart, not me. I hoped. "Do you think your *buddy* there is going to have me thinking you're nothing but a puppy, all big eyes and milk breath? Sugar, you're trying to pull the wool over the wrong set of eyes. I know wickedness when I smell it, and you are *rank* with it."

I hadn't noticed it in Becca, but Starling had a trace of a southern accent. Around twenty-four or twenty-five, she had hair that wasn't long like Becca's, but a short cap of dark red streaked with the black stripes of a tiger. It cupped her head less like a gentle hand and more like a warrior's sleek helmet. Her eyes were dark and fierce, but she had the same five freckles. It was incongruous— the same as if you walked the plains of Africa and a tiger lifted its head from its kill to show a spattering of shooting-star freckles across its bloodied muzzle.

Sappy, yeah?

Head-over-heels. What can I say?

Can you blame me? I mean, seriously, a tiger with freckles. Who wouldn't fall for that?

"Wicked? Jesus, Starling, you've known me six months now." And it wouldn't be any longer than that. Bart was the type to piss where he lived. His stays would be short and his exits in the middle of the night, leaving pain and regret in his wake. Sometimes maybe worse. "What have I ever done to you? What have I ever done to anyone?"

His hand relaxed on the fork, but it twitched. It was the kind of movement that made me think that had he had metal instead of plastic, she might have been stabbed with it.

"I don't know. What did you do to Mr. Murphy? How'd you come by his booth? One day he's there, the next he's gone, and there you are with your easy smile, pretty talk, and dead eyes. And don't tell me he sold it to you. Murph loved the carnival, and as far as I can tell, you don't love anything but yourself." A short fingernail painted copper hit Bart in the chest. "So, here it is, Bar-tho-lomew, you don't touch Becca or I'll get my daddy's old bowie knife out and make sure you don't have a damn thing left to touch anyone with ever again."

Eyes narrowed, face flushed with anger, unpainted lips peeled back from her tiger's teeth, she was . . . amazing. And then she was gone, turned and striding out of the tent with her long silk skirt doing nothing to conceal long legs loping after another gazelle to take down.

Bart, unfortunately, was no gazelle. He wasn't a tiger, either. Bart was a hyena through and through. He only took down the weak and the vulnerable, but that didn't mean he wasn't dangerous. If anything, this adversary would make him more dangerous . . . thinking, plotting, and full of an ego that was not going to take this lying down.

And Starling, as demanding and feisty as the bird she was named for, knew him. No one else at the carnival did, but she knew. She might actually be a little psychic, putting truth to that label on her booth. If I'd learned anything in this world, it was that things you think are aren't, and things you think aren't can be. Everything under the sun . . .

Mr. Murphy . . . That was a new name I didn't know anything about. Bart could be a bigger predator than I'd thought, a pack of hyenas all on his own. Which wasn't good—not for Becca. Starling had tried to push around Bart, command him. Bart was a man . . . (a *thing*) . . . you didn't tell what to do, because sure as shit, he'd do exactly the opposite for spite alone.

Well, fuck.

What did I do about that? About little Becca? About her gloriously wild sister? I was Doodle. While the Barts of life walked around with hands dripping pain or blood, Doodles, we didn't get involved. I was always on the outside looking in. I wanted to see the world, I didn't want to *be* the world. It was too complicated. Standing up for something, I didn't know how to do that, to be that. I was content being the camera, not the subject.

I only wanted to watch. I only wanted to see.

What about Starling, anyway? She'd watched me, but she hadn't seen me, not really. Sometimes I blended in a little too well, and blending in with Bart's kind wasn't the way to her heart, that was for damn certain. I shifted a little and grimaced at how that had come back to bite me in the ass. Bart hissed and glared at me, raising a hand to aim a slap in my direction.

Stopping at the last moment, he snapped, low and mean, "Son of a bitch." Then he stared at where Starling had sat. "Or just a fucking bitch—period."

The rest of the evening and night, Bart spent thinking. What he was thinking, he didn't say out loud. I wasn't surprised. If it was close to the thoughts I was working through, words like that . . . they do something to the air. They taint it with shadows and the smell of week-old roadkill. Words like that—I'd heard enough of them in my life, and I didn't care to hear any more of them.

When Bart went to bed that night, I left as I always did. Sometimes I lay in the grass and watched the stars. I waved to them, too, like I did the reflections in the mirror maze . . . just in case. Sometimes I'd investigate the carnival further, which was how I discovered that the magician had four arms and his hat had teeth. No wonder he kept a giant cage constantly full of at least twenty-five doomed rabbits. I let them go. That wasn't much interference.

Tonight I found a family sitting outside their trailer. The mother and father were listening to music, drinking wine, kissing, and laughing, laughing, laughing. Here was the love Bart knew nothing about. I watched from the dark, then wandered behind the trailer, where someone else had wandered as well. Their little boy. He was two, two and a half. Baby ages are hard. Strawberry-blond hair stood on end and pudgy hands were waving in a vain attempt to catch fireflies. He saw me, pointed, and laughed.

I smiled at him and whispered, "Hi." I pointed to my chest. "Doodle."

He pressed his finger against my nose. "Doodle!" He laughed again.

"Doodle," I agreed. I liked kids. Kids were uncomplicated and easy to understand. I didn't have to worry about keeping my head down and not being noticed. Kids accepted. They weren't suspicious or judgmental. They took me at face value and it didn't matter what I knew or didn't know. If I wasn't always sure how to behave, because I was a little different, it didn't matter. To them being Doodle was enough. I was about to ask what his name was, although I wasn't so good with talking—words were difficult to get out for me—when I heard his mother calling. Reluctantly, I trudged back into the dark.

He called after me. "Doodle! Doodle!"

I heard his mother laugh at him. "Who are you talking to, silly bear?"

Those were two nice memories. Love and wine; a little boy and fireflies. I'd keep those when I moved on.

I wandered some more, watched the stars, and got back to Bart's trailer by morning. It was important, as a professional hanger-on, not to be gone long enough to be noticeably absent. That led to second thoughts about poor Doodle. I wouldn't want Bart to get too used to being without me—not yet.

I expected him to start a campaign to win Becca's trust. Buy her a gooey, sugary pastry, all fried dough, cherries, and powdered sugar. Talk to her as if she were a grown woman, not a fourteen-year-old. Try to get her to brush off Starling's warnings as an over-protective big-sister reaction. It would've been typical pedophile behavior.

But Bart proved me wrong. Bart showed he wasn't typical . . . not in this case. Maybe he would be normally, but Starling had stood up to him, beat him down, and seen him for what he really was. She saw through his mask, and of all the things she'd done, that was the worst. No one saw Bart for what he was. If they did, how could he continue being what he was? How could he get away with it?

He couldn't.

She might tell others. They might believe her. Bart couldn't have that.

No, he could not.

While he sulked among the teddy bears, taking dollars in exchange for guaranteed failure, he kept his fake smile plastered to his face, though he mumbled under his breath. I couldn't make out words—just the static buzz of what were likely psychotic ravings.

Bart had been a mistake. I should go now. Before I spent the next night and the one after peeking in the window of Starling and Becca's trailer.

Too late.

No self-will at all, that was me. When Bart turned in, I was at their trailer window. The curtains were the brilliant green of Irish fields, with a crack between the two halves. It wasn't a large one, but large enough that I could see through. It was late, with Bart exhausted by his porn for the night and already asleep. But Starling was still up. She was curled up on a tiny couch with a cup of tea, wearing pajamas patterned with ice cream cones. Her bare feet were pink with copper-painted toenails, her smooth cap of hair was ruffled in completely ridiculous spikes and cowlicks, and the curve of her lips was relaxed. She was a long way from the "gypsy psychic" she'd been while facing down Bart, when she was dressed in silk and beads with black ice for eyes, nails the color of a Burmese sunset, and teeth bared in threat. It was different now, a picture of domestic bliss. . . .

Until you noticed the giant bowie knife that was cradled on the cushion next to her. That made it even better.

Perfect domestic bliss.

I laughed. I couldn't help it. A she-tiger sat in ridiculous pajamas, drinking tea, studying her toenails to see if they needed repainting—and had her knife at the ready for Bart in case some wicked piece of anatomy needed to be treated like a breakfast sausage.

Love could be wine under the stars, but love could be this too.

I'd never felt it before, not really, but love . . . I didn't have the words for how it made me feel. I was Doodle and words weren't my thing. But I felt and I wanted and I dreamed and Starling, she was all of that. She was a tiger, *my* tiger, and she wouldn't ever back down from anything.

Laughing had been a mistake, though. She whipped her head toward the window and was up and moving. She was fast, but I was faster. I'd traveled far and wide and learned you had to be fast to survive.

Later I returned and tried the back where the bedroom would be. It was a small trailer, only big enough for one foldout bed. I saw Starling and Becca tangled up like children under the blankets. Becca slept curled up on her side, doing her unconscious best to scoot Starling out of the bed onto the floor. Starling slept—out of self-preservation, probably—on her stomach with one arm hooked around the edge of the mattress as if it were a lover of last hope. Lavender and tiger-striped hair mixed together in the dark, inseparable.

My heart warmed. Becca was less Starling's sister and more her cub. Starling would kill Bart and wouldn't shed a tear over it. Such was the way of the wild, and that was another good thought and memory to keep. Fierce protection and soft hair mixed under piles of blankets.

It was enough. I didn't spy anymore. I wanted to see new things, but I didn't want to dirty them . . . unless they were already dirty, and then there wasn't much more I could do there anyway. I learned that when one of the poodles chased me back to Bart's trailer. I nearly lost a strip of my hide to a fast-moving tentacle, but I still loved the little monsters. They were so damn funny.

THE NEXT DAY was the same as the others. Or so I thought until that night, when Bart spent three hours digging up Mr. Murphy and moving him farther away into the woods. Starling had spooked him. And Bart spooked me. He didn't know I was there, watching. He wouldn't have known if the whole carnival was there, cheering him on. He was muttering to himself with flecks of saliva flying from his mouth and a body tense with absolute molten rage. This time I could hear what he was saying: "Bitch, bitch, bitch. Fucking whore. Telling me. Telling *me* what I can do. She'll be sorry. She'll be so fucking sorry, she'll beg. She'll beg and beg and beg—she'll beg. . . ." After that it was more incoherent, the rage a language all its own.

Shit, Doodle, I thought with grim resignation, *what have you gotten yourself into now?*

Breakfast was not good. I kept wondering why I was still here and not in the wind. That was my number one rule, the Doodle motto: *Watch but don't participate. Don't get involved.* You're different, you're weird, and no matter how harmless I tried to look, people wouldn't want me around once they knew me—the real me. I was a freak.

Wasn't that ironic? In a carnival where there were no freaks anymore and the word itself was now bad and wrong, I was still a freak. Just a different kind of one.

Facts were facts: if people knew me, they would shun me. That meant I couldn't let anyone see behind the mask or through the reflection. I wanted to talk to Starling and tell her all the places and things I'd seen. The world was huge and its mysteries and secrets never-ending. I wanted to see her small, fiercely suspicious face smooth into smiles. I wanted to see her throw that neatly shaped head back in reckless laughter. I wanted to make fun of her pajamas and have her make up an outrageous fortune for me. Most of all, I wanted to sharpen her bowie knife for her and tell her never to warn men like Bart first, to just go ahead and put them down.

I wanted all those things, but I knew that Starling, for all her wild ways, wouldn't react differently from anyone else when it came to me. I was too different, and while the world changed all the time, that wouldn't.

Couldn't.

I watched as Bart shoveled down his breakfast. Wondering. Wondering. *What should I . . .* The thought was interrupted. The couple from three nights ago walked by, swinging their little boy hand in hand. He saw me and squealed, "Doodle!"

His mother, ponytail swinging, looked over and smiled. "There *is* a Doodle, isn't there? Hey, Doodle." She laughed cheerfully. It wasn't the throaty wine laugh from before, but I still liked it.

Bart was not thrilled. "You get more action than I do, asshole," he mumbled under his breath while waving at them and giving them the patented Bart smile, that cork against a human bottle of psychopathic rage and hate. See the smile, but never look past it.

The mother didn't, and they were past us and gone. I relaxed slightly. Bart had something planned for either Becca or Starling, I knew that. I didn't want to add any further collateral damage.

By that time Bart was done. He left his plate and cup on the table, uncaring, which wasn't a good sign. You didn't do that in the carnival. You cleaned up after yourself—always. The mask was slipping.

THAT NIGHT IT dissolved and Bart—the real Bart—came out to play.

I could hear a thousand crickets when Becca slipped out the trailer door and Bart approached her with, "Hey, sweetheart, where you going?"

I saw the flash of wariness in her eyes. Her sister had told her about Bart and, unlike most girls Becca's age, she believed. She listened to her big sister, and now she wanted nothing to do with Bart.

"Oh . . . Bart . . . and Doodle." Her smile was a small, pained thing, because it was meant to include me. But as everyone had seen that I stood with and behind Bart since I'd arrived, it didn't throw Bart off. Her voice wasn't casual and breezy as she hoped. It only showed her fear and her weakness, and I could see Bart was already high at the sight of both. "I'm just going to Bartleby's." She tilted her head toward the next trailer. "We're out of milk for Star's tea."

It was barely dark. It was just next door, but even so, I found it hard to believe Starling would let her go alone . . . not when the big bad wolf lived just across the way.

"Tea." Bart rolled the word around his mouth. "She drinks tea. The bitch drinks tea. How fucking boring. I'm surprised she doesn't drink acid, for all the shit that comes out of her mouth."

Becca was frozen. In her life probably no one had ever talked to her that way, not even in a carnival. Bart used that. And he clubbed her down with one blow of his fist. She was a puddle of green and heather and ivory silk at his feet.

I hissed. This was wrong. Wrong. The world could be a bad place. I knew that. From the beginning I knew and had promised to stay out of it—for the very reason that I was as wrong in my way and my help might not be any better than the things I tried to stop. I watched. That's all. That's . . .

Why, Bart? Why, you asshole? Why'd you have to go and screw everything up?

He buried a hand in Becca's hair and dragged her back into the trailer, dropping her on the floor and locking the flimsy door behind us.

"Doodle this and Doodle that," he sneered at her. "You never had a word to say to me until *goddamn Doodle* came along."

That was why. It was why Bart had messed things up for me and Becca, and it was why I had to fix it. If I hadn't been here, this wouldn't have happened. Mr. Murphy would've—already had—but not this.

"Becca? Did you open the door? I told you not to go outside after dark without me." Starling came out of the tiny bathroom and stopped short at the sight of the unconscious bundle that was her sister. "Becca?"

She sounded lost, but she wasn't. I don't think Starling had ever been lost in her life. She stood, short hair damp, the wet gloss of red-and-black stripes screaming "Beware!" Wrapped in a scarlet robe, feet bare like before, she was a queen and Bart should've feared her. But Bart was an idiot.

I wasn't. When she whipped that man-eating knife from behind her back and lunged to stab him in the chest, I applauded, unnoticed. Bart spat curses and grabbed her neck to throw her to the ground, the knife still in him. Starling was a fighter, but she was small. Five foot three at best. Barely a hundred pounds. But no matter the size, a tiger is still a tiger. She was back on her feet in a fraction of a second, her hands back on the handle of the knife, trying to shove it in deeper. It had gotten hung up on a rib bone, more's the pity.

This time Bart grabbed her throat and held on, choking fast any screams she might've made. With the other hand he pulled the blade out of his flesh. "You fucking bitch." His teeth were bared, his eyes full of fury, but a cold fury. When rage burns, at least it's quick. When it's cold, it can make a death last forever. Slice by slice by slice.

Holding the knife just under her chin and above his hand, he seethed curses that seemed to crawl over both of their bodies. "I'm going to kill you—don't think for a second there's a way out of that. But first I'm going to hurt your little sister. Hurt your Becca. I'm going to fuck her five ways to Sunday and then I'm going to cut every inch of her so the next man that looks at her pukes from the sight. And then I'm going to leave her alive on top of your fucking entrails. If 'alive' is what you can call that. In fact, I'll call her up in a few years, ask her. Ask her if she's alive or if she's a corpse walking around with a beating heart. How's that sound, Starling my darling? Well? How's that sound? Fucking answer me, bitch!"

I was different. I was a freak, maybe. I was the passive watcher, blending in and never getting involved. Speaking only to kids too little to know how strange I was. That's who Doodle was. That's who Doodle had always been.

Until now.

Now . . . now I got involved.

Now I spoke.

Because now I was fucking *pissed*.

"Time to go home, Bart," I said, stretching against the tightness of being still. Shedding the inertia of blending in.

Past Starling and the knife I could see the three of us in the bathroom mirror. I could see the surprise on Bart's face, the bulge of his bicep where he all but held Starling off her feet. And I could see me.

On his bicep. On his skin.

A cute, happy monkey with a cheerful grin, the hat of a clown, several balloons of red, blue, and green held in one paw, the tail wrapped around Bart's arm and below that, my name: Doodle.

Bart's drunken vacation had him waking up with a tattoo he couldn't even remember getting. Everyone in the carnival had loved it, though. Loved me. Joked about his new friend with the funny name, Doodle. Bart had been pissed about me, thought I was goofy and stupid, until people started talking to him to look at me. He regretted it less then, that mysterious tattoo. Bart, who'd take any advantage he could get.

Me? I'd just wanted to see life in a carnival. See this world. I'd spent millions of years in a different place and, once out, I wanted to see it all. It was brand-new to me and much better than home. Home . . . well, home was hell. Plain as it came.

Once, when especially bored, a demon had sketched me in the burning sand. Hence my name—hilarious, huh? I was a demonic doodle, who after endless years had finally escaped Hell, snaking through the smallest of cracks. I was a line of sulfur and will, and I could shape myself into any form and color. I thought a monkey was good for a carnival and particularly appropriate for Bart. He didn't fling his feces, but he bit and he bit hard.

So did I.

I slithered out of the monkey shape, shed those colors, and went up Bart's arm, winding back and forth at a speed even a rattlesnake couldn't have managed. In less than a breath I was wrapped several times around Bart's neck and that breath . . . it wasn't something he had to worry about any longer.

I tightened until he turned blue and dropped the knife from Starling's throat. I tightened again until he was purple and dropped himself, too, beside the knife. He foamed at the mouth a bit, like they do, and then he died and shot straight down to the burning sands I'd escaped.

Of all the predators that prowled the carnival with strange appetites and stranger shapes, the human was the truest monster of them all. The truest evil.

I know what people would think. I'm from Hell. Big *H*, little *e*, double-hockey-sticks Hell. I should be evil myself, pure malevolence, every part of me. Eh, not so much. You live in Hell for millions of years and you realize something about evil: it's boring. You can say it's wrong and morally reprehensible and all that, and you'd be right. But mainly it's just so damn boring that after a while you don't ever want to see it again. Life, even when it lasts millions of years, is too short for boring.

I wasn't putting up with boring again.

Bart was wrong. Bart was boring. And now Bart was gone.

"Doodle?" Starling was crouched on the floor, staring at the tattoo line garroting Bart, finally seeing me.

I slid from around Bart's neck and re-created the monkey shape and offered her the balloons.

"Doodle," I confirmed.

She reached out and took them. Hesitantly, but she was a tiger and feared nothing, so she accepted them. The painted colors poured over her hand like a melting rainbow before disappearing.

"You . . . what are . . . ?" She shook her head, because this was Starling and even if I'd known her only days, I knew her still. She was infinitely practical. She didn't second-guess, she definitely didn't look a gift Doodle in the mouth. "You saved us. Thank you."

My monkey tail curled around her wrist, black and brown lines of ink. "Doodle loves you." I couldn't talk much. Throats and voice boxes and tongues, they're beyond a simple doodle, and I hadn't regretted it before, but I did now. I eked out the words anyway. I couldn't have held them back.

Because, yes, love is a bitch and doodles and tigers can't be together, but love is still worth saying aloud.

"Doodle loves you." I let go of her wrist, unraveled this shape, and slipped away through the small crack under the door and into the night.

Soon enough I'd find someone else to hitch a ride with, see something new, and maybe fall in love again. It was possible. Evil was boring, but love was interesting and exciting—everything I could imagine—and covered the world. I could meet love over and over.

Love is a bitch, I thought sadly, yet fondly, too, as I disappeared from the carnival and into a promising darkness.

Love is a bitch.

But she's my bitch, and I couldn't wait to see her again.

"The Three Lives of Lydia"

A Blud Short Story

Delilah S. Dawson

Lydia woke to the curious sound of a calliope. Opening her eyes to a swaybacked, star-studded sky, she shivered. Something was deeply, deeply wrong, as if she had just fallen out of a nightmare, heart pounding and head spinning, limbs still too numb to run away. A chill breeze played over her naked skin, making the tall grass around her whisper and sway. She sat up and contracted into a ball in one breath. Running a finger over the crooked heart tattooed on her left wrist, she inhaled the scent of crushed grass and cold iron and waited for something to happen.

"Am I dead?"

Her voice was overloud in the moon-bitten night, and she suddenly felt like an extra in someone else's movie. The background sounds descended with a vengeance: the cheery calliope, squealing metal, an excited burble of voices overlaid by the amplified shriek of a barker, like at an old-fashioned carnival. The tall form rising above her turned out to be a train car, one of a wide circle of wagons enclosing a cluttered meadow. Lydia was on the inside of the circle, and the warmth and laughter were all on the outside. Crawling to the dark wall, she put a hand against the freezing enamel, curious as to why the wagons were circled, why the inside of the ring was abandoned while the outside was full of life. From under the wagon's belly, warm light flickered and twitched, beckoning her close with curling fingers.

She parted the grass and jerked her head back when she found a gleaming coil of razor wire. Just out of reach, hundreds of people swarmed through the brightly lit space. Lydia's eyes danced with leather boots, the hems of jewel-colored gowns, gaily striped parasols, and tapping canes from another century. It couldn't be real. This had to be heaven or hell or purgatory. It had to be a dream, and a beautiful one. The vision was too lovely to inspire terror, even if every cell of her body knew it was wrong.

As if a golden hook had wrapped around her heart, she knew she had to get to the other side, to the carnival there. But first she needed clothes. She stood and ran a hand along the side of the wagon until she found a doorknob. The car was completely dark, and she was willing to bet it was empty.

The door creaked open on more darkness, and stepping through it she fumbled along the interior wall until she found a button. A series of Victorian-looking sconces lit with an orange glow. She was in luck: the room was a jumble of mannequins, hats, and sequins. Costumes sprouted from dress forms, half finished in harlequin diamonds or lurid stripes. Feathers exploded from upturned top hats, and bolts of cloth swooped across the ceiling like gypsy tents. When no one appeared to challenge her presence, she went to a rack to borrow some clothes.

Half of the outfits revealed far too much skin, while the other half laced up so tightly at neck and wrist that she dismissed them on the grounds of claustrophobia. At last, she selected a long green gown with a low neck that covered her full sleeves of tattoos but neatly framed the sparrows on her clavicles and the banner strung between them. The dress covered every other tattoo except the one on the back of her neck. She chose a hat that would hide that and her hair, tying the ribbons under her chin with more determination than she'd felt in a long time. Finding a pair of worn slippers under an ancient sewing machine, she slid her feet in, turned off the lights, and slipped back out the door to face the darkness where she'd begun.

She paused outside and leaned her back against the wagon, her head tilted upward to half-familiar constellations partially hidden by swirling wisps of cloud. This place—it couldn't be real.

Then again, considering reality had failed her, did she care?

Lydia breathed out, low and long. Whatever this place was, she had to go to the carnival. It called to her, whispered in her ear with every caressing breeze, drew her inexorably forward. The dress swished around her as she stepped down the stairs and crept around to where the wagon hooked on to the next car. The path to the carnival beyond was blocked by a strange contraption. As Lydia approached, a demonic head on a long neck swung toward her with a metallic creak. Red eyes flashed in her face, and she stumbled back as steel teeth clanked inches away from her nose.

She'd almost been bitten by an animatronic giraffe.

There was no way around it. She slunk back around the wagon, only to find a unicorn at the next juncture between cars. Then an elephant after that. Then a panda bear. She began to feel very much like Alice in Wonderland, met at every path by blockades of her own feverish imagining. It made no sense; why would robots guard the spaces between the train cars? Wasn't the point of the carnival to attract an audience? When she came to a trio of ridiculous flamingos, she decided it was time to take control of the limbo world and force her way through.

The dancing flamingos were made of metal scraps held together with rivets, their legs coiled springs. Lydia was about to dart past their pedestal when one of the heads sprang back toward her, the banana-shaped beak opening to show sawtooth ridges. With a determined grunt, she pushed it to the side and tried to duck past. Another head appeared in her way, the beak latching onto her arm.

Lydia stumbled back, jerking her sleeve away. Stunned and shaking, she looked down at her torn gown and the red scratch across her arm.

So she could be hurt here, then, wherever here was. The flamingo's head turned, the beak wide open and spinning with saw teeth.

"You lost?"

Swallowing a shriek, she jerked her head to the side. An oddly fierce man stood in the scant light, far too close for comfort. His face was narrow and pale under a mop of wild hair, his dark eyes outlined in black. He was dressed in a loose shirt, suspenders, and striped pants that accentuated his wiry build. He had appeared from nowhere, and it unsettled her.

Trapped between the stranger and the chainsaw teeth, she whispered, "Yes."

The man's eyes widened. "Come on, then." He jerked his head away from the flamingos, and she nervously followed him across the wide patch of grass circled by the ring of linked wagons. When he slowed a little and half turned to her, she could barely see the shadow of a smile.

"Settle down, girl. I'm not going to eat you. I promise." She didn't say anything; she couldn't. "How'd you get back here, anyway? This area's off-limits." He focused on the rip in her dress, nostrils flaring. "Did one of the carnivalleros bring you back here? Take advantage?"

Lydia shook her head no before realizing that gestures weren't enough.

"I got lost." Her voice was small, swallowed up by the night.

"That don't explain your undressery." He started walking again, and she felt every pebble through the slippers. "Pretty lass like you might get in trouble, letting that much skin out. You foreign or something?"

When he said *something*, his mournful British accent turned it into *sumpin'*, and she smiled a wobbly smile. It was hard to be scared of a guy who looked and sounded like John Lennon.

"Or something, I guess."

He stopped walking when they reached the patch of light between two train cars. The shadow of a large mechanical ostrich danced over them, and the man ran a hand through wavy auburn hair and held out a red-gloved hand.

"I'm Charlie Dregs." His smile was crooked but contagious, and Lydia reached out to shake.

"Lydia Beckwith."

He bowed and went gallantly to kiss her hand. As his lips brushed her skin, he breathed in deeply and let out a small moan. Lydia snatched her hand back and crossed her arms protectively over her chest.

"Are you some kind of creeper, Charlie Dregs?"

Charlie swallowed and glanced around the field as if someone might step forward to vouch for him. Lydia took a step backward, on the off chance he was checking for possible witnesses. Her instinct was to trust him, but her instinct had been wrong before.

"I ain't a creeper. Plain enough to see I'm a Bludman."

"A blood man?"

"Bludman. A man who drinks blood."

She reared back, panicking, looking for a place to run, but he just snorted.

"If I was going to attack you, don't you think I would have done it when you wasn't looking?"

It was true. It was crazy, but it was true. And he wasn't attacking her now. And she was trapped back here, in the field, thanks to the robot animals. Trusting Charlie Dregs was the only way to the carnival. She wrapped her arms more tightly around herself and glared at him.

"Why aren't you attacking me, then?"

He stared at her for a moment; then his eyes lit up, and he let out a bark of laughter.

"I get it now, Lydia. You're a Stranger."

"What?"

"This ain't your world, is it? That explains your smell, why you'd dress like that, how you got on this side of the clockworks, how come you got ink when you ain't a Bludman. It's true, right?"

"I don't understand."

"You just woke up here, naked. And it ain't where you're from."

Lydia looked up at the sky. The stars seemed all cattywampus, tilted and dizzying. She blinked, and the world coalesced around her like a new coat that already fit perfectly.

"No, I guess it's not."

A brilliant grin lit Charlie's face. "I always wanted to find a Stranger. We got to tell the caravan master, but then we'll see the sights, eh?" He raised his eyebrows at her and smirked, but sweetly. "Unless you're scared?"

She stiffened. "Should I be?"

"Plenty in this world to be scared of, but you needn't fear me. I've not drunk blood straight from the source in at least ten years. Only vials." He jerked his chin at the carnival beyond. "You're going to need somewhere to stay, you know. You won't last a night on the wild moors alone. Master Criminy likes to take in Strangers, so long as they don't mind work. How about it?"

"I . . ."

Lydia stared at the glittering dreamscape beyond. Women in corsets and bustles and bell-shaped skirts flitted about like tropical birds on the arms of men wrapped in tailcoats and doffing top hats. The calliope music had segued into something familiar that sounded like "Yellow Submarine." The air was chill with autumn, spiked with the scents of caramel and apples and pumpkin and topped with the buttery kiss of popcorn. Her mouth watered. She still didn't understand what was happening or why this friendly yet strangely fierce man had fangs. But she couldn't stand on this side of the wagons any longer. The carnival tugged at her. She had to get to the other side, where the magic was.

She shrugged. "What do I have to lose?"

Charlie stepped close to the clockwork ostrich, saying, "Orangutan posthumous grotesque." Before she could ask him what he meant, the dancing bird froze. "That's the passcode," Charlie explained, stepping under its neck and holding out his hand. With a deep breath, she ducked under the unmoving bird and into the carnival proper.

Everything was different on the other side of the wagons. The air was full of glitter, the lanterns glowed like jars of fairy dust, and music danced on a sugar-frosted breeze. Laughter was everywhere. It was like a dream, like every Christmas morning should have been, like prom looked in movies. And it was contagious. Lydia's smile broke out, stretching until her cheeks ached. She wanted to be part of this place, this moment, forever.

"You never been to a carnival before, Lydia?"

She shook her head, stars in her eyes. "Never."

He held out his arm, and she took it. As they walked under a tightrope strung high overhead, the pretty girl balancing there on one leg shouted, "Oi, Charlie! What do you think you're doin', lad?"

"Bein' philanthropic," he shot back. He gave Lydia a fond but sharp-toothed smile and a look she couldn't quite puzzle out but that nevertheless made her blush.

Charlie scanned the crowd, nostrils flaring and head cocked to the side like that of a dog hunting for bacon. Lydia danced back when a small monkey made of metal scampered past, tail in the air, but Charlie pulled her along to follow it. They wound through the crowd in giggling pursuit, stopping short when the copper robot scampered into a cluster of velvet-walled tents with fluttering flags on top. A golden rope was strung all around as a barricade, and the curlicue letters on the sign said simply *Freak Show*.

"Is the boss inside?" Charlie asked the leather-clad man standing by the money box.

"Yeah, but the girl has to pay admission," the man snapped. Charlie pointed to Lydia's sparrow tattoo.

"New act."

The man sneered but let them by. They ducked into the maze of tents, and Lydia barely had time to take in the lantern-lit wall of strange jars filled with horrors and miracles before she heard a ruckus behind the display.

"Lads. Lads. Not again. Which head shall I cut off first, eh?"

Charlie held back a curtain to reveal the strangest scene Lydia had ever witnessed. The copper monkey they'd just followed perched on the shoulder of a seriously sexy ringmaster, who had his fist wound up in the jacket lapels of a two-headed boy while a well-dressed wolfman watched from the sidelines.

"She asked for it, Master Stain. Begged to be bitten, really—"

"Perk of the job—"

"One less vial you got to feed us, right?"

The two heads kept interrupting each other, muttering through bloodstained teeth. The ringmaster tossed the boys to the ground at the feet of the wolfman, whose face looked more like that of a smug Yorkie than that of a wolf.

"I'm not one for upholding the law, lads, but I'm rather against having my caravan shut down, and Pietro caught you fair and square." The ringmaster fetched a copper coin from his waistcoat and threw it at the wolfman, who fumbled with dark-furred fingers before shoving it in his pocket with a grin. "Catarrh, Quincy. This is your last warning. I know how delicious they are, but if I can abstain, so can you. No more drinking from the customers, or I swear I'll toss the uglier head to the bludbunnies if I can ever figure out which one is more repugnant."

The ringmaster turned around, noticing Charlie and Lydia for the first time. Behind him, the two-headed boy stood and launched himself at the wolfman, who yipped and howled and snapped. With a dramatic bow, the ringmaster closed the curtain on the tussle.

"I'm Criminy Stain, proprietor of Criminy's Clockwork Caravan." His cloudy eyes traveled hungrily over Lydia's tattoos. "Welcome to Sang, pretty Stranger."

Lydia turned to Charlie. "How did he—"

Criminy laughed. "I know everything. Almost. You practically scream it, pet. And you don't even look gnawed on, so that's a plus. Where'd you find her, Charlie?"

"Inside the wagon's circle. By the costumer's."

Charlie sounded melancholy, and he was hunched over like a kicked dog. Lydia couldn't imagine what had dampened him, making him look at his boots instead of meeting the ringmaster's ferocious glare.

"Well played, lad. I'll take over from here." Criminy straightened his cravat and hat, gave Lydia a sizzling grin, and held out his arm. "Care to see a hell of a show, love?"

He was dangerously gorgeous and, frankly, scared the hell out of her. She stepped closer to Charlie, giving his arm a squeeze.

"Charlie's taking good care of me," she said, and he squeezed her back.

Criminy's eyes narrowed, focusing on her throat.

"You got a magic locket?" he asked, voice clipped.

"Nope."

He snorted and looked down, his cocky confidence exchanged for chagrin.

"Then you're not the one I'm waiting for. Still, I never thought I'd see the day Charlie Dregs got the girl."

Charlie growled low in his throat, and Lydia blurted, "Are you hiring?"

Criminy's mouth quirked up. "That depends. What's your act?"

She rolled back the velvet arms of her dress, showing full sleeves of tattoos. Magical beasts, flowers, spiderwebs, sugar skulls, all chosen from the same artist's portfolio.

"Is that all you've got?" Criminy's sharp eyebrows went up as if daring her.

"Not even close." She hiked up her skirt to show feet and ankles likewise inked. "They go all the way up."

Criminy whistled and took off his hat to run a hand through ink-black hair. Charlie went on alert as the ringmaster leaned forward to reach behind Lydia's ear. He pulled out a copper coin and held it out to her. "For a show like that, I'll be your first customer. *Lydia, the Tattooed Lady.* It has a nice ring to it."

She took the coin but not the bait. "So what do I have to do?"

"We'll have a tent ready for you tomorrow night, right here. The costumer will set you up in the morning, so be prepared to show some skin. All you have to do is sit there and be beautiful while people gawk. You'll get a hundred coppers per year, plus room and board. You'll get to see the world of Sang. All your dreams come true—for as long as you last." He twirled a white-gloved hand in the air. "Et cetera."

"Wait. As long as I last?"

"I take on any useful Strangers I can find. Some stay only a few hours before disappearing back to your world. Some last forever.

Some die. There's no way to tell how long you'll be here, so make it count."

"What about tonight?"

His eyes twinkled, and he grinned. Reaching into his waist-coat, Criminy pulled out a scarf the color of shadows and smoke and tossed it to Lydia.

"Tonight, pet, you have but one assignment: cover your ink and enjoy your first night in Sang. Charlie, the puppet show's been canceled, and you'll deliver the lady to Abilene's wagon before dawn. If you wouldn't mind?"

Charlie's answering grin lit up his face and straightened his posture, making him seem more like the lively man who had found her in the field.

"It would be an honor," he said. Lydia gave Criminy a nod, tucked the coin in a pocket, and turned away to arrange her scarf.

Criminy held back the curtain, displaying the ongoing struggle between the two-headed boy and the wolfman. "Stop fighting, fools. I need my freaks in one piece."

As Charlie guided her out of the tent, a shiver ran up her spine. She felt hungry eyes on her back, a predator's sharp smile in her wake. There was danger here, that much was sure. She would have to watch out for Criminy Stain and his dire, unexplainable warnings.

AS THEY REJOINED the murmuring crowd outside, Charlie bent close to murmur, "Thank you for that, Lydia."

Feeling brave, she nudged him with a shoulder. "I know what it's like to feel invisible."

He chuckled. "Tonight's your last night of that. People will pay to see you from now on."

She looked down. "They won't see the real me. Just the ink."

"Isn't that why you got it? To stand out?"

She pulled back her sleeve to look at the crooked heart on her wrist, the only piece of art that was of her own design. "I always thought beauty was only skin-deep. I'm not sure that's enough anymore."

"If they can't see the beauty underneath, that's their loss. But tonight is just for you. What would you like to see first?"

She spun, a small cog in the grand machinery of light and chaos. She couldn't say why, but it felt like she belonged there. And whether Criminy was dangerous or kindly, she would take his advice and enjoy this place, whatever it was, for as long as she could.

"I want to see everything."

He looked left and right and shrugged. "There's really no right place to begin on a wheel."

"Then we can't mess up, right?"

He gave her the strangest look, as if measuring her in some way she couldn't understand. Instead of answering, Charlie guided her toward a collection of food and drink carts, each treat more mouthwatering than the last. Leaving her by a roasted-chestnut dispenser, he fussed with a potbellied copper contraption. He soon returned with a steaming paper cup. Lydia took it with murmured thanks, savoring the heat of the thin parchment and sipping carefully. Not until she'd gulped down half the strangely spiced hot chocolate did she remember that drinking things in other worlds was a mythological no-no. Hades, Olympus, the faerie world—most places would punish her for that transgression. But what was done was done, so she gulped the rest down fast, scalding her throat. As she threw the cup away and took his arm to stroll some more, Charlie sighed in relief and relaxed as if he, too, had felt her thirst and was sated.

As they skirted the crowd gathered around the strong man,

Charlie said, "What's your world like, then? I've heard stories, but never straight from the source."

"It's . . . not that great. I like it better here."

"No Bludmen, right?"

"No Bludmen. Just humans and animals."

"Speak of the devil." Charlie knelt to snatch a black rabbit as it lunged from the shadows toward Lydia's feet. It kicked violently in his grasp, dangling by its ears with panic in its eyes. Lydia was outraged and opened her mouth to protest the cruelty . . . until it hissed, revealing fangs that would have fit better on a German shepherd. In a heartbeat, she understood that rabbits here were vicious predators, far from the innocent bunnies of her world. A trickle of fear settled in her belly. As if sensing her disquiet, Charlie swiftly twisted its neck.

"One more for the stewpot. Can't have him hopping around, biting the audience." He shrugged. "Or you." Seeing the horror on her face, he slung it over his shoulder, out of sight. "You're a tender-hearted little thing, aren't you?"

"I'm a vegetarian." It came out as a squeak.

"I'm not. Neither was that rabbit."

Lydia had some familiarity with dangerous predators hiding behind sweet exteriors. But Charlie was the complete opposite. She looked at him, so different in every respect from every man she'd ever known. He called himself a monster, a Bludman, yet his behavior revealed a kind soul with hidden depths. He felt like the missing piece to a puzzle she'd never tried to solve. Something still felt off, but she liked where she was now, liked the warm light of the lanterns and the taste of the wild wind on her spice-dusted lips. And she liked being with Charlie.

Their twined arms took on a new significance, and when Charlie led her into the darkness behind the sword-swallower's painted backdrop, she thrilled with anticipation.

But he didn't pull her close for a kiss. Instead, he went to the corner of the wagon to hang the dead rabbit with dozens of others on a hook and put a mark by his name on a chalkboard.

"We get a copper for every ten bludbunnies we bring in," he explained.

The tangled mass of rabbits twitched, and Lydia jumped back.

"Does it trouble you?" Charlie looked down at her, one fang biting nervously into his lip.

"Not as much as it should, and *that* troubles me. Where am I, Charlie? And why don't I feel more upset? More lost?"

Her voice shook, and he drew her down beside him to sit on the steps of the wagon, away from the half-dead rabbits and hidden in the thickest shadows behind the bare wood backdrop. It was strangely intimate, being so close to hundreds of enchanted people skipping through lantern light and yet completely invisible. Without meaning to, she leaned against Charlie, noticing that he smelled of comfortingly forgotten things, of fire-heated wood and old paper and night wind and, vaguely, of red wine. He put his arm around her and set his cheek against her hair as if soothing a child.

"Criminy says most Strangers end up in Sang because they're asleep in your world, or hurt. So did you go to sleep, or did you get hurt?"

Tears sprung to her eyes when she realized she knew the answer. "I got hurt."

"What happened?"

"I don't know. There was this guy, and things went to hell, and then one day I looked in the mirror, and . . ."

"And what?"

"It's like no one ever saw the real me. I was just so sick of being invisible."

His arm tightened around her. "I know that feeling. But I see you, Lydia, and you're beautiful, on the surface and inside. You invade my senses and bewitch my heart. It feels like madness. But better." He chuckled, and she felt it against her hand, which had crept up to his chest. "It's as if I've been waiting for you. Something about you is just so . . ."

"Right?"

"Right."

The way he looked at her made her pulse flutter faster, made her remember the day she'd gotten the sparrow Charlie was gazing at with a mixture of tenderness and hunger. She still remembered the way she'd felt, her skin buzzing along with the needle, Jayson's glove-covered hand pressing over her heart while they laughed together. That had been her first bit of ink, a piece of his flash impulsively chosen from the wall. Over the next year, they'd enjoyed a storybook romance as he reverently branded her body with his artwork, hands, and lips.

Her father had tried to break it up, quoting Michelangelo's saying about how skin is more beautiful than the garment that covers it. She had replied that beauty is only skin-deep, but ugly goes straight to the bone.

Everything had been perfect until the day she found Jayson in the alley, ramming his tongue down the throat of a skinny freshman with perfectly straight blond hair and mud-brown eyes and not a single tattoo. The look he had given her then—like she was nobody, like he'd never seen Lydia before—it had killed her, and she had reacted poorly. Lydia still loved the ink, but she had come to hate the artist.

She had been so sure that they were meant to be together, and he had betrayed her completely. And, sure, she had flipped out a little. Her father had sent a car to bring her back from college to recuperate at their summerhouse by the shore. It hadn't helped. She hated it there, hated the money and the perfect, empty house and the way her father stared at her as if wishing she were someone else. He'd always hated tattoos, and she'd always hated him.

"Your mind's far away, girl. Come back to me."

Lydia looked up, smacking Charlie in the nose with her hat. With a grunt of annoyance, she untied the limp bow beneath her chin and threw the bonnet on the ground. The shocked look on Charlie's face was priceless.

"Is that your real hair?"

She dragged a hand through the hot-pink spikes, twisting a few curls to make them stand up. "What, women don't do weird things with their hair here? Don't you like it?"

He chuckled. "Lydia, love, you're in one of the few places in the world where weirdness will earn your supper. I would like your hair no matter what, but the brightness suits you. Perhaps this is where you were meant to be. D'you mind?"

Before she could ask what might she mind, he ran his gloved palm over her prickly hair, his palm caressing her skull. A shiver shot down her spine, a melty sensation spreading through her belly under the velvet.

"They say Strangers can disappear." He traced her hairline to the nape of her neck, making her gasp. "I hope you don't."

The sincerity in his kohl-rimmed eyes drew her in, and she looked down, his hand still warm on her neck. "Charlie, are you real?"

He shrugged with an amused smile. "I think so. Are you?"

Her voice was tiny, unguarded, and raw. "I think so. But I'm not sure. Maybe I'm dead."

Tipping her head back with a finger under her chin, his eyes traced the lines of her face. "To tell you the truth, when I first saw you, I thought you were a dream. A lost ghost haunting the field. When you spoke, it probably scared me as much as it did you."

Giving her every opportunity to pull away, he gently touched his lips to hers, a tentative brush of warmth and question. She held perfectly still, afraid that the slightest movement would break the fragile thread connecting them, that either one of them might disappear or lose their nerve. She trembled and closed her eyes as he pulled away.

"That made me feel more real," she whispered.

Charlie pulled her face closer with one hand at the nape of her neck, and her lips parted. His mouth was firm, bold yet soft and seeking. His thumb gently stroked the ticklish place on her spine where a tattooed luna moth spread bright wings as if forever taking flight, and her shawl fell away. One of her hands found his cheek, the other landing on his forearm, bare where his shirt was rolled up. Cradled between the warmth of his body and the chill of midnight, she shivered. He touched her only where the dress left off, gently tracing the tattoos and lines of her neck and shoulders as if he knew the secret places no one had touched, where planes met planes and the breeze alone could raise goose bumps. As if those places had been his all along.

His mouth opened, his questing tongue stroking hers. Never had she imagined being kissed with such thorough delicacy and patience and worship. He pulled her closer and turned his head, just a little. The flavor of his kiss took on the heady spice of passion and hunger, and she welcomed him, lips wide, answering his need with her own. Whether she was kissing an angel or a vampire or a construct of her own mind no longer mattered. Whatever Charlie was, inside and out—it was enough.

A rousing cheer went up, and Lydia drew back, a blush hot in her cheeks. But the applause and whistles were for something happening in the light of the carnival; she and Charlie were still alone backstage.

Charlie drew a line down her neck to stroke with reverence the tattoos along her collarbones. She could barely see him in the shadows, but he could apparently see her quite well, and his touch woke her skin, making her breathe faster.

"Finest ink I've ever seen. What's the words say?"

"It's Latin for 'Don't let the bastards grind you down.'"

His fingertip slowly traced the inked words to the faceted jewel that disappeared into the V of her gown, leaving a trail of fire along the already feverish skin of her chest. "I can see that. And that's why a diamond, right? For the irony." His dark, black-lined eyes looked straight down into her soul. "You been ground down, but you didn't break. It makes you all the more beautiful."

Lydia wrapped her arms around his neck and pulled him close, her cheek against his. He didn't just see her; he saw through her to what was really there. Charlie swallowed hard, gently untangling her to stand and step away.

"We stay back here any longer, and I'm afraid you won't think me a gentleman. I waited for you too long to let that happen. And there's more to see tonight."

Lydia studied him with new understanding, committing his wavy auburn hair and fierce eyes and sharp cheekbones to memory should she suddenly disappear. He held out a hand to help her stand and rearranged the fallen scarf around her shoulders.

With a soft peck on her cheek, he drew her out into the dancing light of the caravan. It was blinding at first, the sights and sounds overwhelming. But soon she was giggling and chatting with Charlie as she pulled him from one act to the next. They saw the lizard boy, the acrobats, the contortionists, the dancing fembots of the Bolted Burlesque. He told her of the small island where he had grown up, riding wild bludponies along the shore at his mother's side. Lydia said nothing of her family, and he was wise enough not to ask.

As they paused, trying to catch their breath after laughing at a malfunctioning fembot, a dark-skinned Amazonian woman strode past with a giant snake around her shoulders, a train of small children singing and eating popcorn in her wake. The woman looked at Lydia and Charlie, white teeth flashing in the glowing ebony of her face, and murmured, "That's powerful magic."

Before either of them could respond, she held up a torch and blew a long plume of fire that rippled through the air in the shape of a winged snake. The children clapped and squealed as she moved on, and Charlie hissed under his breath and took Lydia in the opposite direction.

All along, the calliope's song had been dancing in the background, and finally they were close enough to see the instrument and its master. Massive pipes shaped like octopus tentacles curled from a contraption of polished wood and inlaid brass and danced smoothly with the music. The man at the keyboard was movie-star gorgeous, his copper hair rippling down his back as he shifted from something classical and circus-y to "Octopus's Garden." The tiny hairs rose along Lydia's arms.

"Do you know that song?" she asked Charlie.

He shook his head no. "Never heard anything like it until the Maestro showed up."

Lydia stepped up to the calliope to watch the Maestro play, noting that his rolled-up sleeves showed ink of his own. "Do you know 'Hey Jude'?" she asked quietly, and the man turned sharply to stare at her, his hands still playing.

She'd forgotten her hat, and when he saw her hair, he broke out in a huge dimpled grin.

"Where you from?" he asked with a Southern accent.

"Nashville. You?"

"Atlanta. You sticking around?"

She looked back at Charlie. He stood at a respectful distance, but his entire being was focused on her, his eyes intent as if he didn't trust the Maestro, didn't trust anyone around her. From this far away, he was beautiful and frightening, and she wasn't bothered by either truth.

"I want to stay. But do you know what this place is? Are we dead? Is it a dream? Or are we both crazy?"

He chuckled with a hint of madness. "Darlin', I just play the piano. I've been here for months, and I still have no idea what it is. Sang is weird as hell, but you get used to it." He looked her up and down. "You should probably put on a hat and some gloves, though. You're asking for trouble, walking around like that."

"Charlie'll take care of me." She moved back to his side, and his arm settled around her waist like it belonged there. "See you later, Maestro." She had a thousand questions to ask him, but he hadn't stopped playing the piano, and she had so much to see, and she would run into him later, anyway, if she stayed. He gave her a be-mused nod, and she let Charlie guide her to the next act, a mer-maid in a glass aquarium.

Lydia stepped close to the tank, and the mermaid swam up to the glass. So far as Lydia could tell, she was the real deal, with gleaming gray-green scales and a long mane of undulating blond hair. The mermaid looked her over in turn, one eyebrow going up when she reached the spiky pink hair. Then the blond girl looked over Lydia's shoulder and burst out laughing, bright bubbles float-ing up to pop against the surface.

"Really? Charlie Dregs?" The words were muffled but unmis-takable.

Lydia looked back at Charlie, but she saw nothing laughable. His dark eyes were hard, his mouth frozen in a snarl.

She gave the mermaid the finger and turned to take Charlie's arm. As they walked away from the tank, Lydia said, "What's her problem?"

Charlie didn't answer right away. They had reached a wagon with no lights. The crowd gave it a wide berth, keeping to the lantern light around the outside of its blocky shadow. The painted puppet stage out front looked abandoned, and Charlie left Lydia front and center as he ducked behind the curtains with a smile.

Something rustled in the darkness; then a white rabbit popped up onstage, startling her before she realized it was a puppet. It hopped about exactly like a real rabbit and nosed the air before standing upright to dance a jig. In a voice that wasn't Charlie's, it said, "You might've noticed I'm different from the other Bludmen. I prefer puppets to people. Keep to myself. Not an alpha male, like Criminy. Not a beast, like the two-headed boy. Not cruel, like the mermaid. Not as big, not as good-looking, not as powerful. They don't really know me, much less like me." With a click, the rabbit's eyes turned red and fangs shot out of its mouth. "Truth is, I don't really like them, either."

She paused, afraid to break the puppet master's spell.

"I like you, Charlie Dregs," she whispered.

The rabbit disappeared, and Charlie emerged to face her. "That's enough, then."

"Even if I'm not real?"

"You're the realest thing I know, Lydia. If you're not real, we're all just pretending."

His hand slipped down her arm to entwine their fingers, and she decided that she, too, would pretend. She would pretend that her other world was the dream, that Jayson had just been a nightmare and that she'd never gone back to her father's house. She would pretend that she could stay here forever, have a future with Charlie and a place to belong, where she would be valued. She would pretend that she had hope.

They wandered back into the lights of the carnival, stopping to watch Criminy's magic show and clapping when glitter and streamers shot out from his top hat. They saw jugglers and dancing clockworks and played games of chance and rode the small Ferris wheel even though they were much too large. Laughing, smiling, they ended up near where they'd begun, by the tightrope. Far above, the girl in stripes wobbled on a unicycle.

"Where to next?" Lydia asked, and Charlie had just opened his mouth to reply when the crowd around the tightrope gasped.

"She's going to fall!" a woman shrieked.

Charlie let loose Lydia's hand and plunged into the throng of onlookers with superhero speed. The girl on the tightrope was in the process of a slow, melodramatic fall, her eyes wide and her arms pinwheeling. Finally, she swooned and plummeted toward the ground amid a chorus of screams. Lydia couldn't see what was going on, but judging by the clapping and whistling, Charlie must have caught the girl. More and more people arrived, craning their necks to see the spectacle, and Lydia backed away uneasily from the press of wide skirts, proud of Charlie's heroism but wishing he would come back to her soon.

She turned away. The moors beyond the lanterns were mesmerizing, rippling like a midnight ocean, beautiful and fathomless and otherworldly. Tiny, white night flowers bloomed amid the indigo-painted grass, and she couldn't help thinking of the Asphodel Meadows outside Hades, which her Classics 101 prof had called the Greek purgatory for those who led lives of inaction. She shivered at the night's cold emptiness and followed the path of a meandering stream with her eyes, curious if its icy waters would taste alive and invigorating or creep down, down into her chest, bitter with forgetfulness and oblivion. Her eyes were wet, her throat was dry, and taking in each ragged breath was a struggle.

When a sly voice asked, "Lost again?" she nearly jumped out of her skin.

But it wasn't Charlie.

"Yeah, she's lost," another voice answered.

"We can help you find your way."

A hand clamped down on her shoulder and she spun around. It was the two-headed boy she'd seen earlier, and their matching grins made her blood run cold.

"I'm fine," she said, shrugging out from under the filthy glove.

The boys took a step forward and she took a step backward, her head barely missing one of the lanterns. The chill of the moors hit her back like a punch to the kidney, and she gasped for air. The boys' body was broader than a usual person's, the arms stretched out in a gesture that might have been welcoming but felt far more sinister. The two heads looked at each other, and one snickered.

"She won't be missed," he hissed, barely a whisper above the mad yammer of the crowd.

Lydia stepped fully into the darkness of the field, her entire body going cold with panic. She couldn't see Charlie or Criminy or a single familiar face in the caravan—just hundreds of strangers swarming in the light. She was invisible again. She would have to take her chances in the field.

She had just sucked in a breath to run when she heard a voice from the moors behind her.

"Attacking innocent women again, boys? Honestly." The figure that stepped to her side smelled heavily of wet fur and fetid breath. It was the wolfman.

"Aw, Pietro. We'd share her with you."

"You can have the body, after. A nice, juicy femur?"

"Just give us the blood first. It's a fine deal."

Pietro growled, stepping between Lydia and the boys. "Go. Now. And I won't tell Master Stain. This is your last warning."

The wolfman's voice was cultured but thick, as if there weren't enough room in his mouth for all his teeth and tongue. One of the boys' heads spit a glob of blood at Lydia's slippers before he disappeared into the crowd. She stepped back into the light and craned her neck for Charlie, but couldn't find him.

"You'll be looking for Mr. Dregs, I wager. I can sniff him out for you." Pietro gallantly held out his arm, and she took it, careful not to show distaste at the odd squish of damp jacket on thick fur.

"Thanks for saving me," she said.

"You're very welcome, my dear. I take it you're new to the caravan?"

He guided her around the crowd, and she turned to look back. "But Charlie—"

"We can't get near him right now, not with that nosy rabble. But I'll drop you off at his wagon and send him along. Locks from the inside, you know. The twins won't be able to touch you."

"I want to wait for him."

She tried to slow down but tripped and stumbled, and he slung her up to carry her pressed uncomfortably against his lapels as the alarm bells in her head began to ring.

"You're understandably upset. But with all these Bludmen around, I can see why."

The wolfman was strong, and they were already beyond the crowd. When she opened her mouth to shout, his hand latched over her lips, digging claws into her flesh and making her retch. Lydia kicked and struggled in his arms, but he was solid and unrelenting. One black lip lifted in warning.

"Don't try me, girl. I'm doing you a favor."

Lydia squealed and tried to kick him, but the little slippers were barely anything, and one flew off to land in the dirt by Charlie's puppet stage as they passed. Pietro ducked behind a painted backdrop, pushed through the door of a light-blue wagon, and dumped her on the floor. She landed hard as he locked the door and turned on the lights. The humming orange lamps showed a genteel sitting room replete with oil paintings and curly-legged tables and an ornate full-length mirror. Pietro stopped in front of it, slipping off his coat and inspecting his teeth with a black-padded finger. He smoothed the brown and black fur on his face before turning to her with a sinister grin.

"The twins were right about one thing. You won't be missed."

Fierce resolve blazed through Lydia as she realized that she would do anything, fight any fight, to stay alive, here and now, in this world. She looked around the room for a window, another door, a weapon, anything. There was nothing.

"Oh, no. Wait. They were right about two things. I do enjoy a nice femur."

She gasped before she could stop herself, then scrambled to her feet. Pietro walked toward her slowly, his boots heavy on the wood boards. Lydia picked up a chair and slung it at him, but he dashed it to the ground in pieces. When he threw his head back in a howling laugh, she grabbed a jagged chair leg off the floor and stabbed him in the thigh before dashing to the door. She barely had time to turn the top two bolts before heavy paws landed on her shoulders, knocking the shawl away. The wolfman shoved her against the mirror, and the ice-cold glass kissed the nape of her neck.

"There's nowhere to run. Nowhere you can hide from me."

She kneed him in the wounded thigh and dodged for the door again. His claws raked the mirror with a harsh squeal, right where her throat had been seconds before. She had the last two locks unbolted before he caught her again. If she could just live long enough to open the door, maybe she could escape or call for help.

But not this time. The wolfman's arms wrapped around her waist, pulling her to his chest with an intimacy that made her squirm.

"You sick bastard," she shouted, and he dug his fingers into her sides.

"I'm not sick, dearest. It's only natural."

With a growl of her own, she sunk her teeth into his arm, gagging on the hair and fabric, and he threw her to the ground. Bruised and trembling, she scrambled backward until she fetched up against the wall beside a claw-scratched sofa. Her assailant went into a crouch, the animal movement at odds with his dapper outfit. She kicked a table at him, and he batted it aside. There was nothing left to throw, nothing left to hide behind, and his smile said he knew it.

"Look at it this way. I'm protecting you from that vile Bludman. He would suck you dry, given half a chance, perhaps even turn you into a monster like himself. This way you stay pure. Retain your virtue."

She was getting ready to aim a kick at his balls when the door burst open.

"Lydia!"

Charlie charged across the room, eyes wide with fury. His lips pulled back to show fangs even sharper than Pietro's as his talons sought the beast's neck.

"Charlie! Be careful!"

With a snarl, Pietro leaped on top of Lydia, crushing her against the wall. She threw an arm up to protect her face, and wicked teeth closed around her wrist, ripping into the flesh and scraping on bone. The wolfman didn't stop chewing when Charlie roared, but the Bludman's sharp kick to his stomach got his attention, forcing him to drop her. Lydia scooted away, clutching the mauled and bleeding wrist to her chest, her body running hot and cold with shock and fear. Charlie wound his fingers into the wolfman's hair to tip back his head. A vicious swipe of the Bludman's white claws ripped out the thickly furred throat in one wet gobbet.

Tossing the limp body aside, Charlie cradled Lydia against his chest, his hands hovering over the numb, shivering wreckage of her useless arm.

"It'll be fine, love. He's dead. It's over now," he whispered in her ear.

"But my wrist. The veins. The blood. I'm dying again, aren't I?"

"Maybe." He swallowed hard and kissed her forehead. "Maybe not. I can try turning you. That would heal over right quick if you were a Bludman."

"And then I could stay here?"

"I don't know, love."

She took a ragged breath and gazed into his eyes. They shone with hunger and what might be love.

"What have I got to lose?" she said.

He brought her wrist tenderly to his mouth, his lips soft and searing. She was enveloped in warmth and numbness. And then, with a frightening familiarity, everything dissolved into darkness.

LYDIA WOKE TO sunlight and the robot breath of air-conditioning set just a little too low. Outside her window, the ocean lapped restlessly at the shore. She was in her daybed, the sheets pulled up to her chin and tucked tightly over her arms. Her stomach twisted as she recognized her bedroom, and she squeezed her eyes shut, hoping to wish it away.

"Welcome back."

"Charlie?"

"I thought his name was Jayson."

She knew that voice well. "Dr. Werner. Why are you here?"

He had been her private physician since her mother died giving birth to her, and she wasn't surprised when he sat on the corner of her bed. She didn't open her eyes. She'd always despised his artificially benevolent smile.

"Your father called me. He's worried about you."

"Can you put me back to sleep?"

There was an uncomfortable pause. "Your father pays me to keep you alive, Lydia. Now, can you tell me why you tried to kill yourself?"

She shook her head. "It doesn't matter. I want to go back."

"Back to college? Alone? You know you can't do that."

"Back to sleep. Back to Sang."

He sighed sadly. "Lydia, you can't go back to sleep. Open your eyes and look at me. We have to talk."

"No."

"I know you wanted your father's attention, and now you've got it. He trusted you. You promised you wouldn't go back to that tattoo parlor."

Tears stung her eyes, and she wrenched an arm out from under the blanket and flung it over her face. The gauze was soft against her forehead as it soaked up the tears.

"I had to go back. I had to see him again."

"Lydia, Jayson doesn't know who you are. Your father asked me to talk to him. Jayson doesn't even know your name. Whatever romance you've concocted in your head—it doesn't exist." Dr. Werner leaned close and whispered, "I'm going to be brutally honest. You're just an overprotected little rich girl, playing at suicide and making Daddy angry with your obsession with that tattooed sideshow freak."

"Don't you get it, Dr. Werner? I *am* the tattooed sideshow freak!" She pulled her other arm out from under the sheet to show him her forearms, even though her wrists still stung. "I'm a legal adult, and even if he does own half of Nashville, he doesn't own my skin—he doesn't own this unicorn, or this sparrow, or this winged snake. They're mine, and he can't take them away. And I finally found a place where they make me special and beautiful, a place where I fit in."

The pause spun out longer this time, but she utterly refused to fill the silence or open her eyes to a world she'd already abandoned and the room she'd outgrown at fourteen. Dr. Werner sighed deeply.

"Lydia. I need you to open your eyes. Please. Look at your arms."

Her breath caught in her throat. What was he playing at? Surely the cuts hadn't messed up her ink too much, not if he'd sewn them with any care.

She opened her eyes just a little and immediately squeezed them shut again.

"Lydia."

"No."

"Lydia, there are no tattoos."

"There are. I have a job at the carnival. Ink like mine—it's rare. Charlie likes it."

The doctor placed his hand against her forehead, and she shook it off.

"Your father wants me to stay nearby while you recover. After your little trick with the mirror shards, he's put up cameras and taken the door off the hinges. You can't hurt yourself now. We can help you heal."

She swallowed a sob. "Am I allowed to use the bathroom, at least?"

He looked away, cleared his throat. "I can't leave the room, but I'll turn my back."

Lydia slid out of her bed, stunned to see the uninked skin of her legs poking dully out of a flower-sprigged gown. As she passed the empty place that had once held an ornate floor-length mirror, she was struck by a series of fun-house-mirror memories that seemed as ephemeral as the ringmaster's glitter strewn against the stars.

Passing a tattoo parlor while walking from the bookstore to her posh condo. Watching the artist through the plate glass, laughing with a pretty girl with spiky pink hair as he tattooed sparrows on her clavicles. Going back the next day to watch him drawing art at a table, running his hand through long, dark hair. Making a daily pilgrimage past the shop to see what he was doing. Skipping class to sit at the café across the street and imagine him undressing her on the black leather sofa by his station. Checking his website daily for new flash and printing out every design, pinning them to her blank, white walls. Buying a rainbow of Sharpies and sitting alone in the cold apartment, drawing on her skin and imagining the buzz of his needle, the brand of his eyes, the endorphins shuddering through her as his wrist rested gently against her pounding pulse. Scrubbing the Sharpie away before Sunday brunch with her father.

And finally, catching Jayson in an alley, kissing the pink-haired tattooed girl.

Things went dark after that.

Her feet were leaden as if still bruised by stones through thin slippers. The bathroom door was gone. So was the mirror, leaving behind scarred plaster. At least she didn't have to look at her perfectly straight blond hair and mud-brown eyes and uninked skin and the beautiful face that didn't match who she was in her heart. The father-daughter photos with their glass frames and the gilt cup that had held tweezers and eyebrow scissors were also gone. Her father was so determined to keep her here, to keep her safe, to keep her pure. To keep her for himself.

Sitting down on the gleaming tub and breathing in the scent of blood washed over with bleach, Lydia turned her face away from the life of splendor she'd always known but never loved. She pulled down the gauze on her wrists and saw for the first time how ugly and harsh stitches could be, bristling and black. On the left, the crooked seam held a Sharpie-drawn heart inelegantly together as if it had always been broken.

Setting her teeth against a knot in the stitching, she began to gnaw with an animal's rabid hunger. The blood on her tongue tasted of victory and freedom, and she waited to hear the calliope dancing on starlight, to feel the lanterns' warmth kissing her tattoos and Charlie's fingers in her hair.

Soon she would wake up in Sang as a Bludman. She'd open her eyes to her own Elysium, dance through the flower-dotted fields in the powerful body of an elegant monster, an untouchable predator, a creature of her own devising that carried forever the mark of the man she'd chosen for her own. She would pull him into the shadows, draw his hands down to her inked skin, dare him into abandoning all pretense of being a gentleman. The caravan had called her, but Charlie had saved her, and he would save her again.

She'd bitten out all the stitches in her left wrist and half the ones on her right before the darkness finally fell, before she finally got past the skin and struck bone.

"The Demon Barker of Wheat Street"

An Iron Druid Chronicles Short Story

Kevin Hearne

(*This story takes place six years after* Tricked, *the fourth book of the* Iron Druid Chronicles, *and two weeks after the events of the novella* Two Ravens and One Crow.)

I fear Kansas.

It's not a toe-curling type of fear, where shoulders tense with an incipient cringe; it's more of a vague apprehension, an expectation that something will go pear shaped and cause me great inconvenience. It's like the dread you feel when going to meet a girl's father: Though it's probably going to be just fine, you're aware that no matter how broadly he smiles, part of him wants you to be a eunuch and he wouldn't mind performing the operation himself. Kansas is like that for me. But I hear lots of nice things about it from other people.

My anxiety stems from impolitic thinking a long time ago. I am usually quite careful to shield my thoughts and think strictly business in my Latin headspace, because that's the one I use to talk with the elementals who grant me my powers as a Druid. But once—and all it takes is once—I let slip the opinion that I thought the American central plains were a bit boring. The elemental—whom I've thought of as "Amber" since the early twentieth century, thanks to the "amber waves of grain" thing—heard me and I've been paying for it ever since. The magic doesn't flow as well for me there anymore. Sometimes my bindings fizzle for no apparent reason, and I know it's just Amber messing with me. As a result, I look uncomfortable whenever I visit and people wonder if I'm suffering from dyspepsia. Or maybe they stare because I don't look like a local. I'd fit right in on a beach in California with my surfer dude façade, but at the Kansas Wheat Festival, not so much.

Said Wheat Festival was in Wellington, Kansas, the hometown of my apprentice, Granuaile MacTiernan. We were visiting in disguise because she wanted to check up on her mother. We'd faked Granuaile's death a few years ago—for very good reasons—but now she was worried about how her mom was coping. For the past few years she'd been satisfied by updates from private investigators willing to do some long-distance stalking, but an overwhelming urge to lay eyes on her mother in person had overtaken her. I hadn't been able to fully persuade her that it was a bad idea to visit people who thought you were dead, so I tagged along in case she managed to get into trouble. Granuaile said I could look at it as a vacation from the rigors of training her, and since I'd recently escaped death in Oslo by the breadth of a whisker, I hadn't needed much convincing to take a break for my mental health. We brought my Irish wolfhound, Oberon, along with us and promised him that we'd go hunting.

<Set me loose on a colony of prairie dogs, Atticus. I'll show them what a real dog is,> he told me. <Or point me at some antelope. Can we go after antelope?>

Sure, buddy, I replied through our mental link. *But that's going to be quite a run. Hard to sneak up on anything in flat land like this.*

<You can hum the theme music from *Chariots of Fire* once we hit full stride. It will make the antelope run in slow motion like the movie and then it will be easy.>

I'm not sure it works like that.

Red hair dyed black and shoved underneath a Colorado Rockies cap pulled low, Granuaile had already taken care of her most distinguishable feature in one go. She had on a pair of those ridiculously oversized sunglasses, too, which hid her green eyes and the freckles high up on her cheeks. A shirt from Dry Dock Brewing in Aurora, a pair of khaki shorts, and sandals suggested that she was a crunchy hippie type from the Denver area. I was dressed similarly, but I wore my Rockies cap backward because Granuaile said it made me look clueless, and that's precisely what I wanted. If I was a clueless crunchy guy, then I couldn't be a Druid more than two thousand years old who was also supposed to have died in the Arizona desert six years before.

Everybody in Wellington knew Granuaile's mom because everyone knew her stepfather. Beau Thatcher was something of an oil baron and employed a large percentage of those locals who weren't wheat farmers. A few inquiries here and there with the right gossips—we posed as friends of her late daughter—and small-town nosiness did most of the work for us. According to reports, her mother was properly mournful without having locked herself in her house with pills and booze. She was taking it all about as well as could be expected, and once we expressed an entirely fake interest in dropping by to pay her a visit, we were ruefully informed by one of her "best friends" that she was off on a Caribbean cruise right now, or else she'd be at the festival.

I hoped my relief didn't show too plainly. Though I'd wrung a promise from Granuaile that we wouldn't visit her house, there had still been a chance of an unfortunate meeting somewhere in town. Now I could relax a bit and bask in the success of our passive spying in the vein of Polonius: "And thus do we of wisdom and of reach, / With windlasses and with assays of bias, / By indirections find directions out . . ."

Having satisfied her need to know that her mother was adjusting well, if not her need to see her in person, we enjoyed the festivities, which included chucking cow patties at a target for fabulous prizes. Oberon didn't understand the attraction.

<I don't get it. You guys look down on chimps for flinging their own poo but you think it's fine to fling other kinds of poo around? I mean, you get opposable thumbs and this is what you do with them?>

The town had invited an old-fashioned carnival to set up alongside the more bland wheat-related events. It had some rides that looked capable of triggering a rush of adrenaline, so once the sun set we passed through the rented fencing to see if we could be entertained. Sunglasses weren't practical at night, so Granuaile just kept her hat pulled low.

Though health codes didn't seem all that important to this particular operation, I cast camouflage on Oberon so that we wouldn't get barred from the venue. The spell bound Oberon's pigments to the ones of his surroundings, which rendered him invisible when motionless and as good as invisible at night, even when on the move.

It's odd how a dog roaming around is a health code violation but serving fried death on a stick isn't. The food vendors didn't seem to rank using wholesome wheaty-wheat in their foodstuffs high in their priorities, despite the name of the festival to which they were catering. Salt and grease and sugar were the main offerings, tied together here and there with animal bits or highly processed starches.

Bright lights and garish painted colors on the rides and game booths did their best to distract patrons from the layer of grime coating everything. The metal parts on the rides groaned and squealed; they'd taken punishment for years and had been disassembled and assembled again with a minimum of care—and a minimum of lubricant.

The carnies working the game booths were universally afflicted with rotting teeth and gingivitis, a dire warning of what would happen if one ate the carnival food and failed to find a toothbrush afterward. They made no effort to be charming; sneers and leers were all they could manage for the people they had been trained to see as marks instead of humans. Granuaile wanted to chuck softballs at steel milk bottles.

"You go ahead. I can't," I said.

"Why not?"

"Because the carnie will mock me for not winning his rigged game, and then I'll be tempted to cheat and unbind the bottles a bit so that they all fall over, which would mean I'd receive something enormous and fluffy."

"If the game's rigged, then you're not cheating. You're leveling the playing field. And if you decided to reward your apprentice with something enormous and fluffy for all of her hard work, then there's really no downside."

<Hey, Atticus, I'm enormous! And if you got me a poodle bitch, then she would be fluffy. You could make us *both* happy with a poodle, see?>

"The downside is I'm not on good terms with the elemental here. Using the earth's magic for something trivial like that would hardly improve matters. Camouflaging Oberon so he can walk around with us is bad enough."

<I'd be happy to walk around in plain sight, Atticus.>

You might scare the children.

<What? But I'm cuddly! "Single Irish wolfhound likes long walks on the beach and belly rubs.">

Granuaile went a few rounds with the milk bottles and the carnie tried to chivvy me into "rescuing" her. My apprentice nearly assaulted him for that but showed admirable restraint.

"Whatsa matter, can't hit the ground if you fell out of a plane?" he called to me.

"Whatsa matter, employers don't provide a dental plan?" I responded.

He didn't want to open his mouth after that, and Granuaile finished her game play scowling.

"It's funny," she said as we walked away. "People come here to be happy but I bet they wind up in a fouler mood than when they walked in. Kids want plushies and rides and sugar, and parents want to hang on to their money and their kids. And everybody wants to go away without digestive problems, but *that's* not gonna happen."

"I can't argue with that."

"So why do people come here?"

I shrugged. "Because we pursue happiness even when it runs away from us."

We passed several booths, ignored the pitches of more carnies with alarming hygiene issues, and examined the faces of people walking by. There were no smiles, only stress and anger and frustration.

"See, there's no happiness here," Granuaile pointed out.

Distant screams of terror reached us from the rides. "Maybe you would find it amusing to experience the joys of centrifugal force." I waved toward the flashing lights of the carnival's midway. "Allow the machinery to jostle the fluid in your inner ear."

"Oh." She grinned at me. "Well, if you put it like that."

"Step right here!" a voice cut into our conversation. "Priceless entertainment for only three dollars! Gape at the Impossibly Whiskered Woman! Thrill at the Three-Armed Man and watch those

hands! Chunder with the force of thunder at the Conjoined Quintuplets! Guaranteed to harrow your soul for only three dollars!"

The barker hawking hyperbole was a dwarf on stilts. Dark pin-
striped pants and oversized clown shoes masked his wooden limbs
and remained very still while his torso gesticulated and waved wee,
chubby, white-sleeved arms at potential spectators. A red paisley
waistcoat flashed and caught lights from the midway, giving his
torso the appearance of flickering flames. His eyes were shadowed
by a bowler hat, but his mouth never stopped moving, and it was
working. A line of people queued outside a yellow pavilion tent,
drawn there as much by the barker as by curiosity over the stunned
people coming out the other side.

"Amazin'," one mumbled as he staggered past me. His eyes
seemed unfocused and his mouth hung slack in disturbing fashion.
He didn't seem to be addressing anyone in particular. "Incredible.
Whadda trip. Sirsley. I mean rilly. Nothin' like it."

My first, somewhat cynical thought was that he was a plant by
the management. But then I noticed that more and more people
kept coming out of the tent with their minds clearly boggled, too
many to be in on the shill. The barker kept fishing with his verbal
bait and was hooking plenty of people.

"It's not a House of Horror! It's a Tent of Terror! Add thrills
and add chills and you get *adventure*! Only three bucks to reap
what you sow!"

The last line struck me as a non sequitur and I looked around
to see if anyone else had been bothered by it. It was an odd pitch to
make for a carnival amusement, but people were forking over their
cash to a muscle-bound hulk at the entrance and walking inside as
the barker continued to weave together rhymes and alliterative
phrases in a tapestry of bombast.

"Two tumescent tumors on either side of her nose! Face cancer
ain't for the faint of heart! We have the freaks but you can't get

freaky—all you get is a peekie! See the sights that can't be unseen for only three dollars!"

"Huh," Granuaile said. "That sounds interesting. What do you think they have in there? A woman who let someone draw on her face with a Sharpie?"

"Only one way to find out."

<Can I go in too?>

Sure, if you can keep close and sneak past the bouncer.

We joined the queue and observed a profound lack of excitement in my fellow entrants. The mood was one of passive resignation to the coming rip-off, albeit garnished with a wedge of hope, sort of like stinky beer graced with a slice of orange.

Oberon easily slipped through into the tent with us once we paid the mountain of beef manning the door. We were immediately confronted with a slab of painted plywood serving as a wall and a lurid sign that shouted at us: LAST CHANCE: CHOOSE HEAVEN (left) or HELL (right).

"Is it the same either way?" Granuaile wondered aloud.

"No idea," I said. There was a bit of a backup going to the hell side, so I suggested we go left.

"Well, in case it's different, I'd like to see what's going on in hell," she said. "Let's split up and compare notes outside."

I shrugged. "Okay. See you soon." Then I asked Oberon, *Which way do you want to go, buddy?*

<I think I'll go with Granuaile. Curiosity killed the cat but never hurt a hound, you know.>

All right, keep talking to me and let me know what you see.

<I see a poodle in my future.>

I'm sure you do, I replied as I turned left and followed a couple of switchbacks.

<She is a black standard poodle and her name is Noche. That's Spanish for *night*.>

Yeah. I know.

<We chase squirrels in the morning and then we lie down on a bed of sausages.>

I wasn't soliciting your fantasies, Oberon. I was rather hoping you'd tell me what you see in the present.

<I don't see any poodles at present. No sausages, either.>

I sighed and dropped my eyes to the bare ground over which the tent had been erected. What grass remained was well trampled and forlorn, perhaps wondering why it, of all grass, had to suffer a herd of bipeds to crush it into the earth. Rounding another plywood barrier, I was confronted with a large woman wearing a costume beard, Grizzly Adams–style. The elastic band keeping it in place was plainly visible over her ears. Next to her stood a man with a cheap, old-fashioned prosthetic arm attached to his chest via a clever arrangement of suspenders and bungee cords. He grabbed the forearm with his left hand and raised it a bit, then wiggled it to make the plastic hand flap at me. I shook my head in disgust and moved on, hoping something more inventive would be around the next sheet of plywood.

<Hey, Atticus, is it normal for there to be stairs in a tent?>

What? No.

<We're going down a staircase. Looks like they slapped wood planks on top of solid earth. We've been walking on wood the whole time, actually.>

I spun around and searched for trapdoors or anything else that might indicate a trip down below on my side. Nothing. No wood flooring, either. The idiot three-armed man flapped his prosthetic hand again, figuring I wanted additional proof of his dexterity.

Have you seen anything stupid posing as a thrill?

<No, we turned a corner and *boom*, stairs headed down.>

That's weird. It's completely different on this side. Seems more elaborate than all their costuming.

Maybe it was a thematic thing. Their side was supposed to be hell, after all. If my side was heaven, though, where was the stairway to it? I hurried around the next corner and saw the woman with two "tumors"—they were red gumdrops attached to her cheeks with adhesive. And the conjoined quintuplets were there too: "They" were one guy with two shrunken plastic heads resting on either shoulder.

How could anyone walk out of here and praise this farce? It made no sense, especially since the few other people who'd chosen this side with me were obviously annoyed by the extent of the swindle. I didn't know what to expect around the next wall, most likely the exit, so I was surprised by a little blond girl, maybe eight years old, in a pretty pink dress and shiny black shoes. She would have been adorable had her eyes not been glowing orange. The smile she smiled was decidedly un-girlish—more like inhuman— and her voice was one of those low basso frequencies that shiver your bones.

"You came alone and it was the most amazing thing you've ever seen," she rumbled, and a wave of her power—or perhaps I should say *its* power—did its best to slap me upside the head. Since my aura was bound to the cold iron of my amulet, the mojo fizzled and delivered a small thump to my chest, like someone had poked me right on the amulet. She was standing on a square of plywood. I blinked as I realized that the deception going on here was much grander than a three-dollar fraud.

I kicked off my sandals and stopped hiding from Amber the elemental. I'd been powering Oberon's camouflage with stored magic in my bear charm, but it was running low and the orange-eyed girl demanded more resources, seeing as how she was casually slinging around hoodoo and speaking like she had a giant pair of balls that dropped two feet after puberty. I drew energy through the tattoos that bound me to the earth and watched as the girl repeated the ensorceling phrase for the person behind me. It was a young man in a white cowboy hat, and he rocked back visibly under the little girl's greeting before his expression assumed a thousand-mile stare and he became a mouth breather.

<Atticus, something isn't right.>

No kidding. I activated the charm on my necklace that allowed me to see in the magical spectrum and discovered that wee miss was an imp crammed into a human shell. That shell was the same thing as taking a hostage: If I attacked it and it couldn't bamboozle people anymore, those same people would think I was assaulting a child.

<We just went through this weird door made of this jelly stuff. More like an orifice, really . . . We sort of squirted through the middle and it was gross. It smells bad down here. Blood and bad meat and that poo you like to fling around. It's coming from some-place ahead.>

I frowned. *Stop. Don't go any farther. I'm coming to join you. In fact, go back.*

<But Granuaile is going forward.>

She couldn't hear Oberon's thoughts yet, since she was still about six years away from getting bound to the earth. *Grab her by the shirt or something. Pull her back. Don't let her go.*

I spent a few seconds trying to think of how to beat the imp without a kerfuffle until I realized it wasn't trying to prevent my escape. All I had to do was act dumb and walk out. Picking up my sandals, I did precisely that, vowing to return later. Once safely out-side, I sprinted around to the front of the tent to have another go.

<She's getting mad at me, Atticus. She's telling me to stop and let her go. And there are people cramming in behind us.>

Don't let her go! I'm on my way.

<I'll try, but she's really determined.>

The line at the front of the tent was just as long as when we entered—perhaps longer. The barker, I saw through magical sight, was actually a full-fledged demon. The huge man at the door taking money was an imp, so the barker was the boss. His words came back to me: Guaranteed to harrow your soul. Reap what you sow. And then, in writing, an offer to choose hell. I couldn't afford to wait in line again.

<Um, Atticus, we've moved down the hall a bit. There's another weird door ahead, like a full-body turnstile, and I think these things are one-way. Great big bears! The smell is awful now and people already through it are screaming and trying to get back where we are, but they can't. And the people on this side—Granuaile included—can't wait to walk through to where the screaming is. This isn't any fun and I think you should get your money back.>

Can't you stop her?

<I tried! She *hit* me, Atticus! On the nose!>

That didn't sound like Granuaile at all. She loved Oberon every bit as much as I did. Only one thing could explain her behavior. *Oberon, she's under a spell. These are demons at work. You have to stop her. Knock her down and sit on her if you have to.*

Oberon weighed more than she did. He could keep her pinned.

<Demons? Why don't I smell them?>

Normally demons smell so bad that it takes a herculean effort to keep your lunch down. I shot another look at the demon barker but saw no one violently ill in his vicinity. Neither the man at the entrance nor the girl at the exit had set my nose twitching.

They've sewn themselves up tight in human bodies. Have you got her?

<Not yet. She's not the average human. You've been training her for six years.>

I'm going to dissolve your camouflage and hope the sight of you helps. You have to stop her, Oberon.

I dissolved his spell and then triggered camouflage for myself, which would allow me to slip past the imp at the door.

However, nothing happened.

"Oh, no, not now, Amber," I said, and then reached through my tattoos to speak directly to the elemental of the central Great Plains. *Speaking* was a relative term; elementals don't speak any human language but rather communicate via emotions and images. My recollections of such conversations are always approximations.

//Demons on earth / Druid requires aid//

Amber replied immediately, not even pretending that she didn't know I was around. //Query: Demon location? / None sensed//

//Demons here// I replied. //My location / Demons using wood to mask presence//

The bloody barker hadn't been insecure about his height; he needed the stilts to make sure the earth never twigged to his presence.

Demons were usually the responsibility of their angelic opposites, but I've run into them more often than I would care to. The problem with them from a Druidic perspective was that they kept trying to hijack the earth's power to open and maintain portals to hell, draining life in the process and endangering the elementals. Aenghus Óg's giant suckhole to the fifth circle, for example, had destroyed fifty square miles in Arizona. If there was a gateway underground here, Amber should have felt it.

//Query: Power drain in this area?// I asked.

//Yes / Intermittent//

//Demons responsible// I said.

Amber's judgment and sentence took no time at all. Her anger boiled through me as she said, //Slay them / Full power restored//

//Gratitude / Harmony//

//Harmony//

Had I the time, I might have shed a tear at that—or celebrated with a shot of whiskey. It had been far too long since I'd shared a sense of harmony with Amber—because these were feelings, after all, not mere translated words, and it was impossible for either Amber or me to lie about feeling harmony. But I had an apprentice and a hound in danger of going through a mysterious unholy orifice, as well as another mystery to solve: since the demons obviously had some kind of portal down there, how were they hiding it?

<Okay, Atticus, she's down, but she's hitting me and yelling, and that hurts.>

You're a good hound. We are totally getting you some gourmet sausages for this. Keep her down. She'll apologize later.

I cast camouflage successfully this time and melted from view. It didn't make me completely invisible when I moved, but it was good enough; no one would be able to see me in time to react well.

Except perhaps the demon barker.

"You, sir! What do you think you're doing?" He was staring right at me, even though I was camouflaged and still. Damn it. I didn't have a weapon, either. Since stealth didn't seem to be an option, my only hope lay in speed and some martial arts. I bolted for the entrance and the barker shouted, "Gobnob! I mean George! Stop that man!"

The imp's name was Gobnob?

"What man?" the hulk said as I whisked past him. Apparently only the demon could pierce my camouflage. Advantage: Druid.

Indiscreet shoving was necessary to get past the line of people and down the stairs. I heard lots of "Heys" and "What the (bleep)s" as I endangered ankles and hips.

"Sorry," I called. "It's an emergency."

<Aughh! Atticus, she got away from me! She's heading for the second thingie!>

Grab her pants leg in your teeth and pull back hard. Don't let her get traction!

<Fail! She's through!>
Go after her and protect her!

The first bizarre "orifice" was ahead. An imp in a human suit was stationed there and charming people much the way the little girl imp was at the exit on the "heaven" side, except that this fellow was telling people, "You can't wait to get through the next doorway after this one." That's why Granuaile and the rest of them kept going even when they heard and smelled something awful ahead.

It was time to put a stick in their spokes.

There wasn't any need to think about it: Amber had ordered me to slay the demons, so I was going to do it. Before I passed through the gross doorway, I placed one hand on top of the imp's head and the other underneath his chin and jerked it violently to the side, snapping his neck.

As he crumpled I yelled, "Go back! They're killing people in here!" The "What the (bleep)s" multiplied, and I hoped for their sakes that their sense of self-preservation would win out over curiosity. They were quite confused because they hadn't precisely seen me kill the imp, but they did know that something had gone horribly wrong and someone had been severely injured. Some of them pulled out cell phones and dialed 911, and at least a couple expressed a loud desire to get out of there and headed back up the stairs.

The orifice was wet and smelled fishy and I had to sort of slither through it, since it was a slit cut into a quivering wall of protoplasm; I felt squeezed out through a pastry chef's frosting gun. Dubbing it the Anchovy Gate due to its odor, I decided, for my own sanity, not to dwell on whether its substance had been secreted or shat or otherwise spawned from unsavory origins. It was a kind of gelatinous, semitranslucent slab of dead lavender sludge that filled the space completely from floor to ceiling, a tight sphincter sealing one environment off from another. Its function was clear: Without the protections it provided against smells and sound, nobody would want to continue onward, for the stench on the other side of it made me gag and the howls of people dying ahead filled me with fear for Granuaile and Oberon.

What's happening? I asked my hound.

<Atticus, I don't think we're in Kansas anymore.>

Nonsense. I can still hear you.

<They are killing people in here. Granuaile kind of woke up and figured out we're in trouble. But so did everybody else.>

Almost there.

<Hurry!>

Everyone ahead of me had been charmed. Their need to get through that next gate was the call of a siren. If the first one had been the Anchovy Gate, this was the Needle Gate, I suppose. It was designed like those tire-shredding devices; you were fine to go through it one way, but try to back up and you'd be punctured with slivers of steel.

Still, whatever was happening on the other side, people were opting for the needles and trying to push backward through the needles, getting cut up in the process. Pelting through the charmed victims until I reached the gateway, I drew on the earth's power for enhanced speed and strength—bindings that essentially improved the efficiency of my neuromuscular system and prevented fatigue.

The Needle Gate was a mass of hinged, bloody steel spikes, doubtless constructed in chunks and then assembled here like the tent and the rides and everything else. The metal didn't burn my skin—in fact, it was quite cool, as one might expect metal underground to be. The fabled temperature of hell wasn't in play here; the horror of it was.

I pressed through the clacking hiss of needles and came through low onto a killing floor, rolling out of the way of a desperate middle-aged man whose face was streaked with snot and tears and spattered with blood. He tried to stick his arm into the gap in the gate I'd just vacated and wound up puncturing it on all sides. The needles must have had wee barbs on the outer sides so that as one passed through the gate they wouldn't snag; but once you tried to back up, you'd be not only stabbed but hooked. There were at least a dozen other people crowding the gate, trying to get out as I was trying to get in, and some of them had caught their hands and arms on needles in their desperate attempts to escape, so now they could either tear free or remain stuck, but either way they had pain to deal with on top of their terror. Two people—a man and a woman—had been pushed into the needles by accident or design and were now wailing in agony, unable to win free. It looked like others, in the frenzy of their fear, might be more than willing to tear them lose forcibly or even use their bodies to wedge the gate open if it meant escape. Thankfully, Granuaile wasn't one of those crowding around the gate.

Oberon? I'm through the door.

<Go to the right and help us with this thing!>

I squeezed through a couple more rows of panicked citizens and emerged into an abattoir. The floor was cheap, splintery wood laid over the earth. The ceiling was surprisingly high—we had descended deeper than I thought. The reason for the height lay at the far end of the room, which was about the length of a high school cafeteria: ghouls had stacked bodies nearly to the top and were adding more rows of fresh kills, presumably for later consumption. A demon with a scythe was supplying the freshness, and right then he was after Granuaile.

He wasn't the actual grim reaper but a demon that had assumed the likeness; enough people associated a robed skeletal figure with hell that it made sense for a demon to take that form. It was certainly working on the psychological front.

The reaper had on the iconic long black robe but had pulled back the cowl, exposing the rictus of a merciless white skull. Tiny fires blazed in his eye sockets, and he appeared competent with the scythe, whirling it around by the little handle halfway down the shaft. Granuaile was leaping over or ducking under his swings, and losing steam, but she would have been dispatched long ago if she hadn't trained the last six years with me in tumbling and martial arts.

Oberon had quite rightly concluded he couldn't be a dog in this fight; he was barking and trying to distract the demon but otherwise staying out of range of the scythe.

Like many long weapons, scythes are fearsome if you're right at the arc of their swing. But they're slow and cumbersome to wield, and if you can get inside that arc, you have a decent chance to deal a debilitating blow to an ill-guarded opponent.

Back me up, buddy.

I charged the demon and went for a slide tackle that would have made Manchester United proud. I dissolved my camouflage as I moved so that Oberon could see me, but unfortunately the demon also caught this in his peripheral vision. If he was anything like the barker he probably could have seen through it anyway, but my abrupt pop into view triggered a reflex action. He leapt over my slide and landed astride me, raising the scythe high above his head to harvest my dumb ass. With his eye sockets cast down at me, he didn't see Oberon coming.

My hound—a buck-fifty and all muscle—hit the demon square in the chest, bowling him over. Oberon's momentum caused him to trample the demon and keep going, which was just as well, because the reaper rolled and regained his feet with a backward somersault, still holding on to his weapon and facing me.

Well done, Oberon. Stay behind him but don't charge. He knows you're back there. Growl and keep him nervous.

The reaper advanced on me, swinging his weapon in a weaving pattern that forced me to backpedal. But once I had the timing of it down, I lunged inside the blade following a backswing and turned my right forearm to block the shaft, continuing to spin around to the left so that I could ram my left elbow into his teeth. Seeing that stagger him, I followed up, shoving the heel of my right palm as hard as I could underneath the reaper's jaw. The skull, bereft of convenient muscles and tendons to anchor it firmly to the neck and shoulders, popped clean off, and the flames died in the sockets.

<Attaboy, Atticus! Don't fear the reaper!>

This isn't done.

I checked on Granuaile. She was breathing heavily and looked exhausted but didn't look wounded.

"You okay?" I asked. She nodded in the affirmative right as a chorus of roars erupted from the far side of the abattoir. The ghouls had just realized I'd killed the reaper, and their rage was answered by a new wave of screams from the carnival goers. A few stragglers had poured in during the fight and the nightmare set before their suddenly cleared minds was of the brick-shitting sort.

Ghouls are unclean, since they feast on the dead or on bits of the dead and get exposed to all sorts of filth and disease. Conveniently, they're immune to infection and poison, but wild ones like these weren't terribly worried about spreading such things around. Their fingernails—which should probably be classified as claws— are coated with all sorts of virulent shit. One scratch would probably spell a death sentence without a source of high-powered antibiotics nearby. Of course, if a ghoul is trying to open you up with its claws, the likelihood of you living long enough to die by disease is small.

Back in Arizona, there was a small group—or I should say a shroud—of ghouls that had learned how to blend in well with the population. They were incredibly handy lads to have around because they made bodies disappear and cleaned up scenes that would be difficult to explain to local authorities. Most paranormal communities rely upon such shrouds, for obvious reasons—they were

key to keeping humans oblivious and believing that the only predators out there were other humans. Antoine and his boys drove
around a refrigerated truck and were able to pass for human so long
as they didn't get too hungry. They were also quite scrupulous about
waiting for people to die on their own before eating their bodies.

These ghouls weren't in Antoine's class, however. If Antoine's
shroud went to Harvard, this shroud was illiterate. Savage, gray-
skinned, black-toothed, and covered in viscera, they looked only
too willing to kill their food if the reaper couldn't do it for them.

"Take the scythe," I told Granuaile. "I will throw them to you
off balance. Finish them or else get out of the way."

"Ready," she puffed, and nodded at me. She looked ready to
hurl; the smell of death and sulfur was inescapable. But she could
handle the scythe; I'd been training her primarily in the quarter-
staff, and she could adapt some of those moves.

I approached the shroud, wagering that since dead bodies
rarely fought back, they'd be rather unskilled fighters that de-
pended largely on their strength and claws to win the day. There
were eight of them, though, and I doubted they would politely wait
their turn to take me on one at a time. The wood flooring that con-
cealed the demons from Amber also cut me off from drawing any
more power; I had to fuel everything on what I had left in my bear
charm. Perhaps a gambit was in order.

The laws of Druidry tend to frown on binding animated creatures, and it's impossible to bind synthetics and difficult to mess
with iron. But apart from that, anything goes. The flooring wasn't
nailed down—they were simply plywood sheets atop the dirt. I
created a binding between the middle of one sheet and the denim
jeans of a body halfway up the stack on the far wall. Normally this
would make both the jeans and the plywood fly to meet each other,
but since the body wearing the jeans was crushed underneath so
many others and couldn't budge, it was only the plywood that was

free to move. Once I energized the binding, the plywood flew up and back to the wall and, functioning like a giant bookend, mowed down a couple of ghouls on the way, though without doing them much harm. More importantly, it left some exposed earth where I could access more energy.

I stepped into the space, felt the earth replenish me, and set myself in an aikido stance. The shroud of ghouls saw the challenge and charged me.

Not for the first time, I wished ghouls were truly undead like zombies or vampires. If that were the case, I could simply unbind them back to their component elements. But ghouls were living creatures, a human variant now mutated into a dead end, har de har har. Back when I was a much younger man—in the second century or so—an idiot wizard somewhere in Arabia had created the first *ghul* by summoning a demon to possess a poor young man. The demon had a taste for necrotic flesh and grew stronger by it, forcing the host to gorge himself on bodies that the wizard provided. Eventually the wizard realized he'd made a horrible mistake—perhaps because he was getting tired of procuring bodies—and exorcised the demon. He didn't realize that the man was forever changed, despite the exorcism. When the wizard went to kill the man—for dead men tell no tales—he presumed him as weak as any human, only to discover that the man was quite strong indeed. Said man instead killed the wizard and escaped. Continuing to hunger for dead flesh, he noticed that his skin was turning gray. He soon realized that if he fed that hunger on a steady basis—defiled graves and feasted on what he found—he could maintain a normal appearance and even enjoy strength beyond that of ordinary humans. His abilities—and his curse—got passed down once he married and had children. Perfectly normal until they hit puberty, when his kids began wasting away and turning gray, Daddy took them to a cemetery and said,

"Here, kids—what you need is a nice corpse snack. Clotted blood! Om nom nom!"

All ghouls were descended from that common ancestor, but this particular branch of the family had clearly decided to throw in their lot with the demons that created them. They weren't making any effort to appear human. Or to charge me with a modicum of respect, considering that I'd just taken out a reaper. Their tactics seemed confined to run, leap at my throat, and roar at me.

Aikido is a discipline ideally suited to redirecting energy and using the opponent's momentum in your favor, and it includes a training set, called *taninzudori*, in which one practices against multiple attackers. I'd found it a refreshing twentieth-century adaptation of older styles. The ghouls, therefore, found themselves thrown or spun awkwardly behind me, where Granuaile was waiting with the scythe. Though the weapon is somewhat unwieldy, it tends to deliver mortal blows, which Granuaile distributed quickly. The last three, seeing what had happened to the rest of the shroud, reconsidered their charge and slowed down. They began to spread out in a half circle.

Meanwhile, behind me, the unbridled panic of the other carnival goers was subsiding just enough for them to start shouting questions, since they had seen us kill some bad guys and assumed we must have all the answers.

"What's going on? Can you get us out of here? What are those things? Don't you have a gun?"

I didn't know how any of this would be explained to the survivors—somehow I doubted they'd believe it was a pocket of swamp gas—but first I had to ensure that there would *be* survivors. And I also needed to find the portal that the demons had used to get here. So far I hadn't spotted it, but I hadn't had the luxury of time to look around, either.

I didn't want to go on the attack because it would leave my

back open and they were set now, so I hawked up something juicy and spit at the one on my right. It landed right on his forehead, and he promptly lost his ghoulish composure. It wasn't that he was grossed out; ghouls find far fouler substances than sputum to be quite tasty. He simply knew an insult when it smacked wetly on his face. Enraged, he lunged at me, and I tossed him at the one on the left, sending them both tumbling. That left the ghoul in the center all alone for a few seconds with no backup. I charged him and shoved my fingers into his eyes. He scratched me deeply on either side of my rib cage, burning cuts I'd have to work hard to heal, but he backed off and would never see the coup de grâce coming. I grabbed one of his arms and whipped him around so that my back was to the wall of bodies, then kicked him in the chest so that he was staggering backward where Granuaile could easily finish him. I backpedaled at the approach of the other two, who had disentangled and were coming now.

Peripherally, I saw that Granuaile had dispatched the blinded ghoul and was also advancing, coming up behind the others as Oberon bounded forward to take advantage. He nipped at the heels of the one on my left, which sent him sprawling and allowed Granuaile to catch up and end him. The last one leapt at me and I dropped onto my back and tucked my knees against my chest, catching him on my feet and then kicking him up and over my head. It threw him into the pile of bodies against the wall. He made a wet impact noise and then crunched down headfirst onto the blood-soaked floorboards. Not a killshot, but it dazed him to the point where Granuaile could hustle over and eviscerate him. Then she dropped the scythe, exhausted.

Ragged cheers and cries of relief rose up from the Needle Gate. There were perhaps twenty people there, crying and clasping hands while thanking me and their gods for deliverance. I smiled and waved at them once before they all died; the Needle Gate exploded and perforated them in at least a hundred different places.

Many of the needles passed completely through the people who had been stuck on the barbs of the gate and went on to sink into the flesh of people in the next rank. None of the needles reached us on the far end of the room; they'd either shot off to either side or punctured the body of some hapless victim. We flinched and gasped and only then saw the cause of the explosion: It was the demon barker, now free of his stilts and stalking toward us dramatically to imbue his wee stature with menace. He still wore his bowler hat but it was pushed back enough now to see that his eyes were glowing orange.

"You two stay back here," I murmured. "He's going to have hellfire."

Oberon and Granuaile agreed, and I ran forward to close the distance between us and get to that bare patch of earth. There was no time to remove any more boards with bindings, and I needed to engage him a safe distance away from my vulnerable companions.

He saw what I intended and rushed to prevent it, acting on the premise that you deny your opponents what they want. With a roar, he shed his human skin. The red waistcoat, the bowler hat, the entire wee man turned to bloody mist as the demon's preferred form burst out. What we then had was a tall, pale, skinny monstrosity with bony thorns all over it, like something out of a Bosch painting. But the lack of muscle tone did not correlate to a lack of strength or an inability to throw a punch. I ducked under the first one, thinking I'd scramble on my hands and knees if necessary, when a sharp thorn from its wrist shot over my back and gashed a deep groove there. It seared my flesh, and when I reared back in agony, the demon connected with a left, the spikes on its knuckles tearing holes in my cheek, sending me spinning.

Hellfire bloomed and shot forth from the barker's hands and

he laughed, thinking he was finishing me. But his punches had been more effective. My cold iron aura shrugged off hellfire, but I screamed and rolled anyway, right toward the open patch of earth. He let me do so but followed close, just as I had hoped. Once I felt the earth underneath me and saw that he touched the earth, too, I pointed my right hand at him and said, "*Dóigh!*"—Irish for "Burn!"

Had I been standing I would have collapsed, because that's what casting Cold Fire does to a guy. It kills demons one hundred percent of the time, but the trade-off is that it takes some time to work and weakens the caster, no matter how much magic is flowing through the earth. Brighid of the Tuatha Dé Danann—a fire goddess, among other things—had given it to me some years ago to aid my fight against her brother, Aenghus Óg, who had allied himself with hell. For the next few hours, I'd have trouble fighting off a hamster, much less a greater demon.

"So what's all this, then?" I asked, twitching a hand to indicate the room. "Upward mobility for you?"

The demon bent and wrapped long, sticklike fingers with too many joints entirely around my neck. He began to crush my windpipe, and all I could manage by way of defense was a feeble Muppet flail. I hoped the Cold Fire spell would take hold sooner rather than later. Its delay could well kill me. The demon grinned at my weakness.

"Yesss. Months have I prepared. Small harvests in small towns."

I couldn't breathe and my vision was going black at the edges as his fingers continued to constrict my throat. Why wouldn't he die already?

"But now I provide a bounty for hell. I will harvest more souls than—" He broke off and his eyes widened. He released me and I sucked in a desperate breath of foul air. He clutched at his chest and said, "What—" before he convulsed, coughed blue flames, then sizzled to a sort of frosty ash and crumbled on top of me, burned from within by Cold Fire.

Seeing that there were no more immediate threats to her person, Granuaile vomited.

Oberon trotted over and licked the side of my head. <Atticus, you're still bleeding.>

Yeah, so a wet willy was exactly what I needed, thanks.

<You're welcome. Can we go now?>

The way was clear through the Needle Gate. I didn't know if the Anchovy Gate was one-way or not. I had to believe that police would be arriving soon; there had to be some response from all the spectators that had fled after I'd killed the imp in the hallway. While I might have welcomed their help earlier in getting people to safety, now there was no one left to save. All they would do was get in the way of the work I still had to do.

Not yet, Oberon.

I sent a message to Amber through my bond to the earth: // Demons slain below / Two imps remain above / Search for portal beginning//

//Harmony// was the only reply.

//Query: Collapse tunnel between this chamber and surface if it is clear of people?//

Amber's answer was to cave in the hallway. That would buy us some time.

"We need to find the portal to hell," I said. "There has to be one around here somewhere. I don't care how dodgy carnivals are, reapers don't travel with them."

<I don't see anything on the walls.>

Granuaile, looking up, said, "It's not on the ceiling. It's probably underneath one of these boards."

I didn't have the energy to lift them all up, and I wanted this over as soon as possible, so I bound each sheet to one of the side walls and sent them flying. We found the portal close to the Needle Gate, near the spot where Granuaile had played dodge-the-scythe with the reaper.

Hellish arcane symbols traced in salt formed a circle a bit bigger than a standard manhole. Inside of this circle was nested an iron disc, which was itself etched with symbols similar to those on the ground, but it covered up the inner halves of the salt symbols, neatly bisecting them.

"Clever," I said, leaning on Granuaile a bit for support as I inspected the setup. "It's still active, but dormant while the iron shorts out the spell. Remove the iron cover and the portal flares open. Drop it back down and the mojo fades. They can get their people in and out in seconds. No wonder they were able to keep this on the down low."

"Keep what, exactly?" Granuaile asked. "What was this all about?"

"Souls. The demon barker wanted to move up in the underworld and this was his scheme. Make people willingly choose hell and then kill them."

"But how could they possibly get away with it? I mean, look at all those poor people. Nobody noticed?"

"This was likely the first time they tried it on a large scale. On the heaven side of the tent they have an imp slapping a memory charm on people as they walk out. Keeps them from searching for their friends when they don't come out, and when they finally realize they've lost their friends, their memories will tell them they couldn't possibly have lost them here. By the time Missing Persons Reports actually get filed, the carnival is on its way out of town. The ghouls would have stayed in this chamber and eaten until all the evidence was gone, and you know how it goes—no body, no crime. The mass disappearance would get explained as an alien abduction before somebody suspected a mass murder underground."

"Well, we're not just going to leave them all here, are we?"

I surveyed the ruin and shook my head. "No. Their families deserve closure. The elemental can move their bodies to the surface for us when the coast is clear."

"Okay." Granuaile returned her attention back to the portal. "So if you lifted that cover right now, we could jump into hell?"

"Or something could jump out, yes. And it would drain a lot of power from the earth while it was open. We can destroy it pretty easily, though."

Binding like to like using the energy of the earth, I bound all the salt crystals together so that they lifted from the ground and met above the iron cover, forming a ball. I let it go and it dropped onto the cover. The salt had rested in shallow troughs traced by a finger, so I erased those as well by smoothing out the ground. I checked the circle in the magical spectrum to make sure it was safe before moving the cover. There was no telltale glow of magic anywhere around it, and the cover could be broken down and reabsorbed into the earth.

"Kick the cover a bit for me?" I asked. I doubted I could make it budge in my condition. Binding spells, by comparison, were simple, since they used Amber's energy, not my own. Granuaile pushed the iron disc a few inches with her foot and the ground underneath remained satisfyingly solid. The ball of bound salt on top rolled off. Satisfied that the situation couldn't get any worse, I informed Amber that the portal was destroyed and asked her to create a path to the surface for us. As we watched, the earth itself created a stairway leading up from the base of the nearest wall.

I cast camouflage on all three of us, since appearing in the midst of a carnival dressed in blood might excite some comment. We emerged behind a row of gaming booths and the stairway closed behind us. We took a moment to reacquaint ourselves with what fresh air smelled like. The voice of the carnie running the milk bottle booth was taunting new marks.

"Be right back," I said, and left them to check on the tent, though I couldn't muster much of a pace. Still, I saw that the hulk at the entrance was gone and someone had called the police. The exit was manned by officers, too, and there was no trace of the little imp girl or the people inside who'd served as the bearded lady, the three-armed man, and so on. The police clearly hadn't found any bodies yet or they would have been doing more than simply closing the exhibit. Any report the police received would have been for the imp whose neck I'd snapped—a mundane affair as far as they knew. No one who had seen the supernatural had survived except for us. The imps who'd escaped would have to be hunted down as a matter of principle, but they didn't have the power to reopen a portal by themselves. We could afford time to recuperate and think of how best to proceed.

I returned to Granuaile and Oberon behind the game booths and dissolved our camouflage, since we were alone, and if someone spied us, they wouldn't see the blood right away in the dark. Granuaile was squatting down and staring at the ground, arms resting on her thighs and hands clasped between her knees. All around us, oblivious carnival goers continued to seek entertainment. The lights and sounds of the midway, bright and alluring before, now grated on my nerves. We couldn't be amused by those rides anymore. I squatted next to her in the same position.

"I told you once what choosing this life could mean for you personally, but those were just words," I said. "Now you know."

Granuaile nodded jerkily. "Yes, I do." She was trembling all over, coming down from the adrenaline and perhaps entering shock now that the enormity of what had happened was settling in.

"But you did well in there," I said. "Thanks for the assist."

"Same to you." Granuaile's lip shook and a tear leaked out of her eye. "I didn't have time to think. My mom could have been in that room."

"Yes. I'm relieved she wasn't. Great time to go on a cruise."

She wiped at her cheek and sniffed. "But somebody's mom is in there. Probably some people I know too."

"That's most likely true. But we couldn't have saved any more than we did. You do realize that we definitely saved some people tonight?"

"Yeah. But I can't feel good about that now."

"Understood."

Oberon moved closer to Granuaile, dipped his head under her hand, and flipped it up, inviting her to pet him. She hugged him around the neck and cried on him a little bit, and he bore it in silence—or at least silent as far as my apprentice was concerned.

<She doesn't remember hitting me down there, does she?>

I don't think so. Probably best not to bring it up. You can see that she loves you. And so do I.

<That so?>

You know it is. But to erase any doubts, I'm going to see if we can arrange a liaison. An amorous rendezvous.

Oberon's tail began to wag. <You mean a black poodle in season?>

We will call her Noche. There will be sausage and occasion to frolic.

Oberon got so excited about this news that he barked, startling Granuaile. She reared back and he turned his head, licking her face.

"What! Oberon!" She toppled backward and hit her head on the back of the gaming booth. "Ow!" Then she laughed as Oberon swooped in and slobbered on her some more.

Dogs make everything better.

Except my fear of Kansas. I still have that.

"The Sweeter the Juice"

Mark Henry

The fruit cart vendor on the curb is persistent if not articulate. He alternates shouting "All da lovely ladies love da frew-its" into his PA system with slapping his palm against his Plexiglas surround.

"You!" he pleads, his voice echoing. "You take. You try!"

He's annoying me, and I'm already edgy from three days dry off the Jimmy. This can only end in bloodshed.

The drawer embedded in the side of the cart's guard glass slams out toward me, a slice of mango glistening inside. The dark fruit rests *not* on a polite napkin but directly on the greasy metal bottom. A red smear of juice sets it off like a gory still life, makes it pop . . . and makes my stomach turn.

I wave my hand, shake my head as apologetically as I can fake.

As I pass, I notice the body in the gutter. A woman's, perhaps. The pink bouclé Chanel knockoff suit appears part of its flesh, the body's rot seeping through the weave of the fabric, turning it a murky green in spots, sludgy. There's a hole in its dimpled forehead, and a sliver of mango dangles between its still-twitching fingers.

I hear a sharp tapping and look up to see the vendor rap a

Glock against the Plexi. "Samples for customer who pay-ay!" he says into his mic, and gives me a big gummy grin.

He's clearly known for his comic banter. Or at least he thinks so.

Zombies don't pay for fruit any more than they do for dry cleaning. A shame. The suit was actually cute at one time. But worse than a fashion tragedy, the thing's thin hips and sturdy legs belie a truth I'd rather deny.

The dead woman was a Sister of Perpetual Disappointment.

And by *sister* . . . I mean the kind with a penis.

The order is strictly my terminology. Don't get me wrong, at times I feel like a nun, but there's no convent, unless you consider all the transgendered gathering around Dr. Bloom's office cloistering.

When death became passé, none of the Sisters expected the harsh toll the epidemic would exact on our small community. The hospitals were hard hit by the infected; doctors and nurses and worse—plastic surgeons specializing in gender reassignment surgeries—were some of the first casualties of the plague. It's hard to maintain a practice from the inside of a zombie's intestinal tract.

Go figure.

Needless to say, a heavy blow to transsexuals everywhere. It's no wonder I took up the Jimmy. A few puffs and I almost didn't care that I might be stuck with these disgusting crotch accessories forever.

A few of the sisters simply gave up, running windmill-armed into a nest of the undead just to get it over with, leaving behind a crimson concrete smear and an empty pair of stilettos—licked clean, naturally. Sure, suicide by zombie is a tad dramatic, considering handguns sell out of hot dog carts like condiments, but it's undeniably effective.

It's easy to go from dead to undead—a cinch, in fact: get bitten—but a bitch to go from man to woman . . . or vice versa.

As the virus began to weaken and some of the newly deceased started to stay dead, you'd think it would have become easier to find a doc somewhere in Manhattan. That they'd ship some in from Buffalo or Amish country, somewhere less affected. But no, for the longest time, it was damn near impossible to find any sort of medical care, let alone a pharmacy with some damn hormones to take care of my hot flashes.

That is, until we found Dr. Bloom, the last sex-change surgeon in New York City.

I PRESS THE buzzer of her building on the Upper East Side—too far east to be a decent address, and not far enough for a river view. No doorman, so that tells you something—in this case, that he's probably dead.

"Yes?" the receptionist's voice crackles from the circle of black mesh.

"Jade Reynolds for Dr. Bloom," I say. "I have a two-thirty appointment?"

A quick note about the name. Jade. Exotic, right?

My given name is James Dean Reynolds. But my mother, God rest her soul, took to calling me J.D. when I was in single digits. The sound of those two letters together was the one thing I wasn't willing to give up about my life as Gloria Reynolds's son.

So I didn't.

The door buzzes and I push inside. Three floors up in the coffin-sized elevator and I'm dumped into a cramped waiting room full of ugly men in makeup and hard women in stenciled sideburns.

Don't get me wrong, I love my people; just don't expect me to be attracted to them.

Speaking of unattractive . . .

"Jade!" Gretta Graves waves a gloved hand from a love seat nearest the receptionist's window and then lets it flutter dramatically to her distended abdomen.

"Oh, hello" is all I manage.

Gretta pats the seat next to her. "Come on over, doll. Let's chat."

I wince, glancing at her belly, but decide to humor her. She could get pretty testy on fake-pregnancy days.

You might want to sit down for this next part.

Gretta is what's called a maternally fixated transsexual. She goes through cycles of believing she's pregnant, complete with terribly detailed prosthetics and a delivery routine that's *not* a hit at parties. The amniotic fluid is a shoe killer—Gretta uses at least three times as much of that shit as is even necessary to emulate water breaking. When she blows, it's *The Poseidon Adventure*. I'm told the "baby" is a disturbingly lifelike infant doll called an Exactie—the breast-feeding is apparently nightmare inducing.

It's this specific delusion that prevents the doctor from moving forward with Gretta's surgery.

That's rule number one: Crazy people have to cut off their own dicks.

It doesn't stop Gretta from haunting Dr. Bloom's office, though. Not a bit.

As I scoot in beside her, she leans in close and whispers, "She's really active today."

I glance at her swollen belly and before I can shove my hand under my thigh, Gretta locks her fist around my wrist like a handcuff. "Wanna feel?"

Snatching my hand away, I hiss, "No, I don't want to feel your fake baby! I need to get smoked. I need some Jimmy."

Gretta nods and leans in close, eyes narrowing shrewdly. "I've got a line on something new."

"You said that last time."

"Something newer." Gretta pulls away and nods at me, eyebrows raised lasciviously; then, when I don't respond, she scrunches up her lips testily and leans back in.

"I'm talking about drugs," she says, so loud that everyone in the room hears.

The receptionist raises her overly penciled eyebrow in judgment.

"Absolutely not!" I say, loud enough for the judgers amongst us. I have to think on my feet. Scramble. I hate that. "They don't know what Pitocin will do to the baby! She'll come out when she's good and ready, that's what I say."

The rest of the waiting room looks away, satisfied Gretta and I are having the kind of regular conversation you might have with a schizophrenic, and not a heated argument between junkies. My gaze settles on the pinched face behind the front desk. The woman's expression weakens into disinterest, and though she keeps an eye on me, she doesn't reach for the phone or call Dr. Bloom for a know-it-all report.

Rule number two: Drug addicts are in the same dick-severing boat as crazies.

You have to be of sound mind to mutilate your body—never mind that the predicament itself is enough to drive a person crazy. Imagine spending your day trapped inside someone else's body.

And not someone awesome.

"When I get done with this appointment, I'll get you a hot dog and you can fill me in on all your maternity issues. Okay?" I pat Gretta's belly.

She covers my hand with her meaty mitt, pressing it tight against the arc of the prosthetic. I try to pull away, but she's persistent and stronger than I am, bullish. A moment goes by before I feel it, a sharp thud in my palm. A cold shiver snakes through me. There's something in there. Something not a doll.

"What have you got in there, Gretta?"

Her only response is a smile.

"A cat?" I ask. "You'd tell me if it was a cat, right?"

She lets go and turns away, ignoring my questions. But I can't shake the feeling.

DR. BLOOM'S EXAM room doesn't have windows; it's lined, floor to ceiling, with library cabinets, and above them a domed fresco of clouds floods the room in a pink hue that seems almost natural. It's serene, and I realize I like it so much because the buffered room affords a reprieve from the periodic gunshots and screams we've all gotten used to.

The doctor sits across from me with her clipboard. My physical exam was routine; the counseling portion, while brief, is where my anxiety kicks up.

"How have you been managing, Jade?" Dr. Bloom crosses her legs and watches me intently.

"Fine, of course. I've been working a lot lately," I say, hoping it's enough to indicate a lack of free time. Free time in which I might get myself into trouble.

She jots down a note. "In the same place?"

"Yes. City Restructuring Office. Nothing exciting."

"And you've been going to work as Jade, correct? I know you've had some backsliding."

My jaw tenses. "Of course. It's been fine."

"How about socially?"

I think of my lover, H.G., probably passed out on dirty linoleum in some public restroom, a needle pegging his arm like a mosquito. He was nearly eaten the last time it happened. Lucky. But he doesn't have any luck left. Once he's gone, there won't be any social life for a while.

"Fine." I nod, producing a faint smile. Noncommittal. If she didn't want lies, she shouldn't make the process so damn difficult.

Dr. Bloom taps her pen against the board and waits a moment. "Have you got something you need to share, Jade?"

"Um"—I feign searching for a memory, when I already have one lined up for this moment—"I'm a little concerned about my weight, Dr. Bloom. I've been exercising, but I'm getting a bit of a pudge."

The statement is enough to send the doctor on an exposition about hormones and the natural progression of the transition. I know all about it, but there's nothing like acting stupid to distract Dr. Bloom. She loves to be helpful, and the truth is, despite my habit, I follow all the rules.

I am Jade. Everywhere.

I haven't been J.D. since about six months before the plague hit.

I stand, straighten my skirt, and slip my purse under my arm.

"You're doing just fine, lady," Dr. Bloom says. "You keep it up. And don't worry about a little weight. It's called curves. Enjoy them."

I'm about to close her office door behind me when I hear those jarring words: "Please see Annick on your way out."

ANNICK IS A Hun—as in Attila the Hun—both brutish and brooding. She hunches behind an aging computer that's been hollowed out and turned into a stash box for the bartered items she accepts for Dr. Bloom.

Her lip curls back from clenched teeth. "You're late with your bill, Mr. Reynolds."

She's also decidedly unambiguous about her disdain for transsexuals, which is always pleasant.

"I'm sorry. I couldn't get the ham. My source is out of stock."

She takes off her glasses, letting them dangle from a knot of twine around her neck. "From the looks of it, no corn, either."

"Sorry. Next time, I promise."

"There won't be a next time, Mr. Reynolds. This is the third time, and you know what they say—"

"Third time's a charm?" I venture with a crooked smile.

She responds with a smirk and a quick shake of the head. "Three strikes and you're out."

"But, Annick, my progress. I can't backtrack. My chest will start to fur. You know how terrible my cleavage looks with hair!"

Annick sucks at her teeth, her cold stare is unblinking, and I'm certain I'm sunk.

"I'm afraid I have some rather bad news, Mr. Reynolds."

"*Ms.* It shouldn't be that difficult to refer to me as Ms. I *am* wearing women's clothes."

"Yes, well, it's bad news regardless of gender. You see, it's come to our attention that your trades have been consistently irregular. A barter system only works if the patient keeps up their end. That hasn't been happening. We pride ourselves on flexibility, but your doctor can only bend so far before your lack of payment breaks her back. We don't want that to happen, do we, Mr. Reynolds?" Annick shrugs. "I'm afraid we're discontinuing your treatment."

"What? When?"

"Now. Right this very minute."

"But what am I supposed to do?" I lurch forward, gripping the edge of Annick's desk for support. "How can I make this right?"

"You should have considered that before you started taking drugs."

"I—I haven't."

"Of course, not. I'm certainly mistaken." Her crinkled lips form a crooked, empathetic circle. "But not about this bill. You've made promises you haven't kept. And there are others who don't seem to have any problem making appropriate trades." She pouts and puts her hand over both of mine. Pats them gently. "I'm sure you'll find other . . . arrangements."

"Like what? What is there? I'm six months from surgery. I'm in the middle of something here. I can't just live this . . . this . . . half life." I grab my breasts as a reminder.

"Well."

"Well?"

"I'm sorry."

And with those words I feel the hope slip away. One moment I'm a transitioning woman with a plan, the next I'm a thing, with hormone-enhanced breasts and a shriveled dick. I imagine what will come next: the horrible decision to hack it off like the rest of the unfortunates who can't work out a deal with Dr. Bloom, dick in a jar of brine, my balls and groin cinched up with dental floss.

Annick taps a pencil on the desk, her eyes narrowed in thought. "There may be something. We've heard word of an alternative to the surgery. A . . ." She pauses, searches the room for a word and then seeming to find it, her eyes snap back to mine. "Transformative agent."

"What does that even mean?"

"We only know that it's called Zed. We don't know who's supplying it or where it comes from. Just that it's post-pharmaceutical, so there hasn't been any testing done, obviously. No guarantees of efficacy. But there have been claims of transformations. Body changes. Miraculous to hear them tell . . ." Her voice trails away. "If you were to verify this for Dr. Bloom—and bring some back, of course—your entire care here would be gratis."

The words don't register quite right.

"Gratis," I repeat.

"It means free treatment, Mr. Reynolds."

Free treatment. Let's bask in that for a moment. I'm not a lucky person. I never have been. Except surviving the zombies—that's pretty lucky. Still, I think you'll agree, that little trick was entirely offset by being born into the wrong body.

I nod that I understand, lost in thought.

It's not the worst thing that could happen. In fact, it could be a godsend. Black-market meds for Dr. Bloom in exchange for the freedom I've always longed for—freedom from this torturous prison of a body . . . and these horrible, foreign genitals.

The more I think about it, the more I feel like I'd be providing a service to the Sisters of Perpetual Disappointment. Bringing hormones to my people. Like Moses, only instead of slaves from Egypt, I'd deliver the transsexuals from crippling dick dependence. Obviously, there'd be no Red Sea parting—because, FYI, a monthly period cannot be re-created through surgery.

I'm woken from my daydream by fingers drumming.

Annick glares like I've just shit in her oatmeal. "Why are you still here?"

IF I'VE LEARNED anything from the zombie apocalypse, it's that you take advantage of every spot of fortune that comes your way. Those moments are fleeting. Think you're safe enough to relax? A zombie horde pops in for a surprise party—one in which you're the cake. You're well fed and your pantry's stocked? Your place is targeted by scavengers and cleaned out. Sex-change financing in the bag?

Shit. I don't even want to think about how that could fuck up.

I have to move quick. I have to be smart.

Outside, I'm confronted not by the fruit vendor, who's sadly packed up his stand and disappeared—"sadly" because I could really go for a mango now—but by an impromptu street carnival.

It is the smell that hits me first.

Already steamy in the afternoon heat, the air rumples with the all-too-common stench of rotten flesh.

And then Gretta stumbles into me, clutching my shoulders like a railing and pressing the hard shell of her fake stomach against my back.

"Jesus," I mutter.

She gropes and clings and struggles to remain upright. I finally have to twist on my heels and snatch both of her arms to balance her. When she's settled and I'm sufficiently fondled, she looks over my shoulder, lets out a sharp whistle, and says, "Now, that's a float."

And she's right.

An old El Camino fitted with a wooden stage cantilevered over the bed of the truck by a good six feet on either side creeps up the street. It's flanked by several scantily clad women and men, both young and old, some horrendously sagging but all unapologetically gyrating, kick-stepping to big band music blaring from a pair of precariously duct-taped speakers on the roof of a trailing taxi. Atop the stage, in all its macabre glory, a family diorama is on proud display. Three corpses positioned in the roles of swing dancers, two males dressed in zoot suits and a female, hair in victory rolls and a retro dress tight enough to keep her withered flesh from falling apart.

As is customary, the immediate family follows behind, puppeting the movement of their beloved dead, with rods fitted with slipknots strung around decaying wrists, necks, and precarious kneecaps.

These are no ordinary dead. They are the blessed, the unrisen, the precious few who have died since the plague and were unmoved by reanimation.

They are the new American iconography.

I find the entire display almost tasteful. But I've attended some where the celebrants were clearly half-assing it. Shoddy costuming. Incongruent theming. Missing body parts. It's enough to make me want to judge them openly, like when we used to have Olympics.

This float earns at least an eight point three—points off for not working in a Mexican theme with the El Camino.

But festive nonetheless.

"Annick made me an offer," I say. "I need to track down this drug. Zed."

Gretta nods. "This is a job for Neuter."

The name sends a shiver up my spine. Neuter is the epitome of a botched sex change, right down to the name. He represents the kind of failure that terrifies me. A place where we all might end up without the kind of prospects Annick has offered up. Plus he tries to make out with everyone, which is only okay if I'm really really stoned.

"Seriously?" I ask.

She nods.

I groan, but I know it's true. Neuter is also a gigantic drug addict. Nearly to the point of fetishism. He collects information on new drugs and where to get them like girls used to do with high heels. If he doesn't know where to find Zed, no one will.

"Fine," I say. "Let's go."

"After the parade, okay?" Gretta asks. She leans back on the stoop, rubs her belly, and bops her head along to the music.

EVENTUALLY I NOTICE that somewhere behind the music, and outside the possibility of speaker feedback, another sort of buzzing vibrates, familiar enough to have me collecting my things and searching the street for an escape route.

Pat-pat-pat.

Not close, but coming.

The taxi stops first. Its driver, a curious youth with more ink than not and a bulbous head crammed into a wool cap, sticks his needle neck out the window, putting an ear to the wind. He twists off the tunes and the El Camino stops too. The parade goes still.

Slap-slap-slap.

The sound is like cards being shuffled through thumbs. *Slap. Slap. Slap.*

I turn to Gretta; everything about her face is wide open: eyes, nostrils, mouth. That's the look. Zombie radar.

Alleys and streets begin to echo with their footfalls. There are no groans like the films have led us to believe. Zombies have no use for their vocal cords. The only thing their throats are good for is inhaling large quantities of flesh. Gulping back the wet stuff. They don't even bother to chew. I came across one, once, lying on its side like an opium addict, an intestine dangling from its mouth. It slowly pushed the organ down its esophagus with a loose chopstick. It watched me but wasn't interested in anything fresher. They're pretty calm once they are eating.

But there's always that smell. Acrid. Cloyingly sweet. A human innately knows the smell of their own kind's rotting flesh. The first couple of times, it wrenches the bile out of your gut, but after a while you learn to use it as a tool.

A warning.

The approaching horde has either figured out how to hide their own putrification—unlikely—or they are an unusually fresh group of undead. Whatever. They are clearly coming toward the impromptu *carnivale* like the once-happy family staging it rang a dinner bell.

Gretta claws at my back. "Save yourself!" she cries dramatically, hand fluttering at her chest like an honest-to-God self-sacrificing southern belle. "I've already lived a life!"

Normally, I'd be fine with that, but something's wrong here. Something that stops me from climbing atop her like a drowning victim.

In an alley across from where the El Camino idles, its desiccated passengers abandoned by the scattered revelers, shadows begin to stretch up the brick walls. I push us back into an alcove, Gretta's fake pregnancy bump jutting into my suddenly aching back. I feel a thud and worry about whether the cat or whatever she's smuggling in the shell under her dress is getting enough air.

The first of the marauders appears. He's small and angry, and what looks to be a port-wine stain blotches the area around his mouth. Something glints in his hand in the seconds before he bolts into the street. And then it's slashing its way through what's left of the crowd.

A knife.

Knives. His compatriots flood the street.

There are too many of them to be zombies. There hasn't been a decent horde in weeks; they just can't assemble like they used to. These folks are different, and as they each appear from the alley, darting into the street to join the fray, it's clear exactly how different. Besides being blind with fury and armed—zombies never carry weapons—each and every one of them is disfigured by a purpling splotch radiating from their lips. One of them, a craggy branch of a woman, staggers up and points a metal skewer at us. Her stain is as dark as plum and stretches across her cheeks like a black doctor's mask. We make eye contact, and her eyes narrow.

Alive . . . and crazy. Clearly.

I hold up my hands instinctively, but she isn't interested in us.

"Bitch is trippin'," Gretta whispers.

"For real."

The woman's eyes roll back into her head as she catches the scent of what the group is really after, and her head lolls to the side, facing the family iconography. Two men have already heaved themselves atop the El Camino's stage and are busy tearing at the corpses. An arm detaches and lands on the hot concrete, and I could swear I hear the damn thing sizzle before the woman dives atop it, grips it between her clawed hands like a hoagie, and begins to gnaw at the bone end, tugging at the dry flesh as a dog does with rawhide.

Soon the street turns into a smorgasbord for the living carrion. Even the Sister of Perpetual Disappointment lying prone in the gutter isn't immune to their savage foodfest. A pair of the grape-mouthed sickos tear at her clothing and dig into the weak flesh of her abdomen, using their spread fingers to wind up intestines like spaghetti caught in the spinning tines of a fork.

A niggling stitch winds in my stomach as I try to hold back my disgust.

They devour dead flesh like vultures but seem to be completely uninterested in the living. A reversal of what we've become so used to with the undead.

Gretta, who can't be bothered with discretion, retches behind me, bumping me forward onto the sidewalk in the process with that disgusting growth of hers.

"Dammit, woman!" I shout.

The movement catches the feeders' attention, and before I can back away, one of the bigger freaks—a real pushy bastard—rushes past me, sending me spinning into a tumble across the concrete. I hear Gretta's hoarse screams first, followed by the rapid clops of her gigantic platforms.

The man is gaining ground on her and, like any good pseudo-acquaintance would, I reach for the gun in my purse, kick off my heels, and give motherfuckin' chase. I've never shot a person, living or dead, that I recall—though things got pretty hairy in the thick of the apocalypse, so you never stuck around to see if your bullet found a soft home.

That I'd be totally conscious of this, paired with the way my day was going, brings a tiny smile to my face.

Gretta ducks into the gaping doorway of a ground-floor apartment decorated to look like the dash of a third-world cab. A rope of fuzzy puffs garlands the frame, and instead of a knocker, a brass Virgin Mary clings to the open door. The guy darts in behind her.

I leap the three stairs and rush inside, but what I'm witness to isn't altogether clear. The carrion eater has Gretta Graves on the floor, backed into a corner and screaming her head off. Her legs are spread and he's chomping away, and at first I wonder if they'd like some privacy, and then I realize I hear the scraping of teeth against plastic.

"What the fuck?" The words escape without any real control on my part.

Grape Ape's head pivots in my direction and that indigo tongue of his laps at bleeding black gums. Whatever he's been eating is staining them from the inside out. His eyes are crazy, and I'm certain it's drugs. I look past him to my friend's torn dress. The man's blood trickles from the fake navel of Gretta's prosthetic gut. Beside the belly button a dark spot. The freak managed to puncture it, and the hole is just large enough for what's inside to make itself known.

"Oh, Jesus, Gretta," I say.

The freak's head jerks back and it howls, lunging for the gray protuberance. Wiggling out of the hole is a tiny finger. Correction: a tiny dead finger.

Gretta shrieks and bats at the junkie as I lurch forward, taking the gun by the barrel and driving the butt into the man's skull hard enough to crack it open and taste the resulting ferrous spray. He collapses into a heap.

I kneel beside Gretta, who is frantically coaxing the fingers back inside. "Hush, now," she coos. "You're safe in Mama's belly."

I fall against the wall, panting. "You're crazy, Gretta. You're fucking crazy."

But all she can do is smile and stuff the hole with a red bandanna the apartment's previous occupant had been using as an end-table cozy.

WE HIT THE Jimmy on the floor of Neuter's apartment. Nothing says escapist drug use like sucking smoke off of a sizzling pie tin through fast-food straws. Squalor is the perfect design scheme, and Neuter has it down. I collapse into the only chair that's not held together with electrical tape and plastic shopping bags and let the smoke soothe my edges.

"What the hell is causing those people to eat the dead?" Gretta mumbles.

"Here's a better question," I say. "What the hell are you doing toting around a zombie baby?"

"Shh," Gretta scolds. "You're going to make her upset."

"*Her?* It's those things out there you need to worry about . . . and me, when I leave your ass the next time it happens. And I expect it will unless—"

"Lula," Gretta cuts in. "Her name is Lula Belle Graves. And when I birth her, I'm gonna dress her in frills and teach her to spin. Spin so fast."

At some point, hard to say when, Gretta clearly lost what was left of her already paper-thin grasp on reality.

"Sweet Jesus," I sigh, and slump back against the wall, drained from the futility.

But then Gretta reaches across the chasm back into sanity, grasping my hand as though to make a vow. "If we're attacked again, I'll run. I won't leave you with a decision like that. To leave your bestest best friend of all time."

Her smile is genuine. Mine is, well, less so.

"Sure." I nod and then turn to our companion. "How are those cocktails comin', Neuter? I'm gonna need something high-octane to make Gretta sound like she's not going to kill us in our sleep."

"Pshaw." Gretta shrugs off my volley with a jiggle of her head. "You are so funny, Jade!"

Neuter leans over the pan, shaking his pimply face in judgment, and takes another hit. "There's been more attacks than just that one. I heard about one a few days ago. A bunch of trust fund kids committed suicide up on Central Park West and they only found them because of these purple-faced crazies sniffing the place out and chomping away at them where they hung from the rafters. Crazy shit, right?"

"Jesus."

Gretta takes a break from cooing at her abomination to say, "Jade needs some Zed. Quantity. You know who's holding?"

Neuter smiles, thin lips scraping back over a grisly graveyard of teeth. "Yeah. When you need it?"

"Yesterday," I say, but Neuter is already drifting to sleep.

"Gotta go see the Geek," he mumbles.

"ZED AIN'T EASY, ladies," Neuter says, stopping in the middle of the street. "It's about as hard to get as a new pussy."

"Fucking hilarious."

"Didn't mean that shit to be funny. Meant it to sound like you're about to walk through hell to get the transformation you're after. A whole bunch of hells. Starting with this one."

Neuter points down the way a bit. A few people line the shadowed side of the street, avoiding the heat and the black smoke billowing from the subway entrance. He whips the backpack off his shoulder and strides up to a vendor, a crooked little man cowering under a parasol, rubbing a pistol like a lover. Neuter digs out three oranges and drops them in a basket at the guy's feet.

"Rent," Neuter says. "Need three kits to get us through to Coney."

Dark eyes narrowing to slits and brows curling up, thick as caterpillars, the vendor holsters his gun and reaches for the fruit, twisting each around, examining them. "This one got a bruise."

Neuter shrugs. "Don't matter. They're sweet, man. Sweet as fuck. But if you don't want 'em, someone else will."

He hunches over as if to take the oranges back. The vendor, quick to change his tune, drops a hat over them and brushes the basket under his cart with the toe of his shoe. The man pulls out some bulky masks, hoses, and metal tanks from his cart and lines them up on the curb. "Three kits. You need tickets?"

"Don't try to pull that shit. The conductor don't take no tickets." The little man's lip curls back from blackened nicotine-flecked teeth.

"Let's go," Neuter says, still looking at him.

We don't have to be told twice.

A few steps from the hole vomiting up coal smoke, Neuter pulls a mask over his face before helping Gretta with hers, then me with mine. The descent into the subway is surely a disastrous idea, but what choice did they have? Maybe the oxygen will help calm me; that's what it's supposed to do, right? Flood your brain, make you euphoric so you don't mind the fact that you're roasting like a pig in a giant tubular oven?

Keep you alive.

The whole process would have been a shit ton easier if someone had survived the zombies who knew one thing about the trains. Hooking up coal locomotives has caused a whole new set of problems.

The elastic straps pinch the tips of my ears, and the goggles steam up almost immediately, but when the nozzle turns and the oxygen storms in, cool and clean, I feel an unfamiliar surge of optimism. This might just work.

Neuter ties a thin loop of rope around his waist and then ours, linking us. I look into the gaping hole of the stairwell, vomiting black smoke like a chimney stack.

"It's now or never!" Neuter shouts, and disappears into the dark cloud. The rope tied around Gretta's waist snaps tight, and she stumbles forward.

The only thing stopping me from tumbling down the stairs and breaking a hip is my white-knuckle grip on a railing so loose, it clings to the wall by no more than a thick coat of grease. So, not much. It certainly isn't my quaking knees. The way I figure it, there's plenty of residual fear left in these tunnels, smoke aside. We've all heard stories about the subway and what happened down here during the initial outbreak. No need to rehash it.

The lamp on my head does very little to cut through the black cloud, but I can occasionally see Gretta's muumuu and the hint of her body struggling forward into the grim depths. There is a clattering waller that seems to accompany each new mass of smoke, a grating, jarring scrape of a sound so pervasive that it shakes the very air.

"This way!" Neuter screams. "Don't lag, the train's here!"

I'm jostled forward by the rope at my waist. My feet shuffle over the oily cement until the space opens up around us, like we've entered some great cavern. The thick haze clings to the ceiling here a bit, and I'm able to make out Gretta and Neuter and just the impression of a subway car a few steps away.

We've stumbled into a charcoal sketch, but it's all dark-shaded black. We've lost our edges. Our definition. Despite the mask, the sooty air creeps in and crystallizes on my eyelids, each blink scraping painfully.

"Almost there!" Neuter shouts over the din, and the rope tugs at my waist.

Several yards past the base of the stair, a blue light breaks through the gray haze and a figure materializes.

The conductor wears a full hazmat suit, neon glowing around his face like the undercarriage of a street racer. "All aboard," he yells, but when I take a step toward the open door of the train, he snatches my arm.

"Where do you think you're going, missy?"

I sneer. His hand lingers on the girth of my bicep and his expression changes. He turns toward Gretta, who's holding her belly immaculately—or maybe it's merely the halo of light reflecting off the cheap plastic flesh.

"Did you pay me? I'm pretty sure I haven't received payment."

"But you said—"

"I was using the term ironically. By 'All aboard,' I meant 'Pay up, bitch.'"

Neuter sweeps in between us, already digging into his backpack. "Nuh-no see," he stutters. "I got our fare, right here."

The conductor tries to get a peek into the bag, his finger stretching toward the open zipper. Neuter rankles and pivots away.

"Un-unh." He turns back with a paper sack and drops it into the man's gloved palm. "Enough to get us to Coney."

He seems to weigh it, his hand raising and lowering it, and then decides whatever it is is sufficient and tosses it into the darkness.

"Well, then!" he shouts, suddenly perky. "Why didn't we do that right away, instead of getting so snotty?"

My mouth drops open. Did he seriously?

But I don't have time to argue before he starts yammering again. "All aboard! And I mean it this time." He leans in close. Too close. "The ride to Coney Island isn't a short one. And it's been a long time since I've met such a sturdy lady; you're just my type."

"I doubt that," I say, rolling my eyes, and rush into the car before the conductor can launch into any more of his revolting courtship maneuvers. The last thing I need is to figure out that he is turned on by what I'm so desperately trying to get rid of. I'm pretty sure I didn't misread the intent of the word *sturdy*.

I take the closest seat and Gretta crowds in next to me, while Neuter takes up opposite, coiling the slack rope onto the floor at his feet. The conductor peeks in, winks, and then stabs a thumb in the direction of the front of the train.

"Just gotta check on the rest of the passengers." He gives me another wink and then disappears.

"He's into you," Gretta says, elbowing my arm.

"That's what I'm worried about."

And I already have enough to worry about, I think. Tracking down the Zed is the least of it. There seems to be something sinister in the world that wasn't there just hours ago. Something spreading.

What exactly are living people doing eating the dead? Why are there so many of them? And what is that sound in the distance?

Slap-slap-slap.

"Christ!" I scream.

"Shut the door!" Gretta is on her feet and flanking me even as the footfalls get louder. The carrion stampede down the stairs. I lean out of the car and see a hint of blue light ahead.

"Conductor! Conductor!"

Slap-slap-slap.

The lights bounce as he shrugs and he continues to inch toward the smoking coal locomotive attached to the front of the train. He doesn't hear me. I struggle with the knotted rope around my waist.

"Get this door shut, Gretta," I beg as the knot frees. "You

know what they'll be after if they make it down here before we get moving!"

"What about you?"

"They're not coming for me." I point at her gut and she grits her teeth. The realization settles on her like a weight.

I sprint after the conductor, crouching as low as I can to see beneath the smoke, whipping around the concrete columns, passing one empty car after the next until I can see the man's blue aura and something else in the car next to me.

Movement.

Lots of it. Shambling death bumbles behind the glass, some of them looking over at me hungrily, black tongues lapping between loose rotten teeth. And coming down the stairs, a shit ton of two-legged vultures, stumbling and coughing. Coughing.

The smoke is probably slowing them down, I think. But it won't stop them. They're crazy. They can somehow smell the dead down here.

Hell. I can smell the dead.

"What the hell, Conductor!"

He shrugs. "What? It's a shipment for the Geek."

I don't even want to know what this means. "We have to go!" I shout. "Don't you hear that?"

His eyes dart toward the stairs, where the dark haze seems to vibrate. In the distance feet appear, and then faces. The carrion aren't so crazy that they don't stop, drop, and crawl beneath the toxic cloud to get to their dead meat. They scrabble forward, purple smears black in the dim light.

Gagging and coughing.

The conductor's face freezes, shock pushing every orifice wide. I claw at him, scream for him to move, and then we're running, too, into the open engine car. He slams his palm against a lever and suddenly, thankfully, we're moving.

But it's too slow.

The carrion are already attacking the zombie car, desperate for their food. They jack tiles from the station walls and stab at the glass. Toss garbage can covers and benches. Windows shatter, and the dead seem to explode outward along with the shards.

"Faster!" I scream.

And the train does pick up some speed, but as I lean out to watch the melee unfold, I wonder if it's going to be enough. The carrion and the zombies that aren't clinging to the sides of the subway car are locked in a culinary embrace, feeding on each other. Human on the dead, zombie on living flesh.

Blood and bile surge forward across the station floor in a wave and I can't hold back any longer. I lean out, lift up my mask, and vomit as the scene behind us falls into darkness.

I WAKE ON the floor of the engine, the sounds of shovel stabbing coal reminding me of where I am. Where I'm headed and what we've somehow managed to survive.

I wonder about Gretta Graves and Neuter.

Had they been able to get their door shut? If they hadn't, Gretta's special package certainly didn't make it. But would that have been enough for such a horde? Would they have killed just to have more dead flesh later? Are some of them smart like that? Like packing a lunch?

"Why you headed to the carnival?" The conductor's deep voice shakes me out of the dwelling.

"We're looking for something."

"Only one thing to find at Coney and that's the Geek. You jonesing for the Jimmy?" He steps up close to me and slides down the wall until we're real close. "Or is it something else?"

"What do you know about Zed?" I ask.

He winces. "I know it ain't natural. Somethin' the Geek cooked up wrong and took off like new sugar. Tell me a tough chick like you ain't gonna get mixed up with nothin' like that."

"I have to. I don't have a choice."

And I didn't, did I? Whether I took it on my own or as a result of delivering a batch to Dr. Bloom, I was looking at getting mixed up in some Zed.

"Well." The conductor pats me on my leg and stands up. I notice that I can see him more clearly, and it isn't because his helmet light has gotten brighter.

Daylight filters through the greasy glass as the subway train rises from the depths of the tunnel. We're close. I slip off the oxygen mask and gulp at the fresh air. Craning my neck out the side window, I half expect to see an ongoing struggle, but the car that holds the zombies is quiet.

Shredded clothing and gore flap against the sides of broken windows like tattered curtains. The battle has burned itself out, or rather eaten itself still.

The tracks bank slightly, and the full crescent of the collection of cars becomes visible. My eyes scan each for signs of life and then, four cars back, I find some. Gretta and Neuter waving.

As we approach the station, the conductor touches me on the shoulder.

"You know that old saying, 'The darker the berry . . . '?"

I shake my head no.

"'The darker the berry, the sweeter the juice.' That's how it goes. But that ain't true. There's nothin' sweet anymore. You remember that." He withdraws his hand and eases the train to a stop.

I suppose he's right. There isn't a whole lot of sweet to go around.

And all I can think about at the mention of berries are the stains on the carrion's faces. Purple as blackberry jam.

"Jade!" Gretta's big heels clop across the platform toward me. Her smile fades as she passes the zombie car but she doesn't stop to inspect it. Nothing springs out, so that's some luck.

"You managed to keep that baby, I see."

"Yep. Ain't that somethin'? I'd have thought for sure a night like what we just went through would have set off my labor quicker than a shot of Pitocin, but nope. She's hangin' in there. Don't want to be born just yet and that's just fine with me." She rubs at the curvature, secures the bandanna into the gnawed hole, and smiles again.

To that, all I can say is, "Just remember your promise."

CONEY ISLAND USED to be a shambles on a good day, but post–zombie apocalypse it turned into an actual garbage dump. Trash drifts dwarf the already short buildings, turning them into mountains of junk. To get from the elevated train platform to the street level, we climb down, carefully avoiding the hypodermic needles and skinny rats.

But it's the larger vermin moving in the distance that I'm worried about. Carrion wander the streets. A few people without the purple stains, too, but they're much less frequent. We have to move quickly and quietly.

As if it's heard my thoughts, the dead thing in Gretta's gut scrabbles against the plastic shell.

"Shut it up, Gretta," I hiss.

She pouts, rubbing her belly. "We're fine. Just fine . . ."

We tumble into the shadows between buildings and wait, observing the carrion. They stagger to and fro, stumble, and half of them wallow in the refuse like they can't figure out how their appendages work. Something's different about these, disorganized to the point of being slovenly and not the predators the others are.

But we can't risk them noticing. Even if they are high or completely stoned out of their minds.

"This place is magical," Gretta quips, holding her stomach as she crabwalks down toward where Nathan's used to sit, now just another pile of rotting waste and enough of it to provide some cover.

"So where is this guy?" I ask. "The Geek."

Neuter juts his chin toward the water and we follow. The boardwalk is impassable; chopped into shards and used for firewood, it's a valley of splinters and spears. So we cut along the empty street side, diving into alcoves and busted storefronts as we need to, until we arrive at the carnival.

Clouds roll in and cast a dark shadow over the crumbling amusement park. The rides are rusted and still, the cotton candy kiosks empty, unmanned. Rotting husks of stuffed animals decorate the empty game booths, termites and roaches having turned them into prime real estate.

In the past, this kind of place would have been crawling with homeless people. That particular social issue had been completely eradicated by the undead's appearance.

A sharp grinding noise draws my attention to the Wonder Wheel. Strung with lights, it rotates slowly.

"There," Neuter says. "That's where we'll find him."

We crouch in the darkness as more of the stained freaks pass. Up close, they appear asleep, purple tongues thrusting from their mouths like those of overmedicated mental patients. Their faces aren't nearly as stained, but those tongues are unreal.

Amethyst.

I glance at Gretta, a.k.a. the target on our back. If these carrion snap to and get the munchies, I just know I'll trip her to create a diversion.

Neuter is right, though, and we hear the Geek before we see

him. His voice is mechanized, as though he's speaking through a megaphone.

"Rest easy, friends. The conductor will be here soon. Restocking the lake! You'll have your fill and these will come to you! Right to you."

I creep up to a junction and cast my eyes up a glowing gallery lined with torches and strewn with dozing carrion up toward a Roman-esque scene of debauchery. Bodies curled around each other, lazing in their purpled stupors like a new litter of puppies— if puppies ate the flesh of the dead and somehow weren't cute. Some writhe and clutch their guts and even those of their neighbors as if in sympathy. Beyond them sits a raised dais and atop that a man . . . or what looks like a man, from this distance. He's dark as an oil slick.

"Friends, friends—rest easy!" he shouts, and taps a megaphone-topped scepter like a gavel against the grit under his feet. "We have visitors."

My breath hitches in my chest. He's spotted us, which shouldn't surprise me—at six foot six in these heels, I'm not exactly inconspicuous. But it does.

The Geek himself sits on a throne that sparkles like a cell phone kiosk, and as I approach I realize, instead of the bones of his enemies, the man has embedded his chair with those memories of a more connected time. That he's chosen the most blinged-out cases makes me think we might have something in common— until I get a good look at the Geek up close. He wears a black leather hood, and as he watches us approach, he unzips the mouth to reveal his jagged smile and metal teeth.

"Hello!" he shouts pleasantly. "Welcome!"

I push ahead of Gretta and Neuter and advance. "Hello . . . Mr. Geek, is it?"

"You may call me *the* Geek. There's no need to get caught up in gender trappings, is there?" He nods as though we have an understanding.

"I suppose."

"Now, how may I help you? A sample, perhaps?"

"Zed," I say.

"Zed!" he laughs.

A rustle of interest sweeps across his entourage, an unconscious lavender lip-licking that sets my nerves on edge.

"Of course. It's all anyone asks for now." The Geek stands, slips his hand around the crook of my elbow. "Walk with me."

We move closer to the Wonder Wheel, to a stand set up with levers and buttons, and the Geek presses one, causing the giant Ferris wheel to shudder and rotate. From this angle I notice there are bars on the window, and as each car passes I see that it carries a load of passengers, mostly dead and thudding their heads against their prison, others drooling purple juice.

"Don't mind them, they're in process." He shrugs.

"Process of what?" I ask, but I remember Annick's description. *A transformative agent.*

"They are changing. Becoming something different. Who knows what, eventually? Aren't we all becoming something that we're not yet?"

I nod, but without enthusiasm, with the beginnings of fear.

"You yourself appear to understand this more than most." The Geek smiles broadly, shiny teeth grinding. He runs a pink tongue across his likewise flesh-toned lips, his silver teeth glinting.

"You're unstained." The words pop out before I can evaluate whether it's wise to note the difference.

He continues to smile. "Transformation is not my end goal. My medicinal need is for something . . . different. My friends, on the other hand, are freshly dosed and eventually will head off on their own journeys. God bless their souls. It's a wonderful age we live in, full of new possibilities. 'Momentous' is the word—don't you think?"

With a flick of a lever the Wonder Wheel stops its noisy rotation and a dark car sits before us. I am coaxed toward it by the elbow of mine he holds, and when I look back over my shoulder, I'm terrified by the scene playing out behind me. While the Geek has been distracting me, Gretta has been quietly tied to a telephone pole, while Neuter lies in a crumpled heap. A pair of carrion sniff at Gretta's belly, tug at the bandanna, rap at the prosthetic, and listen—all while the big tranny just smiles and nods as if she's witnessing some tribal custom.

Crazy bitch.

"Wait!" I cry, but the door to the rocking room is already open and already I'm being forced inside.

The door clangs shut behind me.

"I don't want this. I don't want to become a carrion. I don't."

The Geek shrugs nonchalantly. "What you seek is there before you."

I turn slowly to find a crate in the center of the gently rocking cell and atop it a box, wooden on all sides but one, where a metal plate is set into a grooved frame, a handle in its center.

"It's a nightmare box, to be sure, but it's the source of Zed. It's what you're after. It's what everyone is after—a new outlook to experience!"

"If that's the case," I say, sweat trickling down my face, "then I just need to get it back to my doctor. That's all I need. I don't need to see it."

The Geek smiles again—actually, he never stopped smiling, the gold glinting in the darkness like a tiny constellation. "Oh, no. You *do*. You need to see it. And you will. After all, you've already brought your payment and everything. I don't renege on deals."

"We haven't made a deal! I haven't paid!"

He motions toward Gretta. "You've brought us a wonderful gift, and in return, you'll have your transformation."

"No, I won't. Let Gretta go!"

"Let me rephrase. You'll have your transformation. Or your friends will die."

Gretta's eyes are wide with terror now, and a few more of the carrion begin to sniff around her; one thunks her belly like a watermelon. I glance at the box and then back to the Geek.

His smile is insanity. His shiny teeth grinding out sparks.

I'm out of choices.

I reach for the handle on the metal plate. When I wrap my shaking fingers around it, I feel a thud jar the wall of the crate. There's something inside. Something moving. I release it and push back, shaking my head.

No.

I can't do it.

What the fuck is it?

"Go on," the Geek coaxes in his hoarse, overly amiable voice.

I can't stand to look at him again, and outside of the cell I can hear Gretta moaning. Or maybe it's inside the cell. A guttural gurgling reverberates all around me. Coming from inside the box.

Three steps. Grab the handle and lift off the side and then I'll know.

Pull off the bandage, I think. *Do it quick enough and it won't hurt.*

I lunge forward. The thing inside thuds against the wall as I feel the metal plate's weight. I lift, slipping the square up and out of its tracks, and fling it to the floor with a clatter.

But all that's behind it is another flat surface. I can see this one has an oval cut into it, though a dirty pair of curtains mostly covers it. Something flutters against them. I swipe them open frantically, unable to take the nightmare a second longer.

What I see there stops my breath dead in my chest.

The rotten ear and gray flesh of a corpse.

A zombie. Trapped in a cell within a cell. Its head braced with leather straps nailed to the ceiling of the box so it can't turn.

But something else too. Something I've never noticed in any of the walking dead I've come into contact with—this one is leaking something from its pores. Dark. Gelatinous.

Purple.

More of the juice trickles as the thing cranes its neck, teeth snapping.

"Lick it!" the Geek hisses. "Lick it and transform!"

I scream. Fall to my knees and hold my head in my hands. There is no hormone. No easy fix. Annick has sent me on a doomsday mission. Did she know? Was she just trying to get rid of me?

I look back at the zombie and see myself. We are the same, all of us trapped in our own cells. The juice trickles.

"No!" I cry. "No!"

"You must!" The Geek giggles both words.

"I'm not turning into one of them."

"No," he agrees. "Not turning."

I don't need him to elaborate. We are them. We feed. We consume. It's all a trap. Carrion, zombie, flesh. All the same.

"I'm done with this," I say, scanning the distance for Gretta, who is sobbing softly. Her prosthetic torn open. Empty.

"Is that your choice?" the Geek asks.

I train my eyes on him, muster up all the hate I have, and hiss, "Fuck you." I cram my hand into my purse and wrap my fingers around the gun that waits for me there. The door of the cell clangs open and suddenly he's there, a knife raised, lunging across the cell toward me. I lift the purse in the Geek's direction and fire. And he's on me.

I feel a stitch in my side. And then warm wetness. And I damn myself for not practicing with the gun more.

The stitch turns into five.

Twelve.

I WAKE IN the darkness. I'm hungry.

Insatiable.

I'm bound about my chest and legs. I can't tell by what. I can't see. My arms are shackled behind my back. But I don't care. There's that. I don't care.

I hear a sharp swipe to my left ear. Close.

And then light pours in and I strain to see a familiar face. Neuter. His eyes are downcast.

"I'm sorry," he whispers, and leans in as though to kiss me.

To comfort me.

I try to forget the pangs scratching at my gut. The scent of him. The sweet iron of his flesh. And I close me eyes, tilting my cheek toward his lips.

But it's not a kiss he delivers.

It's a slow, wet lick.

"THE WEREWIFE"

Jaye Wells

Brad should've turned around and left the minute he saw the kitchen. His first hint of danger was the penicillin growing on the plates. Annie never left dirty dishes in the sink, much less piled on the counter. He glanced at the wall calendar next to the phone. There he saw what he'd been dreading—a huge red *X* over that day's date.

Oh, shit, he thought, *it's that time of the month.*

Work had been crazy and he'd been out of town for a couple of days dealing with a crisis at the Bridgeton warehouse. Still, that was no excuse for forgetting. With Annie, you always had to be careful.

He cupped his balls as he walked into the den—just in case. Annie lay on the couch with an arm covering her eyes. Tiptoeing through the room, his silent feet dodged dirty clothes and empty dog treat boxes. He prayed she'd just ignore him.

"You're late," she barked. "Did you get the steak?"

Brad winced and turned slowly. *No sudden movements,* he reminded himself.

"Sorry. I forgot." Like he hadn't had enough on his mind with the business trip. Why couldn't she have gone to the store herself before nightfall? He swallowed the question when he saw her ferocious scowl and knew he'd never win this argument. "I'll go now."

Her eyes glowed in the dim room, a predator's stare.

"Don't bother." She swiped a furry hand through the air. "I'll eat out tonight."

Brad felt the blood leave his face in a rush. "But, honey, last time—"

His words died as she hunched over, grabbing her belly. Sympathy and terror duked it out in his gut. Then she got on all fours and let loose an unholy growl.

Screw sympathy, he thought. The last time he let it influence his actions, he'd ended up pissing blood for two weeks.

As he ran the usual path toward salvation, Brad took some comfort in the fact that he was near the basement this time. He hadn't always been so lucky and bore the scars to prove it.

He skirted the bistro table and the fridge before leaping over the overflowing basket in the laundry room. Her rage-howls nipped at his spine. But then a frantic skittering sound echoed as her claws struggled for purchase on the slick floor. Just before he slammed shut the basement door, he saw a blur of teeth and fur barreling toward him. The third dead bolt slid home an instant before the heavy body slammed into it.

Claws screeched over the coat of semigloss he'd applied exactly a month earlier. High-pitched yips and low, angry growls sneaked under the doorjamb and made the hair on his neck stand at attention. He closed his eyes and slid down the wall with a shotgun cradled in his lap like the baby they'd never have.

Finally, after what felt like hours, the snarling stopped.

Toenails clicked on the linoleum.

Shattered glass and splintering wood followed.

A mournful howl split the night.

Brad leaned his head back. Light from the kitchen spilled under the jamb to illuminate the weapons and cans of soup he'd stashed there. It really wasn't so bad in his makeshift panic room. He had plenty of beer and food to get him through the full moon. And he knew that when the moon time passed, his Annie would go back to making his breakfast and ironing his shirts. They wouldn't discuss what happened, of course. They never did. But at least he'd have a few weeks of relative peace before the next full moon.

Still, he thought, he probably should go ahead and install that doggy door.

THE NEXT MORNING Brad unlocked the basement door and went to find his wife. His stomach pitched when he found Annie naked in the backyard.

Her pale body was smeared with blood and brown smears he could only hope were mud. Sighing, he bent and threw her over his shoulder. She murmured something but barely stirred as he carried her over to the side of the house. Her body instinctively protested the cold water from the hose, but he knew if he didn't clean her off before taking her inside, he'd hear about the stains on her white carpet for weeks.

Once he had her dried off, he helped his sagging wife inside and tucked her into bed. She rolled over and was snoring before he made his way back out the bedroom door.

His body felt heavy, like he had lead weights tied to his wrists and ankles. He hated this part: the cleanup. He never knew what grisly surprises waited for him in the neighborhood, but he had to hide Annie's trail of destruction before the neighbors woke up for work.

Luckily, it had been a light night. No human bodies this time. Just the remains of two feral cats in the alley. He made quick work of burying the evidence in the abandoned lot that had become his makeshift graveyard. The pets of several neighbors had been laid to rest there without anyone being the wiser.

Leaning on the shovel, he wiped the sweat from his brow and watched the sun come up over the peaked roofs of Holiday Lane. How much longer could they go on like this? In the year since Annie changed, he'd almost filled up the lot with remains. Soon they'd have to move—or find a cure. But how?

The walk back to the house was like a death march. His hands were blistered and bloody and his heart felt heavy in his chest. A whisper in his head suggested he just keep walking and never look back. Start a new life in a new town. Find a new wife who didn't need flea dips or kill the neighbors' pets for fun.

"Hey there, neighbor!" Ernie Rasmussen jumped up from behind his midsize sedan like a jack-in-the-box. Brad jerked and dropped the shovel with a loud clang. His heart was doing some clanging of its own in his chest.

"H-Hey, Ernie. You're up early."

"Oh, you know how it is. Early bird gets the worm and all that jazz. What ya got there?" He shot a pointed look at the shovel, which lay between them like evidence in a murder trial. Ernie winked. "Doing a little grave robbing?"

Brad scrambled for an explanation. With an awkward laugh, he went for the sort-of truth. "Something killed a feral cat in my backyard. Wanted to take care of it before Annie saw it and got upset."

Ernie nodded sagely. "That damned coyote again. I tell you, I've called animal control out here must be five times after that blasted animal got our Muffy, and they still haven't done anything about it. We need to start a petition or something."

Rasmussen's little fur ball used to shit on Brad's pristine front lawn and shred his newspapers every morning. That particular kill of Annie's had been one of the few Brad hadn't mourned.

"I hear you." He needed to change the subject. "Well, I guess I'll let you get to the office."

"Hey, listen." Ernie's eyes lit up like he'd had a brilliant idea. "Lisa and I were planning on going to that carnival this weekend. Would you and Annie like to join us?"

Brad perked up. "Carnival?"

"Oh, you know. Came here last year?" Ernie snapped his fingers, trying to remember. "Carnival Diablo or something?"

"Carnivale Diabolique." Brad's heart picked up pace again, only this time with excitement. "I hadn't heard it was back," he said, trying to sound casual. "When's it start?"

"Friday night, I think. Lisa picked up a flyer at the Piggly Wiggly. Can't stand the things myself," Ernie said, shrugging. "But Lisa gets a kick out of having her palm read, and I suppose the rides are okay. What do you say?"

Brad had every intention of going, but not to have a double date with the Rasmussens. "I'll have to get back to you. Annie said something about cleaning out the gutters this weekend."

"Okeydoke." Ernie nodded like a man who knew the tyranny of the honey-do list. "Just give us a jingle if you want to come along."

After that, Brad extricated himself as fast as he could. He walked away at a dignified pace, though the minute he was out of Ernie's line of sight, he broke into a run. Ernie Rasmussen, despite his annoyingly sunny disposition and love for yappy asshole dogs, had just offered Brad the solution to all of his problems. He couldn't wait to get home to tell Annie.

"I WON'T GO!" Annie shouted in her best and-that's-final voice.

"But, honey, do you really want to spend the rest of your life howling at the moon?"

It's not so bad, she thought silently. *It's the only time I feel really free.* Not that she could tell Brad that. He'd just sulk.

She stared at him hard for a full minute before answering. With each passing second, Brad's posture fell another centimeter. Finally, she said, "This again?" Her words dripped with disdain. "How many times do I have to tell you? I have a *medical condition.*" She enunciated the words like he was one of the mentally impaired kids she used to work with before her condition made her unsafe around children.

Brad just stared back at her. His chin had the stubborn tilt it sometimes got when he remembered he was a man.

"I'm not going." Her voice tremored a little, and she hated that she was so close to admitting she was afraid.

Brad looked her dead in the eyes, leaned forward, and delivered his trump card. "If you don't, I will leave you."

Her stomach bottomed out. An icy wind passed over her skin, causing gooseflesh to rise. If he left her, she'd surely end up dead. It was only a matter of time until the neighbors or the authorities realized she was the one who stalked their quiet neighborhood at night.

"I just don't know what you think it's going to accomplish," she said, keeping the rising panic from her tone.

"Maybe nothing," he said. "But we have to *try*, Annie. Aren't you tired of waking up naked and covered in blood every month?"

No, the beast whispered. *The only time I'm happy is when I'm on the hunt.*

"There's evil there," Annie—the real Annie—whispered to Brad.

His mouth set into a grim line. "There's evil in you, too, Annie."

The words hit her squarely in the gut. For the first time, she allowed herself to see the fear and revulsion Brad tried so hard to hide from her. She'd done such a good job of not noticing the weapons he'd stashed around the house, the locks on the insides of doors, the silver cross he'd taken to wearing.

Her pride reared up. "If you love me, you won't make me go."

He wiped a callused hand—earned from all those graves he'd dug—over his haggard face. "If you love me, you will."

With that, her husband rose from his chair and walked away, leaving those awful words to hover over the table like a hangman's noose.

ONE YEAR EARLIER

ANNIE ALWAYS HATED carnivals. She hated the mud and the hay. She hated the scent of fried dough mixed with horseshit. But most of all, Annie hated the sideshows and the freaky carnies who ran them.

To her, the tops of the moth-eaten tents drooped over like drunken clowns. The rides clanked and groaned like arthritic performers. And the screams of the riders weren't joyful but instead had the high, hysterical pitch of terror.

"The Carnivale Diabolique?" she snorted. "Give me a fucking break."

"Don't be such a downer. It'll be fun." Brad pulled her arm. "C'mon, I'll buy you some cotton candy."

Fun was the opposite of what it was, and cotton candy sucked, but the counselor had warned her that she needed to learn to keep some opinions to herself for the sake of their marriage. So instead of telling her husband she'd rather brush her teeth with barbed wire than go stare at the ridiculous freaks in the red-and-black tent, she pasted on a smile and let him lead the way.

Just like when we have sex, she thought—another observation she wisely kept to herself.

While Brad chatted with the pimply teen behind the cotton candy machine, Annie turned to look at the freak tent. The structure itself was a large affair with vintage posters tacked to the red-and-black panels on its outside. One image was of a man in a pin-striped suit whose face was dominated by an elephant trunk. Another depicted a woman in an evening gown swallowing a sword. The bearded lady, the dog-faced boy, and the Fiji mermaid all stared from their own posters with grim, if misguided, dignity. And there, on the very end—almost in the shadows—was a different sort of image. The background was bruise purple and midnight black. Against it, a picture of a pale man in nothing but a black loincloth. His face was upturned, as if he were praying for salvation. Not surprising, Annie guessed, since his entire chest was skewered with what appeared to be metal hooks.

Out front, a woman stood on top of a large round drum while she called out to passersby. Annie took in the tight harlequin pants, the leather corset, the cropped jacket, and the black top hat with the thick tulle veil with only passing interest. Because it wasn't the audacious outfit that demanded attention when you looked at her—it was the mask.

White porcelain provided a smooth canvas for the perfect doll-like features painted on the surface—long lashes, Cupid's-bow mouth, rosebud cheeks. Over the forehead and chin, scrollwork and lace patterns were painted in blood red.

That mask, Annie thought. It reminded her of death. Her memory offered up a documentary she once saw about how Victorians would create plaster casts of their deceased loved ones' faces. *Yeah*, Annie thought, *it's like a death mask*. She stared into the deep dark holes where the woman's eyes glowed in the dusk like twin embers.

Two bright green cat's eyes landed on Annie with the impact of a punch. She stumbled back a step but was held captive by the compelling gaze.

Those eyes woke something inside of her. Some long-forgotten—or never-recognized-at-all—urge for adventure. It was a reckless feeling, one that reminded her of summer afternoons driving with the top down. Of sneaking out of her parents' home at midnight to meet a bad boy. Of feeling deliciously immortal. *Free*.

What Annie didn't know was that the woman actually could see inside her. She recognized that red spark zinging through her veins—the restlessness Annie had ignored in favor of security—and smiled evilly behind that mask.

Brad handed over the cotton candy like a warrior bestowing a prize upon his maiden fair. Without breaking her stare, Annie lifted the pink cloud to her mouth. It tasted like graveyard dust on her tongue.

If Brad noticed the woman or the mask, he didn't comment. And Annie didn't say anything, either, because at that moment the woman in the mask curled her long, black-lacquered nails in a gesture of invitation.

"Come on," Annie urged. The cotton candy fell, forgotten, to the brown earth.

Now it was her turn to pull Brad's hand.

The air inside the tent smelled dusty and yellow, like dry hay, and of something darker—something spicy and rich and unsettling. A ticket booth sat just inside the entrance. A stooped old man sat inside and grunted at people as they entered. Brad marched over and handed over the four tickets required for the attraction.

The old-timer pushed two of the tickets back across the surface. "She's free," he wheezed.

Brad frowned at the man. "Why?"

Annie scooted closer to hear better.

"Boss says she's free."

Annie glanced toward the closed flaps that led back outside. She had a good idea who this mysterious boss was, but she couldn't figure out why she'd earned a free ride or, more disturbingly, how the masked one had communicated this decree.

"Sounds good to me," Brad said. He'd always loved a deal.

Annie looked at her husband of almost ten years and bit her tongue. She wanted to demand an explanation, or demand that Brad demand one, but the voice of their therapist wriggled in her head like an annoying earworm.

Your constant questioning of Brad's decisions undermines his confidence. If you want him to be more assertive, you have to stop second-guessing his every move.

Since her husband was already at the curtain that led to the exhibits, she mumbled thanks to the old man and turned to follow. Maybe she was overreacting. It was nice that she was getting in free. No reason to be so fucking critical all the time, as Brad so eloquently put it all the time. Besides, that new spark inside of her danced at the prospect of exploring the forbidden world inside the tent.

But as she turned, the man in the booth caught her eye. Maybe it was a reflection off the glass separating them, or maybe the whole freak show vibe was getting to her, but she could have sworn his wrinkled face smoothed over for a split second to reveal a younger face. A handsome face with a square jaw and sparkling eyes and . . . fangs. His shirt was gone and sharp hooks pierced his skin. Thin rivulets of blood trickled down, and a tattoo just under his collarbones read "Adeline."

She blinked.

The old man's face had returned to normal. But his cackles danced down her spine as she walked through the curtain.

FRIDAY NIGHT

THE FREAKS TENT hadn't changed. Brad looked up at the colorful panels and the flags and the vintage posters and felt suddenly like he was back on that fateful night a year earlier. The scent of cotton candy saturating the air only intensified the feeling. Only this time Annie didn't make any flippant remarks. Instead, she slipped her sweaty palm against his and squeezed like she was afraid he'd run off and leave her.

It was the first time she'd touched him in weeks. *Scratch that,* he thought. She touched him plenty when the beast was behind the wheel. Threw herself at him when the predator needed sexual release. Back when she'd first been bitten, the sweaty, animalistic joinings were a dream come true. He'd worn the scratches down his back like badges of honor. Now those marks had hardened into scars and the beast never asked anymore—she just took.

He squeezed Annie's hand back and shot her a wan smile. The logical part of his brain told him he should have left a long time ago. But the other part, the dutiful one, demanded that he give it one last honest effort before he made his exit.

He led her to the ticket booth. A woman with a shock of purple hair on her head and more piercings than a colander blinked at them from behind the window.

"We'd like two tickets to the freak museum, please."

"Closed." She smacked her gum and looked back down at the magazine she'd been pretending to read.

Brad's heart thudded into his diaphragm. "What? It can't be!"

She dragged her eyes back up. "Mistress Valentina closed the museum tonight because there's a special performance."

"What kind of performance?" Annie asked.

"It's kind of a circus thing."

Brad glanced at Annie, who looked like she hoped he'd give up. He gritted his teeth and made his decision. "We'll have two tickets for that then, please." When Annie made a noise of protest back in her throat, he squeezed her hand. "We'll just talk to her after."

Annie's head bowed and he found himself enjoying the rare show of submission.

"Here," the girl behind the glass snapped. "Show starts in five minutes. Better shake a leg."

A FEW PEOPLE believed Valentina was born evil. A couple of others theorized she had to be some sort of demoness. Everyone else died too quickly to form an opinion.

If you asked her, however, she'd tell you she was a collector. A connoisseur. An admirer of the utterly mundane.

And one year ago, the minute Valentina laid her cold, hard eyes on Annie, she knew she'd found the newest treasure for her collection.

Of course, she'd also realized it wouldn't be easy. She had to get rid of the man, for one thing. He was doughy and dense. Mundane, certainly, but utterly forgettable. He'd have to go. But not before she made him spend some time suffering for his lack of spine. A year would do it. *Yes*, she'd thought back then with a smile, *a year serving the beast would break him totally.*

Also, Valentina realized with a frown, Annie's shrewd gaze was still troubling. Valentina didn't like her pets to be too smart for their own good. They were harder to break in. Not that she didn't enjoy that part—some of her favorite pets had been the hardest to break—but it was time-consuming to destroy someone's free will. Still, there was great joy in watching a person's will totally shatter, their back bow, and their face fall with utter submission.

Delayed gratification had never been her strong suit, but in this case, she thought, it might well have been worth it. She had a very special evening planned for the citizens of Brooksville, and the guests of honor had just arrived.

Valentina licked her lips at the thought as she watched Annie move toward the tent.

Yes, breaking Annie would be fun, but watching her kill that husband of hers would be delicious.

THE ONLY THING worse than entering that tent behind Brad was seeing him wave at that jerk Ernie Rasmussen and his insipid wife, Lisa. On cue, the couple waved them over and pointed to two open seats beside them.

"Brad, no," she hissed.

"Relax," he said. "It'll be fine."

No it wouldn't. Annie was beginning to believe nothing would ever be all right again. She could feel that woman—that evil, evil masked woman from last year—watching her from somewhere inside the tent.

But more than that, she could feel the beast pacing restlessly inside her. The instant they'd walked through the tent flaps, her blood heated and her skin crawled with nervous energy.

Annie hated carnivals, sure, but she *loathed* small talk. So when the Rasmussens started chattering on about the local school board referendum, Annie tuned them out and focused on locating the dark energy pulsing through the space.

She turned to take in the other audience members. Smiling families filled the stands, several of whom she knew from her previous life, before this illness. She considered warning them about the darkness pressing in on her chest, or maybe it was like smoke filling her lungs? She couldn't put a name to the bad feeling, but she knew with every cell of her being it was a sinister omen.

But she didn't warn them. Because the beast that lurked under her skin felt that omen too—and it excited her. She licked her chops and put a claw over Annie's loudmouthed conscience and waited impatiently for the fun to begin.

Annie glanced at Brad. He showed no signs of worry. In fact, he looked totally comfortable as he chatted with the neighbors she knew he couldn't stand. *How does he do it?* she wondered. Even before the start of her condition, he'd been the one who always kept his cool. Nothing seemed to faze him. Not car trouble or the never-ending bills or Annie's screams of frustration. Their arguments had been the worst—with her red-faced and screaming while he sat looking as serene as a still mountain pool. She'd hated him the most in those moments. Because after several years she'd realized it wasn't that Brad managed his emotions better than she did. It wasn't that he was more mature or calmer by nature. No, she finally understood that his calmness betrayed a complete lack of conviction, an utter disconnectedness from any emotion stronger than contentment or mild annoyance.

Annie shook herself. She hadn't thought about her issues with Brad in a long time. For the last year, she'd been so caught up in trying—and failing—to manage the beast that she just . . . forgot, she guessed.

To keep from analyzing her relationship with her husband, she went back to watching the audience, like they were her own private freak show. The clean-cut husbands in their polo shirts and pressed pants. The mothers with their tight, forced smiles as they patiently listened to the excited exclamations of their rosy-cheeked children. Annie tilted her head and really looked. For a moment she thought she could see secrets crawling under their skin. Were the private things they hid under their twinsets any less shocking than her own?

Annie knew better. She'd been friends with women like these her whole life. She'd listened to countless confessions whispered over warming glasses of chardonnay. Fevered admissions of longing to run away, of hating children for ruining their bodies and their dreams, of wanting to smother snoring husbands in their sleep. Of wanting to take their delicate, pink razors and carve thin red lines up their arms.

No, Annie decided, she wasn't the only woman in Brooksville with a beast lurking in her blood. She was just the only one who let hers off the leash.

ANNIE WAS TOO quiet, Brad thought. Out of the corner of his eye, he watched her scanning the crowd. What was she thinking? Her hands were clasped in her lap, the knuckles white. Had he made a mistake bringing her back here?

". . . ask my opinion, we should form a posse and go shoot that damned coyote ourselves . . ." Rasmussen was saying.

Brad swiveled back to his neighbor. While he struggled not to look horrified by the prospect of someone hunting down his wife, the statement made him realize he'd been right to come. Whether Annie liked it or not, they needed to settle this business once and for all. Sure, she was upset, but eventually, once everything—once *she*—returned to normal, she'd thank him.

Rasmussen was waiting for his response. Brad cleared his throat and said in his most diplomatic tone, "Hopefully it won't come to that."

He was spared further debate when the lights fell, casting the entire tent in complete darkness.

Brad blindly reached for Annie's hand. He had to pry her fingers apart, and even once they surrendered to his grip, they felt clammy and stiff. He leaned over and whispered, "This will all be over soon."

She didn't respond.

"Ladies and gentlemen, children of all ages, welcome to the Carnivale Diabolique," a husky female voice announced over the speaker. "Take a seat if you dare. Your Auntie Valentina is about to spin hair-raising tales and share with you her private collection of weirdoes, freaks, and abominations. Lights up!"

A single light burst to life over the center ring, illuminating a long figure. Brad caught his breath. It was her—the lady in the mask.

The crowd tittered anxiously at her odd appearance. Annie's hand spasmed in his suddenly sweaty palm. Time had dulled the memory of the shock he'd experienced upon first seeing Valentina. The corset hugging her torso like a lover. The long legs encased in fishnet stockings and knee-high fuck-me boots. The firm breasts glowing in the spotlight. The sex and danger that swirled around her like a mysterious and enticing scent.

But then she removed her porcelain doll mask, and Brad's spontaneous erection deflated. The scarred planes of her face clung to the bones like melted wax. Her red lips slashed across her face like two fresh wounds. And those green eyes glowed with malevolent fervor.

"Ah. That's better. Yes?" She stilled and focused her attention on someone in the front row. "Oh, my dears, why are you crying? What's that?" She tilted her ruined face down, as if speaking to a child. "Auntie Valentina looks scary, doesn't she? Yes, yes. This is what happens when you don't listen to your mommies and daddies."

Nervous laughter tittered through the crowd. Was this all a part of the show?

"There, now, I'll put on my mask and cover those nasty scars so we can get on with the grand spectacle."

Three more lights exploded the darkness behind Valentina. Under each glowing pool, a different freak from Valentina's collection.

"Behold! My greatest treasures!" She spread her arms wide and gazed adoringly at her pets.

"First, we have Bambi." She motioned to the right, where a woman with antlers tipped in metal and hooves for hands posed proudly on a jutting rock. She wore brown and white body paint fashioned to look like fur. "I found her in the mountains of Colorado. She longed for strength to fight off her abusive husband."

The antlered woman pawed at the rock and huffed an angry breath from her nose.

"Bambi stabbed the bastard with her antlers," Valentina whispered dramatically, like she was sharing a juicy bit of gossip. "Isn't that wonderful?"

The audience gaped back in frozen horror.

"Next!" Valentina moved to the far left. A mermaid swam in a large tank of water. Her green tail flashed in the light like sequins, and she wore twin pink shells over her breasts. She crested up over the side of tank with a mighty splash of her tail.

"Nicole's husband liked to rape her in her sleep—now he's sleeping with the fishes, right, Nicky?" Valentina's grotesque laughter echoed through the tent and skittered up Brad's spine and lodged in his brain, bringing with it the horrible knowledge that Annie had been right—coming here had been a terrible idea.

"But in the center is my favorite pet." Their ringmistress motioned to a shirtless man hanging from the steel beams supporting the tent. "Dylan's wife cheated on him. He wished to be able to empty her like she'd done to his love."

His body formed a cross supported by steel hooks piercing his skin. Blood trickled from the wounds, but he wore a serene smile on his face that revealed two blindingly white fangs.

"He sucked down every last drop of his Adeline's blood," Valentina said, her voice high with excitement. "Now he punishes himself every night with those shiny hooks. But they always heal by morning, don't they, sweet Dylan?"

The man yearned forward to make the hooks dig deeper. A rivulet of blood ran down his chest and his expression bordered on bliss.

Outraged shouts and cries rose from the audience. Brad had seen enough. He jumped out of his seat like someone had lit a fire under him. Beside him, Annie jerked and pulled at his hand.

"Brad?" she spat.

"Come on," he urged. Annie rose but seemed uneasy about it, like she was worried the move would earn them attention they didn't want.

And just like that, a light swiveled violently to shine on them. Brad raised his free hand to shield his eyes as Valentina's voice exploded over the speakers.

"*Tsk, tsk, tsk.* Back to your seats, now. You might as well settle in, because the doors are locked." A beat of silence. "Besides, you won't want to deprive these lovely people of the main attraction, would you, Brad, Annie?"

Hearing their names come from that monster made Brad's bowels go watery. He looked to the right and to the left, judging the distance to the tent flaps. But just then two enormous women—at least, he guessed they were women, but it was hard to tell because they also wore masks—came to stand at either end of their aisle. All around, panicked audience members rose and shouted and pushed, desperate for escape. And in the center of the tent, the single spot of calm among the chaos, Valentina's smiling mask glowed under the lone light.

Over the noise, her voice rang out, calm and confident: "Maestro, a dirge if you please."

Brad spied a large hunchbacked man picking up a violin. Gripping the bow with a touch too delicate for his ham-hock hands, he closed his eyes and tucked the instrument under his chin, seemingly oblivious to the chaos. And then . . . then the first strains of a haunting melody lifted up from the strings. At first the people continued to push and claw their way toward the exits, but after a moment they paused and turned their heads up. Brad ignored them and took advantage of their distraction to pull Annie farther down the aisle.

It took effort to force Annie to follow—what was wrong with her, anyway? But once he reached the end of the aisle, he found himself looking up, up, up, at a very large woman. She looked like she was descended from a race of giants. Her meaty hands were larger than Brad's head. He tried to duck around her, but she grabbed him easily and lifted him from the ground. Tucked under her armpit, Brad watched in horror as she turned to Annie.

ANNIE DIDN'T KNOW why, but she couldn't move. One second, she was as eager as her husband to flee, but then the first sweet violin notes caressed her ears like a lover's whisper. She ignored Brad's shouts for help and stared at the hunchback and the masked woman who swayed beside him. Her conscious mind screamed at her to run, but something more compelling froze her limbs. From the corners of her eyes she saw Brad struggle against the giantess. She also saw that everyone else, including the annoying Rasmussens, had stilled as she had.

"Sit down, my doves," Valentina commanded over the music. "Listen to Drude's song." She motioned to the hunchback, whose eyes remained closed as he played a melody that called to a dark place inside Annie.

As one, the entire audience dropped to whichever seats were closest to them. Only Annie remained standing. Those two green eyes behind that mask were locked on her.

"Come."

The single word ricocheted inside Annie like a bullet, destroying what remained of her resistance. She ignored Brad's screams and began to make her way toward the center of the ring. The bouncer at the end of the aisle stepped back and allowed her to pass without comment.

She knew Brad would not be joining her, just as she knew that Valentina had prearranged this entire spectacle for her benefit. The idea should have scared her, but with the hypnotizing music, she couldn't feel anything other than total submission.

"Annie, no!" Brad screamed from far behind her.

"Annie, yes," Valentina cooed, and held out her hands like a mother welcoming her child home.

SHE WAS THINNER than Valentina remembered. Leaner but sinewy, like a young wolf. Behind her mask, the evil one smiled. She knew she'd chosen her newest acquisition wisely. And if there was one thing Valentina enjoyed more than staging spectacles, it was being right about a person's potential.

Valentina always believed murder was more fun in front of an audience. So, she'd been worried all these months that Annie's beast would grow weary of the weak man and eat him for a midnight snack. But whatever humanity was left inside the woman still held some sway. However, the time had finally come for Annie's inner beast to take charge for good.

Annie's cold hands landed in hers. Valentina swiveled smoothly and turned her prize toward the audience.

"Say hello to Annie, everyone."

The audience was still under Drude's narcotic musical spell and did as instructed. "Hello, Annie," they said in stereo monotone.

"She is our guest of honor tonight." Valentina patted Annie's arm and whispered in her ear, "I'm going to make you a star." She turned back to the crowd. "Behold: the Werewife!"

Loud squeaking announced the arrival of the show's special prop: the metal cage that had been specially made for the occasion. Valentina had to admit that Hephaestia—the metal worker from Detroit whose philandering husband had been encased in bronze—had outdone herself. The frame of the cage was covered in delicate silver filigree, not unlike a massive vintage birdcage, and the bars themselves were forged from the strongest steel inlaid with more silver. Inside, the ceiling was covered in a mosaic of moonstones Valentina had purchased from a gypsy in Romania. The old woman had done such wonderful work, it had almost been a shame to kill her. Almost.

The entire contraption was as large as a lion tamer's den and set easily over the ring next to them.

As the door to the cage opened, Annie's body went instantly stiff; even Drude's music couldn't override the beast's instinct to remain free at any cost.

Valentina opened a box set next to the door and removed a squawking chicken. Its wings flapped and its feet kicked, but the demoness held it out by the neck for all to see. "You like hunting, don't you, Annie?" She slashed at the bird's breast with a sharp fingernail. A red line of blood bloomed through the feathers.

The beast reared up and forced Annie's head back. Her mouth fell open and a long, mournful howl filled the tent.

"Come and get it!" Valentina tossed the frantic bird into the ring, where it commenced to running in panicked circles.

Annie hunched over and loped toward the door with her tongue hanging out and the fur already sprouting in dark tufts around her neck and the backs of her curled hands. Once inside, the chase truly began, and the tent filled with the chicken's ear-piercing squawks and Annie's monstrous growls, which were only interrupted by the metallic crash of the gate slamming home.

Valentina twisted the lock with a flick of her wrist and dropped the key in between her breasts. "Enjoy your appetizer while I prepare the main course."

BRAD FOUGHT AGAINST his captor like a wild animal. He kicked, he clawed, he cursed. But the Amazon held him as if he were nothing more than a child throwing a tantrum.

Once the cage had been lowered, he knew exactly what Valentina had planned.

His stomach felt like a nest of vipers had taken residence. Cold sweat coated his chest and back.

When the evil woman said, "Bring him," the giantess who held him lumbered forward. The movement made his stomach revolt and fear made sweat pour like tears from his skin. With a frantic sideways glance he saw Ernie Rasmussen beaming at him like some sort of creepy doll.

But the creepiest doll of all waited for him at the bottom of the bleachers. The startling white porcelain glowed like a full moon under the spotlights.

As he struggled against the large arms that held him, they only grew tighter until his vision swam with stars. The fear and the panic and the disorienting sensations made his mind retreat into the past, where he suddenly remembered that day. The first day they'd seen Valentina at the carnival. The day that had damned them all. And a voice in his head whispered, *You did this.*

The giantess reached the ring and set him down unsteadily on his feet. He swayed but pushed away, stumbling toward their captor.

"I didn't want this!" he screamed over the haunting violin music, over the staccato thrum of blood in his ears, over the buzz of malice in the air. "Do you hear me? I changed my mind. I want my old Annie back!"

Valentina cocked her head to the side like a dog hearing evil in the distance. She turned slowly toward him, leaving the tusked woman to handle Annie. "Changed your mind?" she said on a huff of laughter. "What on earth gave you the impression you had that option?"

Her laughter reached inside him like a fist clenched around his intestines. It squeezed until frigid sweat coated his back and chest. It twisted until he doubled over with nausea. He retched and fell to his knees.

"I didn't want this to happen," he cried. "I didn't."

The laughter cut off abruptly. "Yes, you did." Her tone was whisper soft, but the words themselves were knives on his skin. "You asked for it."

Behind her, Annie let out a triumphant howl as she finally captured her prize. With her back to the crowd, she bent over the struggling bird, her wet, violent sounds adding a vile harmony to the violin's melody. A spray of red decorated the cage's bars.

"No! ANNIE!"

The wolf whined.

"Shh, dear," Valentina soothed his wife. "He's learning a lesson about being careful what he asks for, aren't you, Brad?"

"No! You're wrong. I didn't ask for this!"

Tears blinded his vision and guilt and fear roiled in his gut like acid. He hadn't asked for it. Had he?

"You did!" Valentina announced in a joyful exclamation, like a preacher shouting from the pulpit. "You remember, don't you, Brad?"

Lord help him, he did. He remembered the first moment he'd seen Valentina. He'd been at the cotton candy booth, waiting for his turn. Annie stood sulking nearby, and he remembered a hot spot of anger in his chest that once again nothing was good enough for her. And then, just past Annie's mousy hair, he saw the striking masked woman by the entrance. His instant erection was quickly covered by some creative shifting, but he couldn't hide from the images that flashed through his head. Erotic tableaus, desperate longing for excitement and raw sex. A yearning for freedom from Annie's constant nagging and control-freak tendencies.

And his heart had whispered, *Why can't Annie be more wild and mysterious?*

"Dear, stupid Brad, if I could stage all of this"—Valentina motioned to the spectacle inside the tent—"if I could arrange to have your wife bitten by my pet JoJo the dog-faced boy, then how can you doubt that I could also snatch that wish right out of your feeble mind?"

Done with her meal now, the werewolf that was his wife stood at the metal bars, growling as she watched him with glowing, yellow eyes. The fur of her face was matted red with blood.

"I'm so . . . so . . ." His voice cracked. "I'm so damned sorry, Annie."

Valentina laughed again. Brad cried out as more cramps wracked his lower abdomen. "Oh, she's not innocent in this, either."

Brad sniffed and swiped at his eyes. His muscles felt rubbery and his brain wasn't firing on all cylinders. "*What?*"

He glared at the beast, whose yellow eyes looked down.

"Annie, what does she mean?" he shouted.

The violin was the only sound.

When she finally looked up, the yellow irises were shadowed with guilt.

Brad stumbled back a step.

Valentina opened her mouth, but it was Annie's voice that passed from between her demonic lips. "Could he be any more pathetic? Look at him, so weak and predictable." She waved wild hands in his direction. "Always whining, whining, whining about how we don't have sex enough and then pouting like a baby. Why would I want to have sex with a man-child, Brad?!? Why?" Valentina paced in front of him like a caged animal as she channeled Annie's innermost thoughts.

The crowd started clapping and chanting: "More, more, more!"

"I was so restless, crawling out of my skin." Annie's voice continued to spill from the stranger's lips. "I wanted to howl at the moon and run free without you hanging around my neck like a choke collar."

"If that's what she wanted," Brad shouted, "why didn't she divorce me or just leave?"

At this, Valentina smirked, and returned to possession of herself. "Because once she unleashed the she-wolf, she realized how vulnerable it made her. Lone wolves rarely survive."

Brad cringed, remembering that first full moon. The blood and the tears and the begging. The next morning's carnage. "She stayed because she needed me."

The wolf in the cage raised its snout and howled at the moonstones overhead.

Valentina shrieked in delight. "She was stuck with you!" She tossed her head back and laughed. As if on cue, the entire audience laughed with her, and the grating sound surrounded Brad, invaded him until it felt like thousands of ants chewed away on his brain stem. He was going to go crazy if he stayed in this fucked-up nightmare of a place. He lunged forward and punched the mask.

The porcelain cracked. The demoness shrieked in rage.

Drude's violin fell silent, but the crowd in the stand erupted into panic. As they climbed over each other, yearning for the exits, Brad moved forward to deliver more vengeance.

His fury was so complete that his blood felt like acid in his veins. His heart galloped in his chest and he panted like a dog. The shattered mask blinded the bitch long enough for him to deliver a series of jabs to her midsection, her neck, her jaw. With each furious punch, she staggered back another step. On some level, he was aware of all of Valentina's pets circling them, but none came forward to aid their leader.

Valentina swiped at him with her sharp nails, but his rage made him impervious. Even the swollen knuckles of his punching hand didn't hurt. Instead, he felt elated. Powerful. Like a man awakened from a long slumber.

Behind the bitch's head, he spied the hunchback with the violin approaching. Brad kept striking her, but braced himself to take on the other man too.

Only Drude didn't come to his lady's aid. He set down the violin and picked up something shiny from the ground, then turned toward the cage, which was only six or seven feet behind where Brad and the demoness struggled. The rest happened quickly.

The gate opened, Brad delivered his final punishing blow, and Valentina stumbled backward over the metal threshold of the gate.

Once she landed on her ass, Drude slammed the cage door and locked it with an audible click.

A beat of silence while both Brad and his foe realized what had happened. Their gazes both landed on the silver key held high in Drude's pale hand—Valentina's key, her only hope for escape.

Each of Valentina's pets snapped to and began circling the cage.

"Help me, you idiots!" she screamed.

No one even blinked. Their faces didn't look guilty or afraid. Just eager and shining, like a child's on Christmas morning.

Annie crouched low to the ground and growled. Her sharp teeth glistened with saliva under the heat of the lights, the reflections of the cursed moonstones. The moonstones Valentina had stolen from a gypsy she murdered in Romania. The gypsy who had cursed the stones with her dying breath. The curse that only lacked Valentina's blood to come alive.

Valentina turned slowly. Her melted wax face contorted into a grotesque mask of fear. "If you let me go, I'll change you back. Don't you want to be like your old self?"

The responding snarl sounded nothing like "Yes."

Instead, the beast took two slow, predatory steps forward. Her head lowered and her tongue jutted out to taste the demoness's fear, which tainted the air.

"Brad!" Valentina shouted. "I—I made a mistake."

"Damn straight you did." His voice was low but infused with a power that had never existed in him before. "And now you're about to experience a little poetic justice, you crazy bitch."

Valentina opened her mouth to argue, but the sound dissolved into a shattered scream of pain. Two huge paws wrapped around her head and pulled her to the ground.

Brad crossed his arms and smiled. "Bon appétit, my love," he whispered.

THE WEREWIFE DIDN'T play with her food. She probably would have enjoyed the delicious sounds of Valentina's pleas for mercy, but she just wanted the thing done. Canines slide easily into human flesh, especially the tender meat of the neck. Valentina's blood tasted like brimstone and ashes, but Annie swallowed every bitter drop.

No matter what movies want you to believe, no one's death is ever easy or pretty. The demoness thrashed and wailed—a loud death rattle accompanied the spastic jerking of limbs and the evacuation of her bowels. Annie felt the moment the woman's vile heart stopped beating.

A shock of electricity zapped through Annie's nervous system. She fell back and vomited on the packed dirt. She was vaguely aware of the sounds of cheering, and the sensation of being naked in the night air, but she was too busy trying to figure out what caused her to switch so rapidly from wolf to woman form.

An instant later Brad was beside her. He helped her up and cradled her in his arms. "You did it, honey. You broke the curse." He raised her trembling chin. "Look."

Annie blinked through the tears filling her eyes. All around the cage, the members of the demon's menagerie had each transformed back into their normal human forms. "Killing her must have lifted all the curses."

She should have felt elated and victorious. Instead, she felt hollow. Now that the beast was gone, what would become of her and Brad?

* * *

ONCE AGAIN—BUT HOPEFULLY for the last time—Brad was digging a grave. He should have felt exhausted after their ordeal. Instead, he felt invigorated, strong. More awake than he had in years.

While the other former freaks had ushered the remaining confused stragglers from the audience outside, Drude had helped Brad carry the evil ringmistress's body out back.

Annie tagged along, wrapped in a glittered cape she'd found in a costume trunk. As Brad and Drude discussed the perfect place to dig, she shivered from her perch on a barrel, watching her husband with glinting eyes.

"If you'll excuse me," Drude said, "I'll go check on the others."

The hump on his back hadn't disappeared with the curse, but he carried himself with slow dignity. If Brad hadn't been so busy digging, he would have indulged his curiosity about Drude and asked the man how he'd ended up in Valentina's clutches. Instead, he simply nodded over his shoulder. "Thanks for your help."

With the man's departure, silence wrapped its arms around the couple. The only sound in the clearing was the *shush-thump* as Brad methodically dug Valentina's final resting spot.

"You need to make it wider." Annie's voice rung out into the quiet like a gunshot. Brad jerked to a halt and spun to face his wife.

"What?"

"Wider," she enunciated, as if he were both deaf and dumb. She nodded at the hole. "And deeper too."

His eyes narrowed. "How many graves have you dug, Annie?" His voice was quiet. Too quiet.

She sniffed. "Any idiot could see that hole is too damned small, Brad."

He stabbed the tip of the shovel into the earth. "Would you like to do it?"

"No." Annie raised her gaze and met his stare. "I just want you to do it properly."

Something popped inside Brad's chest. His hands tightened around the wooden handle and he imagined the satisfying crunch of metal on skull.

"Why are you looking at me like that?" Annie shied back. "Stop it."

Brad shook himself and let the shovel fall to the ground. "*You* stop," he whispered. "Just stop."

"You're wasting time. Bury the bitch so we can go home."

"Do it yourself." The shovel hit the ground with a thud. "I'm done digging for you, Annie. Do you hear me? I'm done!"

She rose from her seat and crossed her arms. "If you hadn't brought me here in the first place, there wouldn't be a grave to dig, you idiot."

Brad realized with sudden clarity that Annie was like one of those fun-house mirrors. When he looked at her, she reflected back a distorted version of him. One that was weak and helpless without her.

"Valentina couldn't give you what you wanted," he said, almost to himself. "So I will."

With that, Brad turned and walked away.

"Brad! What are you doing? Get back here and finish this job! Brad?"

With each step he took away from Annie, his posture straightened a little more, each breath came a little easier, his smile grew a little wider.

"Goddammit, Brad, you get back here or I'll . . . I'll . . . Brad!"

When he reached the front of the tent, the audience had all disappeared. He found Drude by a line of motorized gypsy wagons.

"No one remembers a thing," the hunchback said. "Some even demanded their money back because the show was canceled."

Brad smiled and nodded. In the distance he could just hear Annie's shrill shrieks coming from behind the tent. "What are you all going to do?"

All the former freaks had formed a loose circle around the pair. Their faces were somber, but there was also palpable excitement in the air.

"Carnival life is all we know," Drude said with a shrug. "We'll carry on with a new name." He smiled and winked. "And all new acts, of course."

Brad nodded. "You got room for one more?"

A murmur rose up from the other performers. Nicole, the former mermaid, smiled shyly at him, and Brad felt a stirring in his center.

Drude held up a hand to silence the group. "You got any skills?"

Brad thought about it for a moment. "Don't mind getting my hands dirty." He held up his callused hands. "I'm not the fastest learner, but as long as you don't make me clean up after any animals, I'll do any job you give me."

Drude smiled. "Hop in."

Five minutes later, the caravan rolled out. Brad looked out the back of the last wagon in the line and watched the dirt-smeared, pissed-off woman come around the tent. She dragged the shovel behind her. When she looked up and saw her husband in the back of the van, she screamed, "Brad!"

He smiled and blew a kiss at the woman he used to worship. "Good-bye, Werewife," he whispered.

Annie raised her face and howled her rage at the waning moon.

"THE COLD GIRL"

Rachel Caine

It took me two days to die. On the first night, I met Madame Laida, and on the second night, I met the Cold Girl.

And this is how it happened.

This is me. I'm Kiley. I'm sixteen, and I have good taste in clothes and mostly crap taste in boys; I'm kinda pretty, I guess, but that never mattered really, because I've been in love since I was about eight with Jamie Pierson.

Oh, Jamie's pretty, too, in that boy kind of way: glossy black hair, really blue eyes, perfect skin. When he first smiled at me, I fell head over heels in love. It took me about two years to convince him to even hold hands with me, but by twelve we were kissing, and by fourteen we were officially In Love, with all the doves and bells ringing and sparkles from heaven. Cue the music, bring up the credits, the story's over and we all live happily ever after.

Or at least, I thought that was the story. I mean, not that my friends didn't try to tell me. Marina, she was my best friend until I was fifteen, but we had a blowup slap fight about Jamie and how he was treating me. I thought she just didn't understand him. I thought she was a liar when she said he was a douchebag. By then, Marina was my last friend; everybody else had already shrugged, moved on, figured me for a lost cause.

Smithfield isn't exactly a metropolis; it's stuck in the middle of nowhere, and any kind of diversion is welcome. Still, the arrival of a creaky, ancient carnival was something new. I'd thought Smithfield had long been scratched off all the traveling-show lists, but this one looked to be just barely surviving anyway. Even the flyers for it posted around town looked old, not just in design, but even the paper they were printed on.

Still, some of us didn't care about quality; when word went around school that day that a carnival was setting up outside of town, the quality of the entertainment was the last thing on our minds. We just wanted a good time: some cotton candy, some rides, some screams, some cheesy fun.

At least, I did. And I texted Jamie instantly from my last class of the day. CRNVL 2NITE?

And Jamie texted back thirty seconds later: Y.

So. It was a date.

I called my mom to tell her that I wouldn't be home until late because I was going to the movies with Marina. (She never checked; she just assumed that once a friend, always a friend, and I was careful to never use Marina for anything that would bring on awkward parental phone calls.) Mom didn't worry. You didn't much in Smithfield. Little town, comfortable, boring, nothing ever going on here, right? Why do you care if your sixteen-year-old goes to the movies with a friend?

You don't.

But I'm here to tell you . . . maybe you should.

School let out at 3:30, but I had band practice after, so it wasn't until 5:00 when I was at the curb, and the late fall afternoon was getting crisply cool by the time Jamie rolled up in his car. It was black, and shiny, but it wasn't new—he just loved it more than anything else in his life, except (I supposed) me. I put my clarinet in the backseat, on the floorboard, because he'd yelled at me before when I'd put it on the seat (*"You'll scuff up the leather, what's wrong with you?"*) and ducked into the passenger side.

"Hey," I said, and he bent over for a quick, almost nonexistent kiss.

"Hey," he said. "Let's go, the guys are already there."

I didn't know it then, but Jamie was already bored stupid with me, his dumb grade-school crush, and I was too in love to notice. He hardly even looked at me; his attention was on the road as he roared out of the parking lot and onto the street before I'd even had a chance to buckle my seat belt. I did it quick, because I knew the local cops would be on the lookout for anything Jamie did wrong; they didn't like him. I didn't understand why—he was such a good guy!

Stupid, I know, right?

Smithfield was a six-stoplight town in any direction from the school, which was more or less in the center. At each stoplight, instead of talking to me or even glancing at me, Jamie pulled out his cell phone and would watch . . . something. I couldn't see what it was because he had some kind of privacy screen filter over the screen, so you had to be looking straight on to see what was displayed. He was smiling, though, and it wasn't a nice smile. It was tight, hard, and a little disturbing.

I tried, though. "Hey, how was your biology class? Did you pass the test?"

"You could say that," he said, and the smirk got deeper. "Even though Mr. Harrison doesn't think so. Dumbass."

"So . . . you didn't pass?"

"I got a D. Good enough."

A grade of D wasn't passing, and he knew it, but he just shrugged as if it didn't matter. And he kept on smiling.

Dropping the phone on the seat between us (it was one of those long bench seats, the way old cars sometimes have), he gunned it when the light shifted to green. I had taken my phone out too. We had matching ones—isn't that sweet?—except mine had a little crystal dangle on it. Suddenly he hit the brakes hard and I yelped, dropped my phone, and grabbed for the dashboard as the seat belt slammed hard against my chest. His phone slid off the seat and fell, too, bouncing on the floorboard.

"Shit!" Jamie spat, and tried to fish around for it beneath the wheel. "Get it, Kiley!"

He'd braked for some old grandma who was going twenty in a thirty that he'd been blasting through at fifty, so now he whipped the wheel hard over and roared past the other car. He didn't flip her off, but I could see he thought about it.

I unlocked my seat belt and crawled under the dash. Two phones. I grabbed them both and backed out, settled back in the seat, and buckled up.

Oh, no.

"Um . . ." I showed Jamie his phone. A giant crack ran across it, like lightning. He cussed—a lot—and slammed his hand into the dashboard; his face got very red, and then, suddenly, he got real quiet. He took the phone and put it in his jacket pocket.

"I'll sync it up when I get home," he said. "No problem."

"Okay." My voice sounded small. He scared me when he was angry, but this was almost as bad. All of a sudden switching from fury to utter calm? Weird, and wrong. I fumbled for something to make it sound better.

"You know, they can get stuff off your phone at the store, import your contacts and transfer—"

"I just need my photos and vids," he said. "All the rest of it is bullshit anyway. Contacts?" Jamie laughed, and it sounded bitter. "Jesus, Kiley. How many people do we know, anyway? How hard is it to keep track in this ass crack of a town?"

Well, he was kind of right about that. I only had maybe five people in my contacts these days, since I'd deleted Marina. I'd thought he had lots, though. Jamie was popular, right? He seemed to be, anyway, but I guessed over the last year maybe not as much.

Like me.

I shut up, because Jamie clearly wasn't in any mood to hear me try to make things better. I hastily shoved my own phone into my pocket and sat quietly for the next few blocks and stoplights.

Finally, we were out of town, into empty flatlands. The carnival was in the empty parking lot of a long-shut-down superstore, and in the falling night you could see the glow of the flashing lights a long ways off. Traffic wasn't much to speak of in Smithfield, but there were more cars on the road than I'd expected, and they were all heading to the same place we were.

Jamie turned the car into the parking lot and found a spot near the back, in the dark. He always parked out of the way. No door dings that way. I unbuckled and scrambled out of the car, but by the time I'd emerged he was already six steps ahead of me, walking toward the registration booth.

The flashing multicolored lights (some were burned out) distracted from the overall crappy look of the booth; the red-and-yellow canvas was dirty, the countertop was cracked and ancient, the plastic shield was scratched, and the middle-aged woman sitting on the other side really needed to lay off the red hair dye. That, and the way-too-heavy makeup, made her look desperate.

So did the way she eyed my boyfriend—like she knew him, or at least had expected him. She got this strange little smile . . . and then she turned her head and looked at me, and her eyes—I could have sworn they changed color. Just for a second.

I stepped closer to him and took his hand, but he shook me off impatiently and reached for his wallet. He asked how much and the woman pointed at the sign pasted on the plastic as if she was way too exhausted to answer that stupid question one more time. Jamie peeled off bills and passed them over and got a couple of strings of generic tear-off tickets in return. He handed me some, turned, and walked into the carnival. I could tell he was still pissed off about the phone, but honestly, it hadn't been my fault, it *hadn't*.

It only took about half an hour before we ran out of tickets, because the prices on the skeevy games were ridiculous, and I'd wanted to ride the Ferris wheel so Jamie would have a chance to kiss me (he didn't). After that, Jamie went off to buy more tickets. He was gone a long time, long enough that I bought myself a hot chocolate and sat down at one of the splintered wooden tables set up next to the concession stand.

"Hey," said a tentative voice.

I looked up. There was a boy standing there. I knew him, I guess; he looked familiar, anyway, but there wasn't really much to recognize about him. A round, bland sort of face, nothing to make you pay much attention.

"Hey," I replied, and got out my phone, just in case I was going to need to look busy.

"Um, I'm Matt. I'm in your English class," he said. "You're Kiley, right? Just wanted to say hi."

"Hi." I felt strange about this, and worried—not about the boy, about Jamie coming back and finding him here. "Sorry, um, I have to get this."

I pretended to get a call and held the phone up to my ear. The kid probably knew it was a lie, and rude, but he just nodded, put his hands in his pockets, and walked off, head down.

I felt a little bad about it, but truthfully, he shouldn't be talking to me. Jamie didn't like it when boys came around, even if they were harmless.

Since I had the phone out anyway, I figured I'd better check my messages. I turned it on and felt a weird, almost world-shifting shock.

This wasn't my phone.

I didn't realize it at first . . . I expected to see my apps and background, but instead I got sports scores and game apps and a pinup-girl background.

This was *Jamie's* phone.

I understood then: somehow the dangle that should have been there had snapped off my phone when it fell in the car. *My* phone had been the one that had broken, and I'd picked up Jamie's by accident.

Well, he would be happy, I thought, that his phone was okay after all. Mine was no big loss.

I waited for him to come back, but he didn't. I knew his swipe code. He hadn't shared it with me, but I'd seen him put it in often enough on the keypad.

As I entered the numbers slowly, I still wasn't sure I wanted to do this.

His phone accepted the passcode. I waited some more.

Eventually, though I knew it was wrong, I couldn't resist looking through his call lists—you know, to see who else might have been calling and texting him.

Boring. His besties, mostly. Nothing drama-worthy.

He did have a lot of pictures and video on there, which was what he'd been so worried about losing. I thought at first the pictures were of me, and some were—but not all of them.

Some were of girls I didn't know.

I hesitated over the first video, my heart pounding now, the aftertaste of hot chocolate turning sour in my mouth.

I shouldn't, I thought. *He'll kill me.*

But I had to do it. I had to know if he was cheating on me.

The girl in the video looked like me, kind of—dirty-blond hair caught up in a messy knot at the back of her neck. The video showed her laughing and teasing whoever was holding the camera, and then the phone got put down, angled, and Jamie slipped onto the screen with her.

Kissing her.

I felt sick and dizzy, and almost shut off the phone.

Maybe I should have. Maybe if I had, none of this would have happened . . . but maybe that would have actually been worse, in the end.

I sat there with my cooling hot cocoa on the table in front of me, rooted to the spot, holding his phone with both hands as I watched him kiss this nameless blond *whore*, and I wanted to kill her for trying to take him away from me because I needed Jamie, I *needed* him. . . .

And then Jamie put his hands around her neck and started to squeeze.

I honestly thought it was a joke, or something kinky, I really did. I thought: maybe it was some amateur movie or something, and it was all just acting, and at the end they'd laugh and it would all be okay.

But I couldn't believe that, not really. For one thing, the camera stayed on the girl's face, and she was scared. Really scared. Her skin turned redder, redder; her eyes got bigger and bloodshot; and she clawed at Jamie's hands and wrists, slapped at him weakly, and her eyes rolled up in her head so they were all white, and he kept on choking her—tighter, tighter, and her mouth was open and her tongue was swollen and purple. . . .

And then, right when I knew she was dead, he let her fall back. And he laughed. And started stripping off her clothes.

Like undressing a doll. Like posing one too.

And then he unzipped his jeans and knelt down.

And I couldn't help it. I watched all the way to the end, and when it finished, I felt empty. It was like I'd died, too, like I'd had all the life squeezed out of me. All I felt was dizzy, and all I heard was a vast, ringing silence.

I couldn't think what I was going to do. I couldn't think at all.

I put his phone away with shaking hands. The bright, cheap carnival lights around me whirled and blinked, and the dirty, chipped rides spun, and people screamed and screamed, and I wanted to run but I didn't know how, and I didn't know where to go.

I found myself staring at a banner that flapped in the cold night breeze overhead. On it was a girl as white as ice, apparently frozen, except that her eyes were open and bright silver. It said, SEE THE COLD GIRL! DEAD AND YET SHE LIVES!

I stared hard at it, until my eyes started to water, because it was almost like it was alive, that face. Almost like it *was* looking at me out of that banner.

I was still focused on it when Jamie crept up behind me, grabbed me around the waist, and swung me—and I screamed and he laughed, and laughed, and it sounded just like the laughter in the cell phone, cruel and lazy and awful.

I pushed Jamie away and screamed again. Loud. It didn't matter; my cry was lost in all the noise from the roller coaster rocketing by, trailing the eerie yells of those trapped on it.

He hadn't come alone. There were a bunch of boys with him.

I pushed him back again when he tried to take hold of me, and he stumbled back, tripped over his buddy Alan's feet, and fell down.

"What the hell, Kiley?" he said, and shook off the hands of some of the rest of his crew who were trying to help him up. There were six or seven of them, all kind of the same, the way cliques tend to be; his gang were all tall, good-looking guys. Not jocks, because none of them really cared enough about working at anything to be jocks; not nerds, because they weren't really smart. Just the good-looking upper average of the high school set. They did what Jamie said.

Always.

"'Sup with your bitch, man?" Alan asked. "Where'd the attitude come from?"

Jamie had a kind of cold, black gravity to him when he was angry, and I could feel it now, tilting the world in his direction. His posse drew tighter around him as he stood.

"What the hell?" he repeated, and came right up on me, shoving me against the hard wooden block of the table. It hurt, and a splinter dug into my butt, but I didn't move. I didn't fight back. I never did. I froze, staring into that pretty, cold face, and tried to think what to say. The world had ended—*my* world—and words just seemed useless now. But I couldn't accuse him. I couldn't.

"You scared me," I whispered instead.

That made him smile, like it pleased him to hear it.

"Scared you," he said. "Wow. I didn't know you scared that easy, Kiles. Jeez, it's the middle of the carnival. Nothing's going to happen to you here."

No, it would happen somewhere private. Somewhere dark. Somewhere isolated. Like that girl. He'd left her somewhere, naked and dead, face swollen, eyes bugged out and staring in terror at the dark.

I glanced up as the banner flapped again, with a sound like snapping bones, and for a second I was confused. It should have had the Cold Girl on it, but this time it instead had a fortune-teller on it, with the words MADAME LAIDA KNOWS ALL.

"Hey!" Jamie snapped his fingers in front of my face. "What's wrong with you? If you've got good drugs, you're supposed to share."

His boys laughed. I said nothing, just stared at him. He looked so *normal*. Just like the old Jamie, the one that had existed before I'd seen what was on his cell phone . . . only it wasn't him, it wasn't the one I'd loved so much it hurt.

That Jamie had never really existed at all. I didn't know who this one was, and he terrified me.

"Awww, come on, don't look at me like that. You know I'd never hurt you, baby," he said, and kissed me. I wanted to gag. And scream. And cry. Something chilly had settled over me and soaked into my bones, turned them into fragile ice. I knew I'd never really feel warm again.

"Hey, hey, Kiley? You okay?"

"Okay," I said. I didn't mean it. It was an empty set of sounds that stood in for screaming. He stared at me, frowning, and I knew he didn't believe me. He turned and glanced around, and Alan locked eyes with him.

I knew that I'd shown him too much, and my heart started running faster, faster, faster.

"Hey," Jamie said, in a very different kind of tone. "Let me use your phone a second, okay?"

"My—my phone?" I stared at him stupidly. The lump of it in my pocket seemed hot, as if it might sear right through my skin. "Um—I left it in your car."

"You did?" He smiled, wide and easy, but when he looked back at me, his eyes were flat and dark. "Well, that was stupid. What if it gets stolen?"

"Yeah," I agreed. "Stupid. Sorry. I—I can go get it—"

"No." He nodded at Alan, reached in his pocket, and fished out the keys, which he tossed to his best friend. "Alan'll get it. How about you and me go on a ride while he's gone?"

"A ride?" My brain felt numbed, and with his posse standing around him, I felt like a rabbit cornered by a pack of wild dogs. No way out.

"Yeah, Kiley, a *ride*. What, you don't speak Carnival?" He brandished a long tail of tickets in one hand and grabbed me by the arm with the other. "Just you and me, in the dark. Won't that be fun? Maybe you'll have time to give me a little something before it's over."

"Let go of her," a voice said from behind me. An old man's voice this time.

Jamie looked past me and did an exaggerated double take so fake, nobody could mistake it for anything else.

"Hey, look, guys, it's Coach Lame-ass. Oh, shit, sorry, I meant *Coach Lamar*. Sorry, sir."

I glanced back and saw the boys' baseball coach standing there, holding a hot dog dripping with relish in one hand and a soda in the other. Beside him was a woman about his age, who I guessed was Mrs. Lame-ass. The coach was fireplug-wide and short and totally ugly, with his balding head and pug nose and muddy-brown eyes, and I'd called him "Coach Lame-ass," too, lots of times, but just now I was so grateful to him that I wanted to sob.

He was staring straight at Jamie, and it came to me with a shock that the tight expression on his face was genuine disgust. He didn't like my boyfriend. Not at all. Not ever.

"I said, let her go," the coach said. His wife murmured something to him, looking worried, but he shook her off and put his hot dog and Coke down on the table. I noticed, finally, that he had kids with him, too—a girl about ten, and a boy about twelve. They looked worried too. "Now, Pierson."

"No offense, Coach, but this ain't school," Jamie said. He sounded pleasant enough, but his grip tightened around my arm, and it hurt enough to leave bruises. "Tell him you're fine, Kiley."

I'm not, I thought. *God, please, just let me go. . . .*

But I knew he would never do that. Jamie knew, somehow, that I had seen what was on his phone. I couldn't hide it. I couldn't disguise the terror and horror.

If he let me go, it would only be to let me run into the dark, where there'd be no one to hear, and no one to see except the camera lens when he caught up to me.

So I licked my lips and I said, "I'm fine, sir." If I could stay here, in the lights, I had a chance of finding someone who could help me. Not Coach Lame-ass; they'd beat him to a pulp, and his wife and kids too. "Don't worry about me."

"Yeah, what she said," Jamie said. "C'mon, Kiley, let's go get on a ride while Alan comes back with your phone."

The other boys looked at me like I was a piece of dead meat as Jamie tugged me away, heading for the haunted-house ride. It was a cheap tin thing, creaking as the cars moved through it; a giant, peeling illustration of the grim reaper loomed down over the lines queuing up for it. I looked over my shoulder as we left Coach Lamar and his family behind. Jamie's posse hadn't drifted off, like I'd hoped; they had taken over one side of the long table.

Coach was watching us go, still frowning, and his wife was whispering to him. He finally, reluctantly, sat down with his kids.

There were other people from school around the carnival, but nobody paid attention to me, only to Jamie, who got smiles and nods. I wasn't popular, I wasn't unpopular. I was wallpaper—which was a good thing, since it normally meant people left me alone, but a bad thing, because I was invisible, and right now I desperately needed people to *see*. I felt hollowed out inside, and not only did no one notice, most likely no one would have cared even if they had.

I saw Vanessa Seers, with her glossy perfect hair and makeup and shoes, and her coterie of giggling BFFs. Vanessa made eyes at Jamie and he made them back, watching her as she headed off for some other part of the carnival. The Geek Squad came past us in a tight knot, jabbering to each other about books and DVDs and some lame-ass anime festival they were going to. I even saw Ruth Sheldon and Lyle Garrett, the local brains, who held down the top end of the bell curve. They were holding hands. Nerd love.

I saw Matt, who'd talked to me before, but he was deep in conversation with some other girl I couldn't remember, and he never glanced over to see how much trouble I was in.

My brain felt like it was melting, and I was so cold I shivered constantly. I needed to *do something*, and I knew that; but part of me, the survival part, just wouldn't let me. It was convinced that if I stayed quiet, passive, this would all go away. It was stupid, but I couldn't seem to summon up anything but a bone-deep conviction that somehow, if I didn't fight him, it would all be okay.

You need to scream and fight him, some very tiny part of me, the brave part, said. *People are here. They can help you. They can call the police!*

But my brain shied away from the whole idea of the police— God, no, I couldn't even think about it. I didn't know who the girl was, and maybe—maybe—somebody had just sent him the video, right? Maybe it wasn't Jamie on there at all and I'd gotten it all wrong. Maybe it was some other guy. Maybe it was faked. What would happen if it really was some kind of movie, and I was making a big deal out of nothing?

Then why did he keep it? Why would he want to see that again, and show it to his friends?

I couldn't think about it; it made me want to throw up. I licked my lips and said, "I need to go to the bathroom, Jamie."

"Can't," he said. "We'll lose our place in line."

That was crap, and we both knew it; the lines were maybe ten people at most, and moved fast. I tried to pull free, but he yanked me closer still.

"Listen," he said softly, in a deadly cool voice. "Alan's coming back with your phone. Don't go running off, okay?"

I stared hard at the blinking, flashing, gyrating carnival lights until everything just melted into a meaningless sea of sparkles, trying not to think about *anything*, wishing I was dead, wishing I'd never picked up Jamie's phone at all.

But I had, and that would never, ever change.

My boyfriend's a monster. Did that make me a monster too? I knew girls who covered up for their guys, lied for them to the cops, all that kind of stuff; but it was for dumb stunts or minor crimes, not . . . not this. If I told somebody, would it make me a snitch? Would everybody hate me? His friends would, all his handsome tall buds. Their girlfriends would hate me on principle for ratting him out. Half the rest of the girls in school thought Jamie was totally cute, and they'd loathe me for telling lies about him, even if the proof came out. They'd never believe it anyway.

If I could just get away somehow, I could go home. Talk to Mom. No—I could just imagine how that would work. She'd go to Jamie's mom, and then Jamie would find out, and . . . My imagination just stopped there, because I couldn't honestly think what would happen next. And maybe I just didn't want to think about it.

I stared at the man running the dark ride as we drew closer and closer. Jamie's grip on my arm never loosened, and I knew by now it would be flowering black bruises under the skin.

And I knew, with a sick feeling of anger, that Jamie probably liked it that he was hurting me. So I studied the carnie running the ride. He was a big guy, muscular, shaved head, tattoos running up his neck and down his flexing arms. He didn't smile; customer service was not in his job description. He looked bored, and distant, and he just went through the mechanical process of loading people in the seats, strapping them down, and operating the ride controls. The machinery looked ancient, and in a weird way, so did he. Maybe it was how he moved, because his face seemed young.

It was his eyes that aged him, I decided. Old, angry eyes. And when they met mine, they flashed red. Blood red.

A new chill washed over me, like being hit by an unexpected bucket of water. It was as if something had slapped me with an ice-cold hand and said, *Wake up.*

And then we were at the front of the line.

Jamie climbed into the seat that was open, and to do it, he let go of me . . . and I stepped back when he reached again for me.

He froze. "Kiles, come on. Don't be this way." They were coaxing words, but I knew, from the tight, angry set of his lips, that what waited for me in the dark was—at the very least—a fist, and maybe worse. "Baby, come on."

I felt the sudden heat of the ride operator at my back, and his hand fell on my shoulder. It was heavy, and real, and it should have scared the shit out of me, but instead I breathed in a sudden spasm of relief.

"Get in or leave," he said. "You're holding up the line."

"I'm leaving," I said.

"Good choice."

The words were only a faint whisper, and almost too soft to hear, but I knew he'd meant them for me. Jamie grabbed for me, but the carnie got between us and slammed down the locking bar.

"Your boyfriend's going to be taking a little ride. Madame Laida wants to see you."

I backed up another couple of steps. Jamie shouted my name and tried to yank himself out from under the bar, but the carnie was quick to hit the button on the panel next to him.

Jamie's cart lurched off into the darkness of the ride, and me . . .

I turned and ran.

Jamie's posse was nearby, and some of them got up, not sure

whether they ought to stop me. But just then I saw Alan standing in the shadows of the concession stand, his own phone in his hand. He was watching me.

And I heard the phone in my pocket start to ring, and its glow was clearly visible through the pocket of my pants.

Alan held up something that glittered in the light—the broken dangle from my phone, which he must have found in the car. Then he pointed at me with a finger gun, and pulled the trigger.

I gasped, turned, and ran blindly in the opposite direction, deeper into the midway. People swirled around me talking, laughing, having actual futures and lives. But they felt like ghosts to me. I looked around wildly for a familiar face, or for a cop, or *anyone* who could help.

Another ride operator—the teacup ride—looked up as I passed, and I thought I saw his eyes flash red too. One of the midway booth trolls shilling games watched me with eyes that seemed to shift colors from blue to crimson. I was hallucinating now, I thought, because it seemed as if they were *all* looking at me, as if I was drawing their attention the way a gazelle draws lions.

I ran and ran, shoving blindly through the crowd, and finally I found myself standing in front of a billowing, dirty tent the color of cheap mustard, with a sign in front that said MADAME LAIDA KNOWS ALL. Some kind of fortune-teller—the tattered banner showed the standard gypsy woman in a turban, staring mysteriously over a glowing crystal ball.

I realized, with a horrified jolt, that I'd managed to run out of the crowd, and I knew that Jamie's friends, especially Alan, would be right behind me.

I didn't have a choice. I ran into Madame Laida's tent.

Entering felt as if I had run through some kind of barrier—not a real one, but like an electrical field that tingled cold on my skin. And then I was inside a dim, small space that smelled of mold and incense. There was a velvet-draped table, two chairs, and a crystal ball sitting in the center of the cloth—and no one else in the room.

I spun, short of breath now, sure that Alan and his buds were seconds behind me, but I heard nothing—no shouting, no footsteps. Even the noise and music of the carnival was muted, as if it had moved a long ways off.

"Sit," a voice said, and when I spun around again, I saw an old woman sitting on the other side of the table. She hadn't been there before, and I hadn't heard her come in, but I supposed she must have approached from the rear of the tent when I was concentrating on the other side. She looked like the stereotypical fortune-teller—cheap, shiny robes, scarves, layers of jewelry that chimed together when she shifted positions. Her turban had a fake red stone on it, and a peacock feather that had seen better days. She looked pinched and tired.

When she smiled, I saw her crooked teeth were yellow from coffee or smoking or both. "Sit down, child."

I didn't. I went to the flap of the tent and tried to see outside without moving the canvas.

"If you're worried about his friends, they won't find you here," Madame Laida said, which drew me back around to stare at her. Her thin gray eyebrows raised. "Sit down, Kiley."

I went very still inside. "How do you know my name?"

"Madame Laida knows all," she said. "It says so right on my sign. Don't be afraid. They won't come in here."

I sank down in the chair across from her, blinking now. The room really did stink of mold, and the incense tasted a little rancid in my mouth.

"How do you know me? Really?"

"We have our ways, Kiley Reynolds. Hell, maybe I just used Facebook. If you're worried about Jamie finding his way here, he won't. He and his friends are tearing up the midway looking for you. We're letting him do that to keep him occupied." She seemed to find it cute somehow. "I wanted to speak to you, before *she* does."

It wasn't possible she knew my name, or Jamie's. I felt dizzy and a little sick from the smell in there, and the heat, and the bitter black intensity of her eyes on me. She pulled out a cigarette from a pack beneath her robes, lit up with a cheap lighter, and took a long pull of smoke, which she then breathed out over the crystal ball.

It was as if the cigarette smoke had gotten trapped inside the glass, because suddenly the crystal clouded up, swirling, and shapes began to form.

I froze, staring. It happened in shades of gray, but I watched the girl struggling in Jamie's clenched hands, watched her choke and die, watched him rape her all over again. When it was over, and the smoke went back to random swirls, I realized that I was hunched over, both arms protecting my stomach as if she'd punched me hard.

"How . . . how did you do that?" My voice sounded shaky and thin.

Madame Laida hadn't watched the show in her crystal ball; she'd kept staring at me, though I couldn't really say how I knew that, since my attention had been riveted on what she'd shown me. Now she took another drag on her cigarette, blew it up toward the tent's roof, and said, "So, Kiley, let's get the bad news out of the way: you're going to die. I can't usually see in this much detail, but she's close by tonight, and she's giving it to me in full color and sound. That blows, by the way."

"I—I'm going to—" I couldn't handle that, not at all, so I lunged for the other thing. "What do you mean, 'she'? Who are you talking about?"

"She," Madame Laida said, and shrugged. "The Cold Girl. She

likes carnivals, turns out. The boss thought he was buying some freak attraction, but she was nothing like that. She latched onto us back in the Dust Bowl days, and she's been with us ever since. Doesn't show herself much anymore, though. I think she's taking a special interest in you."

"What . . . what do you mean, I'm . . . going to—"

Laida's eyebrow cocked upward. "Do you really need the details? Honey, really, it's lots better if you don't know. You can't avoid it, so there's no point in getting all upset about it. I'm sorry to be so blunt, but we don't have a lot of time to waste here; your prince of a boyfriend isn't going to let you just vanish. Here. Give me your hand. I might be able to do something to help."

Instead of doing as she said, I clutched my hand closer to my chest and stood up so fast I knocked the chair over onto the worn old carpets. Madame Laida looked unsurprised. I wasn't sure anything ever surprised her. She shrugged and took a long pull on her cigarette that transformed half of it into embers and ash, and behind the smoke I saw her eyes flash red.

"Well," she said, "how you go about it is your business. I was just going to give you a little comfort, but if you don't want it, I guess we're done here. Sorry, kid. Life sucks sometimes, and my job isn't to change that."

"But—" I couldn't get my head straight, couldn't get my breath now. "What am I supposed to do?"

"Run," she said, and tapped the ash off her smoke into a silver tray I was sure hadn't been on the table before. "Go on, girl. Run for your life. Cold Girl's waiting out there somewhere for you. She'll find you."

"Help me!"

"Can't." This time she smoked her cigarette all the way down to the butt and stubbed it out in the tray. She blew the smoke at the crystal ball again, and inside, gray mist swirled in nauseating patterns. "And wouldn't if I could, hon. People like me don't get involved if we want to keep on breathing; this is the business of immortals. It's the way it works. Time for you to go now."

She made a little fluttering motion with her hand, and I felt myself getting physically shoved, as if a strong wind were pushing me . . . but there was no wind. My hair didn't even flutter.

I fought it, but I couldn't stop myself from being pushed to the opening of the tent, and when I grabbed for the fabric to stop my slide, it seemed slippery under my fingers.

And then I was outside, and there was no opening at all.

"Hey!" I shouted, and grabbed at the fabric, trying to find the way back inside. "Hey, wait, you can't— Madame Laida! Help me!"

"Hey, Kiles," said a voice from behind me that stopped me cold. Frozen. "Help you with what?"

"Nothing," I whispered. Tears suddenly bloomed in my eyes, and I shook all over. "I'm sorry."

"Sorry? Guess you are. Guess you shouldn't have gotten all up in my business, bitch. Did you like what you saw?"

All of a sudden Jamie's arm was around my throat, pulling me off balance, choking me. I gagged for breath and went up on my tiptoes as he pulled backward. He still had friends with him—only three of them, including Alan. I didn't know where the others had gone. Maybe he didn't trust them enough. I gagged and gasped and hoped that one of his buddies would do something, anything . . . but they just stood there, not looking at me at all.

Jamie's breath puffed hot against my ear as he said, "I will break your neck if you try to run," and I felt all the resistance go out of me. He meant it.

"We're going to walk now," he continued. "We're going to just go quietly to my car, right, babe?"

Jamie pressed something sharp into my back, low and to my side. "This is a knife. And it's right over your kidney. You know what happens if I cut your renal artery, Kiley? You really want to learn how fast you can bleed out?"

I was terrified, and I kept walking. Maybe it wasn't actually a knife, but this was Jamie, and I didn't know him anymore, I really didn't. The others fell in behind us, and we moved through the outer darkness around the tents. The noise and glitter and cheap tinsel shine of the carnival fell behind us. There weren't any lights out in the parking lot.

Or any people.

"Kiley?"

I stopped. The blade dug in a little, and I stopped breathing.

"I want my phone back, bitch."

I don't know where it came from—maybe from the matter-of-fact way Madame Laida had told me I was going to die. Maybe it just didn't matter anymore.

Or maybe I'd finally grown a spine.

"You're a monster," I said. "You want your phone? You want to show everybody what you did? Brag about it? Fuck you, Jamie! Go crawl around and look for it!"

I took his phone out of my pocket and threw it as far as I could into the dark. Far enough, I hoped. At least it would keep them occupied for a while. If I was really, really lucky, maybe it would be lost in the dark, and the cops would find it later. Game over, Jamie.

Alan took his own phone out and tried to call Jamie's, but it really was busted this time; nothing sparked out there in the shadows.

"Go!" Jamie barked at his friends, and Alan and the two others loped off to search. "Don't come back without it!"

He hit me in the head when I started to laugh, so hard that the world wobbled and went black and red, and then he hit me again and it went completely, utterly dark.

* * *

I WOKE UP in a ditch, and I knew I was dying. It was dark, and cold, and I felt the sticky warm trickle of blood down my cheek.

I couldn't move. I was facedown in the sand, covered with trash and weeds, and whatever he'd done to me, I couldn't feel anything much from the waist down; my legs were useless lumps. I was too weak to move my arms much, and when I tried, the pain was white-hot, boiling like lava inside me. I screamed, weakly, but the night and the wind swallowed it.

So alone, but I could hear the distant tinny chaos of the carnival music. He hadn't bothered to take me far before he'd done it.

I guessed he thought that my murder would be blamed on the carnival workers. And he was probably right about that, though Coach Lamar would tell people he'd seen me with Jamie. Still, nobody would believe that Jamie would do a thing like that. No, it'd be the strangers in town, and I'd be just another random, sad victim.

I drifted, and eventually the music went quiet. It turned darker, I suppose because the carnival shut off the lights. I passed out at some point.

WHEN I WOKE, it was brighter. The sun beat down on me. I could hear the rattle and growl of cars and trucks passing on the road. I couldn't have been too far from people, from *help*, but everything seemed as far away as the moon.

When I turned my head, I could see the sloping sand walls of the ditch. They stretched up to infinity. I couldn't do it. I couldn't pull myself out. When I tried, the sand slipped through my fingers and the pain, oh, God, the pain was like being drowned in acid.

I slept, or went unconscious, numerous times. The cut from

my head stopped bleeding but I was still losing blood somewhere else.

I felt so tired.

THE COLD GIRL came, on the second night. There was a sound she brought with her, a hissing rattle like sleet against windows. She was pretty but unreal, like a mannequin, and her skin was as white and cool as snow in moonlight when she stood in the ditch and looked down at me with a strange, beautiful, terrible smile.

Then she lowered herself gracefully to her knees. I'd never seen anything as beautiful as she was, or as awful; and when she leaned over to look into my wide, staring eyes, I felt a surge of cold go through me, as if what blood I had left in my body had frozen into hard chunks.

Her eyes were black. Not like the night sky that wheeled overhead; that was really a dark blue. No, this was *black*, true black, an absolute absence of light and color. A well into nothing at all.

And then, slowly, they swirled into a brilliant fiery red.

"I smelled your fear miles away," she whispered. Her pale white hair brushed my face like snowflakes, and her voice sounded like it was echoes of screams. "Many towns ago. You were marked already for this. That means you're mine."

I couldn't talk. My mouth was as dry as sand. The best I could do was croak something out, and it didn't actually sound like "What are you?" but she smiled anyway and brushed my lank, blood-stiff hair back from my face. I'd thought her smile was cold, but her fingers—it was like being brushed with liquid nitrogen. I could feel my skin freeze and crystallize under that loving touch.

"Your people have lots of names for me," she told me in a thousand voices, all screaming, screaming. "But I guess the one you really understand would be *vampire*. I can save you, if you want saving. Do you?"

You'd think I'd say *yes*. Something in me struggled and squealed still, like an animal in a trap, but that part was already dead, really. It just didn't understand that it was gone.

"No," I whispered. I could make that understood, at least. "I don't want to hurt anymore."

"Such a bright child." She kept stroking my face, and the cold pain, that felt good now—it felt hard and cutting and *right*. "Shhh. This is the second night of your dying, and there's no one to watch over you while you slip away. I could just take you if I wanted. I don't always ask, you know."

The cold, oh, God, it was in me now, over me, weighing me down and tying me into the earth with bonds of ice and stone, and I felt everything, everything go. No more blood. No more pain except the cold whisper of her touch, the bright shine of stars, the rattle of sleet.

"Let me show you," she said, "what your life with me could be. Now, rise up."

I couldn't, but somehow I did. I stood to face her. I was moonlight and chill white flesh, and I knew the crimson was in my eyes, just like it was in hers. I felt so . . . so different. So *other*. I had the shape of Kiley Reynolds, and the knowledge, but all that humanity . . . that was gone, tied to the sad little beaten piece of flesh lying in the ditch at my feet.

"You have until the sun rises to drink," she told me. I heard the dry clattering sound of sleet again, felt it on my skin. I heard screams and music rising inside me, and something else. Something powerful. "Right now, you walk as a shade, a shadow. If you drink, you will rise in flesh and join me. But only if you drink. Otherwise, when the sun rises, you die. Drink, and be like me."

I wasn't like her. Nobody was like the Cold Girl—I understood that immediately and instinctively. She was the spirit, and I was an echo . . . but an echo she had shouted back at the world, defiant and full of fury.

But I did know what she wanted. What she expected. It rose up inside of me like that smoky gray replay of Jamie's brutality inside Madame Laida's crystal ball.

I looked down into the ditch. It wasn't deep after all, only a couple of feet, really. My body lay there, half covered in blown dirt and trash. A snake had slithered up on my legs and fallen asleep, though I couldn't have been very warm for him. My eyes were open, dark and blind, but I was still breathing, just a little.

Still dying, drop by slow, agonizing drop.

But human pain didn't hurt anymore.

The whisper of ice faded, and when I looked up I saw empty flatland, stars, and realized that the Cold Girl was gone.

The moon was up, full and white, and it showed me the road I needed to follow. The carnival was in full swing, music wheezing, lights flashing. People moved like ghosts inside of it, but I wasn't going there. Not yet.

It wasn't far, only a steady, relentless glide back to the borders of our small town. I passed silent houses, blind black windows reflecting like empty mirrors. I passed winter-stripped trees, and as I did, their branches whipped and rattled and icicles formed on their tips.

I was passing the park next to the high school when I realized that I wasn't the only wanderer in the night. There was someone sitting on the child-sized swing, slowly rocking it in small, depressed arcs. I couldn't see clearly, but it looked like a boy.

I didn't mean to turn his direction, but there was a sense of loss around him, something that shivered dark in the air around him. The closer I got, the thicker it became, like a living cloak of darkness . . . and it smelled sweet and delicious.

He was dressed in a black hoodie, and I couldn't see his face. His jeans were ripped; his kicks were filthy and battered. He looked up at me and took in a deep, startled breath, but he didn't say anything. He stopped the motion of the swing and sat perfectly still, hands tight around the chains. I didn't say anything. He hesitated, then let go with his right hand and pulled his hood back.

"Kiley?" he said. "Kiley Reynolds?"

I didn't answer. I wasn't Kiley anymore. I was something else . . . but the name reminded me of who that crushed, bleeding thing was lying in the ditch. Still dying.

"It's Matt," he said. "Matt Saretti. From your English class. I saw you at the carnival."

One of the wallpaper people, just like me, Matt ate, he slept, he existed, and no one cared. I'd never really looked at him before. He seemed . . . nice.

"People are looking for you," he said. "Your mom—your mom's going batshit. They've got flyers up all over town. Where have you been?"

Somewhere on the other side of this park, Jamie was sleeping. I could feel him out there, taste the strange, bitter discord of his nightmares.

I had time.

I sat down in the swing beside Matt and pushed just a little to set it rocking back and forth, a slow pendulum movement that scraped my bare white feet over the dirt. To make myself real enough to affect wood and metal was a little difficult, but with concentration I managed to do it. The plain white dress I was wearing fluttered in the breeze of movement.

All around the park, dogs howled, and nightmares bit, and the innocent shivered and slept on, troubled.

"I've been busy dying," I told Matt. It was hard to talk. Hard to find the words when everything inside me was frozen solid, locked tight. All the pain and fear and despair. "I'm still dying."

He swallowed hard. "Are you . . . are you a ghost?"

I considered that, because I wasn't sure. "I think so," I said. "Because I'm mostly dead now."

"But not all the way."

I shrugged.

Matt let the silence go on for a few seconds, and then he said, "Do you want me to find you? Save you?"

I looked at him and smiled. He made a thin, terrified sound, and I think he would have run away if he could have, at that point. "I don't need help," I said, and every word was as bright and sharp and cutting as ice. "I'm what happens when there is no help."

He licked his lips and asked, "Are you going to kill me?"

For the first time I realized that the warm, sweet, tantalizing fragrance that had drawn me to him was his life. His blood, pulsing through his veins. I could see it running under his skin in faint red trails, sweet, so sweet, and I felt so hungry and empty.

But something stopped me. Something odd in his voice. "Why do you want to die?" I asked him.

He flinched as if I'd hit him. "Why do you?"

"I didn't ask to die," I said. "He killed me. There's a difference."

"But you said you're still alive. You could be saved. But since you don't want me to save you, you must want to die, right?"

I waited for an answer to come to me, but nothing did. There were no reasons, really. Finally I said, "I'm tired of hurting."

Matt stared at me without blinking. "Yeah," he said. "Me too."

And for a moment, just a moment, I felt the ice shift inside me. Felt something melt, just a little.

Just enough to make me resist the hot, pure whisper of his blood.

"I'm sorry, Matt. I'm not here for you. I can't be here for you."

"Why not?"

"Because you're not the guilty one."

He flinched, face tight and drawn. "I am," he said. "I'm guilty."

I shook my head very slowly. "I'd know if you had great sins," I said. "I can taste it, all the guilt out there. It tastes like blood. But yours ... yours isn't real. It's in your head."

"But—"

"You want me to prove it?"

I pointed at one of the houses out there in the dark. "That one's a thief," I said. "He breaks into houses and steals stuff to pawn, for drugs. He raped a woman four years ago when she caught him in her house." After a second, a light went on in the house, and a shadow passed across the window. Inside, the man was shivering, chilled to the bone, and he didn't know why.

I pointed at another one. "That one beats her children. One of them died, but her husband told the cops the boy fell down the stairs." I heard a thin cry of anguish from the woman inside as her nightmares twisted hard. Another light blazed on.

I pointed to a window of yet another house, and then another. "That one poisoned his wife twenty years ago. And that one, he and his friend beat up a homeless man just for fun."

All the nightmares, screaming, and it felt good to bring them out.

To punish.

I looked back at Matt and said, "You see? It's not in you."

He watched me stand up and finally said, "Where are you going?"

"I have something to finish," I said. "And tomorrow I'll be gone."

I started to walk away, across the grass. Where my feet touched it, the blades turned silver as they froze.

"Wait!" Matt called. I looked back at him. "Tell me where to find you! Let me help you!"

"I'm not worth saving," I said. "I should have done something when I had the chance."

"You're worth it to me," he said, and stood up. "Kiley. You are to me."

"That's sweet," I said. "But you can't save me now. Good-bye, Matt."

"Kiley!" I kept walking. "Kiley, I'm going to find you! At least tell me where to look!"

"Ask Madame Laida," I said. "She knows everything."

I didn't look back as I left him.

JAMIE'S HOUSE WAS a quiet ranch-style place with floral curtains and neat hedges, and as I came up the walk, I left footprints of slick white ice behind me. The hedges turned into a lacework of silver and glass and shattered at a touch from my thin white fingers. The window frosted over as I drew closer, and behind me the tree branches hissed and rattled and writhed.

I shattered his window with a whisper and climbed inside.

Everything turned blue and white, frosted with my rage, my despair, and on the bed Jamie's breath fogged up white like steam as he shivered and burrowed beneath his covers. It did no good. The blankets turned to hard sheets of ice and locked him down, and as his eyes opened in terror, I leaned over him.

"Hey, baby. You miss me?"

He screamed, but it came out as a thin scratch of sound, and I breathed it in and added it to the screams that were already inside me, echoing in my voice.

I leaned forward and brushed his lips with mine. His turned frost blue, and when he tried to speak they cracked and bled. I licked the sweet crimson away, and my tongue left trails of ice behind.

He tasted so good. So good. So warm.

I froze the skin over his wrist and shattered it with a tap so that his blood fountained out, warm and desperate to escape. It made dark icicles where it dripped from his arm, and I broke them free and ate them like frozen treats.

Jamie was stiff with terror in his bed, and I couldn't imagine how I'd ever thought he was anything but pathetic. Less of a monstrous threat, he looked like a scared little boy. His own evil ate away inside him like cancer, eroding every good thing that had ever been there.

He was seventeen years old, and he was lost. There was something broken in him that would never be fixed, ever.

"Kiley," he whispered. Blood dripped from his frozen lips. "Please, Kiley, please don't hurt me."

I licked red drops from his skin. Where my tongue touched it, the flesh turned brittle and dead. He tried to scream, but I put a hand lightly over his throat and froze that too. "I think I said that to you when you were killing me. I think that other girl tried to say it while you were choking her to death."

His frozen lips whispered something that looked like *Please*.

I pressed my palm against his chest. "You broke my heart," I said. "And now I'm breaking yours."

Then I plunged my needle-sharp teeth into his throat and drank out his hot, salty, bitter life, and as I drank it turned cool in my mouth, cold in his veins, and his heart froze and broke inside of him.

Jamie died, quietly, with frost on his lips. It was a moment of perfection, of cold and silent peace . . . but it was broken by something strange.

I felt a jolt of warmth.

I was melting.

I looked at my fingers. They were thin now, translucent as icicles. Fading. All of me was fading.

"No," I said. "No, not yet." I stumbled back to the window and out, falling into the grass. I put my back to a tree and felt heat coming from the sky, a blast of intense warmth that brought only pain. The tree limbs clattered together in the wind, and icicles rained and shattered on the blacktop like breaking chimes.

The sun was coming up.

No, I did it, I drank—

I ran, fast as the winter wind; I blurred past the trees, the grass, past the empty swing where Matt had been sitting. I ran through the empty streets and over the blacktop. Impossibly, the carnival's lights were still on, its music still blaring, and ahead, ahead was the ditch, and the horizon was pink now, pink and soft and ready to burst with morning . . .

The Cold Girl rose up out of the ditch and gave me her death-sweet smile. "Is it better now?" she asked. I could hear my own unvoiced scream in there now, distinct as a bell. "Is it?"

"You said—" I was struggling to breathe now, and I felt sick and faint with remembered pain. "You said if I drank I'd stay with you!"

She plucked a falling icicle out of the air. It became a white rose in her hand that shattered into a million pieces, too fragile to survive. Like me.

"You have to be colder."

"But I am!" I said. "I *am* cold, I *want* to be cold! Please!"

"Then why didn't you take the boy who offered himself to you? You had compassion. You felt for him."

The pain was back, aching and hot, real and horrible. I wanted to run away from it. I wanted to be winter, locked in ice. Safe.

The carnival went suddenly silent, and all the lights went out, and I could see Madame Laida standing next to the Cold Girl now, smoking another cigarette. She gave me a bitter smile.

"Come on, kid. You want to be one of us?" she asked me. "A cheap bed in a tent, a carnival that never stops moving, looking for just the right victims? Because that's what you are, honey. A victim. You're just looking to trade one monster for another, and you'll never get away from this one."

The Cold Girl gave her a look, and Madame Laida shrugged and walked away, back toward the silent carnival.

"Your choice," she called back to me. "But once you're hers, it's forever. She's giving you a choice. Make it."

I struggled to think. The pain was back, so intense it was like burning alive, and the sun was just bursting over the horizon, and I had no time, no time at all. . . .

"I just want to stop hurting," I wept. "Please, let me stop hurting."

"Ah," the Cold Girl sighed. "Then you cannot be mine. Because we may be cold, we may be immortal, but we never stop hurting. That is our curse."

She bent and touched her lips to mine, a kiss of ice-cold peace, and then she faded into a stinging mist of blown crystals.

In the dirt I opened my eyes and took my last conscious breath. The darkness came over me just as the sun turned the dirt pink around my head.

Turns out, the darkness was but a shadow falling over me, and then there was a shout, and sirens, and so much noise it made me tired.

WHEN I WOKE up in the hospital, I felt nothing but absolute surprise. How could I be alive?

It was Matt, the boy from English class. They told me that he'd searched all night, and at dawn he'd woken up the carnival and demanded to see Madame Laida. Whatever she told him, Matt headed for the road.

He'd found me at dawn in the ditch and he'd carried me all the way back to town wrapped in his black hoodie, protected against the chill. He wouldn't put me down at the hospital until they made him. I'd stopped breathing a couple of times along the way, they said, and he'd managed to revive me with CPR.

Madame Laida had told me the truth: I'd died, all right. But I'd been saved.

For a week I slept and dreamed of the cold, and Matt never left my side. When I awoke, his was the first face I saw—pale, regular, nothing like Jamie with his flash and beauty and cruelty. Matt was holding my hand in his, and his smile—his smile was fragile, and sad, and warm.

So warm.

"Hey, Kiley," he said. "I promised I'd find you. Remember?"

I thought I remembered the warmth of his arms around me, out there in the night. Of him bringing me back here, to pain, and to life.

"Jamie had a heart attack," he told me, very quietly. "But . . . I guess you know that?" He seemed a little afraid to say it, but I liked that he didn't look away.

I nodded, just a little.

"The police said he killed somebody else too. If he's the one who did that to you, I'm glad he's dead."

I felt so warm inside now, so warm. And I knew, as sure as the slow beat of my heart, that I'd never see the Cold Girl again.

And I'd never need her again.

"Matt?" My voice was just a thread of sound, but he heard it, and his smile was like sunrise. "Stay with me."

He raised my fingers to his mouth, and the touch of his lips made me shiver, but not from the cold.

Not ever again.

I fell asleep then, and I dreamed about the carnival, with its ride operators and ticket sellers, roustabouts and fortune-tellers. They'd all made a bargain with the Cold Girl over the years— victims, every one of them, taking immortality in exchange for revenge. Now they'd never stop moving, never stop hunting for their next recruit. Their next paying customer marked for death.

But it wouldn't be me.

I heard a whisper of tinny music, a glitter of lights at the edge of my vision, and I shivered just as sleep took me away.

It wouldn't be me, this time.

"A Duet with Darkness"

An Abby Sinclair Short Story

Allison Pang

The spotlights shine upon my face, but I barely notice, caught up in the way my fingers rock over the strings, my thoughts nothing more than a blur of white as the music converges into a single strand of color. As always, something dances below my consciousness, a perception that no matter how good I am, no matter how hard I try, there is more to come if I only dare reach for it.

I crack an eye open during a slight pause in the beat, my vision drawn to the man in the front row. Sitting next to my mother, her white coat a shining pearl of righteousness. But who the man is, I'm not sure.

He stares right up at me from the center front, his spiky hair glowing silver and orange, one brow arched as my fingers caress the strings.

You can do better than that, those glittering eyes say. Stop toy-ing with me.

A jolt thrums through my arms at his smugness. His reb[l] [text cut off by page curl] *rows into my bones until all I want is to leap from the st[age to the] door. To run.*

To fly.

But instead, I finish my set, my mother's cold, fish-belly gaze sliding over me. Never good enough for her.

Inside my skin, an inferno burns.

When I exit the stage that night, I do so without the intention of ever coming back. I leave the girl I was by the roadside, sloughing off her life, her very skin. I slither out of her like a dying snake, only to emerge into a world I somehow always belonged to.

And I know about them. This strange affliction that allows me to see music, to lock it into a tawdry rainbow of pure, aching color— it allows me to see them as well. The very words they speak, those wonderful syllables—they drip from their mouths and ring through my bones. Their presence assaults me, teases me, taunts me with what I can never have.

Nobu says most mortals have to be awakened to the presence of the OtherFolk. To recognize the existence of the CrossRoads.

But not me.

THE VAN STINKS of fried chicken and musty clothes. Bong water. Stale sex. Dried sweat. A shag carpet that probably hasn't been cleaned in decades. Elizabeth tries to air it out from time to time, but the Thai sticks she lights do little more than give everything a vague patchouli odor. Like spritzing a pig with Chanel, I guess. The flavor of the road and a handful of bodies slumbering in close quarters has a way of clinging to the skin.

Nobu and I share a joint in the back, surrounded by a Stonehenge of amps and monitors. In the front, Elizabeth's head bobs up and down in Bryston's lap. It's all panting breath and wet sucking sounds as the incubus's fingers fist through the golden blond curls at the nape of her neck in a desperate clawing motion.

Nobu snorts and takes a final puff before flicking the roach to a plastic bag. A long, masculine groan echoes from the driver's side and I roll my eyes, inclining my head toward the rear door of the van.

Not that we all aren't used to it. Traveling with an incubus leads to certain eventualities, and copious amounts of sex is apparently one of them.

I find my violin case on one of the crates and swing it over my shoulder as Nobu opens the lift gate. Once outside he knocks on the window of the driver's-side door in some sort of dude-bro Morse code.

Gig soon. Don't take too long.

A moment later a middle finger presses against the inside of the window.

"Asshole."

"At least they're in the front this time." Brystion wasn't exactly known for his tact when it came to finding fuck space. "Why do we keep him around, again?"

"Because he brings the ladies. And it's his band." Nobu smiles wryly and tips his head to where Marcus slouches on a nearby tree stump, his fingers picking out a fiery Spanish melody on an acoustic guitar. He's in human form, complete with jeans and a wool skullcap, but there's a feral gleam in the werewolf's eye when he raises a brow at us.

Scarlet shimmers in my head as the music hits my ears, whisks me away into a flamenco-filled haze. I shut my eyes against it, but the colors continue to swirl.

Synesthesia.

Both help and hindrance, my own special oddity ensures I see music in the form of colors, each note and chord blending into some new hue.

"Come on." Nobu nudges me away. The others in the band know about this particular "skill" of mine, of course, but none of them really understand it. At most, it's a parlor trick I can trot out onstage. I can always be counted on as a sort of living tuning fork.

But it also makes me far more sensitive when things are played off-key.

Years upon years of training, always searching for perfection. To suffer the indignity of anything less was anathema. One doesn't get into Juilliard on "almost good enough," after all.

Before we'd joined the band, Nobu and I busked together on the streets—me on my battered acoustic violin and him on his electric Jordan Holoflash. Pretentious fucking instrument. It suited him, even though I'd never be caught dead playing it. But it was easy, the two of us meshing with a simple grace that filled me with joy.

Joining the band changed all that.

After several weeks of me butting heads with Marcus and Brystion on arrangements and never quite finding a groove, Nobu took me aside and suggested I ought to tone it down a bit. Which in my case meant no more solo playing. No showing off. Learning how to be a supporting member or some such bullshit. I do my best, but sometimes it chaps the hell out of my hide. I'm better than they are. To hold myself back merely to fit in is so far counter to everything I've been taught.

But I've been on the stage nearly my entire life. I know how to hide behind a smile.

I give the restrooms a sour side glance as Nobu and I approach the fairgrounds. If we could just manage to swing real showers on a regular basis, I'd be all set. The romanticism of making music on the open road certainly has its appeal—but so does hot water.

Nobu chuckles when he sees where my gaze is headed. He pushes his violet tea shades onto his forehead. "All in good time, little bird."

"Easy for you to say," I mutter. "You always look good."

And he does. Nobu is a fallen angel—a sin-eater, to be specific. Most of the time he looks as though he stepped out of the pages of some *bishōnen* manga. Between the copper tint of his skin and the ebony hair spiking from his head, dyed in a multihued brilliance, there is something about him that nearly makes my eyes burn.

Sometimes I marvel at it. That such a creature deigns to travel with me. Teaching me. Protecting me. Loving me.

Tonight his hair is shades of aqua and emerald. He's a gorgeous leather-clad peacock, even if the feathers of the wings he sometimes displays are of the darkest night.

"I still wouldn't mind a real shower." I stretch my arms to the evening sky.

"Soon." He presses a quick kiss against my forehead and leads me through a second field where a small oasis of cars are parked, heading for the CrossRoads fairgrounds.

Nerves run in soft waves down my spine. As gigs go, I've never played openly for so many OtherFolk before, and the unfamiliar anticipation leaves an odd taste in my mouth, gritty and dank. Even if we're mostly doing covers this time. I pat my violin case out of habit, my fingers suddenly eager to showcase my talent among them. To show them all what I can *really* do.

Nobu's lips quirk and he chuckles, the sound soft and low. "If your mother could only see you now," he muses. His wings fade away beneath a Glamour as the glaring lights of the midway hit us.

My mouth compresses into a bitter smile. My mother would be aghast at how her little prodigy had escaped her, eschewing the propriety of Juilliard for lessons learned upon the road. "No need to guess there. She'd garrote me with my own violin strings."

Abruptly, he kisses my palm and then my cheek, his mouth brushing over my jaw to linger on the sweet spot where I lean against the chin rest of my violin.

The violinist's hickey.

Nobu often kisses me there. Some sort of manly claiming ritual, I suppose, but I don't mind.

I shiver. "How much time before the show?"

"Not enough," he says, regretful. "Come on. Let's get the lay of the land, shall we?"

Clasping our hands together, we emerge from the shadowed safety of the trees into a gaudy world constructed of hot fluorescents and creaking metal, screaming children and come-ons from the ride barkers. The scent of cotton candy and funnel cakes floats over the breeze.

"I would have thought there would be something more exotic here," I note as we approach a cluster of small stands proclaiming the world's best hot dogs. "Chocolate-covered Faery wings? Deviled Ding Dongs?"

The sin-eater shrugs. "We crave mortality and its trappings, though most of us deny it. Besides, there are enough humans in attendance to make things awkward should we choose to call attention to ourselves that blatantly."

Part of me wonders why it would even matter in a place like this, but I already know I won't get any answers from Nobu about it. OtherFolk business is their own, of course.

I tug on his obnoxiously scarlet snakeskin jacket with the high collar and no sleeves instead. "Attention, eh?"

"Makes two of us," he murmurs, poking at our reflection in the fun-house mirror. His fingers run up the center of my dark blue corset, lingering on the leather eyelets. My face is distorted, monstrous, but my hair flares in fiery curls from my head, and my rainbow thigh-high socks pool from beneath my loose-fitting skirts like a bowl of melting Lucky Charms.

He kisses me hard, his tongue darting over my lower lip. I nip his chin, smirking as he lowers his glasses so they cover his eyes, and we lose ourselves in the crowd again.

The edge of dusk darkens the sky, but the waning sunlight does little to diminish the excitement of the people around us. Nobu's observations of humans are fairly accurate, but I notice the OtherFolk slipping between the islands of humanity with an odd grace that's so prevalent among their kind.

Some are overt about it, hiding their magic behind shoddy costumes. People see what they want to see, after all—and if this fair was more fantastical in nature, no one was complaining. Pointed ears and furry tails, a hint of feathers, a smattering of scales. Tiny differences, easily overlooked by drunken patrons and overly imaginative children.

I have no such issue. I can't see through Glamours exactly, but the tones the OtherFolk put out when they talk or laugh or sing cuts right through my synesthesia, shining vibrant in my mind's eye. I am blinded to their Paths, though. With three options—the Dark, the Light, and the Fae—I can only know what they tell me themselves. Nobu, Brystion, and the rest of the band fall squarely upon the Dark Path—mostly daemonic in nature, they are the bad boys of the OtherFolk. Their presence is negated by those of the Light Path—angels and the like—and the Fae are smack in the middle.

Some, like Nobu, have moved from one Path to the other, though how or why he's never told me.

I'm not sure I want to know.

All I really understand is that the OtherFolk and their respective Paths are connected to the CrossRoads in some way, traversing the space between the worlds at certain times of the day to dwell among mortals at their own discretion. Beyond that, I am ignorant as to the mechanics, and happily so.

All I need is the music. And Nobu.

Speaking of which . . .

"I think I'm going to go check out the acoustics before we set up. Last time things sounded a little flat."

Nobu shakes his head but gives me a soft shove. "Go on. You won't be happy until things are set up the way you want."

"Probably not." A hint of annoyance lances through me. "After all, if you had to rely on anyone else, we'd never manage to sound good."

His face darkens. "We've talked about this, little bird. We're a band for a reason—and that's not to be your personal showcase."

I snort. "You need me. I'm awesome."

"Not if you're going to act like that, we don't." His tone drops into something serious, and I steel myself against the lecture. "Listen, I *know* what you can do. You are more than your talent. You always have been—but arrogance makes you blind."

The words sting. I bite back the retort that threatens to erupt from my mouth. "What's the point of even having me tag along if you won't let me be who I am?"

I turn away before he can answer, but I still see the flash of hurt upon his face. "I'll meet you at the van in a little while." It's all he says, and a moment later he's gone.

I love Nobu. I do.

But sometimes he can be so damn overbearing.

Next to me, the merry-go-round starts up, and a cacophony of color blurs my vision.

And then I hear it—the familiar sweep of a violin.

Playing a concerto?

Ah, yes. Mendelssohn. E Minor.

My fingers twitch. Familiar, yes, but these notes . . . they cut across my mind like golden rain, shoving through any other sounds, wrapping them away in a delicate webbing until all I can hear is the music.

I move as though entranced; I might walk forever if the player wills it. Like a child following the Pied Piper to my fate inside the mountain, and I will gladly follow and follow and follow. . . .

I duck beneath the tent flap leading to the stage. In a short while it will be full of people—watching, dancing, clapping—but it's empty now except for a few curious bystanders and some roadies setting up.

What holds my attention now isn't the stage itself, though, but the man upon it. Tall, long-limbed, and fully dressed in clothes that wouldn't seem out of place in a Jane Eyre movie. There isn't a bit of sweat upon his brow beneath the russet curls or the neatly trimmed sideburns, despite all the layers. His face has a certain ageless quality, as though time has stood still for him, but a cocksure twinkle gleams in his eyes.

My Doc Martens are somehow graceful as I step through the tangle of wires on the floor, narrowly avoiding the techs. The man's gaze falls upon my violin case and his smile grows broad.

He finishes with a flourish and bows. "Care to join me?" A flush of pleasure rushes through me, and he holds out his hand as I mount the steps. "Call me Nick."

"Melanie. Melanie St. James." The name drops from my tongue easily enough, though I don't usually give it out. My former identity is a ghost, haunting every decision I make.

His hand grasps mine and I know in an instant that this man is a master musician. The tips of his fingers brush over my knuckles; the faint thickness speaks to a lifetime of performing.

He turns my hand over to get a better look at my own fingers. "Exquisite." Next to his, mine seem almost short by comparison, although perhaps it's more that his are so oddly elongated.

"You aren't like the rest of the OtherFolk." I pull my hand away cautiously, wondering if he's Glamoured.

His eyes light up in amusement. "I assure you, I'm quite human, good lady."

"A TouchStone, I'm guessing?" *Like me.* A mortal bound to OtherFolk through a written Contract allowing the OtherFolk to move freely between the worlds, just as Elizabeth has with Bryston. It had seemed the natural thing for me to do at the time too, to sign a Contract with Nobu. It was an easy bargain to make with the man who had rescued me from life in a gilded cage.

"But of course. What else would I be in such a place as this?" He gestures about the tent wryly.

Nick's ageless mien suddenly makes sense. I've heard there are interesting perks and side effects to being a TouchStone, though Nobu and I have never hashed that out. My TouchStoning him had nothing to with material gain.

My eyes fall upon Nick's violin and I frown. The wood is warm, burnished with a golden hue unlike anything I've ever seen. He draws the bow across the strings teasingly. The sound shivers in a quiet sob, but the color in my mind . . . oh, the color! Tiny sunbursts echo each perfect note.

I have no idea what he's playing, but it doesn't matter. A rush of longing fills me with a desire so thick, I can taste it.

Unbidden, I reach toward the violin as though I might pull some of that gold into myself, bask in the glow.

He stops playing, and I jerk my hand away just as my index finger brushes the tip of the scroll. I flush. Touching another person's instrument without permission is rude on a number of levels. "I'm sorry. I didn't mean to."

He shrugs it off. "Please, why don't you take out yours and we'll play something."

I can only nod, unable to shake away the craving for those brilliant notes from my mind. A pleased expression flickers over his face, and I turn to remove my own violin.

The case is battered on the outside, the cracks breaking up the leather like the web of some deranged arachnid. I undo the fastenings and stare down at it. It suddenly seems shoddy compared to

Nick's. I shake myself inwardly. Why the hell am I even thinking this way? Instruments can make a difference in the quality of musical sound—but it's the player that matters, far more than any level of superior carving work.

And yet I can't help stealing another glance at Nick's, envy building even as I tighten my own strings and rosin the bow.

I close my eyes to concentrate and an immediate sense of calm washes over me when my fingers bend around the neck. My nose fills with the gentle wood smell that reminds me of rain and Nobu. My right pinky twitches as it brushes over the slight scratching on the back.

My initials, scrawled there in a childish act of rebellion.

But now it only makes me smile, and I raise the violin to my shoulder, my cheek moving to press against the rest. The bow hums over the strings in a slow, sonorous sigh before I start a quick drill, pausing to turn the pegs in the scroll here and there until the colors align in my head just so.

Perfection.

Finally I glance up. "Did you have something in mind?"

"I thought we might try a duet." Nick runs his bow up the strings pensively.

I shrug. "Whatever you want." He raises a brow at this, and my hackles rise. I'm more than confident in my ability to pick up anything he attempts. My classical repertoire is extensive, and playing with Nobu has opened a new world of "less classical" pieces. Everything from rock to Romani—it's all fair game.

But I'll do it his way for now. He eyes me thoughtfully. "A little 'Table Music for Two'? I don't have the sheet music, but . . ."

Also known as "The Mirror," this was a playful Mozart duet where each musician played from the same sheet, but one played it upside down. "I know it. I'll play upright."

As pieces go, it's fun, not too long, and an amusing way to

gauge each other's talent. I nod and count off the beat. One. Two. Three.

Four.

Our bows hit the strings at the same instant and the music pours forth even as my mind lights up with its usual accompanying visual display. My fingers know where to go before I've finished processing the song from my memory.

But the colors are anything but smooth. The rainbow patterns of certain keys show up in their typical vibrant greens and blues, but it's separate from Nick's music. Instead of our parts blurring into a whole, his golden notes shine brighter, seeming to wrap around mine.

It's too much. Instead of complementing my playing, his side threatens to overwhelm it.

A thin line of anger threads through me. It's been a long god-damned time since I've met anyone who's my equal, not counting a few of my instructors at Juilliard—and even then I could match a number of them.

And Nick is holding back. The look in his eye when our gazes meet is full of pity. *You will never be as good as me.*

Fury forces me to renew my efforts and I finish up with a savage flourish, blinking against the fading gold.

"Rather impressive." He's all politeness and lies. My fingers turn white around the neck of my violin in answer.

"Don't patronize me," I snap. "Let's try something else."

"Whatever you like, I'm sure."

My teeth grind together at the casual dismissal even as my mind sifts through the music in my head. The perfect song falls into place.

Paganini.

Caprice no. 24.

Considered one of the hardest pieces for the solo violinist, it's one I've spent more hours than I care to remember learning. Years of practice and cramping fingers. I'd bled for it.

"Let's see you try this, you bastard," I mutter beneath my breath. Any calm I have skitters away, my nerves struggling to stay in focus. A moment later and I'm off, the playfulness giving way beneath the difficulty. I stay on target, every ounce of my training now at the forefront. The need to prove that I'm better lends an edge to the sound, rage trembling through every scrape of the bow.

I frown when I realize there's an echo.

No.

Not an echo. He's accompanying me, mimicking every movement . . . but playing just a tad off-kilter. The colors blur into a discordant miasma that makes me dizzy. My jaw tightens until my teeth nearly pulse with each chord.

He's doing it on purpose.

A *challenge*, my inner voice crows, sending my fingers into a frenzy of effort I haven't made in ages. The air crackles around us and then I gape as the music changes. Not mine.

I know how the piece is supposed to go, but he's turning it into something else.

Improvisation.

The color shifts and I attempt to follow. A note behind, a chord too slow, but I've got his number in the span of a few seconds. The pattern solved, I surge forward, meeting him note for note until suddenly it's over.

Blood rushes through my ears, met only by a silence that seems all the louder for the absence of the music. I'm panting, air flooding my lungs as I attempt to quell the shaking in my wrists.

"It was a good attempt." Nick bows, but his mouth curves into a mocking smile.

I fight to keep the scowl from my face. He's outplayed me,

but how much of that was due to his violin versus his actual talent? My pride stings as I reach for excuses. I underestimated the hell out of him.

"Whatever. I wasn't asking for your opinion."

"Says who?" Nick asks mildly. "A song played is a song released to the world, to be interpreted by the listener. Your playing was admirable, yes, but it lacks something."

"Yeah. That violin." I lay my own instrument in its case. "There's something funny about it."

"You have no idea," he murmurs, handing it to me. "Feel free to give it a go, but I really don't think you'll care for the results."

My fingers curl around the neck and I pluck a single string. The resulting *plink* lights up my vision like a thunderbolt.

Nick's jaw drops, but I've already placed it beneath my cheek and the bow slides over the string, notes of such perfect clarity and resonance emerging . . . and my mind stills.

The world drops away until all that's left is the sweetness of the sound, the soft sigh and hum. The first strains of Tchaikovsky emerge, the gold swirling, swirling until it seems as though I stand on the brink of the universe.

I have but to reach out and I could hold it all, play it all . . .

The violin is snatched from my hands, something akin to pain vibrating through my fingers.

"That's enough." Nick's smile remains, but it's brittle and his cheeks are flushed. "That was . . . unexpected." He waves me off. "No matter. I look forward to seeing your performance later this evening. I'm sure you'll play to the best of your ability."

"Easy words from someone with a magic violin." Nobu's accusation rumbles thick and dark behind me, the distaste of his words butting through my vision with black precision.

My head snaps toward him, even as I gloat triumphantly. "Called it."

Nick shrugs as he puts his violin away. "It makes no difference what you think. You are an inferior musician."

Nobu's brow cocks high. "Is she? Then how do you explain that?" I crane my head to where he's pointing, nearly sinking to my knees when I see the crowd pressing at the entrance of the tent.

OtherFolk?

Nobu's eyes flick toward me and his voice softens. "She called us—and we came."

"I what, now? Called you how?"

Nick continues to pack his things, silent. I move toward him, but Nobu's hand around my ankle pulls me up short. *Later*, he mouths from below the stage. I scoot off the platform instead, my own violin cradled safely on my shoulder.

The crowd shuffles forward to get a better look at me as I stalk out of the tent. I'm used to adoration, but there's a hunger here that speaks of something far less innocent. Even Bryston and Marcus gape at me. Nobu thrusts past, though, his wings opening wide to clear the way.

I wonder at this flashy display of magic, but apparently the rules of the game have just changed. Nobu's wings curl around me to shield the view, and he manages to return me to the safety of the van, our bandmates close behind.

My mind whirls with the implications of Nobu's words earlier. I was "calling" OtherFolk? What the hell was all that about? I've almost always been aware of their presence, but I don't think that's what he means.

"Do you want to explain what just happened? In English this time?" I slump on the floor of the van, my arms crossed. Beside me, Bryston leans against Elizabeth. Her blue eyes are wide as she stares at me, and the silence stretches out until I punch Nobu in the shoulder. "Hello?"

"The Wild Magic," he mutters. "Somehow you reached it while you played and called us to you."

"The what?"

"You know the CrossRoads work via magic, right?"

I shrug. "Everything's magic with you guys. Why would that be any different?"

"It's the Wild Magic that holds all it together. The glue." He cocks a brow at me and I can't tell if he's scared or proud or what. "And you just managed to use it. Via your music."

I shake my head at him. "It wasn't me. It was that violin. Magic, like you said."

"No. It wasn't just that." Bryston pauses a moment and he shares a glance with Nobu. The angel's nostrils flare wide and in that moment I realize there's more going on than they've said. "You've done it before, Mel. Not call to us, exactly, but sometimes you skirt the edge of it when you play. The magic of the violin probably just amplified it."

"Well, that's news to me." I focus on Nobu, dread knotting my gut. "Did you know about this?"

He doesn't even have to answer. His face barely moves, but that little twitch in the corner of his left eye gives him away as discreetly as a neon billboard.

"I see." The tension fills my lungs with cement, weighing me down so I can't breathe. If I exhale, I'll shatter. No one says anything, and I stare at my fingers. "So where does that leave us for tonight's gig?"

"There isn't going to be one. We're going to can the show and get on the road." Nobu nods to himself as if somehow that makes it all better.

"You don't get to make that decision for all of us. We need the money." Bryston gets to his feet. "I know you're all for this romantic living-on-the-road bullshit, Peacock, but some of us are getting a little tired of it." Elizabeth nods. These are her words spoken from his mouth. As though she had her hand up his ass like some kind of incubus puppet.

I choke back an ugly laugh. "What's the matter? Tired of playing Whac-A-Mole with your mouth in the public view?" The words slip out before I can stop them, but the damage is already done.

Elizabeth blinks, a hint of scarlet staining her cheeks. Without a word she exits the van, the door slamming shut behind her so hard the entire vehicle rocks.

Brystion's eyes flare wide and I catch the crisp slice of gold at the edges. "Go and apologize," he commands. "Now."

"Don't you tell her what to do." Nobu's wings snap open. "She's only saying what the rest of us aren't. You think listening to the two of you rut at all hours is a bag of peaches? Everyone knows it'll never work out anyway."

"That's none of your gods-be-damned business." The golden shimmer about Brystion's eyes grows brighter as he turns toward me. "Perhaps another mortal with brighter dreams?"

Nobu's fist cracks the incubus in the jaw and the two of them hit the floor. Feathers scatter everywhere like ebony snowflakes. For a moment I can't tell who's who.

Until the sound.

The awful cracking sound of splintering wood.

I whimper, but it takes a moment before the men hear it and by then I'm already pushing them out of the way, no longer caring if I'm accidentally hit. My violin case lies beneath Nobu, but I already know what I'll find.

The two daemons pull away. Horror flits over Nobu's face as I open the case. A thick crack shatters the neck of the violin, arching deep into the board.

"'That's that, then." It's my voice saying the words, but I hardly recognize it. A flood of memories slams into me, everything from the last few months and before. If I look at the thing for too long I'll start crying, and I don't want to do that.

Not yet.

Nobu captures my wrist. "Little bird?"

"Fuck off," I snap, not wanting to hear him say it was an accident or that he was sorry. It wouldn't matter anyway.

I escape to the outside, leaving the two men to figure out what to do on their own. Marcus stands guard on his tree stump, hands resting between his knees. He twitches as though he wants to run. I can hardly blame him.

"Elizabeth?" Her name hangs in my throat.

He jerks his head toward the far end of the field, but he eyes me cautiously. "She took a walk. She was crying."

"I know." Shoving my hands into the pockets of my hoodie, I trudge in the direction he indicated, the grass squelching beneath my boots. The field is empty of all but moonlight, but a faint scent of cigarette smoke trails on air thick with tension. I follow it to where Elizabeth perches on a fallen log, puffing on her usual Marlboro Light.

She doesn't look up when I approach; her mascara streaks faintly on her cheeks. "Don't say anything. I don't want to hear it." She takes a long drag and closes her eyes. "You think I don't already know what you all think of me? I'm no musician. No artist. Just some fucking groupie banging the lead singer of a band that's going nowhere."

A puff of smoke drifts from her lips as she exhales. "And even that's in question." Now she does glance at me, and the whites of her eyes glitter bitterly. "You're such a cunt."

My head jerks as though I've been slapped. "Excuse me? I came out here to say I'm sorry. I shouldn't have said what I did, but I hardly think that—"

"Like I care. I was so happy to find out Nobu was bringing you along. Another woman in the band I could at least commiserate with over the little things." Her mouth curls into a sneer. "But you're nothing but a goddamned diva."

Anger runs hot through my ears. "You don't know shit. You have *no* idea what I've given up to be here." I thumb behind us. "You think I enjoy sleeping in a van? I could be in a five-star hotel right now. With room service and a fucking shower. Playing with the world's finest orchestras. Flowers at my feet and people kissing my ass left and right." I pace around her, heedless of the smoke she blows in my face. "But here I am, trying to keep a roof over our heads by pretending I'm something I'm not."

"Poor thing," she mocks, flicking the cigarette on the ground and stomping it out. "You're a spoiled brat who wouldn't know a good thing if it bit her on the ass. And by the way, the band doesn't mesh right *because* you're holding back."

"What are you talking about? Nobu said he wanted me to stop hogging the spotlight, so I did."

"Whatever. Everyone else is just waiting for you to show what you can do. And then you put on this act, like you're surprised people love your music. It's fake. Everything about you is fake." She heads for the van before I can respond, but pauses, the edge of her face crested silver in the moonlight. "I'm not anyone fancy and I don't really know the first thing about music. But I always thought a good musician shouldn't play down. She should lift others up."

And then she's gone, walking swiftly away with her head down.

Shame floods my cheeks. "I'm sorry," I mumble after her. For a moment I wish I were anywhere other than here. Even Juilliard. I have the sudden urge to give my old roommate a call, but I barely said good-bye to Abby when I left. I have no right to expect advice from her now.

My feet find a rhythm as I walk around the log, trying to figure out where I'd gone so wrong. I'd been so trapped in my life. Everything structured. Preplanned. Unable to make my own decisions. Form my own opinions. Every move and concert decided on. Every piece I was supposed to play scheduled well in advance.

I'd been dying. Trapped between the outer layers of my skin and the music inside, battering itself upon my bones to get out. And now I was free, wasn't I? Free to call the shots. To play what I wanted. To dress how I liked. To be where I wanted to be.

So why was I here? Drifting among the masses of OtherFolk and traveling like a vagrant, playing music—*that Nobu insisted I play?*

The realization that I've quite possibly traded one cage for another hits my stomach. I want to vomit.

"With great power comes great responsibility," I quip to myself, but it's a hollow joke. Abby would have understood, though. It's not even about power. Simply being free isn't enough. I have to take control of my own life.

On my own.

I could, right? Just grab my things from the van and disappear on the road? Hitchhike, maybe.

Oh.

That's right. My violin is broken. Without it, I won't have a way to earn any money. I swallow bitter disappointment. Trapped again. Even so, there was still Nobu. Would he understand?

In the distance an electric guitar wails, the familiar riff of Chris Isaak's "Wicked Game" resonating with a sultry twang. I wince. Brystion normally sings this, and I'd have added backup. I can picture him singing to the audience with those rolling hips and that seductive smile, using his incubus charm to leave the ladies in a swooning mess of hormones.

It hurts to realize they've decided to go ahead with the gig, but it's a moot point. I can't join them. I can't even fault Nobu for not coming out to find me, given the last thing I'd said to him. Might as well just head for the stage to watch the show.

At least I won't have to deal with Nick gloating at me during the whole set. Maybe it was a blessing in disguise.

An uncomfortable idea threads itself through my mind. Surely Nobu hadn't attempted to break my violin on purpose? I push it away, not wanting to entertain the thought.

But it lingers, even as I make my way to the fairgrounds. The music has changed up and I easily recognize Marcus's sultry guitar playing. As a band we all had our strengths, and everyone had gotten a chance to showcase their abilities.

Except me.

Anger grows ever deeper, and by the time I stomp up the center aisle beneath the tent and plant myself in the empty seat next to Elizabeth, the only color I'm seeing is red. The blonde's eyes remain pink and puffy. She nods at me, but there's nothing particularly friendly about it. Onstage, I catch a glimpse of Nobu singing, his wings spread wide and unashamed as he covers the Lucifer song "Datenshi Blue."

"Fallen Angel Blue."

He'd told me what it meant once, but whatever the lyrics are, the liquid Japanese syllables all sound like a good-bye.

He gives me a tight smile when he sees me, but I turn my head away, unable to look at him. The song ends, leaving him breathing hard into the microphone. Normally at this point in the set Brystion and I would do a version of "The Raggle Taggle Gypsy." But not this time.

One of the amps blows out with an ominous crackle, and the band disappears backstage as a roadie fusses with it.

"I'm sorry about your violin," Elizabeth says during the lull. "Brystion thought you might use Nobu's electric one instead, but Marcus said you'd never play it."

"Electric violins have no soul. No . . . life." I chew on my lip, stretching my legs out in front of me. "I can't explain it. They don't sing. They just parrot what you tell them to play. I'd take a busted-up piece-of-shit acoustic over plastic any day."

"Well, if it's an instrument you need, I've got one you might borrow." Nick's voice cuts through our conversation like a splash of ice water. Elizabeth's face grows stony as our eyes meet. Whatever our enmity was, in this we would stand together.

"Go fuck yourself, cheater." I don't turn all the way around to look at him. "I don't need magic to play music."

"Well, *that* isn't mine to lend, my dear—but the one I'm Contracted to has indicated I must make amends for my earlier rudeness."

"Yeah? Well, tell him to buzz off too. Don't. Want. Any." My heart quavers at the lie. The mere thought of getting a chance to play that golden violin again makes me tremble. I could get up on the stage and cut loose, as was my due.

But I refuse to take the bait.

Almost.

I finally glance at Nick, but whatever I expected to see, it wasn't abject misery. "Please. We offer you the chance to borrow an instrument of exquisite quality. Enough to get through the show. Or perhaps more, if you would agree to a Contract."

I give him a sour look. "I wasn't born yesterday. There's going to be a catch and I don't want to pay the price."

"No catch. He merely wishes to let you try it out. If you don't want it after that . . . well, then. You move along."

"And what do *you* get out of all this?"

He swallows. "A chance at honor."

Even Elizabeth snorts at this. "Who are you Contracted to? I want to know what I'd be stuck with." I say the words seriously, but I'm not even remotely entertaining the possibility of anything but playing this gig and then returning the instrument. I have a life to find. Somewhere. One that doesn't involve Contracts to strange OtherFolk.

"He wishes to remain anonymous for now," Nick replies. "But after the show, we can meet and discuss everything. All the arrangements, should there be any." He pops open the case beside him, to reveal—

"A Stradivari?" I blink. "Are you shitting me?"

"It is a Guarneri." Something sad flits across his face. "An old friend of mine. One of many."

I hardly hear him, my hands already reaching for it, the gloss of the polish beckoning. Inside, I tremble at the idea of touching it, let alone playing the thing. *But you could. Play it . . . give it back. Get on the road and be gone. . . .*

Responsibility.

Fly away, little bird.

And yet.

"And you just happen to be waltzing around with an instrument worth millions of dollars? Right."

"And yet you're holding it."

I blink and realize he's right. I'm holding a motherfucking Guarneri.

What the hell.

"Fine. I'll borrow it for this set, meet with your guy, and that's it, right?"

"What are you doing, Mel?" Nobu rumbles, a storm cloud striding toward us.

"Our friend Nick here has offered me the use of his spare violin. I'm going to get on that stage and play what I want and then give it back. That's it."

Nick's mouth quirks. "Assuming your keeper lets you play it at all, that is."

"Don't," Nobu growls, snatching me out of the chair to march me behind the stage. "I'm begging you, do *not* do this."

I pull away from him. Nick's last words sting with their truth. He's goading me, but at the moment I don't care. "I'm making my own decisions, Nobu. Not you. Not anymore."

"Yes. Poor ones, it seems."

"You're worse than my mother. At least *she* was honest about using me." I stare at Nobu, rage burning inside. Where the intensity came from, I'm not sure, but once unleashed it wouldn't fade.

Before I realize it, my hand is at the top of my corset, fingers pulling out a folded piece of parchment.

Our Contract.

Fire flashes back at me in the depths of his eyes, disbelief warring with anger, and somehow it's enough that he doesn't think I've got the guts to go through with it that drives me to tear it in half. He flinches as the fluttering remains scatter upon my boots.

Without pausing to look at me, he stalks off. A sharp twang lances through my chest as though something has broken.

Wait. The words form on my lips but I can't give voice to them, pride warring with incredulity. I grip the neck of the violin with fingers made of ice. "Good-bye it is," I mutter.

I would deal with it later. Figure out Nobu later. My life . . . later. I just want to play.

I quickly mount the stage and run my bow over the strings. An answering hum fills the tent. I spend a quick moment warming up, nearly weeping at the perfection of the tone.

Unlike the golden violin, these notes ring silver in my mind, with a richness I can only guess comes from the instrument itself. I step forward into the spotlight. Where I'd been in for nearly the entirety of my life. Where I belong.

Bach's Sarabande in D Minor slips from the strings.

Nobu's presence looms behind me, filling me with sadness.

My eyes meet Nick's in the second row, but they're hollow, as though whatever spark that gave him life had fled long ago.

With each note, the voice of the violin grows stronger, pulling and pushing until I lose myself to it completely. After all, this was the song I was playing when I first met Nobu.

Might as well be the last.

And then I'm not even thinking of him at all.

When the final note fades, the silence is . . . well, it's one of those pin-drop things, except I can barely notice anything but the spotlight shining and the terrible chasm inside me. As though I've poured every ounce of myself into the audience.

It should feel good, but I'm oddly empty.

A breath shudders out of me, the bow hanging between my limp fingers, and I sink to my knees, spent. I glance over at Nobu, surprised to see the look of horror on his face.

"What is it?"

"You . . . you're—"

"Mine." A dark voice shatters my thoughts, the sound's color blacking out all other knowledge.

For a moment I'm transported to a despair so deep, I may never find my way out of it, and it's all the more horrifying for the pleasantness lingering just out of reach. But through it all rings a chord—at once familiar and terrible.

The flattened fifth.

Also known as the Devil's Chord.

"Don't look, Mel! Whatever you do. *Don't look at Him.*" Nobu barrels into me, shoving my face into the floor, his wings arched protectively. "Don't look."

I try anyway. I have to. The sheer presence of the man wrapped in shadow behind us insists on it. Nobu catches my face to hold it still.

"Please, don't."

"Why do you deny what is mine by rights, *lapsis?*"

Nobu winces. "I'm sorry . . . my Lord."

The words send a new thrill of horror racing down my spine. "My Lord"? I swallow as I realize who it must be, but I can't form the name, even in my mind. "I don't understand," I whisper.

"The violin." From the corner of my eye, Nick approaches the stage, even as the rest of the crowd hangs motionless. Statues.

"I don't want it. You can ha—" My words are cut off by a strangled yelp as Nobu covers my mouth.

"Shhh! Anything you say is binding here."

I struggle to sit up, but Nick's next words chill me even more. "I offered you the use of the violin. All you have to do is return it and we're done here."

"Right . . . but—"

"It has your soul, Melanie." Nobu voice is anguished. "When you played . . . somehow the violin took it. You can't give it back or He will own your soul."

A ripple of amused laughter sounds behind me, at once joyful and wretched.

"Indeed. Give me what is mine and your soul belongs to Me. Or enter a Contract to become my new TouchStone."

Nick flinches as I glare at him. "Honor, my ass."

He gestures to his own golden violin. "You weren't supposed to be able to play this. Only His TouchStone may do so. But you did."

"You can't Contract her," Nobu says suddenly. "She's *my* Touch-Stone."

"There is a torn Contract that says otherwise, boy." Nobu curses, and my heart drops.

"So that's it?" Panic flutters like an epileptic butterfly in my chest. I eye the front of the tent. Surely if I ran, I could get away. A hand grips my shoulder.

"There is no way to flee the sin of your pride."

"But you don't need me." I point at Nick. "He's better than I am." Inside, my cowardice cringes upon itself, but he's thrown me under the bus just as quickly.

"Nicolò has served me well, but I grow bored with his jaded assumptions."

"Nicolò," I say weakly. "*The* Nicolò?"

"But of course. The Devil's Violinist has ever been My servant."

My mouth drops. Paganini. I'd been playing against Paganini. No wonder he'd been able to outplay me so easily on the Caprice. He'd written the fucking thing. My head snaps toward him, and he gives me a wry shrug.

"Bastard," I snarl, trying not to cry against the unfairness of it all. In my arms, the violin glitters silver, the strings humming in agreement.

Nobu's arms and his wings wrap around both of us. "What do I do? I can't—I can't do this." His lips fall upon me, kissing my mouth and cheeks. "I'm so sorry, Nobu. I'm so sorry. . . ."

"No. I'm the one who's sorry, little bird. Everything I did was to protect you from this. I should have told you, but I was afraid . . ."

And then he sighs, wings drooping. He tilts my head as though to kiss me again, but this time he aims for that sweet spot beneath my chin.

His mouth brushes over it, and I utter a sharp cry at a thin sliver of pain twisting though my neck, thousands upon thousands of tiny pinpricks. And then nothing at all.

Until I touch it.

A tiny fire erupts beneath my fingers. "What did you do to me?"

His mouth quirks into a sad smile. "The prickle of pride is something that must be borne. Your sin is now mine."

A snort sounds from the shadow. **"An interesting proposition, *lapsis*. And unexpected. I accept."**

"Peacock?" Brystion says hoarsely. "Are you sure?"

Nobu sighs. "What else can I do? I love her."

I blink back a rush of tears. "Nobu?"

"I'm a fallen angel, Mel. But not completely fallen. And thus begins my true descent." He sets his tea shades on my forehead. "For luck."

His mouth presses against my ear. "I've bought you some time. Use it wisely, because you won't get a second chance. I'll wait for you. When you've learned how to use your power . . . when you're ready, come find me." His voice drops lower still. "The Wild Magic lives within *you*. It always has. With it, you can do anything. Anything you want."

"I want you," I sob. "I wish I'd never picked up this fucking thing."

"The price must be paid. Now or later—but either way, you *will* belong to me."

I sag at the Devil's words, but a razor-swift hand snatches my chin, pulling until I'm forced to look the Devil in the eye. I can tell you only that He didn't look anything like the stories said, but more than that I will not say.

It is enough that I saw Him and still breathe.

His fingernail traces the spot where Nobu kissed me. **"A gift."** And then pain lances through me, the sweep of magic and brimstone and the hum of what I could only guess was the Wild Magic surging through my body until every limb tingles.

The Devil smiles, and I know no more.

"MEL? WAKE UP. Come on, now . . . you have to get up." Brystion's voice rumbles in my ears, and for a moment I think I'm still in the van. I rub at my eyes.

Sand and gravel stick to my face, grinding into my cheeks. A deep ache ripples through my mind, the colors a sickening blur. I roll over and retch into the dirt, heedless of whoever is pulling the hair out of my eyes.

"Wha . . ."

"Open your eyes."

I blink. I'm in the middle of an empty field. Any signs of the fair are no more substantial than a thrown-away popcorn box. I glance down to see the violin beside me. Still glittering. Humming. Crooning.

I touch it briefly, and the power of it sings through me.

"Where's Nobu? *Where is he?*"

Brystion squats and throws an arm over my shoulder even as Elizabeth looks away miserably. "He's gone, Mel. He went with . . . *Him.*"

I weep.

For a few minutes. An hour. I don't know. The incubus pats me gently, not answering my soft questions of why. We both know the answer anyway.

Because of me. Nobu is gone because of me. The truth of it startles me out of my self-loathing.

"I'm going to get him." I roll to my feet, the violin in my arms. "You heard them, right? I can do things with this. I can fight back. . . ." My voice shakes with the edges of hysteria.

"Yes," the incubus says slowly. "But not now."

"Then when? I can't just sit here . . . I can't . . . I can't . . ."

Inwardly, I know he's right. I need time to learn how to use this gift—or curse—or whatever it is. Time to figure out a plan of action.

Time to set my own path.

I swallow hard. "Is the van still here?"

"Yes. Marcus is putting things away. He's asked us to drop him off in New York." A twinge of sadness grips me.

Just like that, the band has broken up. I didn't need to look at Elizabeth's face to see the *I told you so.*

I nod, suddenly realizing I have nowhere to go. Certainly not home. And without Nobu? "And you guys?"

Elizabeth slips her hand into Bryston's, her eyes possessive. He gives me a tight smile. "We're headed to Portsmyth. It's a little town in New England. There are a lot of OtherFolk there, but I think you'd like it."

I exhale softly and draw the bow across the strings. Immediately, those silver notes flare into my vision, beckoning me down a path I couldn't quite see. *Hie away, hie away, over bank and over brae . . .*

"All right." I nod. "Let's go."

DOOR MAKER, THEY name me.

Player of the Wild Music.

Rumors say I outplayed the Devil for a chance at winning a violin that would grant me the ability to tap into the magic of the very Cross-Roads itself.

But rumors are rarely more than exaggeration. Only a few know the truth of it, but I let it lie because it suits me. Even though "winning" is a relative term.

The Wild Magic pulls at me, beckoning me to the dance.

I burn with it.

And one day, it will consume me.

"RECESSION OF THE DIVINE"

Hillary Jacques

The fire had ridden up an unfinished four-by-four wooden post and melted the red rubber covering of the gaming booth. Olivia Sarkis snapped photos of all four sides, then crouched to survey the contents. The roof slumped like a gritty tongue and, in the murk beneath it, cheap, once-plush toys lay about, charred and disfigured.

"Holy thunderballs, what happened to those little bastards?" a woman asked, so close that the humidity of her breath invaded Olivia's ear.

Olivia jumped to her feet. Beside her a young woman, red hair short and spiked, stuck her thumbs into her pockets and rocked back until she achieved a gravity-defying angle. She was angular where Olivia was curved, short while the other woman loomed, and ethereal where Olivia was solid flesh. An avatar that well rendered, probably even touchable, could only be the result of centuries on the earthly plane.

"Thalia," Olivia said, her guess confirmed when t[...] lit up. Her pleasure sparked an answering warmth in [...] sneak up on me like that?"

Thalia raised a finger. "Better question, Lady. Why allow me to sneak up on you?"

"I'm working." Olivia tucked stray curls behind her ears. Mortal hair, she had long ago decided, behaved oddly. Thalia bent at the waist and peered under the covering.

"I hate to tell you this, but I think those little bunnies is d-e-a-d dead." Her eyebrows rose expectantly. "Unless you wish to return them to life."

"I doubt that performing mouth-to-mouth on melted snouts will raise them to the level of anything remotely resembling life."

Thalia shrugged and looked around. They stood between shuttered gaming stands, isolated from a seething crowd by a pair of thin ribbons of yellow tape. To Olivia's left, a man on stilts swung a baton, flaming on both ends. Below, the crowd twitched, pointing like dogs, anticipating misfortune. To her right, excited murmurs followed in the wake of a scantily clad bearded lady as she sashayed near the entrance gate. Performers building excitement for the nightly shows. Only at a carnival would a burned building not draw attention.

Kimball and Son Amusements boasted the largest traveling fleet of rides in the United States, but it prided itself on traditional attractions: performers, mind readers, and weight guessers. Freaks.

Thalia scuffed the toe of her boot over the outside of a distinct circle of clean ground.

"Already got it." Olivia pointed to a barrel that had been dragged five paces away. "Someone tossed a cigarette at the trash, missed, and hit something flammable, probably improperly disposed-of cooking grease. Are you now the Muse of loss control engineers?"

"Is that what you're pretending to be?" Thalia extracted a yellow and red nub from the barrel. She sniffed it. "Is this what humans subsist on nowadays?"

"It's a dog made of corn, a rare delicacy. You should try it."

Olivia closed her notebook and pocketed her camera. "I work for insurance companies, reviewing incidents and helping businesses develop safety procedures." She liked the job, finding and sorting the myriad pieces that contributed to accidents. Cause led to effect, and statistics and analysis produced remedies. It was an orderly, controlled profession, and she found she liked helping people. She'd never been useful before.

"For instance, if someone was eating garbage, you'd tell them it would be a good idea to stop before they got dysentery? That's genius!" Thalia mimed an awed expression as she dropped the stick onto the ground. "Why don't you finish up here? There's a great taco place down the road. It's been a nymph's age since we caught up."

"Down the road?"

"Pasco."

"Washington State?" She shook her head. "We're in Kentucky."

Thalia waved absently. "Those laws of space and time are so . . . human."

"I need to complete my investigation." Olivia ground her teeth, then winced. A week ago she'd had a cavity filled, and the tooth was still sore. Discomfort was also a human constant.

"You should investigate more than this fire. This place is a sham." Thalia flicked open a pocketknife and began carving stylized pictures of birds into the singed wooden post.

"Carnivals sell illusion. It's sleight of hand on a mass scale. Stop defacing the premises."

"I don't mean the show." Thalia flashed a pair of jazz hands. The blade made the motion menacing. "There's something nasty under the surface here, something dangerous." Her eyes widened and her voice turned beseeching. "You should fix it. Isn't that your job now, to make things safe?"

"Cease your provocation." The Muse was pushing, using that

subliminal encouragement specific to an essential, professional instigator.

Thalia frowned as she closed her knife. "You can't do this forever, Lady. You may have masked what you are, but you will never be rid of your nature."

The Muse faded, her image wavering like a reflection on water before disappearing. Olivia's head buzzed, the binding over her power quivering in response to Thalia's small trick. To release it meant she would leave this body and disperse like a thread on the wind. She would be stronger, but she would unravel, losing this sense of self she had finally identified and built up. That, she was not ready for.

She bit down, hard, and the resulting pain centered her. Down the lane, a man ducked under the caution tape. He wore pleated gray slacks, a bright white shirt, and thin-soled shoes with real stitching. Her purpose returned to her.

While he had inherited the carnival from his mother when she passed several months prior, August Kimball had the look of a man who, if he didn't own the business, wouldn't have pushed through the turnstile once in his entire life.

"Sorry to leave you out here alone." Kimball met her eyes for a moment before scowling at the ruined booth. "This place pulls me in a hundred directions at a time."

"Not a problem," she said brightly. "I'll send these pictures to the claims adjuster and he'll get back to you soon."

"You're not the adjuster?" Tan fingers tightened around the manila file Kimball held in front of his stomach. He wore a large gold ring inlaid with sapphire on his smallest finger, a token link to some proud university.

"Loss control. And I'm a contractor." Olivia smiled conspiratorially. "I don't really work for 'the Man.'" Nobody liked the idea of someone they paid telling them how to run their business, and sometimes it helped to distance herself. "Actually, the carnival was on my list of accounts that could use some help. You've had some incidents?"

"Yeah." Kimball rubbed his forehead and snuck a glance at the bearded lady's backside. "We had that electrical fire back in July. Wasn't too bad."

"And the other?"

"The other." He drew a breath and held it, his light-blue eyes unfocusing. It was an expression of remembrance, his senses going quiet as he turned inward, walking the steps of moments past.

Images tumbled into Olivia's mind, silverfish snippets of speech, the soft glide of emotions not her own. *August turns away from the collapsed machine, his shaking hands forming fists in his pockets. Behind him, the man yells, "Something has to change, Augie." Patronizing, like he's still a child who can be bullied. August is grown up, in charge, but it seems harder every day to resist that voice.*

Olivia pulled the camera out of her pocket and fiddled with it, resisting the pressure building in her head, the beehive flurry of whispers. His memories were his own; she had no right to them.

She'd spent a hundred years feeding the power of her essence into the shell of a nut, and around that had built her human form. She was aware of the binding—like she was of this aching tooth—but other than a weak pulse in response to the descendants of Olympians she occasionally encountered, it was quiet. Why now did it threaten to wake?

Kimball turned back and forced a smile, all business. "The other incident was a collapse. It would have been on the front page for a week if we were operational, but luckily it happened during setup. The parts are in storage." He glanced at the darkening sky. "Would you rather come back in the morning?"

Normally Olivia tried to be flexible for customers, but something about the place and the queer reaction she was having to it made her want to stay. "Sorry. I'm leaving in the morning. I promise I'll be as quick as I can."

The hope that she'd stop bothering him had softened his eyes. His expression hardened as he handed her the envelope. "These are our incident reports. I'll have to call someone to escort you, since I don't have keys. You can wait in the office."

"If you don't mind, I'll walk around. It's not often I get to go to the carnival. He can find me at the Zipper."

She turned away before he could argue. The file was warped, damp from his hands, though the evening air was rapidly cooling. Olivia held the file between her thumbs and fingertips, slightly away from her body. Paper was an effective conduit for memory, and maybe August Kimball wasn't as worried by the surprise nature of her inspection as he was by the fact that he actually had something to hide.

Olivia dipped under the tape, joining the crowd of fried-meat-on-a-stick-gobbling humanity as it streamed past face painters, walked over spilled popcorn, and gaped and hooted at the attractions. The air beside her shivered.

"You're still here?" Olivia muttered under her breath.

"Maybe I like spending time with you, despite this boring new character you're playing." Thalia materialized at her side. The humans were oblivious. "Do you at least have a secret addiction? Like, do you rescue animals? Are you a hoarder?"

"I'm pretty normal. I enjoy sunsets, long walks on the beach, and snorting copious quantities of cocaine off the backs of the thousands of ferrets I've packed into my home."

Thalia giggled. "At least interacting with humans has given you a sense of humor."

"I interact as little as possible." One of the reasons she freelanced was because she could control when and for how long she was among them. "But I read, and watch their films. All the themes they admire and fear distilled and presented in small, repetitive bites." She hoped to understand the feelings that had sprouted and continued to grow inside her human shell. The unquenchable desire for companionship. The irrational fear of uncertainty. The constant, gnawing need for *more*.

"You really can't sense this corruption?" Thalia snagged a bite of funnel cake from a passerby. "You would if you unleashed all that pent-up goddessness."

"I can't simply flip the switch. It takes time, preparation."

"You should get cranking on that." Thalia sighed and said in a low voice, "Then you could return. We miss you, you know. And things are so different now. It wouldn't be like it was before."

The Muses had a bet, the stakes of which grew each decade. Whichever one could lure Olivia back to the Olympian plane would win. She'd been gone for so long that entire cities probably hung in the balance of that wager by now. Their campaigns were subtle. A suggestion here. A hint there.

Pushing her like this, however, crossed the line. Her powers had been neither lost in battle nor bound by committee; she had chosen to renounce them.

"You overstep yourself, Thalia." She filled her words with ice and dismissal even as her stomach clenched with the knowledge that she was hurting the girl. "Go find a poet to whisper your favor to."

Thalia looked up from beneath her long lashes, contrite. She raised her hand as though making an offering. "At least allow me to do something for you before I go. Please?"

Olivia hesitated, then nodded. There was no harm in taking comfort. A cool grain materialized on her tongue and worked its way to her tooth, burrowing efficiently inside. The grinding ache numbed.

"That's better, isn't it? See you soon." Thalia winked as she faded.

Olivia made it four more steps before her binding twitched. She stumbled into the person beside her, muttered an apology, and hunched into herself as she wove through the crowd. Their minds and mingled histories pressed against her, a blooming riot demanding entry. Thalia didn't have the strength to undo her work. Her design was flawless, down to a release in the event she was threatened and her body incapacitated. And yet she saw no threat. Olivia staggered off the path.

The babbling retreated slowly. After a minute her breathing slowed, after another her heart relaxed. She focused on the bodies and objects around her. The field of the midway writhed and spun, a mechanical organism with a hundred limbs soundtracked by hissing pneumatics, rumbling generators, and delighted screams. The crowd split, slipping into orderly lines beneath the machines. The air hung thick, gravid with some foreign quality.

"Ms. Sarkis." The voice came from beside her, precise and loud enough that her name sounded like an announcement rather than a greeting. It was a voice cultivated to make itself heard. And the person speaking—a slim man with rich brown eyes and black hair styled to wave just so over his forehead—was meant to be seen.

In the old days, he would have been the face of the carnival. *The* barker, walking the streets of a town, his melodious voice sliding under doorways and through cracked windows, beckoning all to come, come see the wonderment.

Aside from the phone clipped to his waist, he seemed to belong to a bygone era as well. Black tuxedo trousers draped his long legs, and dove-gray suspenders intersected a band-collared white shirt. His hands were long fingered, his lips so red they appeared stained.

"Olivia." She offered her hand, smiling when he took it. With olive and gold undertones to his skin, and thick, dark lashes, it was like he'd walked out of her earthly homeland.

"I'm Damon. August asked me to take you to the storage trailers."

"You got here quick."

"Trying to entice people to spend money on a fortune-teller who's been on a drinking binge gets old in a hurry." His gaze locked with hers, and his voice turned slightly suggestive. "I'm happy for the distraction."

"Lead the way." She glanced back. The crowd had been so loud, so messy, before they reached the midway. Now the people hovered in still, sinuous queues. Damon touched her elbow, steering her through the throng. She was tall. He was close to a head higher than anyone else.

"Where are you from?" he asked as he led her between a pair of long booths, pointing a warning at a thick swath of cords crossing their path. "I noticed your accent."

"Greece. The economy has been so bad that I figured I'd have a better chance to put my engineering degree to use here."

"You must miss it." He turned back to her. In the small space she could feel the heat of his body. "I've never been myself, but my grandparents told me all kinds of stories. About the food. All those terraced hills and stone temples. The smell of the sea."

Nostalgia tightened her chest and her head went light, filling with that insistent buzz. The shell rattled, pulling against its moorings until a tiny, essential stitch tore. At her back the sensation surrounding the machines revealed itself in a surge, but it didn't feel hostile.

It felt like sadness.

"You all right, sweetheart?" Damon asked, dropping his chin and peering at her. Above them, a blue electric light clicked and hummed to life.

"Fine. I've got bad night vision," Olivia said, rubbing her eyes while fighting to maintain control. She was here for an inspection, not to be drawn into trouble, not to lose herself in front of so many people. "So the machine's disassembled. Has anyone been out to look at it?"

Damon ushered her onto another path, this one nearly deserted. Without the screen of a crowd it looked shabby, all peeling paint and bored young vendors bent over their phones.

"It's twenty years old, so it's not like there's a warranty. The mechanics declared it dead, so we packed it up. Figured we'd scavenge parts when we had time."

"So, were you in Birmingham when it collapsed?" The claim report hadn't specified where the equipment had broken down, but upon her arrival at the office, August Kimball had proudly recited their progress from Tucson and across Texas and the South before they turned for Louisville.

"Shreveport," Damon said, stopping before five corrugated metal shipping containers. The boxes looked as if they'd been fighting a battle against battery and graffiti for aeons. They hadn't been winning.

"Isn't that where Melanie Kimball passed away?"

"It is." He pulled a fat ring of keys from his pocket. A couple of coins dropped to the tamped-down grass. "You're investigating that too? I thought it wasn't an insurance thing."

"Oh, no. Car accidents after-hours aren't my concern," Olivia said in a rush, intrigued by the naked emotion in his face. He had known the old owner, well and possibly intimately. Olivia leaned back against the box. "I just read about it. In the file."

"You read about her in a file," Damon repeated flatly. Grief painted new and terrible faces on men, but he didn't wear an expression of grief. Or, not of grief alone.

The phone at his waist chirped. He glanced down, then

silenced it. When he raised his head, his good humor had returned. He gestured toward the next container in the line. "That's the one. It might take a moment to find the right key."

It's the tarnished silver one, Melanie thinks with a smile. Remnants of green paint cling to the raised lettering from a temporary office girl's attempt to organize. She frowns, lifts the lock from where it hangs loose. The door screeches when she pulls it open. Her eyes begin to water as smoke billows out. Her stomach falls. What are you doing in there?

Olivia backed away, resisting the urge to brush her shoulder as if that would remove the stark, sour tang of the recollection. Memories were normally fragmented, often occluded by other thoughts. This vision was distinct, the voice and imagery clear. Maybe it wasn't this place that was tripping her power but rather its temporary occupants.

A wink of light in the grass caught her eye. She crouched and plucked up a penny. Her fingers drifted along the back, catching on a small tool mark. It had been rubbed smooth, and the letters *E–M* were scored in the back. A love token. How quaint.

She jerked to her feet when the door creaked open. Damon gestured toward the dark interior. "Here we are."

Olivia pulled a flashlight from her jacket pocket and switched it on, glad for the mundane task. Red-painted aluminum beams were stacked in the front, and green double-occupancy cars blocked the back half of the box. It looked like Christmas in a land of metal giants.

"I think you dropped this," she said, handing Damon the penny.

His fingers dragged across her palm. "Ah. Wouldn't want to lose that."

The flashlight beam wobbled when Olivia stepped into the container. Shadows flitted across the ceiling and walls, rearranging themselves behind the fallen machine.

"It's a Jump-Start," she said, sliding past a large joint oozing brown grease. The air in the trailer was stale and coppery, and her voice echoed slightly, her accent stronger in the reflection. "Any idea what happened?"

"Old Man Kimball got it used off a seaside fair in Southern California. The salt in the air corroded it worse than he thought. A bunch of bolts went, and the holes were being eaten away. We fixed what we could, but when the cables snapped . . ." He raised his hands, then let them fall limp against his legs. "Time to cut our losses."

She sucked in her stomach as she rounded a bar, pressing her hand to the hinge to keep it from touching her shirt. The grease clung to her palm. She stopped. It was warm, and infused with the same sadness she had sensed earlier. Whispers filled her head.

"You okay there, sweetheart?" Damon moved toward her, blocking the light. "Get stuck on something?"

"No," she said quickly. Her hand slipped, and grease slid up to her wrist in a hot lick. *Focus.* "Was there any incident where it was damaged suddenly? That might be covered."

"Not that I remember." Damon steadied her when she rolled her foot over some debris on the floor.

"Not that you remember?" Olivia asked, her voice airy as her mind shuddered.

She still doesn't understand. Damon can see it in her eyes. The stupid woman, believing that everything will work itself out. She's missed payroll repeatedly and left a swath of bounced checks across the Southwest. And now, after he's gone to so much trouble for her and this business that bears her name, she dares to tell him to stop. Nobody will miss the girls. Phoenix. Las Cruces. Lubbock. And . . . where was Melanie from? "Em," he asks, "where were you born?" She thrashes, a gurgle dying in her crushed throat. He pets her hair, and his hand comes away warm with blood. "That won't do, Em. The carnival needs this to stay alive. Isn't that what we always talked about, what it would take to make this place thrive?"

"Miss Sarkis?" he said, in the same voice as the memory. The human part of her recoiled, out of shock and fear. The shell of her binding teetered, fell, and . . . cracked. She gasped.

"Damon."

"Olivia?" Satisfaction in his tone, thinking she was breathless for a very different reason.

"She loved you," Olivia whispered. "How could you do this to her?"

"What . . . what did you say?"

Melanie Kimball. Em. He'd killed her, and others. His hand tightened, fingers biting flesh. He still held the penny, and the ridged edge burned against her arm.

Olivia snapped up the fist holding the flashlight, catching him under his jaw. He reeled back, crashing against a beam, and she ran from the trailer.

She fled the desolate back side of the grounds, seeking safety in the crowd. And now she saw, truly saw, what had looked so odd before. The humans, yammering and excited, eagerly shoved their money into the ticket sellers' hands, then lined up beneath the machines. As they did so, they ceased talking, dropped what they were eating, and stared straight ahead, docile as livestock.

She trawled them, wisps of newly released power moving like a net through rich waters. They would spend and ride until they ran out of money or the carnival moved on, fat with profit. There was no need for new attractions or better help. Damon had created something, a compulsion built from human greed and Olympian power. It was unnatural, familiar, and chaotic, and it was what had climbed into her head and torn her binding apart.

Screams fell from the sky as a spinning metal cage plummeted down. It caught and swooped away at the last moment. The machine moaned, and two men stepped around the fence beneath it, dark eyes narrowing on her. Damon was the barker, charming and commanding. He didn't always need divine intervention to get others to do his bidding.

She bolted into the center of the path. The throng folded around her, tugging at her clothes, snagging the ends of her long hair. The men split up, having lost sight of her. She didn't see Damon, who would be taller than the crowd. He might not be steady enough to pursue her, but he'd been able to call for help. Her head pounded as her essence slithered out, overloading her human mind.

She needed to withdraw to a quiet place where she could unfold the shell, gently dismantle it so that it didn't wash away her own tender memories. She tripped. Her hands scraped the pavement before she regained her feet, and urgency filled her with new strength. Damon had killed Melanie Kimball and was engaged in something far more sinister. He would not allow Olivia to walk away with that knowledge. August would be able to do something. He stood on the periphery of the carnival, over Damon, and no sane man would let his mother's murderer go free. She just had to hold herself together a little longer.

A man lurched out in front of Olivia, the whites showing all around his kohl-lined eyes, his wide mouth stretched into a macabre grin. The momentum of the crowd propelled her into his arms, and his bony hands closed around hers.

"Darling, we can dance if you want to." His breath stank of hard liquor and tooth rot, and he emitted the sound of jangling metal as he moved.

"Release," she hissed, pushing him away. His hands flopped at his sides.

"I know what you are," he called after her, his voice full of wounded pride. "I'm Edwin the All-Seeing! I know."

She reached the office trailer. Shaking, she dragged herself up the grated metal steps and shouldered through the door. It was dark except for a reading light on August Kimball's desk. He dropped a clutch of papers.

"Miss Sarkis! Are you all right?"

She opened her mouth, then hesitated. Telling him one of his people had killed his mother would result in paralysis. She required action. "It's come to my attention that Damon has hurt some of your customers. Do you have security people?"

He closed his eyes but, to his credit, he responded immediately. "Of course. At the gates." He picked up his phone, weighing it in his right hand. "You're sure about this?"

"Yes."

August nodded, eyes unfocused. "I knew this would come back to bite us."

Olivia stilled. "You knew *what* would bite you?" She crossed the trailer and leaned on the desk, barely able to stay upright as her natures clashed inside her. "You knew about this and did nothing?"

"We had a few mentions of sexual harassment. Nothing formal . . ."

"I'm not talking about feeling up employees. I'm talking about murder." And about something far worse.

"Murder?" His thumb hovered over the call button. "Did you . . . did you see a body?"

A body. The carnival moved every other week. There wouldn't be any bodies, which would render human law enforcement impotent.

She could enact justice, or something like it. If Damon fled, she would forget her purpose as she pursued him. For the goddess she'd been, a giver and consumer of memory, the world was a place of swarming distraction. She needed him close when she completed her transformation.

"He's dangerous, Augie. I have proof." It wasn't quite a lie.

He hit the call button and raised the phone to his ear; then a series of lines drove across his forehead. His pale blue eyes rounded. His lips pursed.

"What did you call me?" he asked.

"Augie!" Damon's voice filled the room. Olivia jumped, the corner of the desk gouging her hip when she spun.

"Your mother's pet name for you, her autumnal child." Damon stood in the doorway, his hair wild, hands braced on either side of the doorjamb. "You know, I never would have expected an insurance company to send a mind reader."

"I'm not a mind reader." Walls collapsed inside her head.

Damon's dark eyes glittered. He walked slowly forward, grinning without humor. "Look, Augie, we've won ourselves a prize."

"You said you'd take care of her," Kimball huffed, his earlier hesitation gone. Stalling. He'd been stalling, keeping her there. "What are we supposed to do with her?"

"You can't do anything to me," she said. "My employer knows I'm here."

"Jesus!" Kimball clasped his hands to either side of his head. "I'm not hearing this! Get her out of here, Damon. Just . . . take care of things."

"I've been taking care of things for your family for years, August. When's the last time you contributed to this enterprise?" Damon clasped his hands before him and manufactured a mask of regret. "You're a contractor, Olivia, and freelancers are notoriously unreliable. It's such a shame you never showed."

The light leapt and spun just before the lamp slammed against the back of her head. Olivia collapsed.

HER SHIRT SMELLED of honeysuckle and wax, and the poorly sewn seams chafed her sides. It did not belong to her. She sat cross-legged on a low bench in a small room. The walls and ceiling were draped in dusty black velvet. The cuff encircling her left ankle was attached by a locked chain to a hook behind the curtain. It wasn't the lock that bothered her; it was the cuff. She toyed with it, fingertips tracing the hinge as she wondered at the energy that sprang off of it, stinging nips that warned of large teeth. She had large teeth, too, but she hadn't used them in a long time and they were forbidden in this place.

A couple pushed through the curtain and blinked in the dim light. Sweat marks rusted the man's white shirt beneath his arms, and his dark hair plugs hadn't yet settled the way the clinic had promised. The woman had a heart-shaped face and soft, ash-blond hair. She crept forward in ballet flats and perched on the edge of the tall baroque chair.

"So you're the fortune-teller." The man sneered. "Olivia the All-Seeing?"

Olivia. The name wasn't quite right, but it didn't matter. She had a job to do and this was part of it. "Yes," she said. "Please, sit." She gestured, the bangles on her wrist chiming, disguising the sound of the chain as she slipped her legs beneath the table. The man flopped back in the other throne and tapped his foot.

"How does this work?" the woman asked.

"Ask your questions." Olivia smiled. The man's leg stopped moving and his gaze roved her upper body.

The woman cleared her throat. "Well, our son James—"

"No need to tell her his name." The man forced a chuckle. "She knows it already."

"Oh, don't mind him." The woman's smile was acidic. Olivia tilted her head and sifted through memories: action in the periphery, overheard telephone conversations, the things the couple saw clearly but chose to decipher in a way that did not threaten the lives they'd built.

"You wonder if he's using drugs." The couple shared an uneasy look. Olivia delved further, sampling other memories. "James occasionally smokes marijuana with his friends. It's a matter of fitting in, not of addiction. You should be more concerned with his treatment of the two boys who live at the end of the block." The scenes took shape, and a name crystallized on her tongue. "The McGilroys."

The man lurched upright. "This is bullshit." His teeth ground together. "You've phished us or something."

His face grew redder as his voice rose. A vein protruded on the side of his forehead. Spittle flew from his mouth. The woman bowed her head and systematically assembled a mental shopping list for Tuesday's luncheon. Olivia wondered what day it was, if it was not Tuesday. She was supposed to be somewhere. *Nashville on Wednesday, Louisville on Thursday. Back to Phoenix in the morning.* Phoenix, such a name for a town.

Damon slipped through the curtains, sleek as a dagger. He had a warm smile for the woman, a concerned furrowing of the brow for the man. He captured their attention, commiserated, then pacified them. They went away after a while.

Olivia's eyelids grew heavy and she lay back on the soft pillows. Her mind bobbed idly, a drifting vessel. Damon returned and stood over her, silent for several minutes.

"Olivia," he said. His gaze fell on her hands, resting on her stomach. "What did you get?"

"He'll sell pieces of his father's company at the end of the quarter."

"Which pieces?" Damon sat beside her, his weight dipping the bench and rolling her a little toward him. He looked like someone she should fancy. He'd told her that all she had to do was take moments from the people he sent, and he would give her a good life. It didn't seem like a good life should involve shackling. Her eyes were gritty. This was the dry season in this place, on this plane. She blinked.

"The wholesale operations. He believes the future is in supply chain management, not sales of objects."

"You've done well, sweetheart. I never expected . . . never hoped you would do this well." He paused, switching mental tracks. His eyes sparked, that glimmer that wasn't a reflection of light. "My grandmother taught me the old ways, to respect the gods that once made Greece a great empire. Even after they left the world, my family kept up the rituals. The sacrifices. We were rewarded with luck, easy charm. But I never dreamed I would come face-to-face . . . that I would have one of my own. Which of them do you follow? Are you like Artemis, or Aphrodite?"

More like them than him, she supposed. "Yes."

His shoulders dropped, releasing tension. He lifted her hand and placed it in his. "I knew it. You're a descendant, like me. Not as powerful as they were back in the day, but together we can do something incredible. Go somewhere bigger than this place. You like to make me happy, don't you, Olivia?"

She nodded.

When he spoke, she surged with devotion, but the feeling was thin, too strong, artificially sweet. When he left her, the devotion faded, replaced by real anger.

Damon smiled, the expression both warm and wanting. Her head crunched, and then something cold trickled into it, soothing away the pain. Olivia smiled back. He leaned down until his lips brushed hers. She opened her mouth—and bit him.

He shoved her back and his hand flew up. But he did not strike her. Instead he backed out of the room, lips parted while blood dripped down his chin.

* * *

SHE FOUND THINGS.

    Lost keys.

    Lost rings.

    Lost purposes.

    To strangers she repeated the things they'd told themselves for years, and they took it for advice. She plucked information and handed it to Damon. The power he channeled surrounded her. It wasn't his own, merely borrowed, but it shrouded her like a garment made of ether and absinthe, keeping her mind fuzzy, her body weak. It did not touch the other part of her, which grew daily.

    She lived in the curtained room and woke each evening to find grease rubbed into the skin over her heart. The flesh of her ankle wore away under the cuff. Her tooth ached, and that made her homesick for . . . somewhere. She didn't recall the place, just knew it existed elsewhere, where instead of a distant sky she looked straight into the stars, and they were her brothers and sisters.

    "BUT IT'S A good screenplay," the young man said. Thick brown hair flopped over his eyes.

    "It's a *great* screenplay, baby." His girlfriend snapped her gum.

    "It's already getting buzz, but I want to know if it's going to go anywhere. If it's going to get made." He fingered his bangs, then touched a leather bracelet on his left wrist as he said, loudly, "I'm not in it for the money."

    "Michael Mann would be great for it." The girl flung a leg over the chair arm and banged the heel of her boot against the side.

    "It's a little more artistic than that, babe. Gondry could handle it, maybe." He squinted at Olivia. "So, what do you see in my future?"

She saw nothing in his future, nor in anyone's future. His past contained a clear break. One day he'd changed friends, changed cities, and discarded his family like outgrown clothes. Once he'd dated a girl—not this one—who'd lost an eye in a dart accident, and whose glass eye was prettier than her real one. She was pregnant when he left. But he hadn't asked about that, and besides, Olivia wasn't interested in him.

The screenwriter was white noise beside his girlfriend with the red pixie cut and massive black boots. The girl was opaque, either empty of memories or able to block Olivia. That was new, and after the parade of minds she'd handled, new was intriguing.

"I'm fucking starving here, all-seeing Olivia. Give my man an answer already so he'll buy me a taco. There's a great place just down the road."

"It's not going to sell," Olivia murmured, barely able to hear herself over a rush of noise filling her head.

"I knew it. This is such a scam!" The screenwriter stood and stabbed a finger at his girlfriend. "I can't believe you talked me into wasting my time on this shit. Let's go." He stomped away.

"Way to let him down easy," the girl said. She stretched with a squeak and a gusty sigh. "Don't you want to go, too, Olivia?" She winked and disappeared through the curtains.

The back of Olivia's neck turned cold, and gooseflesh stampeded over her body. She stood. Her legs shook, from fatigue and the searing pain radiating around the cuff. The cold ran down her back, then wrapped around her middle, the arms of a frozen lover. It filled her with strength and a terrible sense of purpose. There was something she was supposed to do.

She raised the hem of her loose skirt and watched the path of the change moving through her. The red ooze around the cuff on her ankle paled and calmed. The skin flaked off, leaving smooth, tan flesh behind. She walked until the cuff caught and the chain stretched taut behind her, then kept moving. The hook broke free with a pinging snap.

The heavy curtains parted, giving her access to a short tunnel. Five even paces and she stepped onto a patch of packed dirt and breathed in the scent of humanity. Food and cigarette smoke, sweet perfume and sour sweat. She angled her head and met the eyes of a short man in a blue vest that said *K&S* in gold script. The cigarette fell from his mouth.

She reached a hand into her blouse and ran it through the patch of grease over her breast. It seeped into the seams of her fingerprint, warmer than her body. She raised it to her tongue. Underneath the harsh petroleum and bitter synthetics, she tasted blood and bone and marrow, hope and desperation. It was the taste of sacrifice.

Damon had begged help from the gods and one had answered. The flavor of the power was familiar, bringing to mind the millennia she had endured the requests and demands of the Olympians. As if she owed them for retrieving her from the prison into which they had cast her even though she had not used her strength against them. The grease on her fingertips caught fire and she blew it out. She couldn't quite put a face to the essence, but that was not her concern right now.

Damon had received a token favor and then wanted more. When she arrived, he had been channeling enough power to capture and enthrall her, which, even weakened as she was, was no small feat. She felt his offering even now. It lingered, open and waiting for all takers.

It had been a long time since Mnemosyne had received a sacrifice. No, not Mnemosyne. Olivia. She had chosen to be Olivia.

She drifted across a gravel aisle and slipped behind a man settling children into the car of a sprawling machine. All around, humans stood in lines, their eyes glazed. Waiting. Grease oozed along the center beam of the ride. She sank her hand into it and called in the tithe. It filled her, a tribute freely given but still full of pain. And beneath that, seeping from the machine itself, a profound sense of sadness. She dragged her fingers down her face, painting slick streaks from hairline to jaw. Damon had wanted the full attention of a god. She would give it to him. She would also give the carnival what it desired.

All around, people rubbed at their eyes and murmured to their companions as they woke from the barker's compulsion. Her power expanded, waving hazy fronds through their minds. The roar of voices—of feelings, expectations, and dreams—crashed over her. Her chain clanged musically against the metal gate, one link at a time, as she walked away from the machine.

She searched, focusing on memories of a tall, slim man with jet-black eyes.

Damon always pays for the drinks. That's enough for me.

Nobody else will let me work for them, not with this record. I owe the man, no matter what fucked-up shit he's into.

We're bringing in half the crowd and getting paid twice as much. I don't care how he does it.

I can't believe I gotta disturb him the one time he says not to be disturbed, but he's got a stone cold hard-on for that chick. He said he'd be at the warehouse.

Olivia turned in place until she spotted the top of the structure in the man's memory. Even set back from the carnival grounds, it towered over the low vending stands. She walked, reveling in the feel of her newly recovered powers as they stretched and constricted, altering to fit inside her chosen form.

She was Olivia Sarkis, and she was the goddess of memory. The years she'd spent learning the restrictions of a human mind now allowed her to function in a crowd, and just enough of the binding remained to dull the flood of sensation.

She'd always been useless in battle, relegated to the sidelines. She had waited behind Cronus when he fought his son, had not raised a hand as she was led into her cell in Tartarus. There she had drifted for years in a flood of screaming misery, bald hatred, and the searing loneliness of the elder gods. It didn't matter that she was a Titan; she'd never been able to focus enough to resist, to fight. Now, though her body was only human, she could.

Damon, through the powers he'd been granted in exchange for his sacrifices, had imprisoned her again. Such tender arrogance.

The lane ended at the Funhouse of Horrors. Chemical smoke billowed from it and menacing, tinny laughter boomed from the jagged, saggy maw of the entrance. Three girls crept up the steps, giggling, while the rest of the crowd turned down another aisle. Olivia strode past the building. The girls looked down at her and shrieked delightedly.

Behind the Funhouse was a bare field. Across it, a building stood alone and unlit, backed up to a dark stand of tall trees. A white door hung ajar on the side, and Olivia slipped through it. The sound of the dragging chain echoed in the large space.

Thirty-foot recreational vehicles, windows papered with sales sheets, and plastic-shrouded pleasure boats on detached trailers filled the center of the building, surrounded by dust. Surplus that couldn't be moved in the bad economy. The owner of these things had stored them, patiently waiting for a better day. Damon, fueled by avarice, was incapable of patience.

Bitter smoke hung low and heavy in the air. The scent of fresh blood assailed her nose, bringing with it the image of the all-seeing Edwin, banging the side of his head against a set of bars over and over and over again.

"I know. I know who you are," Edwin mumbled from nearby, his voice eerily detached.

"And what do we think we're doing, sweetheart? Couldn't

stand to be away from me?" Damon asked, walking out from behind one of the behemoth vehicles. He wiped his hands on a dark cloth. The light from his phone shone through the fabric of his pants. She strode toward him and he froze for a moment before laughing. The sound rippled through the dim space. "How did you get loose? Convince one of your customers to break you out?"

"You tried to make a whore of me," Olivia said.

"No." He was uncertain now. "I would never treat you badly. You know that." His eyes trailed down her body, his brow furrowing when he took in the slick streaks on her face, the smooth skin of her ankle. A puckered line ran parallel to his bottom lip from where she had bitten him. His throat bobbed as he swallowed.

"You treated me very badly," she said. "You took me. You bound me and made me steal for you. But I wasn't the greatest of your crimes." She forced her way into his mind, and he staggered back against the flat side of a slate blue camper.

"Phoenix," Olivia said, plucking the memories from him, "was a blonde with a toe ring. Clarissa. Las Cruces was the drunk woman whose friend didn't want her to go with you. Lani. Lubbock was a sixteen-year-old." She stopped in front of him. "You were her first kiss, Damon. And then there was Melanie, who wished to run her business the old way, and it wasn't enough for you."

The rag landed on the ground in a wet heap. He stared at her as though she were some alien being. That was nearly accurate. His hand latched onto her hip and his fingers dug in.

He leaned forward until his breath stirred her hair. "You *are* good. Much better than Edwin." Somewhere in the dark, the man moaned. "So good, in fact, that I no longer need him." The smoke had a meaty edge. The false mind reader was bleeding, fueling a fresh offering.

"Why not let him go? I've given you information that can earn you much money."

"You've tried." His other hand closed around her wrist. He moved forward, forcing her back. "But rich people, important people, don't come to the goddamn carnival. And that's what I need for the type of money I want. I truly do have the favor of the gods, you see. They've granted me eternal life. I just have to finance it."

"I won't aid you any further." She had started to turn when he shoved her. The flat of his hand struck the center of her chest and snapped the air from her lungs. Her head cracked against cement and her left leg flared with pain. He'd stepped on the chain, keeping her foot in place, and bones broke when she fell. In the rafters, birds took flight, wings beating as they circled, frantic for a way out.

Her breath came harsh and fast. "I won't give you anything else. You'll be on your own. All alone, actually. Your gods? They're done with you."

"I feed them! Nobody else can worship them like I can. I'm their favorite son. They need me." He kicked her. Her still-human body cracked down the side, and she cried out. He knelt beside her and his hands wrapped around her throat, hot and strong. Stars burned in the black depths of his eyes, and she stared back at him while he killed her, there on the cold stone floor.

"LITTLE DRAMATIC, DON'T you think?" Thalia asked.

Olivia opened her eyes. She extracted herself from Damon's new memory. When she stood, her hair fell in smooth ripples down to her waist.

"Oh, he's so confused." Thalia frowned, then held something up. "Dog of corn?"

"Thank you," Olivia said, "but no."

Damon leaned over the avatar she'd left behind. The dead avatar. Olivia squinted, trying to discern what he was doing.

"He's checking to see if you're still breathing. Aww," Thalia said around a mouthful, "I think he's regretting murdering you."

"This memory will replay inside his mind for the rest of his days." Olivia stretched, testing her leg. It was whole. "I closed his offering. Soon he will discover that he is no longer special. Also he'll be out of money. It will drive him mad, knowing he snuffed out his chance at greatness and immortality."

"Oy! When are humans going to learn that immortality thing never pans out?" Thalia looked her over. "Still, that's a little harsh, Lady."

"Justice is not my purview, but I believe he earned it. August Kimball will be bankrupt in weeks without Damon's help. That will be sufficient to break a man like him. Help me free this other one." Olivia turned away as Damon began to moan, an incoherent sound of grief. She moved between the large, boxy rigs, following the smoke and sound of mumbling.

"Eww," Thalia said, tilting her chin toward Edwin. "What's he doing?"

"Being roasted alive, as a tribute. Whatever is left of the tribute after the ritual will be blessed. The barker was mixing remains with the grease he used to lubricate the machines, imbuing the substance with a charm that lured humans and their money."

"You know, pyramid schemes get a bad rap, but they're way more hygienic than this."

Edwin sat in a cage resting on two barrels. The bare skin of his chest and arms was crossed with lacerations, scrawls rather than proper symbols, but in matters of sacrifice intent meant more than accuracy. Small fires burned in the barrels, musky with herbs, and his blood dripped steadily down, hissing when it met flame. Piles of broken boards and a bottle of lighter fluid sat nearby.

The man hurt, and Olivia felt satisfaction at the idea of being useful, of saving him from what would have been much greater pain. In the distance, the low fog of grief that had hung over the carnival began to lift.

"I know who you are," Edwin croaked.

"That's nice."

"I won't tell."

"Doesn't matter if you do," Thalia chimed in. "You're a pedigreed loon. Nobody will believe you."

"Oh." His face fell. He'd had some talent, just enough to addle him. Then, when he drank to quiet his fears, his talent had dried up. "I wouldn't tell anyway."

Olivia plucked the cage off the barrels and cracked the lock. Edwin watched her out of suddenly wary eyes. "What are you?"

"I thought you knew." She glanced at Thalia. "A distraction, please."

The Muse shrugged, tossed her corn dog away, and raised her shirt. She wore nothing beneath. Edwin gasped and leaned forward against the bars of the cage. Olivia ran her hands over his arms and chest. The wounds sealed, leaving behind small, pink welts. His memories of the event she plucked neatly from his sloppy mind. Thalia dropped her shirt and Edwin slumped back, panting.

They left him just outside the door, left Damon as he stumbled in circles, pulling at his hair. They walked into the cool night air. In the distance the rides, now mostly empty, leapt and spun. Melanie Kimball had loved her business and had remained with it, her own essence trapped in the sacrifice Damon had made of her, until it could be set right.

Olivia looked Thalia over. "You came back for me," she said.

Thalia jammed her hands into her pockets and shrugged. "Well, you know, I was in the area. And it's not every day a lowly Muse gets to rescue an elder god."

"It's not every day I get to see my daughter. I've missed you."

The girl flushed and broke out in a grin.

"Where's your screenwriter?"

"Dumped me. And with me went all the inspiration he'll ever have." Thalia sighed, then raised her hand and shook a set of keys. "As well as his economy-size sedan."

"This body is hungry."

"That, Lady, is more disconcerting than referring to yourself in third person." Thalia skipped along beside her. "I'm craving oysters and hush puppies."

"Where are we?"

"West Virginia, I think. Or East Virginia."

"It's just Virginia. West Virginia and Virginia."

"That makes no sense." Thalia poked her arm. "You're still solid, so we'll have to drive. We can be there by tomorrow if we don't stop for pee breaks. How long can a goddess hold it?"

"Let's eat nearby. I need you to take me back."

Thalia stopped, actually going pale. "You're coming home?"

"It was never my home, and I will stay only a short while. That man made a paltry offering, and one of us stooped to honor it. I will speak with whoever that was."

"Times have been tough," Thalia said, jogging to catch up. "A bunch of them are here now, gathering new followers. They'll do anything, stuff you wouldn't believe. They're intercepting prayers not even directed at them. Frankly, it's embarrassing. But this is awesome! So you're coming back to Olympus, and you're going to go all bad mother—"

Olivia grinned. "Shut your mouth."

"Parlor Tricks"

AN ELEMENTAL ASSASSIN SHORT STORY

Jennifer Estep

"A carnival? Really?"

Detective Bria Coolidge looked at me. "You don't like carnivals?"

"Not particularly," I said. "There are already enough people around here looking to con you without you having to actually pay for the privilege."

Bria rolled her eyes. "That's just a stereotype. Not all carnivals are looking to cheat folks."

"I know that," I said. "But I also know that this is Ashland. So if there was any place for a carnival to be crooked, this would be it."

Bria didn't answer me. She knew as well as I did that corruption was a way of life in our sprawling southern city, along with violence, magic, avarice, and greed. Cheating, beating, and even murdering your enemies wouldn't get you jail time in Ashland so much as applause, admiration, and respect—and someone immediately plotting to take you down the same way you had your enemies.

My baby sister and I stood at the entrance to the Ashland Fairgrounds, a wide, grassy clearing that was nestled in among the Appalachian Mountains, which ran through and around the city. Tree-covered ridges towered over the clearing, giving the landscape a bowl-like shape. The fairgrounds hosted a variety of events throughout the year, everything from livestock shows to sporting events to camps for kids. On this warm June evening, it was the site of *The Carnival of Wondrous Wonders!* At least, that's what the banner stretched above the entrance said.

Bria had parked her sedan in the gravel lot, and we'd eased into the stream of people heading for the white picket fence that cordoned off the clearing. Most of the other carnival goers were families with small kids or sullen teenagers looking to escape from Mom and Dad's watchful eyes for a few hours. Bria looked a little out of place with her jeans, her blue button-up shirt, and the gold detective's badge glinting on her belt, right next to her holstered gun. So did I with my boots, jeans, and long-sleeved black T-shirt.

"Well, look at it this way," Bria said in a cheery voice. "The odds of anyone here knowing you are pretty slim. If nothing else, you can just relax and not have to worry about anyone trying to kill you tonight."

Heh. I wouldn't count on it.

By day, I was Gin Blanco, owner of the Pork Pit barbecue restaurant. By night, in the shadows, I was the Spider, Ashland's most notorious assassin. Actually, I suppose these days I was more infamous than notorious, since most of the underworld thought—or at least suspected—that I was the Spider, the woman who'd killed powerful Fire elemental Mab Monroe back in the winter. As a result, many of the crime lords and ladies had sent men after me, trying to take me out, these past few months. With Mab's death, all of the underworld movers and shakers were grappling for power, and some of them thought that murdering the Spider would go a long way toward cementing their position as the city's new head honcho.

"Gin?"

"Okay, okay," I grumbled. "You're right about that. I doubt any of the crime bosses and their goons will be here tonight."

A country-fried clown wearing blue-and-white gingham coveralls, a blue shirt, and brown boots that were about five sizes too big waddled over to us. Bits of straw stuck out of the pockets of his coveralls, while a battered straw hat was perched on top of his curly red wig. White pancake makeup covered his face, although it had started to run in the heat. His painted-on, oversize red lips were curled up into a garish grin, although red and blue tears also covered his face, as though he didn't know whether he wanted to laugh or cry. I'd definitely cry if I had to walk around in that getup. Or kill the person who'd made me wear it. That would definitely turn my frown upside down.

Bria smiled at him, which the clown took as an invitation to dance around us, mock-tripping over his enormous boots. Finally, he reached inside his coveralls. I tensed, ready to tackle him if he came up with a weapon, but he was only going for a red balloon stashed away among the straw. He spent the better part of two minutes not-so-comically huffing and puffing, trying to blow it up, before he eventually succeeded. Then he danced around us again and started twisting the balloon into a man. When he was finished, the clown sidled up to me, probably hoping to get me to smile and laugh like Bria was.

"Go away," I growled. "Or you'll be crying real tears when I make you eat that balloon."

The clown frowned, not quite sure whether I was joking, but I let the coldness seep into my gray eyes, and he got the message. He tucked his balloon man under his arm and quickly scurried away from me.

"Did you have to do that?" Bria asked, exasperation creeping into her light voice. "He's a clown. He was just trying to do his job and entertain you."

"No, I didn't have to do that, but I don't like clowns."

"Is there anything about carnivals that you *do* like?"

I thought about it, then brightened. "Corn dogs. If they're not too greasy."

Bria shook her head.

"Look, I'm sorry. But when you said that you wanted me to help you with something, I didn't expect this. Why are we here anyway?"

"Because I got a report about a missing girl, and this is the last place she was seen." Bria reached into the back pocket of her jeans, drew out a photo, and handed it to me. "Her name's Elizabeth Robbins. Sixteen. Parents died in a car wreck six months ago. She lives with her aunt, Fran, who's one of the police department dispatchers. Fran said she dropped Elizabeth off here with some friends last night. The friends and Elizabeth got separated, and no one's seen her since."

"What else does Fran say?"

"She says that Elizabeth's been acting out a little lately, cutting classes, things like that," Bria replied. "But she says that Elizabeth always checks in and lets Fran know where she is and that it's not like her to just disappear."

"I'm guessing your fellow boys in blue weren't too concerned about a missing girl," I said. "At least, not one who isn't related to someone wealthy and important, even if her aunt does work for the police department. They probably labeled her a runaway."

She nodded. "You know it."

Like almost every other institution in Ashland, the police department had more than its share of corruption. Most members of the po-po took bribes to look the other way, but my sister was one of the few good, honest cops on the force.

I stared at the photo. Elizabeth Robbins was a pretty girl. In fact, with her blond hair and blue eyes, she looked a lot like Bria. She was even wearing a necklace, the way Bria always did, although Elizabeth's was a small diamond heart rather than Bria's silverstone primrose rune. But the camera had captured the tightness in her young features and the shadows that clouded her gaze. This was a girl who was still grieving for her parents. I knew the feeling, since my mother and older sister had also died when I was young.

I started to hand the picture back to Bria, but she shook her head.

"Keep it. I have a copy." She reached into her back pocket and drew out another photo.

I arched an eyebrow. "So you knew that I'd help you after you showed me her picture. Have I ever told you how much you excel at emotional manipulation?"

Bria grinned.

"Well, let's get started," I said. "Before that clown comes back."

WE SPENT THE next hour roaming from one side of the fairgrounds to the other, looking at all of the carnival attractions. Game booths, concession stands, a Ferris wheel, and other spinning, whirling rides lined either side of a long thoroughfare. Smaller paths branched off the main drag and led to other areas, including a house of mirrors, a tent where a magician did tricks, and a petting zoo. Like the clown, everything had a southern feel to it, from the boiled and roasted peanuts sold in the concession stands, to the slow, twangy drawls of the carnival workers, to the Mountain High roller coaster, which, really, wasn't more than ridge-high in these parts.

But the carnival really did have some wondrous wonders, thanks to all the magic users on staff. Fire elementals made flames shoot out of their fingertips before forming balls out of the flickering Fire and then juggling them. Crowds of kids squealed with excitement as an Air elemental took a group of colorful animal balloons and made the creatures float up and down and do loop-the-loops in the breeze, as though the plastic blue and pink bears, lions, and tigers were engaged in old-fashioned aerial combat. Dwarven and giant strongmen and strongwomen hefted miniature cars full of carousing clowns over their heads. There was even a drinking contest for vampires to see who in the crowd could down the most pints of blood in two minutes. The winner got a giant stuffed bat.

I let Bria take the lead. She showed the missing girl's picture to the carnival workers, but they all shook their heads and said they didn't remember seeing Elizabeth. Nothing unusual there. It was Friday night, and the carnival grew more crowded by the minute. The workers were all rushing to get folks their food, get them on the rides, and get them involved in—and shelling out dollars for— the games.

But the more people Bria asked about the girl, the more convinced I became that something was wrong.

For one thing, everyone was too damn *friendly*. Instead of being pissed that Bria was interrupting them, they all smiled and politely nodded at her. Sure, she was a detective, but they had customers to see to and money to make. They should have been more upset that she was cutting into their profit margins. Then there was the fact that staff members were passing signals to each other. As soon as Bria started to move on to the next booth, the worker she'd left behind would either pull out his cell phone and text something on it or make a hand gesture to another carnival member standing nearby. Now, that could have been standard stuff: Be nice to the po-po or anyone else asking questions, but warn each other all the same. Still, the most telling thing was the way all the workers' eyes slid away from the photo and how the smiles dropped from their faces the second Bria turned her back to them.

Oh, yes. Something was *definitely* wrong here.

Bria finished talking to the vampire running the ring toss. He moved off to give some metal rings to a group of kids to throw at the poles that were the targets. She watched him for a few seconds, then turned to me.

"Do you get the feeling all these folks know more than they're telling?" she asked in a low voice.

"Absolutely," I replied. "Not to mention the fact that they're all watching us."

Bria's eyes cut left and right as we walked down the thoroughfare. Her face tightened as she noticed all the furtive looks that came our way from the workers, especially since they stared at her more than they did me, their features dark, troubled, and twisted with fear. I wondered if it was because of the badge on her belt or for some other reason. Maybe they were nervous because she was a cop. Or maybe they were worried she'd figure out what happened to Elizabeth Robbins—and their part in it.

Either way, Bria kept showing the girl's picture and asking about her. I watched my sister's back, ready to reach for one of the five silverstone knives I had on me—two up my sleeves, one against the small of my back, and two in my boots. My weapons of choice as the Spider. But everybody remained just as sugary-sweet as the candy cotton they were selling, and no one made any sinister moves. Still, I thought it was just a matter of time before someone tried something—and I would be ready for them when they did.

Finally, around nine o'clock, a bugle sounded, and everyone headed toward the center of the fairgrounds, where a series of wooden bleachers had been arranged around a circular stage. Bria grabbed one of the pink fliers the country clowns had been passing out, and she read through the colorful, splashy type.

"It says this is the main show," she said as we climbed to the top row. "And that we should be prepared to be awed and amazed."

"Awed and amazed. Check."

We sat down, and the red-, blue-, and green-tinged spotlights focused on the stage dimmed, and shadows fell over the fairgrounds, causing the crowd to slowly hush. A lone white light snapped on, highlighting the center of the stage. A low drumroll rang out, slowly growing louder and louder until my brain pounded from the ominous sound—

BANG!

The sharp, sudden explosion was even louder than the thunderous drumroll, and the noise reverberated through the fairgrounds, echoing up the ridges that surrounded the clearing and back down again. For a moment, everything went dark, making more than a few folks scream in surprise. Then the lone spotlight snapped back on. Pale green smoke billowed up into the starry night sky, and a woman appeared in the middle of the stage to the strains of triumphant music.

Ta-da.

The woman wore a short red ringmaster's coat over a ruffled white silk shirt and black satin short-shorts. Black tights encased her lean, long legs, while a pair of black stiletto boots gave her a few more inches of height. She bowed low, removing her tall black top hat and showing off her hair, which was a rich strawberry blond and piled on top of her head in an artful array of soft curls.

"I thought this was a carnival, not a circus," I muttered to Bria.

"Shhh."

The woman straightened up. She waved her hand, and a summer breeze gusted through the clearing, whipping away all the wispy strands of green smoke that were hovering over the stage. So she was an Air elemental, then—a strong one, judging from the sharp burst of power I felt rolling off her. I was an elemental myself, gifted with Ice and Stone magic. Since my elements were the opposite of hers, the woman's Air power felt like invisible needles stabbing into my skin. Her magic also made the scars embedded in my palms itch and burn. Each of the marks was shaped like a small circle surrounded by eight thin rays—a spider rune, my rune, the symbol for patience. Something I would need a lot of if this show was as cheesy and over-the-top as the rest of the carnival.

I shifted in my seat, trying to get away from the uncomfortable sensation of the other elemental's power, although I knew that it would vanish as soon as she quit using her magic. Beside me, Bria did the same thing, since she had Ice magic as well. She didn't like the feel of Air power any more than I did.

"Greetings, kind friends!" the woman proclaimed in a voice that was almost as loud as the smoke explosion had been. "I am Esmeralda the Amazing, and I'm here to welcome you to our wonderful carnival!"

The crowd politely clapped. Esmeralda beamed and bowed low again, accepting the applause.

"And now," she purred, "be prepared to be awed . . . and amazed!"

Zippy, cartoonish music blared to life, and the colorful spotlights zoomed this way and that as a variety of performers ran, tumbled, cartwheeled, and took pratfalls across the stage. For the next half hour, Esmeralda narrated the action as carnival members performed trick after trick. Clowns goofed off and tried to escape from the strongmen and -women who tossed them back and forth like rag dolls. Acrobats tumble-tumble-tumbled before forming swaying human pyramids, while a guy coaxed a black bear to roll back and forth on top of an oversize red ball embossed with white stars. There was even a woman dressed up like a superhero— Karma Girl, I think—who got shot out of a cannon.

All around me, folks laughed and cheered and clapped and

whistled. But I tuned out the cacophony and looked past the bright lights and blur of movement onstage. One by one, my eyes scanned the shadows and all the workers behind the scenes manning the lights, sound system, smoke cannons, and all the other things that went into such a production.

I wondered if *this* was where Elizabeth had been taken.

It would be easy to snatch someone out of the crowd. With night already settled in, and all the spotlights focused on the stage, deep, dark shadows surrounded the bleachers. All you'd have to do was wait for someone to get up to go get a drink or snack, follow them under the bleachers, and either rob, murder, or spirit them off to parts unknown. Since Elizabeth's body hadn't been found, I was assuming whoever had grabbed her had gone with the third option.

I wondered what they'd wanted with the girl. Lots of terrible things happened in Ashland on a daily basis. Beatings, robberies, murders. Maybe Elizabeth had caught the eye of an unsavory character. Maybe someone had tried to mug her and she'd fought back. Maybe she'd seen something she shouldn't have. Any one of those or a dozen other scenarios could have taken place, and I had no way of knowing which one.

The only thing I did know was that *something* was going on at this so-called Carnival of Wondrous Wonders. The workers had all been too polite to Bria and too prepared to say that they hadn't seen anything at all, almost like they'd been expecting those very types of questions about a missing girl. In fact, the whole thing seemed like a drill they'd gone through many times before, right down to their quick, pat denials.

Finally, the clowns, the dancing bear, and the other performers left the stage, leaving Esmeralda alone once more.

"And now for our final performance of the evening," she said.

The stage went dark. The bombastic music swelled for a few

seconds before giving way to that low, booming drumroll. The lights dimmed again, then—

BANG!

"The Wheel of Death!" Esmeralda called out.

A spotlight snapped on, highlighting a large white wheel with four spokes on it, two at the top and two at the bottom. The crowd oohed and aahed right on cue.

Esmeralda held out her hand, and another spotlight lit up the stage. "Please welcome Arturo the Most Magnificent Bladesman!"

BANG!

More noise, more smoke, more theatrics. Esmeralda used another blast of her Air magic to sweep the smoke away, and a man appeared in the second spotlight—a giant who was almost seven feet tall, with slicked-back black hair and a long, drooping black mustache that curled up at the ends. He was dressed in a sleeveless green silk shirt and black pants, but the most interesting thing about him was the black leather sash he had slung over his wide, muscular chest—one that practically bristled with knives.

I perked up. I liked knives.

Bria noticed my sudden interest in the show. I couldn't hear above the crowd noise, but I thought she snorted, either in disgust or amusement. I wasn't sure which one.

"And now, ladies and gentlemen," Esmeralda proclaimed, "watch in awe and wonder as I brave the Wheel of Death!"

The crowd oohed and aahed some more as Arturo took Esmeralda's arm and escorted her over to the wheel. She threw her top hat into the crowd, blew everyone a kiss, then turned and put her back against the wheel. She reached up and grabbed the two spokes at the top while she rested her stiletto boots against the two spokes at the bottom, forming a star shape with her body. One of the clowns got back up onstage and started turning a hand crank to made the Wheel of Death go 'round and 'round.

Arturo and Esmeralda bantered back and forth for a minute before the giant pulled one of the knives from his sash. He used it to slice an apple that another clown handed to him, supposedly proving how razor-sharp the weapon was, then turned his attention to Esmeralda. Arturo held his knife out and frowned, his bushy black eyebrows drawing together in exaggerated concentration, as though this were the very first time he'd ever done his shtick.

Thunk!

A knife landed beside Esmeralda's right arm, inches away from her dainty wrist.

Thunk!

Another knife, this one close to her left wrist.

Thunk!

Thunk!

Two more knives, one on either side of her legs.

And on and on it went, the crowd gasping at every safe throw, until Arturo had used all the knives in his sash and the Wheel of Death looked more like a pincushion than the cheap plywood it was. Finally, the contraption stopped, and Esmeralda got off. This time she was the one who plucked a knife from the wood. She turned to face Arturo, and the crowd collectively sucked in an excited breath as folks realized what she was about to do. Esmeralda paused and furrowed her lovely brow with the same dramatic effect Arturo had used before, then threw the weapon at him.

The giant caught the knife between his teeth.

Ta-da.

I knew it was a trick, misdirection and sleight of hand, but I had to admit that they pulled it off well. I might have even believed it was real if I hadn't felt another gust of Esmeralda's Air magic sweep across the stage, blowing a bit of smoke over Arturo and obscuring him at just the right moment to help with the illusion.

She took Arturo's hand, and they both bowed low before—BANG!—disappearing in another puff of green smoke.

Everyone in the crowd surged to their feet, clapping, whistling, and cheering. Even I joined in and politely applauded.

"Don't tell me the Wheel of Death finally impressed you," Bria said as we trudged down the bleachers with everyone else.

"Parlor tricks are all well and good if flash is all you're going for," I said. "But we both know that I use my knives for more . . . practical purposes."

Bria snorted again, but she gestured at the stage. "Come on. Since it looks like Esmeralda is the big attraction around here, let's go see if she knows anything about Elizabeth."

"Don't hold your breath."

She shrugged. "If I ask enough people enough questions, somebody will let something slip. They always do."

I followed her to the stage. Esmeralda and Arturo had reappeared and were autographing carnival fliers and posing for pictures. Bria and I stood by and waited until they finished with their fans. I eyed the knives, which had been tucked back into Arturo's sash. They looked like decent blades, if a bit thin, but I could tell by the way the edges glinted that they were as sharp as he'd claimed them to be onstage. The giant himself was extremely muscular and showed off his enormous strength by picking up a couple of kids and bench-pressing them over his head, one in each hand, while their parents took pictures.

Finally, all the autographs had been signed, all the photos had been taken, and the crowd drifted away, leaving Esmeralda and Arturo alone together. My sister stepped up to them and plastered a polite smile on her face.

"Hi, I'm Detective Bria Coolidge with the Ashland Police Department. I was wondering if I might have a few moments of your time. . . ."

She told them about Elizabeth and showed them the missing girl's picture. Arturo gave it a cursory glance and shrugged, but Esmeralda took the photo from Bria and studied it carefully. Then she too shrugged and handed it back.

"Sorry, Detective," Esmeralda said. "I'm afraid I haven't seen her. As you can see, we get quite a few teenagers in here—hard for one of them to stand out. Why, we had such a large group from Cypress Mountain that they practically took over the whole fairgrounds a few nights ago."

Bria nodded. That was pretty much the same line that all of the other workers had given her, although it sounded much smoother and far more sincere coming from Esmeralda. She definitely knew how to sell her act.

The ringmaster looked at Bria and smiled. "But you, on the other hand, are quite striking. Has anyone ever told you what lovely skin you have? Why, it's practically *flawless.*"

"Um, thanks," Bria said.

Esmeralda kept staring at my sister, as though Bria were a sculpture she was admiring. Up close, I could see that the ringmaster was pretty flawless herself, actually. Her skin was as pale and smooth as freshly fallen snow. Rich red highlights shimmered in her blond hair, while her eyes were a dark hazel, with flecks of gold flashing in the whiskey-colored depths.

Arturo noticed his boss's interest in Bria, and he peered at my sister a little more closely before glancing at Esmeralda. He raised his eyebrows in a silent question. She winked at him, and he nodded.

The quick exchange made me wonder what they were up to. I tensed a little, once again ready to reach for one of my knives if Arturo came at us, but he turned and headed toward the main thoroughfare. I wondered where he was going, but I didn't follow him. Keeping Bria in my sights was much more important.

Esmeralda didn't say anything to me. In fact, she didn't so much as glance at me, but I was used to that. My dark chocolate-brown hair and gray eyes weren't nearly as striking as Bria's classic features.

Finally, Bria cleared her throat. "Anyway, thanks for your help. I appreciate it and how nice all your workers have been, taking the time to look at the photo."

Esmeralda waved her hand. Her long nails were the same bloodred as her jacket. "No problem at all, Detective. You look thirsty. Be sure to get something to eat and drink before you head home for the night. The carnival stays open until midnight. Tell Cathy that Em sent you and she'll give you a discount. I always like to help out local law enforcement. Why, it's just disgraceful, the poor salaries they pay such decent, honest, hardworking folks like you."

I had to bite my lip to keep from laughing. She obviously didn't know how corrupt the police were in Ashland. With all the bribes they took, crooked cops around here did just fine. Some of them even had mansions up in Northtown, the rich, fancy, highfalutin part of town.

"Thanks," Bria said, managing to keep her face smoother than mine. "We'll do that."

Esmeralda gave us another beaming smile and moved over to talk to one of the acrobats. But she kept her eyes fixed on Bria the whole time.

"Let's get out of here," I murmured to my sister.

"Yeah," Bria said. "This place is starting to weird me out."

"It's taken this long?"

She shrugged. We left the stage area and walked down the main drag back toward the entrance.

"Come on," Bria said. "I missed dinner, so we might as well eat before we go. I'm starving."

We got in line at one of the concession stands that bore the name *Cathy's Sweets*, although it looked like Cathy was serving up the usual carnival fare—burgers, fries, and all the greasy fixings in between. Smoke from the grill drifted out of the stand, mixing with the smells of sizzling meat, fresh-cut lemons, and cinnamon. I breathed in, enjoying the flavorful aromas, and my stomach rumbled in anticipation. Finally, it was our turn to order.

"What can I get you?" The woman behind the counter gave us a tired, uninterested look.

"I'll have a grilled chicken sandwich, onion rings, and a sweet iced tea," Bria said.

"And you?" The woman looked at me.

"Give me a lemonade, two corn dogs with spicy mustard, fries, a cinnamon-sugar pretzel, and a cone of cherry cotton candy," I replied.

Bria blanched a little at my choices, but she pulled some money out of her jeans pocket and handed it over the counter. A few minutes later, we sat down at a blue plastic picnic table to the right of the stand. Since the main show of the night was over, the crowd had thinned out quite a bit, and we were the only ones sitting in the shadows. I scanned the area. Once again I felt the eyes of the carnival workers on me, but since it didn't seem like any of them were going to be stupid enough to approach us, I took a sip of my lemonade, then picked up one of my corn dogs.

"Do you know how disgusting that is?" Bria asked, wrinkling her nose. "Not to mention what it's going to do to your heart and arteries."

"It's meat on a stick, batter-dipped and deep-fried," I said. "If Finn were here, he'd say that it was nature's perfect food."

My sister smiled at the mention of Finnegan Lane, who happened to be her significant other as well as my foster brother. "Yeah, well, Finn doesn't need to eat that stuff any more than you do."

Instead of answering her, I dipped the corn dog in the mustard and took a big bite of it. The spicy heat of the mustard tickled my tongue, while the cornmeal batter on the meat was crispy on the outside but soft and fluffy on the inside. I was as hungry as Bria was, and we both downed our food. I even managed to convince her to eat some of the pretzel and cotton candy. She grumbled about all the sugar going straight to her ass, but she sighed with contentment after she took the first bite of the light-as-air cotton candy.

"This was actually pretty good," Bria said when we finished.

She stood, grabbed her empty, greasy plates, and dumped them in a nearby trash can. She turned back to me and stopped, slapping at something on her neck. A second later, she crumpled to the ground.

"Bria? Bria!"

I leaped to my feet and started to go over to her, but something stung my arm. I looked down. A red-feathered dart stuck out of my bicep. I cursed and immediately yanked out the dart, even though I knew it was already too late.

"Damn . . . tranquilizer . . . guns," I mumbled as the realization of what happened flitted through my mind.

I whirled around, searching for my attacker, but everything was fuzzy and distorted, as though I were staring at it through one of those freaky carnival mirrors. Still, I stumbled forward, heading toward Bria so I could see whether she was still breathing. Even as I tried to get to her, I was aware of someone slinking through the shadows, moving closer and closer to us. I blinked and Arturo came into focus for a moment. The giant was holding a small gun in his beefy hand.

Esmeralda's voice drifted out of the darkness: "Get them out of sight. Quickly."

That bitch had Arturo drug us, probably with the same tranquilizers they used on the dancing bear. She was going to pay for that—in blood. Even as I tried to palm one of my knives to fight back, everything grew fuzzier than before.

The ground rushed up to meet my face. My eyes closed, and the world went black.

I WOKE UP with my neck twisted at an awkward angle. At first I thought that I was at home in bed, but then the night came rushing back to me. Carnival. Missing girl. Questioning the workers. Esmeralda and her Wheel of Death. The dart stinging my arm.

Since I didn't know where I was or who might be watching, I kept still, although I cracked my eyes open.

I was in a cage.

Someone had tossed me in a cage, although the bars were made of thick wood instead of metal. My body was sprawled across a bed of hay, which reeked of some animal, probably one of the goats from the petting zoo. The musty stench made my nose itch and twitch, but I held back my sneeze. Unconscious people did not sneeze.

I didn't hear any movement, so I risked opening my eyes a little more. It looked like I was in some sort of makeshift barn. Old, weathered boards formed the walls before arching up to create the roof. A few more wooden cages like the one I was in sat inside the building, but the rest of them were empty. Tools and other odds and ends covered the walls, and I spotted the dancing bear's big red ball slowly listing from side to side in the corner.

But the most important thing in the barn was Bria.

My sister was a few feet away from me, propped up in one of the clown cars. I watched her a few seconds. Her chest rose and fell with a steady rhythm, and some of my worry eased. She was still breathing, which meant that everything else that might have been done to her could be fixed. All I had to do was get us out of here.

Too bad I didn't have my knives to help me with that.

Arturo must have searched us, because I spotted my silver-stone knives sitting on a wooden table a few feet away from the clown car. Bria's gun and badge were also lying there—

A low moan sounded, and I slowly turned my head to the side. Elizabeth Robbins lay in another clown car off to my left.

She barely resembled the young, pretty girl in the photo Bria had given me. Her skin was waxy and gray, and her face had a hollow, gaunt, sunken look, as though she was on the verge of death. Her blond hair was matted, and large clumps of it had fallen out. The golden strands littered her slumped shoulders like the hay in my cage. The only reason I knew it was her was because she was wearing the same diamond heart necklace as in the photo Bria had shown me.

What the hell had happened to the girl? I didn't know, but I was going to get her and Bria out of here before things got any worse. I started to reach for my Ice magic to create a set of lockpicks so I could get out of my cage when the barn door opened and Esmeralda and Arturo stepped inside.

"I don't think this is a good idea," Arturo said as he hurried after the ringmaster. "I mean, this chick is a cop. Not some moody teenage girl."

"Are you kidding me? Did you not see her? She's *perfect*," Esmeralda said.

I kept my eyes open just wide enough to watch the ringmaster lean down and stare at my sister once more. She stroked Bria's cheek, lightly digging her nails into my sister's flesh.

"All that lovely, lovely skin," Esmeralda murmured, then clucked her tongue. "Youth truly is wasted on the young."

"But someone's sure to come looking for her," Arturo said. "Who knows how many people she told that she was coming here tonight? Not to mention all those knives that the other chick had

on her. You don't carry quality blades like that unless you know
how to use them. You're taking a big risk with them."

Esmeralda turned to glare at him with cold eyes. "And so are
you, for even *daring* to question me. So shut your mouth and lock
the door. It's time to get started. We need to be gone from here in
the morning."

Arturo stabbed his index finger at Elizabeth, who hadn't
stirred since letting out that one moan. "And what about her? I
thought you were going to drain her the rest of the way tonight."

Esmeralda shrugged. "Not now, not when I have such a fine
specimen here. Crack her skull open and dump her body in some
cave in the woods like you usually do. I don't care—just make sure
that she disappears. At least long enough for us to get out of town."

Drain her? What were they talking about? Esmeralda was an
elemental, not a vampire.

I got my answer a second later when Esmeralda crawled into
the clown car right next to Bria. She spent a few minutes fussing,
moving first one way, then the other, as though she needed to be as
comfortable as possible for whatever foul thing she was planning.
Finally, Esmeralda took Bria's hand, and her hazel eyes began to
glow with her Air magic.

And I watched while she took my sister's life and made it
her own.

The rosy, healthy flush in Bria's cheeks slowly faded away, replaced by a dull, sickly pallor, and her face started to take on the
same gaunt look that Elizabeth's had. Esmeralda sighed with contentment, and I realized that her skin was growing brighter,
warmer, almost as if she was taking the glow from Bria's cheeks
and putting it into her own.

My eyes narrowed. That's *exactly* what she was doing. My
friend Jolene "Jo-Jo" Deveraux was an Air elemental, one who used
her magic to heal folks. Jo-Jo grabbed hold of oxygen and all the

other natural gases in the air and used those molecules to clean wounds, restore vitality, and put ripped skin back together. Esmeralda had the same sort of power, only she was using her Air magic and all those molecules to pull Bria's health and well-being into her own body. Draining the life out of my sister like a vampire sucking someone dry of blood, until there would be nothing left of her and she would die.

I wondered how many girls she'd done this to over the years. The carnival was the perfect cover for something like this. No doubt Esmeralda had Arturo snatch up a girl or two at every town the carnival visited, drained them, disposed of their bodies, then packed up and moved on before anyone realized exactly what had happened. A nice little murderous scheme.

Well, it was going to stop—right now.

Arturo was busy watching Esmeralda, so he didn't see me wrap my hands around two of the wooden bars on my cage. Forget the lockpicks, and fuck being subtle. Not with these monsters. I reached for my Ice magic, letting the cool power bubble up from the deepest part of me. Cold silver lights flared, centered on the spider rune scars embedded in my palms, and I pushed the power outward. It took me only a second to completely coat the bars with an inch of elemental Ice, pushing it into all of the tiny holes and cracks in the wood.

Esmeralda must have sensed me using my magic, because her head turned in my direction. She realized that I was awake and trying to break free. She snapped her fingers at Arturo.

"Get her!" she hissed, tightening her grip on Bria's hand.

"Don't worry," I snarled. "I'm coming out."

I sent out a burst of magic, shattering the elemental Ice that had been driven deep into the wood. My cage bars snapped like matchsticks under my fingers.

Arturo hurried over to the cage, but I was quicker. I crawled out and stayed on the ground, waiting until he was in range. Then I lashed out with my foot, catching the giant in the knee. His leg buckled and he put a hand on the ground to keep from falling flat on his face. He staggered upright, and I got to my feet and darted forward so that I stood right in front of him.

Then, looking him in the eye, I grabbed one of the knives out of his leather sash and stabbed him in the chest with it.

He screamed. I smiled and twisted the knife in deeper, just as I had a hundred times before as the Spider. Blood spurted from the wound, spattering onto my hand, face, and clothes, but I didn't care. The giant would be bleeding a hell of a lot more before I was through with him—and so would his sick, twisted bitch of a boss.

Arturo screamed again and swung his fist at me. This time I reached for my Stone magic and used it to harden my skin into an impenetrable shell. The giant's fist plowed into my chin. The sharp, strong blow didn't break any of my bones, thanks to my magic, but there was still enough force behind Arturo's punch to throw me off him.

I slammed into the dancing bear's ball and bounced off it, but as soon as I hit the floor, I scrambled right back up onto my feet, still clutching his knife. Arturo and I faced each other, about twenty feet of empty space between us. Apparently, the giant thought this was going to be a repeat performance of what he'd done onstage earlier. He reached for the knives in his sash and started throwing them at me—only this time he wasn't looking to miss. No, this time, he aimed for my heart.

Thunk!

Thunk! Thunk!

Thunk!

Since I was still holding on to my Stone power, I didn't bother ducking Arturo's knives. The blades bounced harmlessly off my magic-hardened skin and clattered to the barn floor, tumbling every which way. Instead, I ran toward him even as he backed up. But he wasn't paying attention to where he was going, and he bumped up against another one of the clown cars. Arturo's arms windmilled and he ended up with his ass in the bottom of the car and his long legs dangling over the side. He raised his hands, trying to fend me off, but I smashed my Stone-hardened fist into his face, snapping his head back.

"Catch this between your teeth," I growled.

Then I rammed his own knife into the bastard's throat.

Arturo arched back, clawing at the blade in his windpipe, so I obliged him by ripping it out. Blood sprayed everywhere, as bright, thick, and runny as the greasepaint the clowns wore. Wheezing all the while, the giant clutched his throat with both hands, as if that would save him from the brutal, fatal wound. But after several seconds, his hands slipped off his bloody throat and his dark eyes grew blank and glassy—

A blast of Air magic threw me across the barn.

It was like being picked up and hurled by a tornado, but I managed to hold on to my Stone power as I smacked into the far wall. The tools there rattled from the sudden violent disruption, but they stayed on their pegs. Another gust of wind picked me up and tossed me against the wall again before turning me around and holding me there, two feet off the ground.

I glared at Esmeralda, who climbed out of the clown car and slowly approached me, one hand held out in front of her to help her control the gusts of Air swirling around me. The ringmaster's eyes glowed a bright hazel as she used her magic to keep me right where she wanted me.

"I'll kill you for daring to interfere with Esmeralda the Amazing!" she bellowed.

"Oh, don't make promises you can't keep, sugar," I drawled.

I pushed back against her magic with my own Ice and Stone

power, raised my arm, and chucked the knife I was still holding at her.

Esmeralda shrieked, threw her hands up, and sent out a haphazard burst of Air magic. The sharp gust of wind knocked the knife off course, and the weapon sailed harmlessly off to the left. But my toss had ruined her concentration, and the feel of her Air magic quickly died down to a mere whisper of a breeze. I slid down the wall onto my feet, then grabbed another one of Arturo's knives from where it had landed on the floor and headed in her direction.

But the bitch recovered fast. She tossed another blast of Air magic my way, forcing me back while she sprinted for the barn door. I started after her, but my feet got tangled up in a pile of oversize clown boots. Cursing, I broke free of the mess even though I knew I wasn't going to be quick enough to catch her before she ran outside—

Click.

Esmeralda knew that sound as well as I did. She froze, then slowly turned around. Bria had one hand braced on the side of the clown car to hold herself upright. With her other hand, she pointed her gun at the ringmaster's chest.

Sometime during the fight, my sister had woken up, climbed out of the clown car, and stumbled over to the table where her gun was. Sloppy, sloppy, sloppy of Esmeralda not to have put the weapon somewhere more secure. Then again, she hadn't planned on Bria ever waking up to use it.

Bria leveled the gun at the ringmaster's heart. "Needless to say, you are under arrest," she growled.

Esmeralda stayed where she was, although I could see her trying to think of a way to escape. I moved over to stand beside my sister, careful not to get in her line of fire.

"You okay?" I asked.

Bria nodded. "Other than feeling completely exhausted, I'm fine. What did she do to me?"

"The same thing she did to Elizabeth and I'm guessing a lot of other girls," I said. "She was using her Air magic to pull the life out of you."

Esmeralda laughed, the ugly sound bouncing around inside the barn. "Not the life, you idiot. The *beauty*."

"And what would you need with my beauty?" Bria asked. "You have plenty of your own."

Esmeralda let out another laugh, then gestured at her own face and body. "Please. You have no idea how long and hard I've worked to look this way. The diets, the face creams, the makeup. And when I was finally perfect, do you know what happened?"

Neither Bria nor I answered her, but we didn't have to.

"Old age," Esmeralda hissed, as though it were the vilest thing ever. "Gray hair, wrinkles, sagging skin. Nobody wants to see that. Nobody pays to see the old crone at the carnival. They all want to stare at the pretty young woman in the center of the ring. But I figured out a way to stop it—to stop all of it."

"Yeah," I said. "And all you had to do was kill a bunch of innocent girls."

Esmeralda shrugged. "Youth is wasted on the young—and so is beauty. If they weren't strong enough to keep theirs, then that was their fault—not mine."

"Well, it's over," Bria said. "You're going to jail, where you belong. I wonder how long it will take for all that stolen beauty of yours to fade. What do you think, Gin? Six months?"

"Nah," I said. "Not with all that magic she wasted trying to kill me. I'd give her a month, two tops, before she looks her real age, whatever that is. It won't be pretty, though, will it, Esmeralda? Sad, since we know that's all you really care about."

Panic filled the ringmaster's eyes, and her gaze darted left and right, but there was no way out and nowhere for her to run. The witch had finally been caught, and soon everyone would see her exactly as she was—warts, wrinkles, and all.

"I'd rather die!" she screamed.

Esmeralda reached for her Air magic to throw at us. I tightened my grip on the knife in my hand and headed toward her, determined to end the ringmaster once and for all—

Crack! Crack! Crack!

Bria shot her in the chest three times.

Esmeralda's eyes bulged in pain and surprise. Her mouth opened wide, as though she were going to scream, but the only sound that escaped her lips was a soft rasp, like the air leaking out of a balloon. She toppled over onto the floor, blood soaking into the hay around her.

I waited until my ears quit ringing, then looked at my sister. "What did you do that for? I would have taken care of her."

"I know," Bria said in a grim voice. "But who knew what else she might have tried to do to you with her Air magic? She might have tried to suffocate you with it or something worse. I didn't want to take that chance, and I especially didn't want her to hurt you like she hurt me—like she hurt all those other girls."

I nodded. Bria protecting me, caring about me, fighting side by side with me, was something that I was still getting used to, after her being gone for so many years. But keeping your family safe no matter what was a need I understood all too well. Sometimes I thought it was the *only* thing I understood. Well, that and retribution. And sometimes they were one and the same.

Bria grabbed her badge off the table while I tucked my knives away in their usual slots. Then we both walked over to look at the ringmaster—at least, what was left of her. Death had snuffed out the magic that had sustained Esmeralda, and her body was already starting to deteriorate. Wrinkles grooved her once-smooth skin, gray streaked her hair, and her perfect bloodred nails had come free from her gnarled, knotted fingers. She looked like she'd been dead for months instead of just a few minutes.

"How old do you think she was?" Bria asked.

I shrugged. "Doesn't much matter now, does it? Because she's as dead as can be."

While Bria pulled her cell phone out of her jeans and called her fellow boys in blue to report what had happened, I went over to the clown car where Elizabeth was lying.

I put my hand on her forehead. She was cool to the touch, but she was still alive. Jo-Jo could take care of the rest. Elizabeth jerked awake at the feel of my hand on her skin, her eyes wide with panic and fear. I gently squeezed her shoulder, letting her know that everything was all right. After a moment, when she realized that it wasn't Esmeralda looming over her, her face relaxed.

"It's okay, sweetheart," I said in a gentle voice. "You're safe now."

Elizabeth nodded, and her eyes slid shut in exhaustion once more. "I used to like the carnival," she muttered. "Not anymore."

I smiled, even though she couldn't see it. "I know the feeling."

BRIA AND I were at the carnival late into the night. In addition to calling the cops, Bria also dialed Fran, the girl's aunt. I watched as Fran got out of her car, ran over to where Elizabeth was resting in the back of Bria's sedan, and hugged her niece tight. Jo-Jo would be here in a few minutes to fully heal her, and the girl would be as pretty and right as rain again soon enough.

Bria said something to them, then headed in my direction. I was sitting on top of the picket fence that lined the clearing, and she hopped up next to me.

"Elizabeth should be fine in a few days," she said. "It looks like Esmeralda didn't do any lasting damage. I talked to Jo-Jo on the phone. She said that since Esmeralda didn't fully drain Elizabeth, it's sort of like Elizabeth is suffering from severe dehydration. Some Air magic and a lot of fluids, and she'll be okay."

I nodded. "Good."

"I also called Finn and asked him to do some research into the carnival," Bria said. "He found an old newspaper article from the early 1800s that talked about a traveling Carnival of Wondrous Wonders. The main attraction was a knife-throwing act that featured a particularly beautiful woman."

"Esmeralda the Amazing."

She nodded. "There's no telling how many people she murdered over the centuries to keep herself young. Dozens, maybe even hundreds. We've already started contacting law enforcement agencies in other towns where the carnival passed through so we can look into all of the missing-persons reports."

I figured it would turn out to be something like that. "What about the other carnival workers? Were they all involved in it?"

Bria shook her head. "Apparently, Arturo was the only one who actually helped her abduct and kill the girls. The other workers were never allowed into that barn they set up at every carnival site, so they never actually saw what Esmeralda did to the girls. The workers were suspicious, but mostly they were too afraid of Esmeralda to really look into it. I need to get back and finish interviewing them. It shouldn't take too much longer."

"I'll wait for you," I said.

Bria nodded, hopped off the fence, and moved back into the crowd of cops. The carnival workers also milled around, looking shell-shocked. I wondered what would happen to the carnival now—if it would continue on or if the workers would have to find another one to join. I had a feeling that the wondrous wonders would be no more, just like Esmeralda and Arturo.

Since Bria was busy, I left my perch on the fence and wandered back through the carnival. Finally, I wound up at the main stage. I climbed the steps and looked out at the bleachers. They were empty now, but I could almost hear the roar of the crowd, feel the heat of the spotlight, see everyone's eager eyes fixed on me. Esmeralda had loved this so much that she'd murdered for it. Well, I supposed people have murdered for less—including me.

I was about to leave the stage when I noticed a tin pail of apples sitting next to the Wheel of Death. I looked around, but no one was in sight, so I walked over and grabbed an apple. I skewered the fruit on a piece of plywood that had splintered on the wheel—right where Esmeralda's heart would have been, if she had been on the contraption. When I was satisfied the apple would stay in place, I cranked up the Wheel of Death until it was spinning around and around at a dizzying pace. Then I walked to the opposite side of the stage, several feet behind where Arturo had stood.

I palmed one of my silverstone knives. I hefted it in my hand a moment, then tossed it up, caught it by the blade, and threw it at the spinning wheel.

Thunk!

The apple exploded into pieces.

Ta-da.

I grinned. The wheel slowed down, and I went over and pulled my knife out of the plywood. I flipped the blade up into the air before catching it with ease and giving a low bow to the empty bleachers.

"This old girl's still got it," I murmured, straightening back up. "Parlor tricks and all."

Whistling, I slid my knife back up my sleeve and left the Wheel of Death and the stage behind.

"FREAK HOUSE"

A STRAYS SHORT STORY

Kelly Meding

"How exactly does one acquire their very own djinn?" I ask the dour, mustached man in front of me. He doesn't take offense at the probing question because I inject it with just the right amounts of wide-eyed amazement and breathless wonder to make it sound like I'm gushing over his incredible cleverness.

Which I'm really not. He's the bad guy, and I'm not a gusher, even when gushing is warranted.

Still, the bad guy today is pretty blessed clever, this Stefan Balthazar fellow. He managed to capture and contain a djinn, after all, so I am factually curious about this feat. Not an easy thing for anyone to do, much less a *mortal* magic user (or, more likely in his case, magic abuser).

Balthazar runs a traveling carnival exhibit, but instead of pickled pig fetuses and the shrunken heads of pygmies, he displays the abilities of six different imprisoned Paras (that's Paranormal ~~citi~~zens, to you). Luck bought me an invitation to ~~tonight~~ the outskirts of Denver, Colorado, and what a ~~~~ far—you've never seen beauty until you've seen ~~~~

dance—and now it's mingling time. The two dozen of us who coughed up twenty-five grand a head to enjoy the show get an hour to gawk and chat with our host over plates of crab puffs and glasses of expensive champagne.

I hate seafood, and champagne doesn't do anything except tickle my nose (a benefit of being only half-human), but gulping back the bubbly helps me keep my cover. Wealthy men who are desperate to hold on to their tenuous power and position, like Balthazar, love playing to an audience. Especially if that audience is a pretty, flirty, empty-headed bimbo of a woman, like me. (Or who I'm pretending to be—and managing an Oscar-worthy performance, I must say.)

Balthazar laughs at my question about capturing the djinn. He gives the four other men in our intimate conversational circle a knowing look. A look that clearly asks *Isn't she precious?*

"A magician never reveals his secrets," he says with a chiding tone I want to stuff right back down his throat.

Instead of bristling or retorting like instinct demands, I lean a little more heavily onto Julius, my fellow infiltrator and date for the evening. He's got at least twenty-five years on me, which gives us an oddball May-December look and cements my position as a rich businessman's idiot eye candy.

I tilt my head and twist a strand of my blond wig around my pinkie finger, then give Balthazar a winsome smile. "I didn't know genies really exist," I reply with a pout. "How come no one knows that?"

"Because they're very difficult to summon, my dear."

No kidding. I have more knowledge of the djinn in my little toe than he'll ever hope to learn in his lifetime. I just can't toss that back in his smug face.

Yet.

Very, very few people in the world can summon a djinn, much

less bind one to the Rules of Wishing. Problem one: you have to know djinn exist. Even though vampires, werewolves, and certain types of fey are out to humans, the vast majority of Paras remain hidden while wandering around on Earth. It's much safer this way, for everyone. Problem two: you have to know the binding words for the Rules, which djinn can't speak out loud and which are impossible to write down. Problem three: three wishes are all you get (cliché, but true), and even those wishes are bound to the Rules. And yet Balthazar has somehow turned his djinn prisoner into a dancing monkey, bidden to perform magic on command, and it pisses me off.

Balthazar is no amateur magician, but his experience doesn't worry me as much as it probably should. I didn't travel halfway across the country to Denver just to see the magic show and drink champagne. My entire reason for existing is stuck behind a plate-glass wall, hunched over on a stool in the corner of his tiny cell, as miserable as I've ever seen him. He isn't just any powerful, eight-hundred-year-old djinn over there in that cage.

He is Gaius Oakenjinn. My father.

I SHOULD PROBABLY back up a little bit and explain.

Paras first came out to the public at large when werewolves helped us win World War II in 1944, seven weeks after American forces jumped into France. Vampires followed a few decades later, as did a handful of fey. After a while, though, their celebrity status began to wear off, and humans remembered why they ought to fear what's different. Werewolves now live in state-regulated Packs, while most vampires stick close to their Line Master and avoid human interaction. There's still the occasional violent flare-up, but we're all mostly peaceful. Segregated, but peaceful. Oddly enough, it's usually the human magic abusers who screw things up and incite violence among the Paras.

Kind of like right now.

For most people, an Earth djinn disappearing off the face of the planet isn't going to ding their bell. Djinn live on another plane entirely and they tend to shun human interaction unless summoned and bound to the Rules of Wishing. Likewise, the disappearance of a Pack-less werewolf, a skin-walker, a leprechaun, a pixie cloud, and a harpy won't ding any serious bells, either. Especially not with the human police.

It dinged *my* bell good and hard last week when my dad didn't show up for my birthday.

I hate birthdays, and my gypsy mother knows better than to try anything except a card that sings (because she can't) and a loaf of homemade zucchini bread (her specialty). But this year, birthday number twenty-two, actually did something useful—it clued me in to Dad's new, unofficial status as a missing non-person. As a frustrated college graduate with no real career plans in mind, I decided to make finding him my official business.

Five days later, my snooping led me to a coffee shop in downtown Denver in the dead of winter, freezing my ass off when I'd rather have been soaking up the sun in Florida.

Admittedly, I've always been a bit of a wuss about cold weather—something I inherited from my father's side of the gene pool. All Mom's mix of gypsy and warlock genes gave me is dark hair and a heart-shaped face.

The coffee shop seemed like an innocuous enough place for a clandestine meeting with a dhampir named Peyton. Dhampirs (not to be confused with upyrs) are the offspring of vampire fathers and human mothers. Upyrs are the other way around and way more rare because of the difficulty of keeping a vampire pregnant with a human child alive. Once the fetus reaches a certain age and the mother recognizes it as a potential food source . . . well, it's not important. Or pretty.

Still following me?

Peyton supposedly had information on my father's disappearance, and considering vampires and djinn are immortal enemies, I was taking said information with a barrel of salt. Maybe she was helping me out of some kind of half-breed solidarity thing? Maybe not.

The eighty-year-old dhampir sipping her latte in the rear of the coffee shop didn't look a day over twenty, which made me hate her immediately. Vampire offspring inherit very long life spans. Not so much for a djinn's half-human kid. I'll always age more slowly than my human counterparts, but my biggest magical gift from Dad is the Quarrel. (Oh, stay tuned for that later.)

I slid into the booth across from her without bothering to order anything. I needed caffeine on top of my jumping nerves like a sinking ship needs an extra hole in its hull. She didn't offer me anything, just gazed at me with unblinking eyes shimmering an eerie shade of copper. Without comment, I pulled a paperback novel out of my purse and slid it across the table. Peyton opened the cover, glanced inside, then put the book in her lap.

Hollowing out an old novel and stuffing it with money is way less obvious than using a plain manila envelope.

"There are rumors among the wealthy of a great attraction," Peyton said, her voice toneless and kind of creepy. "An attraction for the wealthy, open only to the wealthy. No one knows what city it will visit until it arrives, and it costs a great deal to attend."

This sounded pretty promising. Or like a really expensive red herring. "What kind of attraction?" I asked.

"A carnival of sorts, or a sideshow, if you will. Paras you know and Paras you've never seen before."

Paras like a bound djinn, no doubt. "Who runs this sideshow?"

"A man named Stefan Balthazar. Some call him an abuser of magic, others a powerful warlock."

Halfway across the coffee shop, a man in a brown leather jacket caught my attention. Not because he did anything more dramatic than add a packet of sweetener to his mug of coffee, and not because he was ruggedly handsome and absolutely worth a second look. I noticed him because, like Peyton and me, he wasn't quite human.

He wasn't alone, either. Another man shared his table, his back to me, salt-and-pepper hair the only thing I could see. The not-human male didn't even glance in my direction, but I couldn't shake the sense of being watched. He was not my priority today, though.

"Power is all in perspective, I guess," I said to Peyton. "And I'm sensing by the lead that brought me here that Mr. Balthazar is in Denver now?"

"Yes. His show is tonight. The cost is twenty-five thousand."

"Dollars?"

"Correct."

My heart dropped right to my feet. No way could I come up with that kind of cash in under twelve hours. I have some djinn magic besides the Quarrel and can be bound to the Rules of Wishing, but like other djinn, I can't use my magic for my own personal gain.

Crapsticks. "How do I let Mr. Balthazar know I want a ticket?"

Peyton arched a slim eyebrow, clearly doubting my ability to produce the necessary cash, probably because I'd haggled with her a bit on her fee. Still, she slid a scrap of paper across the table. "Text a message to this number containing your bank account information. Once the funds have been transferred, you will receive the address."

Quick and efficient, bless it all. Not good. "Thank you. What about the Paras in this sideshow? Are they real, or has Mr. Balthazar just perfected a magical illusion?"

"They are quite real, Ms. Harrison, as I'm sure you will find out for yourself."

I wasn't so sure—not unless I figured out a way to manufacture a whole lot of cash in not a lot of time. "How did you even hear about this carnival?"

"Information is my business."

"Uh-huh."

"I may also have been in the bed of the president of the largest bank in Denver when the call came through. Balthazar personally targets men with money who think themselves . . . adventurous."

I'd call them suicidal, but that's me. "Balthazar only hands out personal invites?"

"To a select few. Word spreads. It is a calculated gamble, to offer up so much money in exchange for what could easily be the work of a con artist. Balthazar plays the odds, and his crowds are often small."

"And wealthy."

"Indeed. Are we finished?"

"Yes, we are. My sincere thanks, Peyton."

"Perhaps we can do business again."

"If this information pans out, you can count on it."

Her mouth twitched in what probably passed as a dhampir smile. "As it should be. Good luck."

After she left, I stayed in the booth and stared at the telephone number she'd given me, as though intense concentration could conjure up the money I needed to attend this little carnival. I had to get in and see for myself if my father was being held against his will by this Stefan Balthazar. Even the man's name was creepy and conjured up mental images of oily hair and a twisted mustache.

The slip of paper couldn't conjure the money, and sitting around while I waited for ideas on getting the funds was a waste of time. My djinn nature made me sensitive to magic as well as the presence of other Paras (like Brown Leather Jacket Guy, who still occupied his table). Wandering around Denver in the freezing cold and hoping I stumbled over a strong, carnival-sized magic signature wasn't really an ideal plan, but it was the only one I had.

And that djinn sense of magic served me well less than five minutes later. I'd made it less than six blocks from the coffee shop when the hairs on my arms prickled and that sense of being watched returned. Mid-morning sunshine meant good odds my tail wasn't a vampire. Beyond that, I had no idea who was following me.

I don't like not knowing things.

Just to be certain of my shadow, I altered my route by slipping onto the next side street. Foot traffic was thinner, the buildings a tad spookier. My tail persisted. The entrance to a public parking garage loomed ten feet ahead. I rummaged in my purse as though looking for keys. Just inside the garage, I slid to my left and hid behind a concrete barrier.

Soft footfalls preceded my shadow, who turned out to be a man about my height with familiar salt-and-pepper hair. Grabbing his arm, I spun him around face-first into the concrete wall and twisted his arm up against his back until he gasped and stopped struggling.

"Now, you can pretend you actually have a car parked here and following me was all a huge cosmic coincidence," I said into his left ear, "or you can save us both a little time and just tell me the truth."

"I don't want to hurt you." His voice had a sharpened edge that made me think of the military, with just a hint of a faded southern accent.

"Well, good, because I doubt you could if you tried." Mostly true—the average punch in the face wouldn't faze me, though knives and bullets were something else.

"Release my arm and we'll talk."

"Talk now."

"*No.*" He put a lot of force into those two little letters.

Who was this guy?

My arms prickled again, too late to do anything about Brown Leather Jacket Guy when he appeared in the parking garage. He froze in place, looking momentarily panicked, before a deep growl rose up from his chest.

Werewolf.

"Julius?" the werewolf asked like I wasn't even there.

"I'm fine," He Who Must Be Julius said to the concrete wall.

A tiny flare of panic hit me in the chest, sharp like a bee sting. I could handle a human male, no problem, but werewolves, even in man form, were strong and insanely fast. This one was less than five feet away and could have his hands around my throat before I screamed. Werewolves also react to fear. I had to put a lid on mine before he caught on and freaked. I couldn't fight him.

My skin flushed all over as my internal magic rose up to protect me without conscious thought. The Quarrel.

Oh, sweet Iblis, this would be bad.

All djinn are not created equal, and Earth djinn—my father's variety—are known for their ability to affect the combative nature of humans. Arguments ensue, sometimes violence. I was ten years old the first time I realized I had inherited this ability, and I'd learned to control it since then—mostly. Sometimes it got away from me when my emotions ran high.

Like now. And making two grown men—one of them prone to lupine adrenaline surges—argumentative and pissy was not going to help my situation at all.

"What are you doing?" the werewolf asked. He took several steps back, stricken, and clasped his hands over opposite forearms like he was cold.

"It's not on purpose," I said. "But this is two against one, and you're freaking me out."

"We are not your enemies, young lady," Julius said. His voice had a new edge, probably from the Quarrel I was desperately trying not to unleash.

"Then why are you following me?"

"Stefan Balthazar."

Surprised, I let him go and skipped out of reach, keeping a safe distance between me and them. "Where did you hear that name?"

Julius rolled his shoulders as he turned around. His gray-speckled hair matched his age-worn face, which was also kinder-looking than I expected. He was in his fifties at least, much older than his companion. "You have your informants and I have mine," he replied.

"What's your business with Balthazar?"

"The same as yours, I imagine. He has something I'm looking for."

"Why do you smell so strange?" the werewolf asked me.

I shot him a glare. "New deodorant."

He frowned. "You aren't completely human."

"Yeah? Neither are you."

"I believe we've all got off on the wrong foot," Julius said. "My name is Julius Almeida. This is my associate, Will Carson."

"Shiloh Harrison," I said. I didn't shake their hands. "You're not cops."

Will snorted. "Hardly."

"We are, however, investigating a disappearance," Julius said. "Much like you are."

"What do you know about Balthazar?" I asked.

"I'm willing to share information, Ms. Harrison, but not here."

"Where?"

"My hotel. Or yours, if you're more comfortable there."

I wasn't comfortable with any of this. Trust two total strangers, or go at this alone and risk losing track of Balthazar's traveling freak house? Both were very bad choices. But if my powerful, eight-hundred-year-old djinn father was in a situation from which he could not extricate himself, I'd never save him by playing it safe. I had to take my chances with Will and Julius.

"My hotel," I said.

Julius nodded. "Do you have a car?"

"Rental's a few blocks from here."

"I'll drive you over. Believe it or not, I actually do have a car parked on the third level."

"I WAS HIRED to find a missing leprechaun," Julius said as soon as my motel room door shut behind him.

If he was waiting for me to act all shocked and confused about the existence of leprechauns, he'd be disappointed. "Hired by whom?"

"By Midas himself."

"The leprechaun king?"

"Yes. One of his sons has been missing for several months."

My distrust of Julius was slowly fading. Slowly. Despite my confidence that he was human, he knew a lot about unknown Paras—information rarely shared with outsiders. He still had a long way to go to gain my full trust, but this was definitely helping things along. Will, on the other hand, wasn't doing anything to ingratiate himself except holding up the wall in tight jeans and that leather jacket. The man—no, the werewolf—was illegally good-looking.

"What makes you think your missing leprechaun is connected to Balthazar?" I asked.

"Balthazar is known in magic circles, and some rumors have

circulated about him abusing his power for monetary gain," Julius said. "Frankly, I wasn't sure of the connection until Will overheard your conversation at the café."

Blessed werewolf hearing. I glared at Will. "You were eavesdropping?"

Will gave me a bland look. "Not on purpose. I'm still learning to control my hearing, and I was curious about the snippets I was hearing from your direction."

Sweet Iblis, a forced wolf.

No scars were visible because of his layers of winter clothes, but they lingered somewhere on his magnificent body. Werewolves came in two varieties: born and forced. The vast majority of werewolves are born and part of state-regulated Packs. They live together in small communities and report to a single state Alpha. Each state's Dame or Homme Alpha controls their own, which includes punishment and policing.

And then there are people like Will Carson—born human and, at some point, mauled by an angry werewolf to the point of death. If the man or woman survives the blood loss and the agony of the wounds, he or she becomes a forced werewolf. Because such individuals can't breed and are considered unnatural, they are rarely accepted into a Pack. Thus they have no protection, no family, and, if found by the government, they are usually "put down."

Colorado is not, thankfully, a Pack state.

"I'm sorry," I said to Will.

He seemed to understand and nodded. "Long story."

No doubt. "Was Julius there during the change?"

His face tightened. "No. But Julius has been helping me adapt to life out here in the world. I'd have gotten myself killed a long time ago if he hadn't found us."

"'Us'?"

Stony silence.

Okay. "Not my business," I said with a shrug. He could keep "us" to himself. And the fact that Julius was helping a forced wolf—who was, by rights, incredibly volatile and dangerous—said a lot about the man. I was starting to like him. "So you and Julius are working together on this case?"

"Yes. Can you tell us more about this sideshow? I only caught snatches of your conversation."

I repeated everything Peyton had told me, including the cost of admission, at which Will released a low whistle, and Julius said with disgust, "A traveling paranormal carnival in which he displays captured creatures in cages for the entertainment of a crowd of rich fools."

"Basically, yes," I said.

"You know, I've heard this story," Will said. "Isn't there a unicorn and a red bull in it?"

Red Bull? "The energy drink?"

Will stared at me like I was nuts. I returned the favor.

"I'd be surprised if our leprechaun was *not* part of this sideshow act," Julius said. "Midas told us that a good deal of gold has gone astray since his son's disappearance."

A brief lesson in leprechauns: contrary to popular culture, they don't hide pots of gold at the ends of rainbows. They are, however, greedy little con artists and thieves. Like the myth of the Midas touch, leprechauns can turn almost any object into pure gold. Unlike the myth, they do this in exchange for a fee—anything from money to goods to services to your firstborn child (and yes, Rumpelstiltskin did collect). The trick is that the object isn't actually altered. It's magically switched out for gold from the leprechaun king's vault. Once the leprechaun who made the deal is safely away, he switches the gold back and is richer his fee. Clever, ancient scam.

Sounded like Midas's kid wasn't able to swap back the gold he was taking. No wonder Midas wanted him back. Balthazar was costing Midas a fortune.

"Since we've shared our interest in Balthazar," Will said, "would you like to return the favor?"

Not really. "One of his captives may be a djinn I'm looking for."

"Someone you know?"

While they both could tell I wasn't fully human, revealing the *whole* truth meant putting my greatest secret on the line. I'm one of the rarest half-breeds in existence, and I like the way I confuse other Paras who can't figure out what I am.

"Yes, he's someone I know," I said.

Julius narrowed his eyes at me, a hard look. "Not someone you'd rather have bound to your will?"

My eyebrows jumped. He continued to surprise me with his Para knowledge. "Absolutely not. This djinn was bound far beyond the scope of the Rules, and I want him set free again."

He studied me in silence, probably deciding how much he trusted my word. Telling him I was half djinn and the target was my dad would be the easiest way to convince him I didn't want to bind anyone, but I wasn't ready to go there yet. Such knowledge gave Julius and Will too much power over me.

"I believe you," the older man finally said.

"Good. Thank you."

"So how many tickets are we getting to this show?" Will asked.

I gaped. Had he forgotten the price tag?

"I doubt Balthazar will believe a new werewolf wants to gawk at other Paras," Julius said. "So just one for me and one for Ms. Harrison."

"It won't work if she isn't a good actress."

"I think she'll do fine."

"You'll both need clothes."

Was I still in the room? "Hello?" I said. "Where are you going to come up with fifty thousand dollars to get us into this little shindig?"

Julius flashed a patient smile. "Midas provided me with a credit line for this investigation."

"Must be nice to have a sponsor with deep pockets."

"It is. I take it you're out here on your own."

"Yes."

"So this is personal."

"Very personal."

"Then you'll do whatever it takes."

"And more." I knew I was young and not all that tough-looking, but I'd be blessed if I'd let him judge my ability to do this. "I'll see this through. Balthazar kidnapped someone I care about, and I want him back."

PLAN HASHING ONLY took an hour, and I learned two important things about Julius in those sixty minutes. First, he was an Army Ranger for nearly twenty years before a forced retirement (no details provided on that) made him seek a new profession as a mercenary. Second, he had a fantastic knack for improvisation. He created an entire backstory for the pair of us in fifteen minutes.

I learned exactly nothing new about Will. Which was okay, because I didn't tell them anything new about me, either. We weren't friends. We were reluctant allies with a common goal.

Over the course of about six hours, everything fell into place. Our request for two tickets for "Mr. David Alvarez" and "friend" was approved, and the coordinates were sent. A quick check located them in the parking lot of a Walmart, so I was guessing that we'd all be picked up and transported to the actual carnival location from the rendezvous point. We also did some quick shopping, and I purchased the tightest, sparkliest minidress I'd ever worn in my life in order to play the part of "Mr. Alvarez's" arm candy. Will's contribution was the blond wig.

Since he couldn't come with us to the show, Will would tail our transportation as long as he was able and provide backup if necessary. We couldn't risk wearing wires, and we had no real plan beyond "locate the targets." Freeing them would be an exercise in improvisation for all of us.

The crowd for tonight's show was larger than I expected. Eighteen other people were waiting with me and Julius. Balthazar was making half a million dollars from the show, and, naturally, I wasn't the only arm candy in attendance. I was, however, the only nonhuman. When the black charter bus finally arrived at 10:00 p.m., everyone was visibly relieved.

The forty-five-minute ride passed mostly in silence. Occasionally someone would start talking business in an obvious "Bring out the measuring stick" way. I hated all of them with a deep, deep anger for coughing up so much money to see other living creatures in captive misery. Paras didn't exist for the entertainment of humans. We roamed the earth long before humans stopped dragging their knuckles along it, and we deserved happy, free lives too.

The bus turned up into the mountains, onto a narrow road bordered on both sides by packed snow. The driver, a silent and surly man, took hairpin turns with enough speed to make me nervous. One of the arm candies started complaining loudly, and I had to stop myself from telling her to shut up. Instead, I took her cue and clung to Julius's arm. You never knew who was watching or why.

The road ended abruptly. When the driver opened the door but did nothing else, a good thirty seconds of silent confusion passed before the first guest—tall, with thick-rimmed glasses— stood and stepped off the bus. I made a mental note to keep an eye on him. Julius and I disembarked around the middle of the pack.

Outside, the air was frigid and still, the only sound the rumble of the bus's idling engine.

My skirt was nowhere near long enough for me to stand around in the middle of the Rockies in January. I made a petulant show of stamping my feet and rubbing my arms. An easy act—I despise the cold.

Trees and packed snow rose up around us like walls, blocking the outside world and keeping our dark purpose contained. And then, in a flash of brilliant blue light that left red dots in my vision for a good two minutes afterward, our host appeared. Decked out in a midnight-black cape and an actual waxed mustache, Stefan Balthazar smiled at us all like some benevolent wizard.

"Ladies and gentlemen," he said in a voice that, strangely, did not echo. "You're here for an experience unlike any other, and I promise you will see sights unlike anything you've ever seen before."

He raised his right hand, and the air crackled with magic. Directly behind him, in what I'd assumed to be more shadows and trees, appeared the entrance to a tent. Not an actual tent, mind you. Just the pulled-back flap and an open maw inviting us inside—the perfect illusion.

My heart pounded. My father was in there somewhere.

"Welcome," Balthazar said, "to the Freak House."

No one moved. I clutched Julius's arm. It would look like I was cold or scared, but mostly I was trying to not storm the tent and blow my cover. Balthazar's intense stare swept over the group, silently daring us, and then he pivoted in a swirl of cape and strode toward the Freak House entrance.

As on the bus, Julius and I moved in the middle of the pack. Magic brushed my skin as we stepped inside the tent, making the hairs on my arms and neck stand on end. This was dark magic, abusive magic. I held on to Julius a little tighter to ground myself and stop my own magic from rising up and unleashing the Quarrel in retaliation. I had to stay calm.

For a good ten feet, the entrance continued in semidarkness before opening up in the perfect clone of a big top tent. Stripes of white and red ran from the ground up to a point in the center of the ceiling. The floor looked like sand but was firm beneath my flimsy spiked heels, and the interior was fantastically warm. A cluster of expensive-looking upholstered chairs held court in the center of the big top.

Balthazar tilted his head at the chairs, and we descended on them as a group. Our host was eerie and had a presence that would demand attention even without the carnival trappings. He must have been a commanding warlock in his day—until he lost himself to the pursuit of power and began abusing his magic.

Julius and I chose seats near the middle as Balthazar gravitated to the front like a minister about to deliver his sermon.

And then the lights went out, casting the tent in complete darkness. I grabbed for Julius's arm, not faking my jolt of fright. I probably even verbalized it, like some of the other guests.

"Beings exist whose capabilities extend far beyond our imaginations . . ." Balthazar said, a voice in the black, still oddly free of echo or actual inflection. His sales pitch continued as the real show began, but I was too focused to really hear him.

Like a curtain rising on a performance, a gilt cage became visible in the darkness.

Roughly the size of the average Dumpster, the cage had a clear front—some kind of glass, I hoped—and shiny gold surfaces on the other five sides. It sat on ornate gold wheels and had a hitch on one end attached to nothing. The cage was illuminated from the inside, but the actual source was yet to be determined. In the center of the cage, seated on a plain wooden stool, was a naked man in his late twenties. He had a long, lean body, and even sitting I could tell he was tall. His black hair and caramel skin hinted at Pacific blood, Filipino or maybe Hawaiian.

He also looked pissed.

"We've all heard about werewolves and their Packs," Balthazar droned. "I'm sure you've all seen a recorded shift on television or your computers, but never one in person. Few have . . ."

The caged man slid off the stool and dropped onto all fours. Black fur sprouted along his spine and spread down his flank. His arms and legs twisted and bent while his face elongated. Someone behind me gasped. The entire shift from man to wolf took about forty-five seconds. He shook himself out, shaggy black fur gleaming in the artificial light. He faced the audience and snarled.

The angry sound echoed long after the cage was engulfed by darkness.

"Werewolves are not the only shifters among us," Balthazar said.

The next set of lights came on to show a new attraction—a skin-walker, a blond man who shifted into an oversized, seven-point stag. Next came a harpy who was insanely beautiful—the body of a woman, the legs of a hawk, and the wide, feathered wings of an exotic bird colored in shades of blue and purple. Her cobalt eyes flashed as she screeched and preened. She probably longed for the freedom of the skies.

The pixie cloud came fourth, a brilliant ball of blinking lights that danced and spelled out whatever words Balthazar commanded. Pixies are generally harmless, unless you anger them; then they'll rip you to pieces with their teeny, tiny hands.

They shouldn't be too difficult to sic on Balthazar.

The fifth time the lights came up, it was on Julius's leprechaun, which meant my father was last. Leprechauns are proportionally small, like someone took an average-sized man and shrunk him down to about thirty inches tall. They're physically weak and rely on tricks to get out of sticky situations. After the audience had time to adjust to this vision, Balthazar requested a donation from an audience member, and one of the arm candies offered up her lipstick. He passed it through the "glass" front of the cage, which rippled around his hand like water and caused magic to caress my skin. The leprechaun touched the lipstick tube with his fingers, and it changed into a solid lump of gold, which Balthazar passed around.

Touching the gold made my stomach lurch, and I quickly handed it over to Julius, who tensed. We'd found his target alive and well.

The lights went out one last time. I held my breath.

"Behold a creature of Arabian legend," Balthazar said. Right then and there I ignored the taunting sound of his voice. He either had no idea of the true nature of the djinn he'd captured or was ignoring the facts of our origin in favor of spinning a familiar story for his paying audience.

The lights illuminating the sixth cage revealed a man much like you'd see walking down any street in any town. Lean and average in height, he sat unassumingly on a wooden stool, hands clasped in his lap, his gaze fixed far in the distance. My father. He looked bored, but I knew better. He was watching, calculating, waiting for the smallest opportunity for escape to come his way. The tiniest flicker in Balthazar's spell to give him an out.

Julius tapped my arm, and I let out a breath. Balthazar spoke again, his words lost beneath the roar in my ears. Magic caressed my skin as my father did whatever parlor trick was required of him and behind me, an arm candy squealed with delight as some menial task was accomplished for her entertainment.

I wanted to turn around and slap her. I hated them all for paying money to see other people suffer. I longed to fly out of my seat and smash the cages with my bare hands. Seeing my father reduced to a puppet was as infuriating as it was heartbreaking. I had to set him free. I had to set them all free.

BALTHAZAR LEAVES OUR small group and migrates to the next, having perfected the part of the gracious host. We have about thirty minutes left before the entire shindig is over, which means Julius and I need to act fast. Still, we need a plan.

I'm uncertain as to the extent of Balthazar's powers and of the enchantments he's cast over the six cages, which are now displayed in a half circle, hitched one to the next like a train of carts pulled by invisible mules.

My father hasn't looked at me, but he has to know I'm here, has to know I'll do something, try anything to set him free.

The pixie cloud, which has hovered in near stillness for the last thirty minutes, alters its shape enough to capture my attention. The little things stretch out in a rectangular configuration, their color patterns blinking more regularly. Intrigued, I nudge Julius forward with me. We stand in front of their cage, his arms around me from behind like a doting boyfriend, with enough space between our bodies so I don't feel trapped. The position puts his mouth very close to my ear.

"What are you thinking?" Julius whispers.

I twist my head back and pretend to kiss his cheek. "Not sure yet."

The pixies are trying to communicate something, I'm sure of it. Their color flashes create a pattern of shapes. Letters in repetition: L. P. H. E. L. P. H.

Help.

Hoping they understand, I give a slight nod. The patterns change immediately. I pretend to be amused and in lust with Julius while they spell out a new word: Harpy.

I laugh, pretending to be delighted by the pretty colors of the pixie cloud. I twist around in Julius's arms and fumble with my champagne flute as though I've had too much. "I have to let the harpy out," I whisper in his ear.

He nuzzles my neck, which almost makes me laugh. "How?"

"Remember the parking garage?"

"The irritation thing?"

"It's not the only party trick I've got."

Did I forget to mention I can also walk through walls?

Okay, so it's not quite so simple as that, which is why I tend not to mention it. I can only move through objects made of natural wood or stone, not metal or man-made materials like plastic, and it hurts like heaven's light when I do it. So I try not to do it very often. Working in my favor tonight is my knowing the limitations that exist on Balthazar's kind of magic—in order to enchant the cages and keep his prisoners contained, the cages must also be of natural materials. Most metals actually repel human magic, which gives me hope that the "gold" decorating each cage is paint.

"You ever going to tell me what you are?" Julius whispers.

"If we make it through this, maybe."

"Oh, good, something to live for."

I laugh, then slip back into arm candy mode. I point to the harpy's cage, giggle, and pretend to whisper to Julius, who leads me over. The harpy stares at me from her stool, her cobalt eyes watchful and deadly. Getting into her cage is the easy part. Setting her free will take a little creativity.

"Pardon the interruption," Balthazar says from behind us, and we turn to face him. He smiles, but it doesn't hide the suspicion that flares briefly in his eyes. "Ms. Lafferty, I cannot shake this feeling that we've met before."

Ms. Lafferty? Oh, that's me. And he's fishing. It's likely he can tell there's something unusual about me; he's just not informed enough to correctly guess.

"I'm sure I'd remember if we had," I say with a flirty laugh. "You're quite unforgettable, Mr. Balthazar."

"So I've heard. You're from Denver, correct?"

"Not originally, but it's been home for the last four years. Before that, I lived in Des Moines."

He clucks his tongue. "Perhaps you simply remind me of someone."

"I hear that quite a lot, actually, that I look like someone's niece or cousin or granddaughter. It's strange . . ." A fine tremor races up my spine and nudges at the back of my mind where the Quarrel resides. Balthazar is attempting to poke into my subconscious, to get a read on me, and it has my instincts going into protective mode.

Which may not be a bad thing. I hadn't planned on unleashing the Quarrel without a proper harpy-release plan, but . . . Oh, well. At least I know Julius is good at improvising.

I drop the mental walls restraining the Quarrel and a warm flush spreads across my skin. The air buzzes with magic. Balthazar frowns, sensing the change immediately, and takes a step back. He gives the crowd a cursory glance as he tries to figure out the source.

"Something wrong, Mr. Balthazar?" Julius asks.

Across the room, voices rise in sharp tones. The Quarrel is doing its job. Julius's arm tightens around my waist as he feels it, too—the irrational urge to contradict someone, to get in their face and challenge them. Over by the werewolf's cage, two of the male guests are facing each other down, arms gesticulating, faces red. Balthazar strides toward them, his black cape flowing behind him.

Now or never.

I slip over to the harpy's cage and touch the smooth surface on the left side. Balthazar's magic hits me like an electric jolt. I ignore it and push through to get a sense of the material—wood, as I thought. Good. Sharp pain stabs between my eyes as I reach for my djinn power and begin vibrating my entire body. Full djinn move through solid objects with no trouble. Being a half-breed means experiencing the unforgettable sensation of being ripped apart, body on fire, while I do this. Add in the burn of Balthazar's magic, and I feel as though I'll explode in a shower of flames.

And then my upper body is inside the harpy's cage. Unhappy with my presence, she reaches for me. I'm vibrating too fast, my body more like a ghost than a corporeal being. Her phantom touch scorches my skin like acid, and I want to scream. She does scream, a piercing shriek that is half bird, half woman. Someone else is yelling. Stuck half inside the cage, the Quarrel going at full steam, my own natural magic battling with Balthazar's abusive magic, I'm a monkey wrench.

I push my vibrations outward, even though I'm terrified of actually turning myself inside out. Agony is my entire world, marred only by a memory of my father's loving face. This is all for him.

I push again.

The harpy screams and rushes forward. She bursts through the front of the cage, shattering the glass in a frightening cacophony of noise, and the burn of Balthazar's magic fades.

Someone yells my name, and I move toward the sound blindly until the fire of passing through a solid object disappears. I pitch forward, landing hard on my hands and knees. My head throbs and my stomach twists with the start of a migraine. I vomit up the champagne I drank, the sour liquid scorching my throat and nose. My eyes sting with tears as I dry heave. Activity around me continues, and I try to focus, to see what results my freeing the harpy has wrought.

Instead, I get a face full of dirt—not vomit-covered dirt, thank Iblis—and the breath knocked out of me. A sensation like a million ants crawling over my skin tells me I'm being touched by abused magic. Black fabric swirls around me, and I struggle to get out from under Balthazar's weight. If I hadn't just walked through the harpy's cage, tossing him off wouldn't be an issue. Unfortunately, I'm wrung out from that particular party trick. I don't have the energy to buck off a chipmunk, much less a pissed-off warlock.

Hands close around my neck from behind. Dad's yelling somewhere far away, audible even through his magic glass.

"What are you?" Balthazar asks, his voice pitched with anger.

"You shouldn't . . . have messed . . . with my dad," I choke out.

"Your . . . *what?*" His grip on my neck slackens, like he's forgotten he wants to throttle me in favor of puzzling through which of his captives is old enough to have spawned me.

I twist hard, and his hold breaks. As I scramble away, a whoosh of air knocks me over. No one attacks, and I'm utterly confused as to what's just happened, so I take a deep breath and lurch up into a sitting position. The tent is practically empty of guests. Only two of the rich patrons remain, both cowering among the chairs. The other five cages are solid, their occupants still caught. Julius is nearby, gazing up.

I crane my neck, which makes my head spin a little bit. The harpy has Balthazar by the throat, and she's holding him near the peak of the tent, her great wings swirling the air as she keeps them aloft.

Her voice fills the tent with its fury. "Free them now!"

"I do not follow the orders of monsters," Balthazar replies, with no less force. "Kill me, little bird, and be done with it."

"No," I croak out, unable to get any volume. Even though no laws exist preventing what Balthazar has done, I want him alive to face justice for the lives he's interrupted. The pain he's caused. But what lawyer will prosecute him? What judge will bother hearing the case? There is no police force, local or federal, capable of handling men like Stefan Balthazar.

We need one. Badly.

This need, however, won't be filled in time to save Balthazar.

"You are a foolish, greedy little man," the harpy screeches. "And your wealth at our expense will bring you nothing."

She cleanly snaps his neck and then releases him. I shut my eyes. I don't see it, but I cannot block out the crunching thud Balthazar's body makes as it slams into the ground. Another sound, like distant thunder, breaks. It buzzes over my skin and right through me as Balthazar's magic dies with him.

I open my eyes to a forest floor covered with dead leaves and fallen twigs. Freezing air wraps around me and sets my teeth chattering. The chairs and cages remain, but the tent is gone, as is the warmth. The illusion is broken. The locks are broken as well, and the pixie cloud has descended on the bus, preventing it from leaving.

Julius wraps an arm around my waist and helps me stand.

The harpy is gone. The skin-walker and werewolf jump down from their respective cages, give each other a look—likely seeing the other face-to-face for the first time—then help themselves to Balthazar's clothes.

The leprechaun toddles over to us, his pint-sized body vibrating with excitement over his release. Julius says something to him in a language I don't know, maybe a greeting, and the little man responds in kind. The only word I recognize is "Midas."

Neither of these men matter as much to me, though, as the man walking toward me from the far side of the circle of cages. My father . . . The pride in his smile as he approaches swells my heart and knocks away some of the chill of the evening.

"Shiloh," he says.

"Dad," I reply. I don't miss the startled look this gets me from Julius.

Dad pulls an epic frown. "I missed your birthday."

I laugh and launch myself into his arms, hugging him, feeling his heart beat, his arms warm around me. We hold each other until I'm aware of low voices speaking behind us. I disengage and turn to the rest of the group, and am surprised to see Will has joined us.

"The bus isn't going anywhere," Will is saying to Julius. "I slashed all four tires, and the pixie cloud seems to be taking it upon themselves to act as guards."

"Good," Julius says.

"The humans won't remember anything in an hour," the skin-walker says with a slight twang to his voice. "Balthazar drugs the champagne and hors d'oeuvres."

That revelation makes me glad I vomited up the champagne I drank, but I give Julius a concerned look.

He smiles at me. "I'm good at pretending to drink in social situations."

Score.

"We owe you a great deal of thanks," Dad says. "Gaius Oaken-jinn."

"Julius Almeida."

Will and I introduce ourselves, too, and so do Kale (the were-wolf) and Jaxon (the skin-walker). The leprechaun stays quiet, lurking near Julius's left leg. The harpy is long gone.

"Are you cops or something?" Kale asks.

"Or something," Julius replies. "Is there someone we can call for you?"

Turns out neither Kale nor Jaxon has family missing them, and, like Will, Kale is a forced wolf. Recently turned, too, and the pair strike up a conversation while Julius and I disperse the pixie cloud holding the bus passengers hostage. Since we have no legal right to keep them, I can only hope the story about the drugged champagne is true.

Who are we gonna call, anyway? The Denver police?

Julius and the leprechaun disappear into the woods. Two minutes later, Julius returns alone.

With that, we remaining six descend the slope and hit up a twenty-four-hour Walmart in order to buy real clothes for Jaxon, Kale, and me (I'm not spending another minute in this awful dress), and then we hit an all-night diner.

It's the first time I've been to a diner—or out to dinner anywhere—with my dad. We make idle conversation over plates of greasy burgers, fries, and coleslaw. The three shifters at the table split an entire blueberry pie for dessert.

"Men like Balthazar operate without fear of capture or reprisal," Dad says once the pie arrives. It's the first mention of Balthazar since we sat down to eat. "There is no human justice for Paras."

"I thought you didn't care about human laws," I say. It isn't an accusation, just a statement of fact.

"I didn't, until they affected my family. You could have been killed tonight, Shiloh."

"I wasn't going to leave you in a cage. None of you deserve that kind of life."

Will makes a soft sound that I can't identify.

"I agree with Gaius's comment," Julius says. "It's something I've considered since before I left the service. There's no recognized authority that polices Para-related crimes."

"Are you thinking of starting one?" Jaxon asks.

"I am, actually. I have contacts in the U.S. Marshals Service, and they've floated the idea to me more than once. I just never realized how it could work until now."

"And how's that?" I ask.

Julius smiles at me. "By populating the teams with Paras."

"But there are no Paras in law enforcement."

"Not yet."

I return his grin, my own excitement growing. We need this,

and I want to do this. For the first time since graduating college, I see a future for myself. A group I can be part of, feel at home with, and help to make a difference in the lives of other Paras. Especially those of my fellow half-breeds, who rarely find a place to belong on either side of their genetic pools.

"If you make this happen, I'm in," I say.

Next to me, Dad grunts.

"Excellent," Julius says. "Will?"

"No." Will shakes his head and puts down his blueberry-stained fork. "No, that's not the life I need right now."

I'm disappointed, but I get it. Everyone has to choose their own path. Jaxon and Kale don't jump on the bandwagon with us, but they don't dismiss the option outright. There are still questions to be asked, answers to be found. Right now a Para-based law-enforcement group is still a pipe dream—one that could just as easily fall apart as it could come to fruition quickly.

"If I can be of assistance in this endeavor, Mr. Almeida, please ask," Dad says to Julius, surprising the crap out of me. I figured on him actively disliking the entire concept. "I owe you a debt, and this is something my people take very seriously." To Will, he adds, "And you as well, Mr. Carson."

Julius and Will acknowledge the debt, but I don't think they fully comprehend the enormity of having a djinn owe you a favor. I just hope that, when the time comes, neither man abuses my father and his generosity.

Or they'll answer to me.

"THE INSIDE MAN"

A JANE TRUE SHORT STORY

Nicole Peeler

When someone comes into your office and tells you that small towns in the Midwest have gone dull, you don't rush out with the cavalry.

But when the biggest, meanest supernatural boss in Chicago knocks at your office door, with the same complaint . . .

Well, then you take notice. It's either that or risk losing an appendage.

Which is how I, Capitola Jones, found myself in a football field in the middle of nowhere, fighting for my soul and the souls of those I loved.

And here I thought the worst thing to be found out in the country were cow pies and rednecks.

They don't tell you about the killer clowns.

EARLIER IN THE week, the assignment had sounded like a joke, even though the guy asking us to do him a "favor" was ⟨…⟩ funny person I could imagine.

"So we're supposed to drive south and find out what makes country towns so boring?"

The man across from me tore his gaze from my breasts to stare at my Afro, then looked back at my breasts, only to return to my Afro. Once again, the hair won. I wear it natural, and as big as I can make it. It's sort of my trademark.

"If you want to put it like that, sure," said Vince the Shark, pulling on his goatee with one of his small hands. Those hands were attached to short arms, which were attached to a lion's body. His face, however, was human enough to leer at me.

But while Vince the Shark looked like something from Dungeons & Dragons and talked like a mobster off *The Simpsons*, he was no cartoon character. A pureblooded manticore with tremendous power, he had tiny arms that hadn't stopped him from carving out for himself a large chunk of one of our most lawless cities, Chicago, using brutal force and extreme cunning.

I stayed well off his grid for a lot of reasons, the main one being that Vince was a psychopath. So to say I was displeased at his sitting in my office with me and my business partners, Moo and Shar, was the understatement of the year.

"So you believe some external force has made your sister . . . dull?" Moo's voice was calm, as always. The daughter of a human woman and an Alfar who'd set himself up as an Egyptian god, Moo had been trained from birth to be his goddess-consort.

Which meant she had lots of daddy issues but great comportment.

"My sister was never a firecracker, but she was never like this. Something changed her." Vince's lion shoulders shrugged like a Mafia heavy, his jowly human face giving me a "What are ya gonna do?" look.

"Is she like you? Powerful?" Shar asked, her usually lush voice uncommonly monotone. Half succubus, my friend had tuned her mojo to zero. Vince had that effect on the ladies.

"She's my half sister. Like you and your friends, she's got a human mother."

I wondered what it would be like to mate with a manticore and decided that was not something I wanted to pursue, even mentally.

Vince also didn't answer my question.

"Moo here is a halfling, and she could tear this building off of its foundations," I said. My friend acknowledged what I'd said with an elegant nod of her head before settling back into her listening pose, her ebony flesh and long braids motionless as that of a statue.

Victor grimaced, his approximation of a smile, and wheezed out a laugh.

"True, but my sister's a more typical halfling than are you ladies. To be honest, she's not gotta lot going for her in any category, and she's a total dud when it comes to power—might as well be a fucking human. But she's family, so I like to keep an eye on her."

"That's very nice of you," I said drily, thinking of Don Vito Corleone.

"She's my sister." Vince gave another wise guy shrug. "But the last time I spoke to her, she wasn't right. So I sent someone to check on her. They brought her here, to me. She's not the same person she was."

"In what way?" Moo asked.

For the first time Vince's face expressed an emotion other than that of a made-for-TV-movie caricature. Genuine grief tightened his jaw and furrowed his brow.

"She walks and she talks, but she's not . . . there. It's like she's dead inside. Her husband and children, they are the same. I sent out my boys to find out what happened. The whole town is like this. And there is a chain of towns, running to the East Border."

Vince didn't mean Indiana, he meant the border where the neighboring, Alfar-controlled lands started. He couldn't cross that line, so we couldn't know if the same thing was happening in other states.

"So what do you want us to do?" I asked, cutting to the chase.

"I want you to investigate. I don't often ask for help," Vince said. It felt more like a threat than an admission, however. "But I've sent dozens of my own people out there, and they have found nothing. Or . . ."

"Or what?" I asked, although I knew Vince was, undoubtedly, going to drop the other shoe.

"Or they didn't come back at all."

I sighed. "Great. So *your* people keep disappearing, and you want *us* to investigate?"

Vince gave me a toothy grin. "You are specialists at this sort of thing, are you not?"

Victims of our own success, I realized. We'd started Triptych intending to be simple private investigators for the supernatural community, but we'd had a few cases that should have been straightforward veer wildly off course into shitballs-crazy territory.

Soon enough, we'd earned a reputation for dealing with the weird.

I gave Vince a curt nod. "Fine. But if your people couldn't discover anything, what are we supposed to do?"

"Simple. Succeed where they failed. Find out what did this to my sister."

At that point, I looked over at Moo, who gave me a small nod, then at Shar, who shrugged. They were acknowledging what I already knew—that we were going to take this case whether we wanted to or not.

Vince wasn't a man who took no for an answer.

"All right, Vince. Give us the facts. What's your sister told you?"

"Nothing. She can't remember anything. But my boys have been digging, like I said. They know there was something that happened all at once. An event. We just don't know what."

"Then how do you know . . ." began Moo. Victor didn't let her finish.

"We have sources, who talked about getting called."

"Like a phone call?" I said.

Vince shot me a Look. I wasn't easily cowed but I felt that Look like the edge of a razor to the thin skin over my throat.

"Who are your sources?" asked Shar, piping up to come to my rescue.

Vince shuffled, obviously uncomfortable. It took me a second to recognize that he was scared, and so not used to being scared he didn't know how to express it. But whatever he'd heard or seen about this "event" freaked him right out.

"In each location there was at least one person who was physically immobile. One guy was in traction with a broken neck. Another lady was so fat, she'd have to take a wall out of her house to leave. People like that, who could not physically leave their premises, told us what happened. They also told us they tried."

"Tried to what?" I asked. Vince's lack of detail was frustrating. I knew he was a badass, used to getting anything he wanted done without question, but we needed something, anything, to investigate this farce.

"They tried to follow this . . . call. They say they suddenly knew they had to be somewhere. And they did try, even though there was no way they could. The guy in traction nearly killed himself, and the fat lady actually clawed at her walls with a hammer."

"A really strong glamour could call people like that," I said. I really wanted this to be a normal case.

This wasn't going to be a normal case.

Vince's lips stretched around his three rows of teeth in a horrible grimace of pain. He truly grieved for his sister, psychopath or not.

"My sister, even though I love her, she hates me. Or hated me. She hated everything I did, everything I worked for. She wanted nothing to do with me even though I was always generous. Now she doesn't care. She let me move her into my house. Her *and* her family. She wouldn't let me within fifteen feet of her children before. Now they are in my guest bedrooms, watching reality television. All day. Reality television."

We three marveled at that.

"Okay," I said, "we'll look into this. But it's going to cost you." Vince may be psycho, but he also knew the value of appearing to be a good businessman.

"I'll pay," he said. "Anything. Just find out what happened to my sister."

I perked up at the "anything."

"We have a deal," I said, reaching out for his paw. "We need to know where you went and what you found out in each place, to try to anticipate where this 'event' will strike next."

Vince nodded, waving at one of his goons posted by the door. As we got to work, I hoped this case would be pretty open-and-shut—a siren with delusions of grandeur, or some wayward Alfar with a god complex.

But while "anything" in the way of money goes a long way in my book, it didn't take much in the way of facts to dent my confidence. Actually, all it took was a highlighted sentence in the notes of a flunky sent to investigate the event.

The line read, "Fat lady heard music, like from a circus."

A circus?

* * *

"IS IT REALLY going to be this easy?" Shar asked, a pair of night scope binoculars obscuring her Middle Eastern features. I couldn't help but smile at the sight of her peering through the window of our Jeep. She looked like Aladdin's Jasmine had decided to become either a spy or a supervillain, what with her soft, rounded body encased in the leather catsuit she'd insisted on wearing.

"I doubt it," I said.

Moo grunted from the backseat, her power stretching out in her own version of radar. If anything used magic near us, she'd know. After all, Moo's father may have been an asshole, but he did pass on to his daughter a tremendous amount of power.

"It will come to this town," Moo said, absentmindedly touching the map at her side. "Our event is predictable."

We had decided to call it "the event." We weren't sure if the fat lady was right, after all, in calling the event a circus.

And I, for one, *really* didn't want it to be a circus.

"Every thirty-three miles," Shar said, repeating the pattern we'd discovered when we'd studied Vince the Shark's notes.

"And Harmony is exactly thirty-three miles from the last site," Moo said. I reached over for the binoculars, nudging Shar when she didn't notice. After she'd handed them over, I took a look through them at Harmony. The town wasn't much: a small main street with a few shops, two half-assed attempts at tiny strip malls, and a clustering of houses that might once have been grand. Well, grand-ish. There were more people than just this in the town, of course—farmers were scattered around in their houses across the countryside. From what we could make out from Vince's notes, the "call" for the event seemed to affect people in a five-mile radius.

"I'd raise shields," I said to Moo, eyeing the clock on our dash, which read 11:30 p.m. The Alfar halfling rolled her eyes at me, but her power boomed out in a palpable barrier that brushed over my skin. Her shields were nigh on impenetrable when she put her back into it, so I wasn't worried. Plus, we hadn't seen any evidence of supernaturals being affected by the event. Not that the lack of supernatural victims really meant anything. After all, not a lot of supes went in for living in Podunk towns, so there may have been no supernatural creatures to victimize. Except for Vince's sister, of course, but she was practically human.

"So what are we going to do if it comes?" Shar asked. We'd not had much time to go over a plan. Vince wanted us on the case pronto, so we'd figured out the trajectory of the event as we drove south from Borealis. Then we spent the day driving, keeping our feelers out for anything or anyone with a lot of power and taking every possible route between Harmony and the town it had just attacked. That town was eerily quiet, its inhabitants shuffling around like asylum inmates on too much lithium.

"I still don't know how we could have missed anything," I said grumpily. Moo's sensors could feel if an incubus so much as got an erection within a hundred-mile radius. How could something capable of sucking the personality out of an entire town sneak past her?

"They would have to be strong to hide from me," Moo said, echoing my concerns.

"You couldn't have missed it," Shar said. "So whatever this thing is, either it can fly or it can pop up out of the ground."

"Or it can apparate," said Moo, and I shivered.

Apparating, the ability to magically move objects or people, meant old magic, and old magic was the real reason we'd earned our reputation and ended up on Vince's radar. Basically, the cases we'd solved that had made Triptych infamous had involved old magic. Old magic wasn't elemental magic, like what my friends and I wielded. It was something older, something darker, and something a hell of a lot more powerful. We publicly attributed our success at dealing with cases that involved old magic to our teamwork and Moo's Alfar power. But that wasn't the whole truth.

I looked mixed-race but, like my friends, I was really a half-ling—my mom was a nice Jewish human and my dad a nahual, or shape-shifter, whose human form looked like an African-American male. My genetic cocktail had given me a lovely complexion the color of demerara and fantastically huge hair, but very little ele-mental magic. Compared to Moo with her nuclear force, I was a Swiss army knife. But—and we kept this on the down low—my genes *had* given me something in exchange for my dud powers: immunity to old magic.

I could face the biggest, baddest elemental being, one with power that could knock even Moo's head off. But anything it sent at me would fizzle, like I had some kind of natural dampening field around me.

That said, even though I was immune to old magic didn't mean I wasn't scared to death of the ancient creatures that wielded it. Es-pecially because they tended to be huge, Godzilla-esque monsters. Being immune to their magic didn't mean a hoot when one tore you apart limb from limb.

"If it's old magic, we'll deal with it," I said, sounding braver than I felt. "And our plan for tonight is reconnaissance. We need to find out what we're dealing with. Don't engage unless we have to."

"Have you ever heard of anything like what happened to those people?" Shar asked. The victims we'd run into hadn't been overtly sick or anything. But they had no affect. Nothing we did raised anything but a polite, disinterested response—not even Shar flash-ing her boobs (her favorite trick) or Moo calling fire to dance in the air.

"My people told stories about an ancient race of soul suckers. Creatures that would trap your soul, eating your memories like candy," Moo said.

I shuddered at that image. "Why memories?"

"We *are* our memories. So much of who we are and who we

think we are is created by how we interpret our lives. I suppose such a creature would eat our memories as a way of consuming our souls, bit by bit."

Shar whimpered, "Gross, Moo. Do these things really exist?"

I watched Moo shrug in my rearview mirror. "I never encountered such a creature. And the evidence was never firsthand, so I do not know." Moo fell silent for a bit, and when I looked in the rearview mirror again, she was wearing her thinking face. "All the stories did have one thing in common, though, when I think about it."

"And that is?"

"Once a person's soul was trapped, the only way to free them was to free the souls. Killing the one that had trapped it or destroying the vessel holding the soul would only destroy that which it contained."

"Huh," I said. "Good to know. But we can't rely on legends. We have to see what pops up— Holy shit!"

That last part was screamed, as I jumped in the driver's seat so high, I knocked my knee hard on the steering wheel.

"What the fuck!" I shouted again, my skin crawling like I was covered in maggots. For in front of us stood my worst nightmare:

A clown.

He was right there, right in front of our car, with a white-painted face and red paint smeared around his eyes and mouth. He wore a big red wig and a green, blue, and yellow romper with white pom-poms flopping down the front.

The red paint around his eyes emphasized the fact that they were a solid black that sucked in the light. They had no pupils, no iris, no sclera. Just an empty, eerie black.

I screamed bloody fucking murder.

I'm really only afraid of two things: my hair losing its volume, and clowns. I've always hated clowns. But who doesn't? So I hadn't made a big deal about the whole circus thing, as who in their right mind actually likes clowns? I assumed Moo and Shar were equally freaked out by all things circus and are equally loath to admit it.

But I was the only one in that car freaking out; at least, I realized that about ten seconds after my last scream died in the air. Shar and Moo sat there watching the clown with impassive expressions as if pop-up clowns were totally normal in parking lots these days.

"Moo, what is it?" I whispered, using my own sad little feelers to try to tell what we were dealing with. My magic came up with nothing, so I physically turned to my friend when she didn't answer.

"Moo, what is . . . ?" My voice trailed off when I saw Moo's expression. She was normally calm, but this wasn't "calm." This was a total lack of expression, like Moo wasn't home.

Shar was no better when I turned to her. She, too, was staring at the clown, and she didn't blink when I waved a hand in front of her face.

"Guys?" I asked, trying to keep one eye on the clown and one on my friends. Meanwhile, I beefed up my skimpy shields and my attempts to read the clown. But I still felt absolutely nothing.

I groaned inwardly, then groaned outwardly as the clown raised a gloved white hand. He beckoned, his thickly painted lips rising in a creepy smile. Shaking my head, I told him "Nuh-uh" even as I locked the doors of the Jeep and started her up. I was just about to drive away when Moo did finally move. I saw her fist coming at the back of my head a split second before it connected. I didn't even have time to swear before I was out cold.

I CAME TO slumped over in the front seat, the car still running. My friends were long gone. The girls had put the Jeep in park before leaving me stranded, but I could tell from the fuel gauge that I'd lost at least an hour.

"Shit," I said, shutting down the car and getting out. It took a few minutes to regain my sea legs, and I took that time to check out the damage to my head.

I'd live, though I'd have a knot. My hand didn't come away bloody or anything. I wondered what Moo had hit me with, and then I saw our gun lying where she'd been sitting. You never knew when good old-fashioned brute force would be necessary in a case, so we kept the revolver handy. That said, we rarely used it with Moo's mojo in our arsenal.

"No chances," I mumbled, picking up the gun and tucking it in my waistband at the small of my back. It felt cold but comforting.

Since I had no idea where the damned clown had led my friends, the first thing I did was shift into something with a better sense of smell. Had I had my dad's shape-shifting abilities, I could have changed into a bloodhound. But with my own more modest talents, I had to keep my too-tall human frame, although I did manage a good long snout and some slightly bigger ears to catch any sounds.

I wore my hair natural, and huge, and I know my Afro looked good. But probably not *as* good when coupled with a hound's snout and an ass's ears. All topping a voluptuous woman's body. I undoubtedly looked heinous to anyone outside of a furry convention, but that didn't matter. I only cared about getting my friends back.

Testing the wind, I lowered my nose to the ground. I could smell where Moo and Shar had alighted from the car. Then they'd walked east, parallel to the town.

Every once in a while I'd see their sneaker imprints in a patch of soft dirt. Inevitably, they were framing another set of enormous shoe prints.

Clown shoe prints.

Following their scent, I ran as hard as my legs and the trail would allow. The surrounding streets were ominously quiet, with no signs of animal or human life. I passed a few houses, the doors hanging open as if the inhabitants had just walked out. Remembering Moo and Shar's behavior, I knew they'd done just that, answering the call of that damned clown. I reckoned we'd gotten a personal visit due to Moo's power. She wasn't the only thing that could sense the deep mojo, after all.

Why did it have to be a clown?

I whined through my long muzzle, but—clown or no clown—didn't slacken my pace. It wasn't till I was approaching what had to be the local high school that I slowed.

My ears picked up the music first. Faint strains that grew into the blaring horns and bashing cymbals of King's circus anthem "Barnum and Bailey's Favorite."

And then I saw it.

Pitched right in the center of the high school's football field stood a huge Victorian-looking tent, replete with pennants and banners. Except the tent was solid black, as were the pennants and banners, advertising nothing. The music played from old-fashioned loudspeakers set high on black poles.

Crouching low, I scuttled forward. Expecting all sorts of circusy things like animals, performers, and more scary clowns, I was surprised to neither see nor hear any activity. I could smell people—lots of people—but I couldn't hear anything besides the music playing over the loudspeakers.

Finally I was at the mouth of the tent, where one panel was folded back, another large empty black banner unfurled over it where you'd expect to find the name of the circus. I peered in, squatting low in case there were guards at eye level. But there was no one watching the door, nor could I see or hear any activity from inside the tent. After a few more seconds of nothing, I raised myself into a low crouch, poking my head through the flap.

There was still nothing, although I could see more of the interior of the tent. Risers were set up to the right and the left, but the light was so dim, it took me a second to see the legs. There were at least a hundred people in the room staring silently at something in front of them, only the backs of their legs visible between the riser slats.

I slipped into the tent, tiptoeing forward till I could see around one of the risers. When I did, it took everything in me not to do a heebie-jeebie dance.

The clown was standing just to the left of an enormous slab of mirror that stood on two silver legs. I watched as the clown's upraised arms adjusted the mirror so it was tilted ever so slightly upward. He kept his arms up and his head thrown back as he glared up at the ceiling with those eerie black eyes. But he never moved a muscle, nor did anyone else in the audience. They all sat rigidly in their seats, staring toward the mirror. I couldn't make out my friends in the gloom, but I knew they were there.

Meanwhile, everyone watched the mirror. But "mirror" wasn't quite the right word. Gray smoke swirled over its surface, and an occasional flash, like lightning bursting, seemed to illuminate it from the inside out.

My brain scrambled trying to figure out what to do next, when the clown finally moved. He lowered his gloved hands, exhaling hard as he did so. Then, on the inhale, he raised his hands again in a wide movement, as if summoning great power. To my horror, sparkling orbs of light rose out of the foreheads of the entranced audience. The clown swept his hands around again, this time bringing them in close to his chest. He smiled, a grimacing leer that brought cold to my bones as the orbs followed his command, bobbing toward him like obedient little dogs.

The orbs formed a line as they floated forward. I stifled a gasp as the first one hit the mirror, only to be swallowed up by that oily surface. Narrowing my eyes, I focused on the people in the audience. One by one they slumped over like puppets whose strings had been cut. It didn't take a rocket scientist to put two and two together.

The clown was collecting their souls or spirits—whatever made them *them*—in his mirror.

Moo's words came back to me about how killing the trapper would destroy the souls, as would destroying its trap. I wasn't sure if we were dealing with the same creature she'd heard about, but its MO seemed to fit.

Which meant I had to get the souls out before I took on the clown.

I focused back on him again. He was still exaggeratedly gesturing, his arm movements expansive. Eventually he flung his arms wide, and as he did so, his whole hand plunged into the surface of the smoky mirror.

Only it didn't hit anything. Like the orbs, his hand went straight through. That wasn't a mirror; it was a portal.

I had a few options at that moment. I could have called for backup. I could have searched for Moo and Shar in that room, hoping I could wake them up or reconnect them with their orbs. I could also have taken on the clown directly and risked killing him before I could free the souls.

Instead, without really thinking about it, I did what I do best. I acted entirely rashly, rushing headfirst into danger.

My legs carried me forward in a sprint that would have made an Olympian envious, and it took me a whole second to realize I was screaming like a banshee. The clown looked as surprised as I felt to find myself hurtling toward him, and I think he was even more surprised when I neatly dodged his outstretched arm, plunging at the mirror itself.

I sort of expected to bounce off of it. But instead, I plummeted—

falling,

and falling,

and falling.

A FOOTBALL PLAYER *was charging toward me. My muscles clenched, the ball solid between my calloused hands. My focus was split between the wall of man hurtling toward me and the man behind me, waiting for me to pass. At the last second, as I saw the pimples marring my opponent's chin, my arm swung with brutal force, sending the ball to my teammate just as the crowd went wild and I went down. . . .*

The shadowy presence of the hulking older man passed out of me, but before I could recover, the shadow of a woman about my age collided with me.

My daughter twirled, her spangly tutu so impossibly tiny on her equally tiny five-year-old frame. My husband watched her with sad eyes, and I wondered what he was thinking. That she was growing up too fast? That we'd miss these years when she was a bratty teen? I reached over to grasp his hand. When his eyes met mine, I smiled and leaned closer. "We made that beautiful creature," I told him, and he leaned in to kiss me. . . .

I sidestepped out of the shadow woman, only to careen into a small shadow, that of a child.

Candy and pop and candy and pop and candy . . . the bright lights twirl past and the boxes are endless and every one has a cartoon and a toy and I want them all and Mom always gives in and lets me have one and I'll ask her again if I can have that, or that, or that, or that, or that. . . .

I pulled myself away from the child's shadow, only more carefully this time. I was standing on a spectral plain of what looked like gray grass. The sky was gray, the landscape was unrelentingly gray, and it stretched forever and forever.

There was no horizon, I realized, a shiver running down my spine. Wherever I was, it wasn't earth with its comforting roundness.

I looked around, trying to get my bearings, but all I saw was a gray landscape and gray people. But then I recognized a few people from the crowd—the silver orbs must have become these ghostlike apparitions.

I also couldn't see a way out. It wasn't till I looked up that I saw, shimmering tantalizingly, an exact replica of the mirror from the circus tent floating just above me in the sky. I thought I could even see the clown, although the image was faint, seen through the other side of the mirror's surface.

That had to be my way out. Unfortunately, there was no way I would reach it unless I could find something to stand on. Peering about, I turned, only to collide with another of those ghostly shadows. . . .

She cried like she didn't want it, but all those bitches are the same. My dick was so hard in her and she liked it, she was whimpering and that wasn't pain, I'd bet my Camaro on that. She kept whispering "No" till I slapped her again and again till she shut up and my hand was bloody, like her lip. "Whore," I whispered, the word making me want to come. . . .

"Holy shit," I said, plunging out of that shadow as quickly as I could. I whirled around to come face-to-face with a middle-aged man with what would have been a powerful build were he not made of something akin to gray smoke. His face was hard, and I recognized him.

He'd been pumping gas into a massive black Dodge Ram dually when we stopped to refuel in Harmony. He had ogled all of us when we got out of the car, the whole time chewing on a toothpick.

I took a deep breath, trying to figure out what these experiences meant. Were they fantasies? Memories? Dreams?

Then I remembered what Moo had said in the car, about creatures eating memories as a way of chewing through souls. I turned back to the guy from the gas station, watching him intently. He shuffled forward a tiny bit, then back, and just for a moment his face crunched up a little—a bit like that of a man having an orgasm. I remembered his thoughts of the woman as his expression again grew slack—and his already ghostly form grew just a tad less visible. He'd faded, infinitesimally, as if something had siphoned off a bit of his energy.

Everything I was seeing corroborated what Moo had said earlier. Which meant I hadn't stumbled into that man's sick fantasy but into what had been a reality.

"I'll remember you," I told his specter, my voice weirdly muffled in the shadow realm. "And if I do manage to get you out of here, don't think I'm rescuing you. 'Cuz we're going to have a little chat."

I'd bring Moo. A victim of abuse at the hands of her Alfar father, she had a special place in her heart for rapists. It was a place full of pain, and expressing that pain was cathartic for her.

I'm all about helping out my friends.

I looked around, scanning the milling shadows clustered in two large groups. The placement seemed odd till I remembered the risers. The good people of Harmony must be standing where they'd once been sitting. They'd pace a bit, their faces blank as if sleepwalking. But none of them moved very far.

I moved away from the rapist toward what looked like a nice elderly lady. Waving my hands in front of her, I shouted. Again my voice was muffled, as if it were underwater. But it was still loud enough that it should have attracted her attention, as should my jumping up and down. Her wide gray gaze never wavered, however, from whatever she was watching in her mind.

After a second I decided to experiment. I walked forward till my solid mass met her insubstantial one. . . .

Twirling in my peach gown, his hands on my waist just like I'd always wanted them. We waltzed all night that night, and then he took me home and told me I was his best girl. . . .

Walking straight through her, I shook off the vestiges of her memory. The clown's method was genius. I couldn't think of a more elegant and efficient prison than our own memories. But how to break these people out, especially since I was trapped with them?

I took a deep breath, putting aside my fear. Panic would get me nowhere. There was an obvious first step I needed to take, and that was to find my backup.

Walking around the periphery of the crowd, I scanned the faces, looking for my friends. It wasn't an easy task, as one insubstantial body would blend in with another as they paced back and forth, trapped in little boxes of their own making. After a few increasingly worried passes, I finally saw them at the edge of the crowd. Shar paced, but Moo stood stock-still.

I ran to them, avoiding colliding with any of the other shadows. I did the whole scream-and-dance thing in front of them, but like the little old lady they didn't respond.

It was like they were asleep. Which meant I needed to wake them up.

And there was only one way I could think of to do that. I had to get in there with their memories and make them see reality.

But did I have that right? They were my best friends—more like sisters, really. And yet plunging into their memories meant I might see things they hadn't ever shared, for reasons all their own. These, however, weren't normal circumstances.

I had to go in.

That decided, I had to strategize. After all, my friends' memories wouldn't be of high school football games or children's recitals. I eyed them, speculating. Shar paced restlessly in front of me, her hand sometimes reaching up to brush against her lips or her breasts. Sometimes lower.

It was pretty obvious what sorts of memories Shar was experiencing.

Moo, however, hadn't moved a muscle since I walked up. She stood like a statue, her eyes haunted. God only knows where she was trapped. Knowing her tragic history, it couldn't be pleasant.

I made my decision. Shar was a famous over-sharer, so any secrets she had were probably things she knew we'd be squicked out by. I could handle a Tijuana donkey show or a romp with Hanson much more easily than I could Moo's vast, undoubtedly horrifying secrets.

I turned and walked right into Shar's shadow.

The smell of sex in the air as the girl's fingers played deep inside me, bringing out the moan lingering on my lips. Her mouth found mine, and then we both turned to the man kneeling in front of us. . . .

The sensuality of Shar's memories threatened to drag me under. Her memories of sensation were more powerful than some of my actual experiences, and for a split second I envied her ability to let go and just be . . .

. . . Now he was moaning, our tongues meeting each other around his hard shaft. . . .

I pulled myself back, the lure of Shar's sexuality too powerful. If I let her suck me in (no pun intended), I'd never leave. But I'd once again pulled out (wink wink, nudge nudge) too far, finding myself again standing next to my shadow friend rather than in her memories, where I needed to be.

I tried again, walking into her . . .

. . . my lips wrapped around him, the girl kissing down my neck, to my breasts. . . .

Yanking out, I stood next to Shar. I swore. I needed to be in the dream, but not *as* Shar. She was occupied, after all, and I needed to get her attention.

The good thing about having a mom who was a staunch New Agey hippie type was that I knew way too much about things like lucid dreaming. I wondered if I could reverse the process of lucid dreaming to make myself real in Shar's dream, like lucid dreamers tried to make themselves "real" in their own.

Clearing my mind of all other thoughts, I imagined myself less a part of Shar and more a voyeur. *I'm a watcher*, I repeated to myself in a focusing mantra as I slid toward the dream shadow of my friend. The metaphor not only worked, but it was appropriate as my perception shifted so that I watched the three figures writhing on the bed rather than being a part of Shar.

Concentrating, I willed myself into solidity. *I'm not just watching*, I told myself. *I am here. I am here. I am . . .*

And just like that, I was. I looked down at my own arms and hands as I stood next to the bed.

Hooting in triumph like a madwoman, I reached out and grabbed Shar's hair, pulling her mouth off the man.

"Shar!" I shouted. "Wake up!"

Shar's face scrunched at me, like that of a sleeper who didn't want to wake. Then the walls around us dissolved and we were in a room. Shar was tied to a bed, facedown and spread-eagled, while a man had his proverbial way with her.

I sighed and walked to the bed, putting my face down to hers. "Shar! Wake up! I'm serious!"

The walls dissolved again. This time, however, Shar wasn't naked. To my pleasant surprise, we were all in our favorite dive bar, Smitty's, laughing so hard we were doubled over. I grinned, remembering that night myself. We'd all been drinking—even Moo, who almost never indulged—after we'd wrapped up a particularly nasty kidnapping case. We'd found the kid, safe, and we felt pretty good about the world and our place in it.

That had been a great night. And it was nice to know that Moo and I ranked up there with sex, in Shar's memories.

That didn't stop me, however, from once again grabbing her dream ponytail and yanking. I also grabbed her dream drink from the dream table, splashing it right in her dream face.

She yelped, and this time the walls around us didn't dissolve into another setting. This time she looked at me, really *looked* at me, and then at the other Capitola sitting frozen as if her DVD were paused.

"Cappie?" she asked, reaching a hand out. I knew what she needed. I dipped my head so she could pat my Afro.

"It *is* you," she whispered. "But . . ." She pointed at the other me sitting across from her.

"That's a dream me, and you're a dream you. Trapped in a dream. It's complicated. What do you remember?"

"We were in the car. Then you were slapping me." Her eyes narrowed. She'd get me back for that one, if I got her out of here. That's how we rolled.

"I had to slap you," I said. "You're trapped in some dream state. Only this isn't even really you. Your body is still in that town. Do you remember the clown?"

She frowned, as if something was tickling her memory. I didn't have time to wait. So I gave her a quick recap and my very succinct plans. "We've got to free the souls and kill the clown."

"Kill the clown?" she whispered.

"Yep. But first we have to get everyone out. If I leave your dream, do you think you can come with me?"

She didn't answer, just took my hand, her liquid dark eyes latched on mine.

We had each other's backs. That's what made us good.

So I did what I'd done before when exiting one of the shadow people. I sidestepped to the left, but this time I kept Shar's hand gripped tightly in mine. For a second there was resistance. Then an audible pop, and then I was standing in front of my best friend. She was still a shadow, though.

"Shar?" I asked, afraid she'd just stare dumbly at me again.

Instead she nodded, then made a tight circle, taking in our surroundings and putting everything together.

"Wow. All these people?"

"Yes. And there have to be more, all the other people from the other towns."

"And Moo?" she asked, turning to our other friend. Moo's face probably would look calm to a stranger, but we could see her agony.

"I'm gonna have to do the same thing to her that I did to you."

Shar winced. "Need me to go with?"

I shook my head. "I don't want to risk losing you again. Stay here. Stay you."

She nodded toward Moo. "Be careful in there. Lord knows what you'll find."

I didn't answer her. Instead, I walked with purpose at Moo's shadow.

"Good luck!" Shar called as I passed into Moo's memories. . . .

THE PRIESTESSES PREPARED *me for my husband, the man I'd called father until yesterday and now was supposed to call lover. They commented over my body, congratulating me again on my budding breasts, still sore from my first bleeding.*

I ignored them, as I'd been told to. They were merely human and we were gods.

Sit, who had been my friend before I learned she was beneath me, dared meet my eyes with her sad gaze. I nearly told her how afraid I was, how I hated this, how I wasn't ready. . . .

But instead I slapped her for daring to gaze upon my person, as I'd been told to do. I was Emuishere, the consort of the Sun God, and she had no right to defile me with her human eyes.

Her whole face went red, not just her cheek, and she turned to fold the elaborately beaded shift that would be my bridal gown. . . .

Drowned in the thousand flooding emotions of Moo's impending nuptials to her own father, I nearly forgot I wasn't her, that I was Capitola Jones, and that I was watching.

I'm watching, I reminded myself, chanting that fact to myself. *I'm watching, I'm watching, I'm watching . . .*

And just like that, I was standing beside the cluster of women working on Moo, no longer inside Moo's actual memories.

I also wanted to get out of here, desperately. Poor Moo. . . .

I shouldered my way through the crowd surrounding her. They shifted apart as if doing so unconsciously. Moo still wasn't aware of anything outside her nightmare.

"Moo!" I shouted. "Moo!" I reached out to touch her, not wanting to pull her hair or slap her as I had with Shar. She was going through enough. But as my hand contacted her smooth dark flesh, she shuddered convulsively and the room spun. . . .

We were in a dark room, and I heard grunts from its center. My eyes adjusted enough that I could see a low dais upon which a man hovered over another figure. He was the one grunting. My heart breaking, I moved forward, knowing I had to get to Moo to get her out of there, but not wanting to see this.

Her face was turned away, toward where I stood, her eyes open and unseeing. I ignored what was happening and laid a hand upon her cheek.

"Moo, this is a memory. It was centuries ago. Lifetimes. You're not that girl anymore, Moo. . . ."

A tear slid down her cheek, wetting my hand. I wanted to kill the bastard who'd fathered her, but before I could move, the room slid away again and there was Moo, a girl still, wearing a white shift covered in blood. She was weeping, holding a battered, bloody dagger.

I hadn't been the only one to want to kill their dad. Moo had, too, and she'd gone ahead and done it.

"Moo," I said, both hands on her cheeks now, willing her to look at me. "Moo, these are memories, you've got to focus on my voice. . . ."

Again the room went black, and we were in that antechamber, the girls dressing her. Again Moo slapped her friend. Before I could reach her, her memories put her right back in that bed, enduring her first rape. Then we were back in that corner, her bloody fingers trembling on the knife.

So maybe the gentle approach wasn't working.

I picked her up from that corner, her child's body depressingly light in my arms. She was too small to be suffering any of this. But that didn't mean I couldn't shake the shit out of her. Not till her teeth were rattling in her head and her dark brown eyes had finally met mine, widening in recognition, did I stop. I'd do anything to get her out of her own mind, short of killing her.

"Cap?"

"Yes. It's me. And you need to wake the fuck up." My voice was rough. I wanted to hug her and cry for her and murder things for her, all at the same time.

The room started to waver again, so she got another shaking.

"None of that, Moo. This is a memory. You have to stay with me."

"A memory?"

"Yes, and it's over. You're not this kid anymore."

She watched me with haunted eyes. "I will always be 'this kid.'"

I leaned my forehead down onto hers, my hands cupping her jaw.

"And she grew up to be a fine woman, and my friend. Come back to me, Moo."

My eyes welled over with hers, our tears mingling down her cheeks to pool on the hands that held her cheeks. Then she was changing, her child's body elongating and growing heavy in my hands till she was Moo again. My tall, strong friend whom I could always count on.

My hands still rested on her cheeks. For a second she let the weight of her head fall against my touch before she stood up straight.

"I am assuming we ended up falling into the same trap that befell Vince's sister. How do you plan to extricate us?"

That's my Moo, I thought, love for her nearly overwhelming me for a moment. But I managed to pull it together, giving her a tight smile instead of the hug I craved.

"First we have to get you out of here. You ready?"

"Yes." It was a short, sharp response. I can't say I blamed her.

"Take my hand," I said. When she did, I gave it a squeeze. Then I pulled her with me. But before we made it, another hand came out of the darkness, grabbing her wrist.

"Daughter, you're mine" came a commanding voice that sent shivers down my spine. Moo cried out, an agonized shout like nothing I'd ever heard from her as the air around us began to swirl in sympathy to her agony.

"C'mon, Moo!" I shouted over the wind. "You're not his, and you never were!"

I pulled on her hand, but the other hand pulled back. We

played tug-of-war for what felt like an eternity, Moo nearly col-lapsed between us.

"Girl, you've got to help!" I shouted, squeezing her hand. "We're getting out, but you gotta help!"

Her eyes flickered to mine, but her face was still collapsed with agony.

"C'mon! You got away from him before! Now, pull!"

I knew it was probably bad form to remind someone they'd committed patricide, but I was pretty sure the situation called for it. And it did the trick.

With a growl, Moo yanked her arm away from her father, plunging with me out and through. . . .

We found ourselves panting, crouched together. She was in-corporeal, still, but she was Moo.

She met my eyes. "Thank you."

I nodded, knowing she didn't want to talk about what I'd seen. Maybe we never would.

Shar, meanwhile, watched us with worried eyes. When we stood, she threw herself at Moo. I noticed they had no problem embracing, but when Shar tried to hug me I was treated to another quick vision of nudie patooties.

"Oops, sorry," she said, although she clearly wasn't.

"No problem," I said, my mind already going a hundred miles an hour. "Wait, you can touch each other?"

Moo and Shar reached out, touching fingertips. They nodded.

I looked around, locating the hulking football player whose winning play I'd witnessed earlier.

"We're gonna have to channel the circus," I said, seeing a plan forming in my brainpan. "Bring him."

I waved them to follow and Moo and Shar manhandled the beefcake football player till we all stood directly beneath the shim-mering mirror in the sky.

"That's the exit. Moo, you need to climb on top of this guy. Shar, you have to climb on top of Moo and get out. Then pull Moo out."

"Then what?" Shar asked. "We didn't stand a chance last time."

"Moo needs to keep our perp busy. You're expecting him this time. Hopefully that will be enough."

"But what about you?" Moo asked.

I thought of the mirror on its two spindly legs.

"Tip it," I said. "Tip it and shake us out."

"Is that going to work?" Shar asked, clearly skeptical.

"I have no idea," I said. "But it's all I've got."

The girls frowned, but they did as I said. First they positioned the man mountain, then Moo climbed up him, Shar helping, after which Moo pulled Shar up. I gratefully remembered all the times we'd forced Moo to play cheerleader when we were little girls, the Alfar our grudging anchor, as she was already an adult then. Channeling those childhood games, Moo boosted Shar up, her feet on the flats of Moo's palms. And just like that, Shar popped up and out of the mirror.

Then Shar's ghostly hand reached down, clasping Moo's. "Grab it! Grab it!" I shouted. A second later, both of my friends were free of the ghost world.

The next few minutes were torture. This plan was as crazy as anything we'd ever tried, and we tended to be successful. But we also sometimes failed miserably, and failing now meant I'd be trapped forever with these shadows. . . .

My negative ruminations were interrupted by the world tilting. I'd never felt anything weirder before or since, and I'd been through some weird shit. But to have the ground beneath you start tilting and never stop . . . My feet stuck on the ground, as if caught in the memory of gravity, but then the ghosts around me started to fall. I braced myself as I tumbled headfirst down toward the mirror. . . .

I managed to tuck and roll at the last second, but pain still flared in my shoulder as I landed hard on solid ground. Solid ground where there was an evil clown lurking, I reminded myself, struggling to my feet. I took a few stumbling steps as my head cleared. What I saw was pure chaos.

The orbs of light that had made such an orderly line when under the control of the clown were now whizzing around inside the tent. Some found their bodies, and a few humans were running around the tent, screaming, trying to find an exit.

Luckily, for our purposes, the tent seemed to be self-sealing, and neither humans nor orbs could escape. We didn't want people getting out and calling the cops before we could glamour their memories away. But having them trapped also meant that there were a lot more lives at stake. At risk were also all the souls of the circus's recent victims from other towns—there must have been thousands of orbs floating around the high, peaked top of the tent. They were so tightly packed as to make a near solid matting of light.

Even brighter, however, was the firefight happening between Moo and the clown. Good news: she was back in her own body. Bad news: she was losing.

The clown was pouring some kind of raw elemental magic at Moo, who looked like she was caught in a maelstrom despite the powerful shields she'd erected around herself. Buffeting magic picked her up, shields and all, shaking her like a maraca.

Shit, I thought, about to jump in to help her, although I wasn't sure how I could.

Before I could move toward my friend, however, someone goosed me. I jumped, turning to find a reembodied Shar behind me.

"What do we do?" she shouted over the din of the flying magic. Around us milled the shadows, their corporeal counterparts still sitting in the risers, staring with unseeing eyes.

"No idea!" I said. "But it's gotta be one of Moo's soul suckers she talked about earlier."

"So how do we kill it?"

"I don't know! I can try jumping it, but I don't know if killing it will hurt the souls it sucked out." Watching my friend battling a creature of unknown origin, I pulled out the only other weapon, besides the gun, that I had with me.

My cell phone.

A few tippie taps later, and it was ringing on the other end of the line.

"Hello?" said a rough, deep voice.

"Hey, Uncle Anyan?" Anyan was an old family friend and one of the wisest men I knew. He was also old as dirt. Before he could say anything, I asked my question. "Do you know how to kill something that traps souls, then eats them by ingesting their memories bit by bit?"

A pause from the other end of the line. "What are you doing, Cap? Are you in trouble?"

"I'm in the middle of something, yes," I said, keeping my voice calm. "So if you could hurry . . ."

"That's some old magic right there," he said, confirming what I already knew from my earlier nonreaction to the clown's call that had felled my friends. "It sounds like you've got a gaki on your hands. They were children of Air, but they're supposed to be eradicated. They're bad news."

"Um, yeah, they are. How do I kill it?"

"Kill it? You can't. They're Air."

I frowned. "This one looks pretty solid to me."

"What?" I'd made Uncle Anyan squawk, something I'd tease him about later. "You're with one?"

I watched as Moo rushed bodily at the clown, her shields so amped they were like a battering ram. But instead of its knocking him down, the clown's arms swung forward, launching Moo at the ceiling. She did some Crouching Tiger maneuvers, all charged with enough mojo that the tent rattled, then swooped down at the clown like a falcon.

For a second I thought she was actually flying, but then I realized she was taking advantage of all the magic in the air by using her shields like a surfboard.

Anyan said "Hello!" into the phone, bringing me back to our conversation.

"Sorry. Yes, we're with one, and it's shaped like a clown."

"It's in a body," he said, all business now that he knew what I was up against. "They enter a body and take possession of it. Take out the clown."

"But . . ."

"Don't worry about the person they possessed. They killed that soul already, to power the possession. Just get it out of the clown."

"Then what?"

"Trap the gaki. Do you have a soul catcher?"

"What the fuck is that?"

"It's a soul catcher," he said unhelpfully.

I closed my eyes to count to ten, but when I opened them I found myself staring at the mirror.

Duh.

"Actually, I may have just that. So the plan is kill the clown and trap the gaki?"

"Yes. I can be there today."

"It's a little late for that," I said, wincing as the clown stopped Moo's airborne attack by swatting her into a tent pole. She hit hard, and she got up slow. "I gotta go, but I'll let you know how we do."

"Cap!" I heard Uncle Anyan shout as I ended the call.

"We have a plan," I said to Shar as I pulled the gun still lodged in my jeans' waistband at the base of my spine. "Can you lift that mirror?"

She went to it, avoiding the mirror's smoky surface. She nodded as she manhandled it awkwardly.

"Good. Here goes nothing."

And with that, I ran toward where the clown was advancing on my friend. He held his stolen arms out in front of him stiffly, magic crackling between his hands like one of those electricity globes from the eighties. As she was still trying to regain her feet, Moo's eyes accidentally flicked to my darting form. The clown caught that slight movement even as she corrected herself, looking squarely at him, but it was too late. He whirled, power booming out at me.

The clown hit me with enough mojo to send any normal supe or human flying into the next county. Luckily, I wasn't normal. His power fizzled when it should have hit me, not even slowing my forward motion. As his eyes widened in confusion, I lifted the gun and shot the clown in the forehead.

As his body crumpled to the ground, I dropped the gun to help Shar with the mirror. We lumbered forward just as an oily black smoke began to rise from the dead clown.

"Trap it!" I shouted, heaving the mirror, smoky surface first, onto the gaki. The black smoke disappeared under its square bulk as it slammed onto the floor of the tent. I panted, my arm muscles singing, as I stared in trepidation at the slick steel of the mirror's back. Then I crouched on my hands and knees, pressing my cheek against the dirt as I carefully raised the mirror a crack.

Rather than merely squished under the mirror, as I'd feared, the oily smoke was inside of it. As it started to reach out, a tendril escaping the mirror, I let the heavy steel fall back onto the floor.

"Smash it, Moo!" I shouted at my tired friend. She struggled to her feet, raising her arm as if it weighed a ton. With one last burst of power, Moo destroyed the mirror. It broke with a resounding crack, shattering into hundreds of tiny pieces.

"Guys," Shar said urgently, and we raised our eyes from the mirror to see the orbs around us dissolving. I swore, fearing the worst, till I saw that many of the bright lights were darting into the people still sitting in the risers. I heard various moans, coughs, and mumbles of "What the fuck?" and then they all started moving.

"Oh, thank God," I said, relief flooding through me. I hoped their orbs had found the other people, from all the other towns.

I especially hoped Vince's sister's orb had found her, or he'd probably have us murdered in our beds. But we could worry about Vince later, as right now we had work to do. The humans whose orbs had hit them earlier were huddled in groups throughout the tent, peering at us like we were the monsters, and those only now coming to were quickly becoming agitated.

"Sit still!" Shar called out, her powerful glamour-skillz hitting the humans like a truck. They all sat back down quietly while we figured out what to do.

"We'll have to wipe their memories," Moo said. She sounded exhausted, and I knew only part of that was because of the firefight she'd had with the gaki.

"Yup," I said. But first I gave the girls a fierce hug.

After that, we did what needed to be done, sending all the humans back home with a vague memory of a fun time at a local fair. They'd never remember the soul-eating clown or the women who'd saved them.

When they were all gone, and we'd set the circus tent alight with the body of the unfortunate possessed human inside of it, we stood to watch it blaze to the ground.

"You okay?" I asked Moo. Shar acted like she couldn't hear our exchange, bless her.

"I'll be all right," she said, affecting Alfar coldness.

"I know you will. But if you ever want to talk . . ."

Moo shrugged.

"In the meantime," I said, knowing I'd said enough, "I think I have something that will cheer you up. One of those guys we just set free is a rapist. I saw it in his memories."

Moo turned to me, dark eyes flashing. "Really?"

"Yup. And I bet we can find him in a town this small."

She grinned. It was a vicious, frightening grin.

"Excellent. Shall we?"

I nodded. "Shar?"

"You know I love a little vigilante justice," Shar said, clapping Moo on the shoulder. We strolled off as the sun rose, arm in arm.

"A Chance in Hell"

Jackie Kessler

A demon was eating my face.

I had a moment of confusion—out of all the ways to wake up, this was nowhere in my Top Ten—and then it sank in that *a demon was eating my face.* I opened my mouth and screamed, "Don't stop!"

Well, you have to understand that "face" in this context was actually my clit.

Between my legs, the demon chuckled. "So controlling, babes."

Before I could reply, that wicked tongue was used for much better things than scolding me. Oh, the things that tongue could do! My hips bucked wildly and my fingers clenched. I might have torn the sheets. Or the mattress. It had been forever since I'd had sex—no, really, vibrators don't count—and the former succubus in me was lapping up how I was being lapped up. My nostrils stung from the stench of brimstone and sweat; my heart danced inside my chest as my breathing quickened. A delicious heat was building inside of me, heating my core, promising to set my blood
Yes, just a little more . . . almost there . . .

In my head, his voice murmured: **Say my name.**

The words hit me like holy water. Getting pleasured by a demon was one thing—one delicious, delectable, but not quite damning thing. But calling a demon's name in the middle of that pleasure would cost a soul. Specifically, in this case, mine. My soul was practically fresh out of the box—in the cosmic scheme of things, being mortal for ten months barely counted—and I wasn't about to trade the essence of what made me human just for a quickie.

My eyes snapped open, and my sword, a Fury blade of magic and steel, appeared in my outstretched hand. My fingers curled around the hilt, and I aimed the weapon down my body until its tip hovered by the demon's head.

I growled, "Bastard."

The demon chuckled again, then looked up at me. My bedroom was shrouded in darkness, so I caught only glimpses of the long blond hair that framed his face, with tendrils cascading around two russet horns that sprouted from his brow. His turquoise skin gleamed in the neon of the alarm clock on my nightstand, and his amber eyes glinted with dark humor as he met my gaze.

He asked, "Problem, Jezzie?"

"With the cunnilingus? Never. With you trying to claim my soul? Yep."

"Can't blame an incubus for trying," he said, kissing my inner thigh.

There must have been some mojo in that kiss, because it echoed in places much, much more sensitive than my thigh. Waves of pleasure hummed through me, making me feel so good that I almost dropped my sword.

Stupid demon mojo.

Gritting my teeth, I said, "What do you want, Daun?"

Daunuan, one of Hell's kings and answerable only to the dread (and insane) ruler of the Pit, smiled lazily at me. "Want? Your soul, of course. An orgasm or two along the way would be nice."

Never mind that I agreed about the orgasms. "You promised to serve me."

"I'd much rather service you."

I nudged the blade until its edge whispered against his throat. "Wrong answer."

"So touchy. Yes, Jezebel, I still pledge my service and the service of all of the Kingdom of Lust to follow you when you finally challenge the Sovereign of Hell for His throne, blah blah." Daun grinned. "But until that fateful day occurs, I'm going to focus on more enjoyable things. Like seducing you."

His eyes gleamed, and I felt another lick of pleasure, hot and slick.

I glared at him. "Stop that!"

"Or what? Will you chop off my head with your pretty Fury sword? Maybe cut out my heart?"

"Demons don't have hearts."

"Of course we do," he chided. "As you know."

Daun was right: I did know. When I had run away from the Underworld and became human not even a year ago, I had soon fallen in love with a mortal. And then things truly had gone to Hell.

"Fine," I amended. "You have a heart. And yes, I'd cut it out."

"Would you?" Daun cocked his head, exposing more of his throat. "Lying naked in your overstuffed bed, surrounded by pillows? I think you've gone soft."

I stared at his neck, and I imagined the edge of my sword piercing that majestic blue skin. My weapon was no mortal toy that would meet only smoke and shadow; now that the sword touched Daun, he'd have no chance to discorporate and flee to the Pit. The Fury sword was an Erinyes-blessed blade of magical steel;

one cut from it would kill. All I had to do was flick my wrist, and that would be the end of the demon Daunuan.

The end of the one who'd been with me for thousands of years—the one who'd saved my life and spared my life and made a holy Hell of my life too many times to count.

The sword suddenly weighed a thousand pounds.

Mental note: Start weightlifting.

I sighed and lowered the blade. "That's your neck, you dumb demon, not your heart."

"So you can't cut your way from my neck to my chest?" He smiled as he sat up. "Like I said, babes. You've gone soft."

"Maybe I just don't want to turn your insides into outsides all over my bed."

"Maybe not."

He was on me before I could blink, his body on mine, hips pressing against mine, his mouth hovering over mine, and for one intense moment I remembered what it was like to give myself over to him completely even as he gave himself to me. I remembered the feel of him, the *feeling* of him, deep inside me, remembered moving with him, bodies rocking, fingers interlocked, our sweat mingling.

And then I remembered that he was still a demon, and I was just a human—a human with a soul to lose.

I tried to tap into Hell's power to blast him away, but now that I was mortal, my connection to the magic that fueled the Underworld was flaky at best and undependable at worst—and this was clearly an "at worst" sort of moment.

I growled, "Get off!"

Daun began kissing my neck. "Working on it."

He did . . . something . . . and I gasped before I could stop myself. Then I thought: *Not like this.* I wanted him—bless me, I was horny enough to want a quadriplegic leper—but not like this.

With that thought, my sword—my wonderful, magical

sword—suddenly was between us, its tip nestled under Daun's chin.

"I said, 'Get off,' as in 'Get your body off of mine.'" I smiled grimly. "Unless you really do want me to spill your insides all over my bedspread."

Daun sighed and leaned back. If the sword pointing at his chest made him uneasy, he hid it well. "Bishop's balls, Jez. You went human and lost your sense of humor. Not to mention your sex drive."

"My sex drive is alive and well, thanks. It's just tempered with a survival instinct."

He snorted. "Damnation would be loads more fun than survival."

"That's a matter of perspective. I'd have to die before the damnation set in."

"So?"

"Not keen on dying just yet. Have to stop Armageddon first."

"You're not keen on that, either."

I wasn't. But unless there was another former demon who could do the job, I was stuck. I'd recently learned that the King of the Pit was bringing about Armageddon, and I was the only one who could stop it . . . by becoming the new Ruler of the Underworld. The only way for me to claim the seat of the Hell was to challenge the sitting King . . . and win. So now I spent most waking moments preparing myself for that challenge and hoping the Apocalypse wouldn't happen along the way. Things would have been much easier if I didn't care. But I did. I'd fallen in love with more than just a human last year. I'd fallen in love with humanity. Terrible trait for an ex-demon.

Daun was one of the few entities who knew what I was fated to do. It was grossly unfair that he also knew the way to my sweet spot.

So I shrugged—which, for the record, isn't easy to do while holding a sword level in one hand. "If the world went away, there'd be no more chocolate."

He shook his head. "Chocolate over sex. You've changed. At least you still sleep naked."

"I might not be a succubus anymore, but I'm not dead." (Ditto the "anymore," but that's another story.) The sword was getting heavy in my hand again, and this time it had nothing to do with emotions or memories or other human crap that I still found difficult to handle. It was also difficult to act menacing when I was in bed. "Get out of here, Daun."

"Before I go," he purred, "I'll give my favorite former succubus two truths."

"Don't bother. Demons lie."

"Only when we want to. Truth number one: I know you don't control that pigsticker of yours."

"Really?" I said lightly. "You hear that from the demons who've crossed me? No? Oh, right—that's because I killed them deader than disco. With the sword you claim I don't control."

His amber eyes sparkled with secrets. "I've been watching you. I've seen you fricassee your former brethren. That doesn't change a thing. I know how you move, how you think." He smiled lushly. "I know *you*, Jezebel. You wield that Fury sword, yes. But you don't control it."

I forced myself to smile. "If that's the case, sweetie, you really should get out of here before I lose control and accidentally poke you with my 'pigsticker.'"

"I'm going, but not before I share with you this second truth." His voice slid into my mind. **You can't cut out what I've already given away.**

Gentle pressure on my brow—a ghostlike kiss, chaste and fleeting.

"Liar," I said, my throat dry.

"Sometimes," he agreed. "But not tonight. Be seeing you, babes."

The stench of brimstone and sex, and then he was gone.

I waited for a count of ten seconds before I lowered the sword. As soon as it touched the bed, it vanished, going . . . well, wherever it went when I didn't need it.

Daun was right. Bless him six ways to Salvation, he was right.

I didn't know how to control my sword. I didn't understand how the sword knew when I needed it, or how it got into my hand just in time, or where it went when I was done. The former Fury who'd passed it down to me hadn't included a user's manual, and the only other Fury left in the world was a big believer in me learning things the hard way. Because the blade did what I needed it to do—slice and dice unruly demons—I had placed the weapon in the "Gift Horse" category of life and not worried about it. Demons took advantage of opportunities and didn't question them; curiosity was a human trait—one in which I was, apparently, sorely lacking.

Whatever. It didn't matter that I didn't know everything about my sword. I could still use it. Daun was lucky that I didn't use it on him.

Stupid incubus.

I buried myself under the covers and closed my eyes and absolutely, positively did not think about the second truth Daun had whispered. Because no matter what I felt about him, or thought I felt about him, demons were liars.

And when they claimed to tell the truth, they told the biggest lies of all.

I sighed. Stupid, stupid ex-demon.

Only one thing could nudge me out of my funk. I poked my hand out from the blankets, opened my nightstand drawer, and pulled out the one tool that I could always count on—at least until I drained the batteries.

Twenty minutes and three orgasms later, I finally got back to sleep.

LATER THAT MORNING I shuffled into the kitchen, aiming for the coffeemaker.

"Won't do you any good," a woman's voice called out. "You busted it yesterday, remember?"

I paused mid-yawn and looked over at the kitchen table. There sat Cecelia Baker, my former coworker and current housemate; she was grinning at me, her teeth a brilliant white against the dark chocolate of her skin. Partially because of the richness of her coloring, Ceci had used the stage name "Candy" when she'd been an exotic dancer; the other part had to do with, she claimed, being sweet as sugar. Which was a total lie, but then, customers didn't pay dancers to tell the truth. Still grinning, Ceci took a sip from a Styrofoam cup.

I said, "Hunh?" It was the best I could do on interrupted sleep and no caffeine.

"You," she said. "The coffeemaker. Yesterday. Remember?"

Blinking, I tried to pierce the cobwebs around my brain. I thought I remembered the smell of burning plastic, but that could have been the remnants of last night's dinner loitering in the air. (Those warnings about some containers not being microwave-safe? Not hyperbole.) But now that I was thinking about it, there had been another kitchen-related scorching yesterday, hadn't there?

Tentatively, I said, "I blew up the coffeemaker, didn't I?"

"Yup."

"Oops."

"Yup." Ceci took another sip. "You were trying to heat it up with your funky Hell-power thing instead of putting a cup in the nuker like a normal human being."

I mumbled, "Yeah, well, I'm not a normal human being."

"That's no excuse. Here." Ceci reached into a paper bag and pulled out a second Styrofoam cup. "Mama's got your medicine, light and sweet."

"You're my favorite person ever." I dragged myself to the table, plopped onto a chair, and gratefully accepted the steaming cup. "I owe you one."

"I'll add it to your tab. FYI, you're up to roughly seventy billion IOUs."

"Duly noted." I took my first sip of liquid deliciousness and sighed contentedly. On a scale of sex to chocolate, coffee ranked somewhere between a nooner and a Caramello.

"Don't linger over that java. You're mine today." Ceci smiled, all innocence. "And I know just the thing."

I sighed. My housemates took turns training me in their own unique ways on how to prepare for my upcoming challenge. It was Ceci's job to help me learn how to be human. Apparently, that was an important factor in trying to save humanity. I'd been trying to convince her that the best thing I could do was overdose on reality TV, but she tended to have other ideas—most of which had to do with charity, empathy, and other shit like that.

Resigned, I asked, "What's on the agenda for today? Not another stint picking up litter by the highway, I hope."

"Complain, complain. No, I've got something a little more fun in mind."

I perked up. "Dancing?"

"Nope. We're going to a carnival."

A pause as I digested this, then I said, "*Please* tell me that means we're going to Rio."

"Sorry. There's a carnie not even an hour away. It's here only for a couple days before it moves on."

I made a face. "A carnival? Seriously? That's a breeding ground for Evil."

"You speaking from experience?"

"No, from watching season four of *Heroes*."

"Don't be all pessimistic," Ceci said. "Carnivals are awesome. I had my first kiss at the top of a Ferris wheel. I even thought it was true love. Brian . . . Haley? Henley? Something like that. Oh, that Brian. Oh, that kiss."

"Oh, my stomach. I can't believe we're going to a carnival because you're a hopeless romantic with a short-term memory. Can't we just see a chick flick?"

She smirked. "You can't learn about the human experience just by watching movies. The carnival will be packed with people of all ages, from all slices of life. It's the perfect place for you to bask in all the humanity and have a little fun along the way."

"Your definition of 'fun' is very different from mine."

"That's a good thing, considering that you're an ex-demon. Get your butt in gear, Jez. We're off to the Pogo Brothers Traveling Show."

I blinked. "Polo Brothers? Will they all be wearing collared shirts?"

"Po-*go*. Go. As in 'Let's get going.'" Ceci pointed at my coffee. "One more sip, then get ready. We're spending the day at the carnival."

Well, it had to be better than spending the day picking up trash, right?

"GLAD WE GOT here early," Ceci said as she shut the car door. "Look at that line to get in."

I glanced at the throngs of people queued up to gain admittance into the carnival, then shrugged, unimpressed. While the wait might have been remarkable by mortal standards, I'd worked in Hell for thousands of years. You didn't experience a long wait until you needed to get inside the Gates that separated the Pit from Limbo. Good things might come to those who wait, but Evil believes in the fine art of anticipation. Demons never complained about waiting. First, waiting was easy when you were eternal and didn't need to breathe. Second, complaining was a good way to get yourself tortured for a few centuries. Hell wasn't big on bitching.

As we walked to join the line, I took in the hundreds of people swarming outside the gates that surrounded the carnival. Most were families, with moms and dads desperately trying to keep their precious little tax deductions entertained while they waited to get inside. There also were a large number of adults without kids, clumped in groups or linked as couples, chatting and checking email on their phones. Clearly, a good portion of the crowd had been there a long time—the grumbles and sighs of exasperation were a giveaway—but no one peeled off to leave. Maybe it was because of the enticing sounds of music coming from beyond the gates. Maybe it was the heady smells of grease and sugar weighting the air with the promise of junk food. Maybe it was those things together—the sounds, the smells—that wove an invisible web around the crowd, pulling everyone close, keeping them in line. Penned.

It occurred to me that all my years as a demon had made me a rather cynical human.

"Does this count as me basking in all the humanity?" I asked as Ceci and I took our places among the masses.

"It's a start."

"I wish humanity had bothered to shower."

"Just be glad it's not the height of the summer."

"Hey, you're not the one who's armpit-level to the world."

"You're not that short."

"Says the woman who could have been an Amazon in another life."

We waited.

We inched forward.

We waited more.

Time did this weird thing where it felt like two hours had passed, but my watch insisted it had been barely twenty minutes. Ceci had been right: I'd learned more about the human experience by coming here. Specifically, all of my practice waiting as a demon didn't matter, because waiting as a human was excruciatingly boring. Who needed Hell? This was an eternity of torture by itself.

"Okay," I said. "I've basked. Can we leave?"

"Bask a little more."

I sighed.

We inched.

As we slowly drew closer to the looming arch at the front of the gate, a man's voice rode the air. The tone was enthusiastic, even infectious; it carried over the grumblings and mutterings of our fellow waiters. Ahead of us, people stilled, some even shushing the folks behind them. Soon, Ceci and I were close enough to make out the words.

"Welcome!" said the voice. "Welcome to the amazing Pogo Brothers Traveling Show! You've waited so long, so very long, and now your patience is going to be rewarded!"

It was a beckoning voice, one that demanded you settle down and listen attentively. It was an entertainer's voice, hypnotic, enthralling. I tensed as I realized two things simultaneously: One, the voice belonged to the carnival barker, who I could see standing up ahead, not needing a microphone for his words to fill the air.

Two, I knew that voice very well.

"A small fee gains you entrance and ten tickets," the barker announced, "a bargain by any stretch! With those tickets, you can buy scrumptious food and drink! You can try your luck at games of chance! And if you're willing to pay a little more—just a little, nothing that would break the bank—you can watch our marvelous shows! Enjoy our breathtaking rides! See all that the amazing Pogo Brothers have to offer! If you're willing to pay, we're happy to oblige!"

He stood next to the admissions booth at the front of the arch, charming in his seersucker suit, grinning as he talked the talk. Dark haired, dark eyed, silver tongued, quick with a smile—the barker was the quintessential showman, winking at the women and clapping men on the shoulder, taking extra time to shake children's small hands before they walked through the arch.

And if I knew him as well as I thought I did, he was fantasizing about how all those souls would look on his record as he filed his claim Below. When I'd said to Ceci that carnivals were breeding grounds for Evil, I had no idea how right I'd been.

"We have to go," I said to Ceci.

"Patience, Jez. We're almost by the ticket booth."

"Seriously. We have to go now." I glanced at the barker, whose back was to me. "Don't run; he'll notice if we run. Just start walking back toward the parking lot."

"What's the problem?"

I turned back to Ceci, saw the frustration in her eyes. "The barker. I know him. He's—"

My voice was cut off as a ripple of power washed over me, and then a warm hand clamped down on my shoulder.

"Why, as my human body lives and breathes," the barker declared. "Jezebel! Have you gained weight? Oh, forgive me, that's just your human soul I'm seeing. It looks delightful on you!"

Forcing myself to smile brightly, I turned to face the demon

Amaymon, one of the dukes of Hell. A glance revealed that he appeared human enough—male, tall, handsome, if a little soft around the edges—except for the telltale glow around his eyes. Most normal mortals wouldn't see the reddish shine, and those who did probably would mistakenly assume the eyes were bloodshot. But if they looked too closely, they would be caught by his hypnotic gaze, and then they'd be little better than puppets. Which is why I made it a point not to look him in the eye.

I quickly inclined my head, showing respect while protecting myself from his mesmerizing gaze. Technically, he couldn't attack me unless I attacked him first—demons had many rules, and that was a biggie—but that didn't make it any less dangerous. If he thought I was impolite, he could take that insult as a personal attack, and then things would get . . . messy. As in: he'd make a mess of me all over the floor. Even with my Fury sword, I was no match for him. So I played nice, and hoped he'd find me so boring he'd let me go.

"Lord Amaymon," I murmured. "Nice suit."

"This old thing?" He motioned to the body he was currently wearing. "He's a former Hollywood lawyer. Made a standard deal with me—fortune, fame, the works. By the time I came to collect, his soul had been so burned out that he was mostly a husk. I decided to try him on for size before dropping him in the Pit."

Demonic possession was all the rage in some circles of Hell. "It's a good look," I said gamely.

"It is, isn't it? Joe here had wanted to run away and join a circus when he was a child. I thought it would be fun to do just that, in case there's anything left of him bouncing around in here." Amaymon tapped Joe's noggin. "Seeing himself do what he'd always dreamed of, while not being able to enjoy any of it, would be a lovely bit of torture."

"Very creative, lord."

"Besides, being carnival talker suits me," he said, hooking his thumbs in his lapels.

"Indeed, lord." Amaymon was an ancient demon of Greed. Unlike his younger nefarious brethren, who were more about whispering into mortal ears and encouraging them to commit the sins that would damn them to Hell, Amaymon was a salesman—he showed people what they thought they wanted, and he let them make their own fate. Modern demons were all about instant gratification, but Amaymon was old-school. He doled out contracts like forward-thinking dentists handed out lollipops: it was the end result that mattered.

I glanced over my shoulder to see how Ceci was taking all of this, but she, like the other humans around us, stood frozen.

"Don't worry about the meat puppets," Amaymon murmured. "They can't hear or see us. I thought a bubble of privacy would be the perfect thing for us to catch up."

"How considerate, lord," I said, trying not to sweat. Even when I'd been a demon, I hadn't been strong enough to portion out time in bubbles. Creatures like him ate ones like me for lunch, and not in the way that a succubus preferred. "Congratulations on your latest business. It seems to be doing well."

"You have no idea," he said smugly. "The mortals line up, all eager to spend their money. Most are content to buy their food and play some games and win small prizes. They're little fish. They can swim away. But for those precious others, the bigger fish who have greed festering in their souls, it's easy for them to buy more and more tickets, to take another chance that this time they're going to win the prize they so dearly want." He laughed, the sound like coins clattering in a pile. "And when they run out of money, I'm happy to make a bargain on the spot. It's amazing how many people are willing to barter their souls for a toy not worth its weight in copper."

I had to admit, it was a sweet plan. Those mortals Amaymon targeted would unconsciously react to the closeness of such a strong demon of Greed. He wouldn't have to do anything directly; his very presence would be enough for those humans to suddenly want some two-bit trinket more than anything else. A Kewpie doll or stuffed gorilla would become something they *had* to have, no matter what the cost.

And when it came to cost, well, mortals tended to be quick to offer what they didn't really believe anyone, or anything, could actually take from them.

"You sound busy, lord. By your leave, I'll say my farewells." And gather my sheep and get the flock out of there.

"Oh, Jezebel," Amaymon said with a chuckle, "I wouldn't dream of it. Let's talk about you."

"There's not much to talk about, lord."

"How modest! Look at you, all human and sparkly souled. What are you doing with the handful of days left to you before you die and are damned? Still screwing anything that moves?"

"Not as much as I'd like," I said, shrugging.

"No, of course not. You're too busy killing the nefarious that are loitering in some pissant little town. I've heard you're quite the hunter."

Careful, Jezebel.

"I'm not a hunter, lord," I said slowly. "I've no issue with demons just doing their jobs. Everyone's got to make a living."

"But you don't deny that you've been slaughtering the nefarious?"

"Only those who get out of line."

"So you're less a hunter and more of an enforcer." A pause, then he added, "One would think you'd be taller."

"I get that a lot."

"Maybe it's your fabled weapon that has your former colleagues so nervous around you. Rumor has it you wield an Erinyes-blessed sword."

Uh-oh. "Me?"

"You. Quite the prize for a former succubus."

"You're assuming the rumors are true, lord. The thing about demons is they tend to lie. No offense."

"None taken. Why so shy, little human? Look me in the eye."

I felt his power tug at me, urging me to lock my gaze onto his. I knew from experience that one look would be enough for him to bespell me, and then I'd be spilling my guts—figuratively, and probably literally. I also knew from experience what I needed to do to break his hold.

I bit my lip, hard.

Ow.

"Tell me true," he crooned. "Do you own a Fury sword?"

Lip stinging, I managed a perky smile, which made my lip sting all the more. To his chin I said, "Actually, lord, I have two of them. One for each hand. The thing is, they clash terribly with all my shoes."

A pause as he absorbed my words, then he laughed. "Amusing! Well, even if you don't have such an exquisite prize, you do have something else that's rather tempting."

I assumed he wasn't talking about my boobs. "I'm just a human, lord."

"Exactly. A human with a soul tainted by Hell." I heard the smile in his voice as he said, "Tell me, how did a former bottom-feeder like yourself manage to escape the Pit, go human, and gain a soul?"

Throat dry, I said, "Just lucky, I guess."

"Then I must invite you to try your luck inside." He motioned to the arch and beyond, to the hidden secrets of the carnival. "Come in, see the sights. Try your hand at the games of chance. Maybe you'll win big." His smile broadened. "Maybe I will."

And that would be my exit cue.

I offered a more formal bow, deep at the waist. "Thank you, lord. But I must respectfully decline."

"Decline? Even when I have something you very much want to win?"

Still bowing, I said, "I'm afraid you don't have anything I want, lord."

"Your friend might disagree."

Oh no.

I whirled around, but I was much too late: Ceci was nowhere in sight.

To Heaven with formality. I turned back to him and glared at his chin. "Where is she?"

"She's in my traveling show somewhere, trying her luck. You should thank me, Jezebel. I allowed her entrance free of charge."

"The Greedy don't let people get something for nothing," I said tightly.

"Little fish," he said, motioning to the archway and beyond. Then he motioned to me. "Bigger fish."

Shit.

"Don't worry about your friend. I'm sure she'll be fine. Until she finds that one prize she wants more than anything. I wonder," he said idly, "what will she offer once her money runs out?"

"Her soul's untainted," I insisted. "You can't have her."

"You mean, I can't have her *yet*. Who knows what she'll be willing to do when she wants something desperately?"

I gritted my teeth. If Amaymon decided to make Ceci an offer, she wouldn't stand a chance. She'd be damned. Forever.

"You're welcome to walk away, little human. Look after yourself. Leave your friend to her fate."

My fists clenched. "I can't do that, lord."

"Ah, Jezebel. I'd wondered if there was any demon left in you.

Apparently, there isn't. You're a selfless human. I think I'm disappointed." He sighed dramatically. "Go on, then. Enter my humble carnival and find your friend before she makes a deal she'll live to regret. If you get to her in time, you may both leave with your souls unclaimed. If not, well . . ." He laughed softly. "We'll just have to see what happens from there, won't we?"

With his words, the time bubble dropped. Not looking back, I ran through the archway.

Behind me, Amaymon shouted, "Enjoy the show!"

THE NOISE HIT me before anything else. Screams, mostly: the joyous shouts from prizewinners; the lamentations from losers; the declarations from the agents running games and rides. Around the screams were the sounds from the attractions themselves, metallic clangs and popping balloons and whirring motors and music—so much music from each venue, all of them attempting to drown out the sounds from other booths and rides, creating a blaring cacophony that threatened to rupture eardrums.

Next, the smells: all sorts of foods, their odors mingling— overly sweet cotton candy; the thick grease of hot cheese on pizza; the meaty promise of hamburgers and frankfurters and sausages; fried everything, from dough to ice cream to onions. Beneath the enticing scent of food was the stench wafting from various portable bathrooms, rank enough to make eyes water. More subtle was the stink of thousands of human bodies, the musk of their sweat and excitement and, in some, a growing sense of desperation.

And then the sights themselves: the garish colors and neon lights; the constant motion of rides, cars zooming back and forth and up and down and side to side; the action from the game booths as customers tried their luck and agents tried their wallets; the steady flow of people to buy food as they waited their turns to be entertained, with the pockets of surges as customers exited an attraction. At the far end of the venue loomed a Ferris wheel, the sleepy giant of the Pogo Brothers Traveling Show. A haze of dust tinged the hot air, the dirt kicked up from thousands of tramping feet.

The sounds, the smells, the sights—everything mixed together in a heady blend of controlled chaos. It made me think longingly of Hell, and I felt a pang of homesickness. I could almost smell the brimstone and hear the laughter of demons.

And then I realized that I really was smelling brimstone and hearing demonic chortling.

I look a longer look around, and this time I saw them: demons flitting among the humans, hovering overhead, crawling below, whispering in their ears. Invisible yet subtle, spreading their influence and encouraging people to act on their baser desires. Eat a little more. Spend a little more. Want a little more—just enough to do something irredeemable. And then there'd be a hot seat waiting, ready to be filled for all eternity.

And there was nothing I could do.

I hated it when demons cheated. That sounds insane, but it's true: demons are supposed to let humans make their own choices. They're not supposed to tempt them into making the choices that will damn them to Hell. That was cheating. But the King of the Pit recently decided that cheating was fine and dandy, which was one of the two major problems I had with Him. (The other one was He wanted me to be tortured in His throne room every day for the next thousand years.)

Usually, I made my point about cheating whenever I came across demons tempting humans, typically by drawing my sword and doing my best Highlander impersonation. But that wasn't an option now. Going sword-happy in a crowd was a great way to (a) accidentally cut down humans and (b) get myself arrested while (c) leaving Ceci to her fate. None of that was particularly appealing.

So I ignored the nefarious and focused on finding Ceci.

If I were better able to tap into Hell's power, I could home in on Ceci's soul and follow it to the end of the Earth. I'm not that good. Luckily, there's an app for that.

I pulled out my cell phone and opened Find My Friend. A few weeks ago, one of our housemates, an überwitch, had worked her mojo to make some creative tweaks to the technology. So this particular app stayed running all the time on my phone as well as on Ceci's, and we never had to worry about getting a signal. A few clicks brought up a map of the entire venue, with a pin indicating Ceci's location: the Ferris wheel. At the far end of the carnival.

Of course.

I texted her, but I wasn't surprised when there was no reply. A call to her phone went to voice mail after four rings. Ceci either couldn't answer or was too distracted to answer.

Who knows what she'll be willing to do when she wants something desperately?

I ran.

More accurately: I sprinted, peppered with lots of sudden stops. There were too many people packed too closely together for me to run continuously. Pushing my way through clumps of customers, I ignored their nasty looks and offended cries, although one of them shouted something so interesting that I had to turn to him and say, "You kiss your mother with that mouth?" That actually made him blush. Grinning, I turned and poured on the speed as best I could.

The thickest lines were in front of the food stands, or maybe just the thickest people. Most had some extra padding—hey, not judging; Satan knows there's a little more of me to love than I'd like—but there were also a number of humans who were very large, startlingly large, stuffing themselves with loaded hot dogs and funnel cakes. They all had a sickly gray pallor; even their clothing, stretched against mounds of flesh, was gray, and all of them seemed to be covered in dust.

No, not dust. A halo of gray.

I blinked as I realized I wasn't seeing most of them as they were now but had instead caught a vision of how they'd appear in the future. With that realization, the hazy image of the obese rippled and vanished. Now I saw the customers as they truly were: humans of all sizes and colors simply enjoying the carnival fare, not knowing how some of them were already marked for Gluttony, courtesy of the Pogo Brothers Traveling Show.

Stupid, flaky Hell power. One day I'd learn to control it. Maybe. I hoped.

Past the concessions were the games of chance and skill, with throngs of mortals vying for an opportunity to try their luck. They aimed toy crossbows and threw weighted darts at balloons; they playfully attacked each other with water guns. None of them saw the demon of Greed lingering by the prizes, its presence transforming the offerings from cheap stuffed toys into fantastic items they simply *had* to have. Three men by the ring toss began to shout and push one another, each accusing the other two of cheating. The demon grinned as the first punch was thrown.

I chose Ceci over strangers. I kept going.

Off to the right was the fenced-off kiddie area, where sweet tykes could enjoy safe rides and games so tame that nuns would have been bored. There was a petting zoo with lambs and piglets, a saucer ride that went maybe a mile an hour, and flying swings that were less about the flying and more about coasting within easy stepping distance from the ground. A small merry-go-round belted out a happy tune as kids rode pretend ponies and shrieked in delight. Parents watched and laughed and took pictures, oblivious to the demons gathered on the other side of the fence. I hastily counted eight: three from Greed, four from Pride, and one from Envy—all of them fixated on the children, ignoring the parents just as the parents ignored them. I grinned as I sailed past. All the demons could do was look and wish; tempting mortals didn't include children, who almost always were innocent. Humans caught a break until they were old enough to wear deodorant. After that, the boogeyman stories their parents told to scare them into behaving were more along the lines of cautionary tales.

At the center of the carnival, an enormous carousel held court, showing off its splendor to the crowd. It was the adult version of the children's merry-go-round, but this ride didn't sport plastic ponies. Yes, there were horses, as well as monkeys and lions and dragons, but their mouths were set in screams of rage as they moved up and down, their bodies skewered by brass poles. There was nothing festive about the animals; they radiated hatred so palpable that I couldn't fathom how the mortals weren't cowering in terror. Maybe the animals loathed the jaunty tune playing from hidden speakers, stuck in an endless loop just as they were, doomed to travel in a loping circle until the end of time. But, I thought as I ran past the line wrapping around the carousel like an ouroboros, it was more likely that the hatred emanating from the animals was focused on the senseless humans who climbed atop their backs.

I wondered if the carousel animals ever left the carousel.

I wondered if the red paint on their mouths was really paint.

Not my problem.

I kept going.

I darted past signs advertising various shows—this astounding magician and that amazing fire-eater; the snake charmer will be center stage at three, and the strongman will perform incredible feats at five: Buy your tickets now—and I silently had to acknowledge Amaymon's business sense. What had started as a lark of possession had led to a phenomenal opportunity for him to mark hundreds of mortals for Hell. And that was just in this town alone. How many places did the Pogo Brothers Traveling Show visit? How many humans unwillingly gave up their souls for wisps and fluff? Thousands? Hundreds of thousands?

If I were still a succubus, I would have been impressed. Instead, I was sickened. Bless me, I hate it when demons cheat.

My pace had slowed to a plodding jog. My legs were well and truly pissed at me, and I was breathing heavily enough to put some phone sex operators out of business. My training to challenge the King of Hell included many things, but doing laps wasn't one of them. Wheezing, I moved past lines for rides like the Tilt-A-Whirl and the Ghost Train, making a beeline for the Ferris wheel. As I drew closer, sounds around me seemed to dwindle and my focus pinpointed onto one car on the ride—the one at the very top. The ride had paused so that the customers could all enjoy the view of the carnival from their vantage points.

But at the pinnacle, the riders in that particular car were doing other things.

I could see Ceci, her black hair shining in the afternoon sunlight, her arms wrapped around a man's form as the two of them sucked face. She didn't seem to be flailing or thrashing, so I assumed he was kissing her and not chowing down on her tongue. Their car bobbed gently in the dusty breeze as overly cheerful music played on and on.

My stomach clenched as I stared up at them. Ceci had fallen in love on a Ferris wheel, she'd said; now here she was, in a demon-run carnival, kissing a stranger like they were long-lost lovers. Unless my life had suddenly transformed into some warped romantic comedy, there was no way this could work out for the best.

I shouted her name, but she was either too far away or too

busy to answer. Desperate, I looked around until I spied the ride's operator, a heavyset middle-aged man.

"Get the top car down now," I said, "and I'll give you a hand job behind the Tilt-A-Whirl."

The man blushed and began to sweat. He also pressed a button, and that wasn't a euphemism for something naughty. The wheel whirred and began to turn. Slowly, the cars made their way to the bottom of the ride, then circled back up. I waited, dread building, until Ceci's car arrived at the ground level. I pushed the operator aside and unlatched the door.

And I knew, even before Amaymon appeared, that I was far too late.

Ceci was smiling deliriously, her head lolling against the chest of an incubus. I'm sure he appeared to be human to everyone else, but I saw him clearly—the ruby skin, the long black hair, the coal-red horns.

Just as I also clearly saw the claim on her soul, red-tinged, black-edged. Ceci had been marked for Lust. She'd been damned.

The incubus winked a neon blue eye at me. "Hey, sugar," he said. "Come here often?"

I had only one option: I could summon my sword and cut down the demon. Once he was dead, his claim would be invalid. Ceci would be free. It was a toss-up whether I'd be arrested by human authorities before or after I was attacked by the other demons in the carnival, but that didn't matter. I had to save my friend.

Before I could call my sword, I felt hot breath against the back of my neck.

"Well, now," Amaymon murmured in my ear. "Looks like you lose."

"So do you," I blurted. "She's marked for Lust, not Greed. You won't get the claim."

"We'll see about that," he said with a laugh. "Come, Jezebel. We have business to discuss."

And there went my only chance of freeing Ceci quickly. Or maybe at all.

Life had been much simpler when I was a self-centered succubus.

As he led me away from the Ferris wheel, the ride operator called out, "Say, Mr. Pogo, sir? Me and the lady here, we were just about to go get acquainted."

"Sorry, Carl," Amaymon said. "I saw her first."

GIVEN THAT AMAYMON was a duke of Greed, I shouldn't have been surprised that his motor home was a mansion on polished aluminum wheels. The living room boasted a leather sofa and ottoman opposite a desk and recliner that belonged in a CEO's office. The kitchen included gleaming cabinets, a marble countertop with a vase full of flowers, a stainless steel sink, a refrigerator, a dishwasher, and a built-in coffeemaker. (Yes, I noticed the coffeemaker. I liked coffee.) A full bathroom gleamed with tile, mirrors, china, and glass. But the crown jewel, as far as I was concerned, was the massive bedroom, complete with a bed large enough to host an orgy and a home theater system to provide the soundtrack. Like I'd said to Daun, I might not be a succubus anymore, but I wasn't dead.

Yet.

Amaymon shoved me to the center of the living room, and I stumbled to the ground. I spat out carpet fibers as the incubus led Ceci inside the mobile mansion. They started to walk toward the bedroom, but Amaymon stopped them.

"You're mistaken if you think I'll let you ruin my sheets," he chided. "Egyptian cotton, you know."

"Lord," the incubus growled, "I marked her. It's my right to consummate our relationship."

Amaymon didn't bother replying with words. With a flick of his wrist, he released a bolt of power.

For the record, charred incubus smells like chicken.

"Shame," Amaymon said, frowning at the mound of ashes that until a moment ago had been a demon. "Decent help is so hard to find these days. Well, at least now he won't complain about me taking my percentage. Have a seat, Cecelia."

Ceci lowered herself onto the sofa and stared blankly ahead. She was Amaymon's now, body and soul—at least, until he killed her and took her to Hell.

"Well, now, Jezebel. Here we are." He smiled at me. "Still on your knees? Some habits are hard to break, I suppose."

That's right. Keep talking. Think I'm completely outclassed and out of options. Well, the outclassed part was very true, but I still had an option. "You said we had business to discuss, lord."

"Indeed." He sat next to Ceci, putting a hand on her knee. "I have something you want. And you have something I want. Let's make a deal."

"See something you like?" I asked, rising to my feet. I ran my hands up over my breasts, leaning forward to better show off the twins. "Want to do it on a pile of coins?" I jiggled closer to him, smiling and winking. "I know you don't want to get your Egyptian cotton dirty."

"No, little whore," he said with a grin. "I want your soul."

"Souls are a dime a dozen," I said, doing a shimmy-bop and stepping closer to where he sat. "If you want to screw me over, let's get physical first. There has to be something that turns you on. A golden shower, maybe?"

"You're not my type."

"Sweetie, I'm everyone's type." I danced in a slow circle, showing him my back as I reached for my flaky Hell power, hoping that it would work. All I needed was a smidge of magic, just enough to emphasize my assets and make my body as desirable as possible.

Luck was on my side: I felt my power come to the surface, flushing my body and making me tingle. I smiled as I peeked at Amaymon over my shoulder. "If you take me from behind," I purred, "you can pretend I'm anyone you want. Any*thing* you want."

Just as demons (and former demons) of Lust were susceptible to the hypnotic gaze of the Greedy, demons of Greed could be seduced by a creature of Lust. At the very least, they could be distracted. Amaymon's gaze was fixed on my ass.

Perfect.

I made sure to move my body slowly, enticingly, as I summoned my sword. Once my fingers closed around the hilt, I spun around and attacked.

And barely pulled back before slicing into Ceci, who had thrown herself in front of Amaymon as a human shield.

Shit!

"That," Amaymon hissed, "was a mistake." He took a deep breath and straightened his lapels. "I could cut you down where you stand, little whore. But this will be so much more rewarding on a personal level. I don't need you alive to claim your soul. Cecelia? Be a dear and kill Jezebel for me."

Ceci launched herself at me, fingers curled for maximum eye gouging. I sidestepped, whipping around as she sailed past me, into the kitchen. She turned as I leveled my sword at her chest.

"Ceci," I implored, "don't do this."

"Oh, Jezebel," Amaymon laughed. "She doesn't have a choice."

Ceci charged.

I jumped out of her path and swatted her skull with the flat of my blade, aiming for a concussion instead of a decapitation. Her head rocked back, but she didn't go down. I shouted as I threw a side kick into her gut, connecting solidly enough to knock her back into the kitchen. She landed hard against a counter, and I winced as I heard the distinct snap of a rib. But the pain wouldn't stop her, assuming she was able to feel pain at all in her possessed state. Nothing would stop her. She'd keep coming at me until I was dead—or until she was. I had to figure out how to take her down without making it permanent.

Mental note: Buy tranquilizer darts.

As Ceci pulled herself up, I reached deep inside of myself and threw a blast of magic at her, hoping to knock her out. I probably would have, too, if she hadn't ducked. The bolt slammed into the built-in coffeemaker, decimating it as well as a good chunk of the countertop.

I really have no luck with coffeemakers.

Before I could take aim again, Ceci grabbed the flower vase and threw the contents at my face. I dodged the flora and the water but walked headfirst into her backhand with the vase.

Blinding pain.

I screamed; I staggered.

I sensed my oncoming death.

I screamed again as I swung my sword in a wide arc—and connected.

Another scream, this one not my own.

Gritting my teeth, I opened my eyes. Through the haze of pain, I saw Ceci fall to the ground slowly, almost gracefully.

Amaymon screamed again, high-pitched and tortured. I pivoted and saw him on his knees, clutching his head. Cutting down Ceci had severed his claim on her soul—brutally. He screeched, lost in the agony of psychic feedback.

I took a moment to savor his torment. Then I did what he'd wanted all along: I gave him my Fury sword, blade first.

The demon Amaymon died screaming.

I watched as the tattered remains of a human soul, no longer bound by the demon, stretched up and out, hovering for a moment before it discorporated with a sound like a sigh. The empty body crashed to the floor.

Untouched.

No blood; no cuts. No nothing. Just a corpse on the expensive carpet. He could have been sleeping, if not for the lack of breathing.

From behind me, a weak voice said: "Jez?"

I turned to find Ceci sitting on the ground, clutching her side with one hand and her head with the other, looking at me with big, wounded eyes.

"I told you the carnival was a bad idea," I said.

CECI HAD THREE broken ribs and a mild concussion. After we got home from the hospital, she went straight to bed. I followed suit, but not before grabbing a bottle of Jägermeister. I retreated to my bedroom and put on awesome music. And then there was much drinking. Dancing, too, but mostly drinking.

I was coasting along on a decent buzz, when I heard a throaty chuckle behind me.

"Drinking alone, Jez? How sad."

Still dancing—well, swaying to the music—I turned to face Daunuan. He was magnificently naked. Looking at him made me feel overdressed in my skin.

"Not alone," I insisted. "I've got Tom Waits."

He wrapped his arms around my waist. "To Hell with him. You've got me."

I wanted to ask if he was vying for my soul again, but I was too drunk and too tired to care. So I leaned my head against his chest and for a moment I simply enjoyed being close to him.

You're feeling sad, he said in my mind. **What's wrong?**

Nothing, I thought at him. *Killed me a demon today and saved my friend's soul. Point, Jezebel.*

Then why are you sad?

I'm not, I insisted. *I'm all sorts of happy.*

And I was. I was very happy that I hadn't killed Ceci when I'd attacked her with my sword. I had even half convinced myself that deep down, I had known that an Erinyes-blessed blade couldn't harm a human—that all along, I had done it to sever Amaymon's hold over her.

Demons lie. But they never lie to themselves.

Only humans do that.

Daun let me have my lie.

Then he let me have three orgasms. He didn't even try to steal my soul. Just went to prove that demons really did have hearts.

And Daunuan's belonged to me.

"HELL'S MENAGERIE"

A CHARLIE MADIGAN SHORT STORY

Kelly Gay

Why did I let her talk me into this? Why, why, why? "Your mother is going to go ape shit. Total ape shit. I'm so dead. And she won't be swift about it, either. She'll drag it out, enjoy it with that maniacal gleam she gets in her eyes. She'll—"

"Rex." Emma turned, stopping Rex in his tracks. "Focus. Mom is in Elysia for the week. She'll never know." Her gaze went narrow and suspicious; funny how she could do that—go from big brown-eyed innocence to shrewd and calculating. "Unless you slip up and tell her."

"Yeah. Right. Not going to sign my own death warrant, kid."

But he probably already had.

If Charlie found out he'd allowed her only child to track a kidnapper to *hell* of all places . . . Christ. He rubbed a hand down his sweaty face. He was in deep, deep shit. This fatherly role was *way* more complicated than he thought it'd be. Who knew that little piece of work walking in front of him could worm her way inside of him like some adorable little parasite and make his heart go all mushy and weak-willed at the first sign of a lip tremble or tears?

Weren't fathers supposed to be stern and solid as rocks? Unmovable as mountains? Sounded way better than being whipped by a twelve-year-old kid.

Emma was just like her mother, too. Headstrong, brave, powerful. But she had a long way to go before holding her own like Charlie. Charlie was trained, had years of experience dealing with the off-world criminal element in Underground Atlanta, and she knew pain, death, and loss on an intimate level.

Emma knew loss, too. Her father, Will, was gone for good, his spirit set free to go to the Afterlife while his physical body remained, a true home for Rex's jinn spirit to take over, to become something more than a simple Revenant who possessed one body after another. Something permanent, in body and in Emma's life.

Rex would be damned if he'd ever let Emma experience the things her mother had gone through—what she *might* be going through even now as she scoured the heavenly world of Elysia to find her partner, Hank. Imagine Charlie coming home to learn he'd allowed Emma to traipse into hell, *hell*, to recover a bunch of kidnapped hellhound pups.

Puppy-napped.

Jesus.

He hadn't really let her 'traipse', though. Em's journey was more of a stealthy escape through a bedroom window, unlocking Brimstone's kennel, then breaking into the League of Mages headquarters and using the portal to Charbydon (aka hell). And he hadn't exactly *let* her do that, now, had he?

He'd been blameless right up until he caught up with her and her hellhound in the capital city of Telmath, where the portal had taken them. Where Emma had cried, completely heartbroken in his arms.

And he was a world-class sucker.

In his defense, what the hell was he supposed to do?

The pregnant hellhound Charlie had found in the warehouse district a couple months ago should have been sent back to Charbydon and set free in the wild. But there were issues with her pregnancy, so it was decided she'd go after the pups were born. The pups arrived, the shelter breached, and Momma and her pups were taken.

Easy pickin's for someone looking for a few exotic animals . . .

Emma had learned that two other kidnappings had occurred in the area, all of exotic animals, all supposedly taken by some traveling circus/menagerie. The things kids learned at school. Little eavesdroppers. In a school full of arcanely gifted children, there was no doubt in Rex's mind that if they put their minds and talents to it, they'd find the culprits and recover the animals.

Emma, however, had taken it personal. The rescued hellhound living in their home, Brimstone, meant more to her than anything. The fact that she could communicate with the beast added another layer of intimacy and loyalty when it came to the breed.

"We look around," he reminded her, sticking close in the crowded city street. "If we find them, we let the authorities know."

She didn't answer. Just kept walking down the dark avenue, in the direction of the three big-top tents they'd spied from Telmath Station's high vantage point.

Charbydon was Rex's place of birth, where he'd fought as a jinn warrior long ago in the war with the nobles. But that was before he died and spent the next few thousand years as a spirit, before he met Emma's father and made a deal that would change both their lives.

The familiar scents of warm tar and stone were heavy in the hot Telmath air. The old city was tucked inside a gigantic cavern in the mountainside. Its buildings were made of thick timber beams and beautifully carved gray stones, and they clung to jagged outcroppings along the cavern walls or were packed together on every available surface where the cavern floor didn't drop off into nothingness below. Bridges linked one area to another, and high above in the cavern ceiling, veins of raw typanum ran through the rock, casting its violet glow onto the gray city below.

This world was the basis for humanity's notion of hell. The beings here—ghouls, goblins, jinn, darkling fae, and nobles—had been the inspiration behind legends of monsters, demons, dark gods, and fallen angels. Heaven and hell had come out of the closet over a decade ago, and now all three worlds—heaven, hell, and Earth—existed in what was usually a very lawful coexistence.

Usually.

Rex glanced up to the sight far across the cavern where an enormous spear of rock jutted up from the cavern floor. Its height was dizzying from where he stood. He'd once stood upon that rock, a place called the City of Two Houses, where the houses of Abaddon and Astarot ruled this world from their dark obsidian temples and palaces.

A cold shiver snaked up his spine as they moved deeper and deeper into the heart of Telmath. He could feel Emma's excitement and awe, but, wisely, she kept silent; she was already in enough trouble and did *not* need to be enjoying this little excursion.

No longer able to see the tents, they followed the music, a slow, beckoning melody that flowed down the streets and alleys like a cool refreshing welcome—tempting the mind and heart. *Come. Come to the carnival.* It wound through the congested avenue, a marketplace where open fires burned in barrels, goblins hawked their wares, cloaked ghouls kept to the shadows, and darkling fae moved their lithe gray bodies in and out of the throng. Rex spotted a few humans and mages, a noble or two, and a small group of jinn warriors standing around a fire.

Brimstone stuck by Emma's side, his hairless gray back coming to her elbow. She placed a hand on his thick neck. Thousands of years ago, hellhounds had trained as warhounds, companions to the hulking jinn warriors who once ruled Charbydon. Then the nobles came, fought for dominion, and the use and training of hellhounds was forbidden. The warhounds were killed and the young ones were turned out into the wild. It wasn't uncommon to see the beasts lurking around populated areas, hunting for scraps of food, or the weak . . . Having Brim with them drew some curious looks, but not enough to slow them down. Not yet, anyway.

Above the crowd, they caught sight again of the tents. They loomed in the distance, their dark, ragged flags limp in the stale air, their black and white stripes dirtied with the dull, dusty gray that made up much of Charbydon's landscape.

"Hurry," Em said over her shoulder, increasing her pace, darting in and out of foot traffic, not stopping until the avenue ended and a massive square opened up. She found a spot under the eaves of a corner shop. "That's it. That's the carnival." Her voice was breathless and low, determined, but with a small note of trepidation.

Rex had a few spotty memories of small faires and festivals in his first life, but nothing like what rose up before him. This was wild, dangerous, and chaotic, a spectacle of fire and darkness, shadows and light.

Freak shows, menageries, performers . . . Jinn strongmen performed feats. Darkling fae used their thin bodies to twist and bend and tumble on wires strung taut above the square. Some wielded fire and blades. Death matches were advertised outside of the larger tents. In the arena, one could pit oneself against beast or being to win prizes. This wasn't any carnival the human world would ever allow.

Ghouls with faces painted white—stark within the frames of their dark cloaks—weaved through the crowd, taunting, advertising, luring spectators. To Rex, their mannerisms and presence seemed more predatory than not.

Rex stepped closer to Emma. Alert and protective, he scanned the crowd. His thoughts and senses went sharp as his warrior traits surfaced with blinding speed.

Emma did that to him. Being her protector, her caretaker, did that to him.

He placed a hand on her small shoulder.

REX'S HAND ON her shoulder pulled Emma out of her awestruck daze. She glanced at him, his profile grim. A muscle flexed in his jaw as he surveyed the crowd. A lump formed in her throat and her heart beat wildly.

Oh God. She was in *so* much trouble!

Her hand shook as she stroked Brim's neck, his presence helping to calm her and remind her of why she'd come here, why she'd done something so monumentally crazy . . .

If the League found out she'd used their portal, she'd be expelled from their school. If her mom found out, she'd be expelled from the world forever. Grounded forever. Guilt had a firm, almost painful grip on her chest ever since yesterday.

Just get in, get out. Save them.

She knew the pups were here. She knew it because Brim knew it. All she had to do was sink into his thoughts and she could feel what he felt. And right now he was still, almost frozen, as his mind weeded through the sensory overload of the carnival. Through the sights, the scents, the sounds . . .

He'd find the female and those pups. They were his, after all.

Emma had visited the mother in the kennel and had gone again when the puppies were born. Three of them. Two males, one female. Three tiny, gray, hairless, short-eared, no-tailed pups with wrinkly skin and thick, heavy bones. One day they'd be as big as tigers, with jaws like pit bulls' times ten. They were intelligent, loyal, and brave. But wild and deadly and feared. Hellhounds were banned from the human world. If one was found illegally imported or, worse, got loose in her world, it was killed. Her mom had pulled some major strings to get the pregnant hellhound slated for the trip back to Charbydon instead of something worse, and she'd pulled even bigger strings to get Brim an official permit to stay with them under some bogus research K-9–type training allowance.

Brim hadn't been allowed in the kennel to see the pups, but the happiness and longing he felt when Emma returned home told her all she needed to know. He couldn't stop sniffing her. And it broke her heart.

Honestly, she was scared to death, coming here, putting not only herself but Brim, and now Rex, in danger. But she couldn't leave Brim's babies to chance, to the fate she'd learned was awaiting them. And she was afraid if she told Rex or anyone else, they'd prevent her from coming, or not take her seriously, or, worse, wait too long by going through proper channels—the pups and their mother would disappear for sure if that happened.

Brim had put his life on the line for her mother when Emma asked him to. No hesitation. He gave his all. How could she *not* do the same for him?

She might be young, but she knew a lot. She knew more than the average kid about fighting, magic, danger . . . Her mom was a kick-ass law enforcement officer, one who had taught her the value of loyalty, family, love. And because of those things, she was here. The adults in her life would just have to deal. They had raised her this way—though, maybe not the sneaking-away-from-home part, or the breaking and entering . . . But sometimes one had to break a few rules for the greater good. Her mom had done the same many times.

"We need to find where they keep the animals," she told Rex.

"The pups won't be in the matches," he said, "but they might be in a cage on display."

Emma knew there was a good chance their mother would be in one of the death matches, pitted against another beast for the entertainment of the crowd or pitted against a challenger.

In her world, carnivals were fun and safe and exciting. In this one, they meant death for many.

But not today, she thought. *Not my hounds.*

Determination settling over her, Emma squared her shoulders and started through the square. Brim remained at her side, growling low and deep, his eyes flashing red when one of the ghouls came too close, its face painted in a grotesque scream of white, red, and black.

They headed for the three large tents. A caged nithyn sat in front of the middle tent, advertising what one might find inside. The menagerie.

REX SHUDDERED. HE remembered those massive flying birds of prey and their penchant for cannibalism more vividly than he wanted to. A flash went off beside him. He turned to see a human snapping pictures. The nithyn shied away, screeching and ducking its bony head under large leathery wings.

The sign in front of the menagerie advertised all three tents. A menagerie, circus performances, and matches in both Charbydon and English. THE BEASTS OF HELL, it said in large, bold lettering in English. Rex wanted to roll his eyes. Laying it on pretty thick, weren't they?

The tent to the left held the performances and a list of times. The tent on the right of the menagerie was where the challenge and death matches took place.

The flash went off again, followed by a distinct crack.

The flashbulb and casing had cracked. The photographer cursed softly in surprise and examined his camera while Rex lifted an eyebrow and turned a knowing, very parental look Emma's way.

Anger had narrowed her big eyes to bright points. So unassuming, he thought, with her ponytail and thin frame, the graphic T-shirt, jeans, and sneakers. He'd felt the flare of her power and knew she'd caused the flash to break. *Good for you, kid.* Her gaze traveled from the photographer to him. Clearly, she could tell he knew. She shrugged in defiance, and Rex couldn't help but smile.

All business, Emma turned her attention to Brim. Rex watched as she leaned down and pressed her cheek to the top of his head. He thought he heard her whisper but wasn't sure with the noise from the vendors and carnival musicians.

The menagerie was open, but the performances and matches wouldn't be held until later that night. They had time to look around and, hopefully, find the pups and their momma.

"They're here," Emma said, straightening.

IT TOOK EVERYTHING Emma had to breach Brim's strong instinctual response and convince him to wait. To let her guide him. To keep him safe. He trembled inside with the need to go, to track his family down and tear into anything in his way.

She'd never command him, never force him. That wasn't the kind of relationship they had. It was one of mutual trust and respect. He whined softly, his mouth open and panting as he stared at the tent. Then he licked his chops and looked up at her for a moment, eyes hopeful and ready and needing to follow the scent.

"We'll go. Don't worry, we'll go soon," she told him.

Rex paid the admission price and they entered the menagerie, where three long rows of cages spread out before them. It was hotter inside than outside. Sweat beaded on Emma's forehead and dripped down her back. The smell of manure, dung, urine, and bedding, warmed in the Telmath heat, made her stomach clench into a hard knot.

They were only a few steps in when someone called to them.

A tall darkling fae approached, scolding the ticket taker as he passed. His skin was a dull luminescent gray. He wore a black suit with a white silk scarf tucked into the lapels, a high-collared white shirt, and a black satin top hat. His wide eyes were a pale mauve shade, and his lips were painted black.

He had a narrow face, all angles and prominence.

His words changed from Charbydon to English. "No beasts allowed in the tent." His voice was deep and almost musical, a smooth, creepy tone that lifted the fine hairs on Emma's arms.

The fae stopped in front of them and eyed Brim with interest.

Brim shifted his weight from paw to paw, wanting desperately to attack.

Please, Brim, no. Not yet.

From Brim's reaction, she knew the fae had the scent of the pups all over him. Sweat trailed down her temples as she tried her best to mentally convince him to wait.

Just wait a little longer. Please, trust me.

REX MOVED SLIGHTLY in front of Brim and Emma, not liking the look of this guy one bit—like hell's version of a ringmaster, with the eyes of a snake and the aura of a weasel—and from the antsy way Brim was acting and the fear he'd glimpsed in Em's eyes, neither did they.

"The hound stays with us," Rex said.

"Humans don't usually travel with such . . . company, and with one so tame, it seems. Still, no *pets* allowed."

"He's not a pet. He's in training under special permit 6673 of the ITF Weapons Research Allowance. He is permitted to stay with us, even in Charbydon."

The fae's wide lips spread to reveal blunt yellowed teeth. "Humans training hellhounds. How . . . novel. Good luck with that." His expression became nonchalant. He sighed. "It's not the most unusual thing I've heard of, I suppose."

"Shouldn't be. You train hellhounds and other beasts for the performances, don't you?" Rex countered easily, when what he really wanted to do was knock out some of those blunt teeth.

The fae paused thoughtfully. "We do. Yes. You should come to our performance tonight."

The fae watched Emma and Brim a little too closely for Rex's comfort. Her hand was on Brim's collar and her eyes were lost in thought—a good sign she was in communication with the hellhound.

"It takes a special person to train a hellhound," the fae went on. "The beasts are such rarities these days, especially the males. Most have disappeared into the Charbydon wilds. Others that lurk on the edges of society are too hard to catch, too dangerous to try . . . They are prized beasts. Where did you get yours?"

"He was illegally imported," Rex answered carefully. "Found by law enforcement. The rest is history."

"Ah. Well, that makes training a little easier, doesn't it? When they're already in the hands of human or off-worlder. Really, they must be born into it. The ones captured in the wild are completely untrainable and put to . . . other uses."

Em gasped. Brim lunged forward, but she grabbed at his collar, struggling to hold him back while muttering to him under her breath. Once he settled, she turned her attention to the fae, her cheeks reddened by rage. "You mean death matches. They don't deserve that. Who are you to decide that for them?"

Saliva dripped from Brim's mouth; his red eyes fixed on the fae with laser focus.

One eyebrow rose, the fae obviously not affected by her outburst. "Who are you to decide the fate which you have given yours, my dear?" he asked, eyeing Brim's collar.

"*He* decided. It was his choice. You don't give your animals a choice. You condemn them to die for sport, for fun." Her voice choked on the last word.

A smug smiled curved his black lips. "I suppose that's true. Such is the nature of our people and my business. I'm Baasîl, ringmaster, beast master, proprietor of Hell's Menagerie." He reached into his pocket and pulled out two tickets. "Please be my guests tonight at the performance. I insist. I'm sure you'll find it most . . . enlightening."

From the look in Baasîl's calculating eyes, Rex was pretty sure the ringmaster had figured out that Em and Brim could communicate in some way. Not good. Not good at all, he thought as the ringmaster left, disappearing through the flap and out into the lovely Telmath air.

Rex exhaled, releasing the tension in his body. "Come on," he said, starting down one of the rows, "let's see if the pups are here."

The cages were on wagon wheels, their bars made of thick iron crusted with years of dirt and grime. Their height put the beasts inside almost at eye level with Rex. He'd been to plenty of zoos in his time and plenty of carnivals, too, and these types of cages were always the most intimate, the animals right there in front of you, staring you in the face.

Emma stopped in front of each cage, giving each occupant her acknowledgment and respect. There were animals from all three worlds. Bears, hellhounds, nithyn, massive sand dragons similar to

earth's Komodo dragons, screechers—hellish monkey-like creatures with webbed hands tipped with long, razor-sharp claws.
They had small, useless milky-white eyes and lived deep inside of
caves, hunting at night, using their hearing to detect prey. There
was a winged griffon from Elysia—rare indeed, and lonely, Rex
thought, as the beast stared back at them with sad, regal eyes.
There was a huge violet-eyed, gray-haired cat similar to a lynx, but
the size of a lion. He'd never seen one before, but he knew they
were said to exist high in the Charbydon Mountains.

Rex was surprised by the rarity of the creatures Baasîl had col-
lected. It must have taken him aeons to gather this many, and it
made Rex wonder how long some of the beasts had been there.

At the end of one of the rows, a massive cage faced them. It
was five times the width of the others and nearly as high as the tent
ceiling. Huddled in the back corner of the cage was a mountain
troll.

They stopped, both amazed by the sight.

It was all muscle under thick gray skin. Huge hands, a bald
head with a thick skull, and small black tusks that curved down
over its mouth and lower jaw like massive fangs. Its wrists and ankles were ringed with wide iron shackles.

Emma approached the cage. Rex followed, the stench of the
beast reaching him long before he came to a stop in front of the
bars.

The troll kept its shoulder to them, shunning them after a
quick, solemn sideways look. It closed its eyes as though pretending they weren't there.

"So sad," Em barely uttered beside him. She started to place
her hand on the bars. Rex reached for her. He didn't want her
touching anything or getting that close. In that split second, the
troll lunged. It happened so fast, Brim yelped in surprise, and Rex's
first reaction was to grab Emma's shoulders and pull her back.

But the troll had grabbed the bars and trapped one of Emma's hands beneath its thick fingers.

Fear swept arctic and instant through his veins. "Emma," he said calmly.

The beast's face was smashed against the bars. Its head was lowered, eyes level with Emma. Its small nostrils flared in and out in loud, snorting puffs.

"Can you slide your hand out?"

She didn't answer. There was no pain on her face, no fear. Rex wasn't quite sure what she was feeling, but she was transfixed by the creature. They stared at each other intensely, as though nothing else existed.

Then the creature pushed away from the bars, snorting loudly as it went back to its corner and slumped down, ignoring them.

Em's hand slid free of the bars. Rex took it. "You okay?"

She seemed dazed, her wide brown eyes lost for a few moments. "Yeah," she said, then shook her head and finally focused on him. "Yeah. I'm fine. Let's keep looking."

THE PUPS WEREN'T in the menagerie. But they had been. Brim could smell their lingering scent. Emma's heart hurt as they left the tent. All those animals ... She knew some were deadly, and poisonous, and would kill as soon as they got the chance, but still she felt for them. They should be free to live in their own habitat, left alone. Not caged. Not spectacles. Not shoved into some arena to fight for their lives.

If she listened hard enough, she could feel their misery, their anger, their confusion, their heartbreak.

She wanted to go home, wanted her mom, wanted to forget she had ever seen this. She never wanted to see another off-world carnival as long as she lived. All around her the performers awed the crowd. Fire whooshed and flashed bright. Music played. Spectators cheered, laughed, and heckled. But Emma had never felt more alone. She didn't realize she'd stopped until Rex turned and put a hand on her arm.

"Aw, hell, kid. You kill me when you cry." He pulled her into a hug.

It was her father's arms, her father's smell—though somewhat different now that Rex had taken up residence. She missed him. But she loved Rex and knew he loved her, too.

"I'm sorry." She leaned back and sniffed, wiping away the tears with her hands. "I knew when we found out about the carnival, the menagerie . . . I knew all these animals would be here." She tipped her wet face up to look at him. "We have to help them."

Rex's expression turned pained and his eyes went glassy, his jaw tight. "I'd give you the world if I could. But not at the expense of your safety. We'll see if we can locate the pups, and that's it."

She didn't answer. What could she say to that?

"We'll figure it out, Em. Okay? We'll figure it out."

He wrapped an arm around her shoulder and led her to a vendor for some water and fresh bread.

REX AND EMMA were given the best seats in the house for the performance that night, which started off with Baasîl sweeping into the arena in his black suit and top hat. His voice reverberated through the massive tent as he promised a night of heart-pounding spectacle. Goose bumps sped up Rex's arms as the ringmaster declared the start of the greatest show in all three worlds with a dramatic flourish of his long arms and deep, booming laughter in his voice.

Baasîl leapt onto the arena wall and then climbed, like some black-clad praying mantis, up the chain-link cage that rose high around the arena as three large cats with lean bodies, short black fur, and long, curved fangs were set loose in the arena as eerily painted fae clowns dodged and tumbled over them like some hyped-up version of rodeo clowns meets bullfighting. Baasîl clung to the cage, telling the crowd that the goal was to turn the cats into clowns by sticking spikes topped with red pom-poms along their backs, which matched the pom-poms stuck to the clowns' outfits. Once all three cats had a set of four running down their backs, it was over.

And when it was, one fae was dead and one seriously injured. The cats were still standing, but they wouldn't make it through the night.

The crowd loved it. Fucking bastards.

It was no place for a twelve-year-old. Sure, there were young Charbydons there, but it was their world, how they'd grown up. Death was as much a part of their lives as anything else; they were desensitized to it. All great and good for them. Not so much for Emma. Rex had assumed these types of matches would be relegated to the match tent, but apparently even the performance-going folks liked a good mauling every once in a while. He'd thought the pups might be part of the show, something fun and cute for the crowd—how wrong he'd been.

The problem was that when they tried to leave before the performance was over, the three jinn warriors who stood guard at the exit to Baasîl's private box prevented them. So they sat back down, Emma tucked next to Rex and Brim on her other side. "Don't look," he told her. And she didn't. But the crowd, the screams . . . There was no way to avoid those. He knew she'd never forget those.

The performance finally drew to an end with trained moon snakes dancing to an otherworldly tune.

Rex breathed a sigh of relief and Emma's tense body went soft as the crowd filed out of the tent. But their guards remained, beefy arms crossed over their chests, huge linebackers' bodies that would've been intimidating had Rex not been one of them once. As it was, it irritated the shit out of him and he had a really bad feeling that letting Emma talk him into "just checking out the carnival" for the pups had turned into something else entirely.

The ringmaster walked into the arena.

Emma slipped her hand into Rex's. He squeezed and bumped her shoulder with his own. "Let me do the talking. Just keep Brim under control."

Rex stood just as two attendants closed the flaps to the tent's exit and stood guard. Quiet settled inside of the tent, accentuated by the murmur of the crowd outside.

"Enjoy the show?" Baasîl walked toward them, leapt onto the wall, and slipped his long bony fingers through the chain links.

"What do you want, Baasîl?"

A gleam appeared in the ringmaster's eyes. A deep growl rumbled in Brim's chest. Baasîl turned his attention to Emma, his strange mauve eyes narrowing. "He's a magnificent beast, you know. Big for his breed. Intimidating. There are those who would pay dearly for him."

"He's not for sale," Em bit out.

"No, I didn't think he would be. And that, you see, is the problem. How about we make a deal, you and me?"

Rex started to speak, but the ringmaster interrupted him, telling Emma, "One second." He nodded to the jinn behind them. Before she could react, Rex was struck with a tranquilizer tag.

"REX!" EMMA REACHED for Rex as he fell over, his body draped along the bench, the side of his face squished against the wood.

Oh God.

Electric fear slid into her, from her scalp all the way to her toes. Her pulse hammered through her eardrums. She swallowed, her mind racing. *Stay calm. Don't panic.* Her mom had schooled her in those very things—how to stay calm and smart in dangerous situations. After her kidnapping, Emma had taken those talks, those self-defense lessons, to heart . . .

Swallowing down the mushrooming panic, she straightened her spine, drew in a deep breath, and looked the ringmaster square in the eyes. He hurt Rex. He. Hurt. Rex. And that made her mad. Mad was better than scared. A smart mad was better than a rash one—her mom had taught her that, too.

"Now that that's taken care of," Baasîl said as the jinn lifted Rex and took him away, "we can deal."

She wouldn't cry, wouldn't call after Rex, wouldn't freak out because she was now alone. No, not alone. Brim was by her side. Brim would *always* be by her side. He leaned into her, sensing her emotions.

Rex was dumped by the tent's exit as Baasîl crawled over the top of the chain-link fence like a spider. Then he was down on her side. In her box. In her space, sitting down on the bench in front of her, his elbows resting on his knees.

Brim could take out his throat in the blink of an eye. But Baasîl wasn't afraid.

He should be, Em thought.

"Doesn't take a genius to figure out why you're here, little one. You show up, two humans with a hellhound. Not here to see the animals. See, I could tell you were looking for something. Had to ask myself what, 'What could they be after?'" He tapped his cheek with one long gray finger. "So here's the deal. You give me Big Daddy there, and you walk away with the pups. Free and clear.

Simple exchange. I'd throw in the bitch, too, but she lost in the ring last night, so . . ."

Instant tears surged, burning Emma's throat. The mother was dead. Her hand clenched into a tight fist, and the one holding on to Brim's neck dug into his muscled flesh. Her anger and grief blinded her for a second and then crystallized into a defined point. That point was Baasîl. "You're going to pay for that," she said in an even, flat tone.

Baasîl laughed softly, indulgently. Another one of his mistakes. Not believing her. Underestimating her. Behind him the arena gate opened and a small wire cage was carried in with the pups in it.

A shudder snaked through Brim's body; Emma felt it beneath her hand. He whined, glancing quickly at her, then back at the pups. Torn. He was torn between leaving her and guarding her. Tears thickened her throat.

"Don't cry, pretty girl." Baasîl's words tried to sound comforting but they came out grim and dark and just wrong. "He would want you to do this. Go ahead, ask him."

"What do you mean?"

"Oh, I saw you, how you were with him when we met earlier. He listens to you. You listen to him. Even among my kind, there are those who can talk to beasts. Rare, but it happens. Maybe even rarer in humans, I don't know." He leaned closer, his bony face harsh, daring her to argue. "I know what I saw. So you ask him."

Baasîl sat back, a smug light coming into his eyes. "It's his choice, remember?" He threw her words back at her, and Emma realized with a sinking feeling in her gut that he had her. He had Brim. Because Brim wouldn't even have to think about it. He'd give up his life to let her and the pups walk out of there safely.

The ringmaster went to touch her knee to nudge her as he said, "Go ahead, ask—"

Brim lunged. Baasîl lurched backward, his back meeting with the chain links as the hellhound's massive jaws and fangs snapped inches from his face. The suddenness of it made Emma jump. The snarl and growl—she'd never seen Brim so angry, so wild . . .

Beyond the ringmaster's shoulders, Emma saw the jinn in the arena reach in and grab one of the pups from the cage and hold it up by the neck. It squirmed, its lower body twisting back and forth. It let out a small cry at the tightening fingers around its neck. Brim's nostrils flared, drool dripped from his bared fangs, and his eyes burned hot and red.

He stepped back.

The ringmaster let out a relieved laugh; the gray color of his skin had gone to pale ash. He straightened his top hat and found his voice. "He's perfect. The crowd will love him."

"You'd trade three hellhounds for one? Why?"

"The pups are useless to me right now. It'll take years for them to grow and to train. But him . . . he'll do whatever I want. Tricks, commands, fights, coordinated attacks. Can you imagine what he'd look like in the warhound armor of old?"

"He won't listen to you," she told him. "He'll turn on you the first chance he gets. He won't forget what you've done."

"Oh, I think he will. See, I've thought this through. I'm a businessman and all. As long as he listens, his pups are safe. I just came from your city, see? Where do you think I got this incredible hat? I have contacts everywhere. No matter where you hide them, no matter what protection you put them under, my guys will find them and . . ." He left the rest of it unspoken, left it up to her imagination.

The jinn put the pup back with the others and took the cage to where Rex lay. Rex was coming around, sitting up with a loud groan and rubbing his hands down his face.

"Go ahead, child," Baasîl said. "Ask him. Give him the choice."

She couldn't think. She didn't want to make this decision,

didn't want to ask Brim anything. She loved him. God, she loved him. She couldn't let him go, couldn't let him do this.

The ringmaster was taking advantage of her, she knew. A lot of adults she'd come across underestimated kids her age, always thought they couldn't think for themselves, couldn't figure things out, couldn't see the flaws and loopholes . . .

Brim could kill Baasîl right now. They even had a good chance of escaping—if Rex could shake off the tranquilizer, Brim made it to the jinn by the exit in time, and her power was strong enough to take care of the other guards.

It was. She knew it was.

But it wasn't her choice. She had to leave it up to Brim to take the risk. It was his family, after all.

She turned to him and slipped her arms around his neck, hugging him tight. Her eyes closed, her nose went stuffy. "I love you," she whispered against his warm skin. *I love you so much, Brim.* He turned his big head toward her, eyes staring right into hers. She held his face, pressed her forehead against his, and sank into his thoughts . . .

THE FOG WAS almost gone from Rex's mind.

It felt like he had just been body slammed by a fucking elephant. He rubbed a hand down his face and remembered where he was and what was happening. A surge of panic went through him.

The gray wrinkly pups were next to him in their small cage, all huddled together, staring up at him with huge, innocent eyes. And there was Emma, sitting in the box across the arena, posture straight, face pale, talking to the ringmaster—the dead man; Rex was going to kill him.

Quickly, he took stock of the situation, put a few things together in his head, and then made to lunge for the jinn nearby. But

Emma stood suddenly. Rex paused. The jinn guarding the box stood aside, and she walked around the curve of the arena toward the exit. Brim stayed behind.

What the hell?

He struggled to his feet, swaying slightly as a wave of nausea nearly sent him down again. Emma finally reached him. She was white as a ghost, eyes rimmed in red, and she looked so small and so goddamn broken, he wanted to hit something. His fists clenched. But instead of striking the nearest wall, he pulled her to his chest and held on tight. He set her back from him more harshly than he intended and looked her over. "Tell me you're okay. Did he hurt you?"

Tears filled her eyes and slipped out in long streams. Her lips had gone thin and trembly. She nodded, sucked in a deep, gasping breath. "Not on the outside," she said. "We have to go now."

He blinked. But Brim . . . He glanced from Emma's devastated face to where the ringmaster stood with Brim obediently at his side, and Rex knew.

Oh, hell no. Hell fucking no.

Shaking from the shock and the tranq, Rex bent slowly and picked up the cage. The flap was lifted for them, and they left. Just . . . left.

He could barely keep up with Emma as she marched through the crowded square, head up, tears streaming. The pups licked his fingers through the wire cage. Once they reached a quieter area, Emma stopped, swiping angrily at the wetness on her face.

She struggled to regain her composure, and it killed him. He wasn't sure what to do, what to say. Slowly, her expression morphed. He knew that look, had seen it a hundred times on her mother. "We need a room somewhere," she said. "An inn or something. Did you bring money?"

Still feeling woozy and sick, and a whole lot weak and shaky, Rex set the cage down, wiping his wet fingers on his pants. "Yeah, I brought money. You mind telling me what happened back there? And what's going through your head?"

He might be about to upchuck in the barrel behind him, but he sure as shit was sharp enough to see that this wasn't over. Despite the tears, sweet Emma Madigan Garrity had morphed into a focused, highly pissed-off version of Charlie Madigan.

He ran a shaky hand through his hair and let out a soft curse. Emma would never leave it at that. She'd never walk away from Brim. She had a plan, and seeing as she was her mother's daughter . . . Yeah. All hell was about to break loose.

"Rex," she said. "A room."

He hefted the cage again and started walking. "You know I'm technically already banned from Charbydon, right? The last thing we need is to cause a scene and get thrown into jail. Prison in hell is beyond miserable."

"So am I if we don't save Brim," she muttered.

As they headed away from the carnival, Rex realized they had only the pups, not the mother. He opened his mouth but then shut it again. No. He'd leave that one alone. Emma hadn't mentioned her, and he had a bad feeling as to why. With a weary sigh, he gazed at the pups. They bounced along as he walked, eyes and ears alert. His chest tightened as he thought of their mother. And Brim . . .

They found an inn off the market street, and after the tranquilizer, the extreme nausea, and subsequent visits to the Inn's bathroom, Rex was not in a good mood. He was downright pissed, angry, and ready to hurt something. Upon exiting the bathroom, he found Emma standing there with her arms crossed and foot tapping. Deep down, he knew she'd never leave without Brim, but he also knew he had to find a way to get her back home. This had gotten way out of hand.

"We're not going back," he said, stepping around her to sit on the bed.

Emma whirled on him. "We're not going home. We can't. And we're not waiting for reinforcements. No one here cares. My mom is rescuing Hank. She's in another *world*, Rex. There's no telling when she'll get back. And if we contact Aunt Bryn or anyone else, then everyone will know what we've done. They'll get the law involved, and you know what Baasîl will do. He'll get rid of evidence."

"And I told you, you're under my protection. If I had to choose, I'd pick you over Brim and those pups. And you know that's the right thing for me to do. Stop being a delinquent and just listen."

"Stop calling me a delinquent! I'm not leaving here without Brim and the others."

Oh, this was new. "What *others?*"

She reddened. "All of them."

"All of them." Jesus H. This was getting better and better.

Her chin stuck out. "Yes, all of them. Every single one of those animals in the cages. You didn't feel them. You don't know how they're suffering. This is what I was meant to do. I can hear them, feel them. Why would I have this power if not to help when I can?"

His voice softened. "You're twelve years old, Emma. It's not your responsibility. Maybe one day it will be, but not now. Look, right now we're safe. Baasîl got what he wanted. But once we go against him, there's no telling what he'll do . . . We'll get Brim back, but not on our own, not tonight. Not without help."

"Then go away," she shot back. "I'll do this myself."

He rolled his eyes. "Uh. No."

"I don't care how old I am or what you say! I'm doing this, Rex. And I swear, if you get in my way I will never forgive you. Never." It hurt her to say that, he saw. Her lips trembled and tears slipped from her sad eyes. "You have no idea what I can do. I've figured it out. I know how to save them. Why can't you believe in me?"

Rex, who had an answer for most anything, didn't know what to say.

He did believe in her. But he was also her protector. And right now those two things seemed at war. He reached for her. "Emma, I can't let you do this. You can't . . ."

"Watch me."

She turned and ran out the door. "Goddammit. Emma!" He ran to the door but then stopped, grabbed their key off the table, and locked the door behind him, securing the pups inside.

Rex glimpsed her darting out of the inn and into the night. He knew the direction she was headed, so he ran, weaving through the streets until he found his way back into the square. For a split second he caught sight of her ponytail, and then she was gone. The carnival crowd had grown, becoming louder, drunker, and more dangerous than during the day.

A knife juggler backed into Rex. Rex shoved the darkling fae away, causing the airborne knives to drop to the ground, barely missing his foot. He didn't care. He was trying to keep up. A dense pack of spectators had gathered around the match tent. He jumped to see over their heads and finally spotted Emma as she snuck down the narrow alley between the match tent and the menagerie.

A myriad of curses flowing through his mind, Rex followed. Emma reached the end of the alley and slipped behind the match tent. Rex edged his way down, wanting to shout at her, to call her back, but he didn't dare. It was too quiet back there, too much of a risk of being found by Baasíl's guards.

He stopped at the end of the tent and peered around the corner. The last thing he saw was a giant gray fist coming out of nowhere. The last thing he heard was Baasíl's soft chuckle and the words, "Put them in the show."

WHY DID I *let her talk me into this? Why?*

Standing in the arena with Emma by his side, facing a twelve-foot-tall mountain troll, was just about as much as Rex could take. He laughed. And to top it all off, he was dressed like a clown. A macabre one. His entire face had been painted white like Emma's, their eyes circled with black paint. They looked like skeletons. Skeleton clowns in tuxedo leotards. No one would know there were two humans in the ring.

Baasîl apparently had no qualms about the law.

It was the finale of the night's performance. And Baasîl had just informed the crowd that Emma and Rex would face the snarling mass of muscle, fangs, and lunacy in front of them. It wasn't a question of if they could defeat the troll, but how long they could last before it tore them apart.

A flat club with serrated inserts of razor-sharp stone hung in the beast's massive hand. Mountain trolls were extremely reclusive, extremely volatile creatures. Once they felt threatened, they attacked with a frenzy that didn't let up until all that remained was a bloody mass of goo on the ground.

The crowd cheered. Money was passed from hand to hand. Trapeze artists swung overhead, and clowns climbed inside the chain links that protected the crowd. They, too, wore skeleton paint and black tuxedo body suits. Anyone inside or above was fair game. You fell, you got caught, and you were dead.

Baasîl settled into his private box. Behind him was Brim in a spiked collar. Attached to the collar were four stiff rods held by four jinn. The rods kept them safe and gave them control over the hellhound. Rex knew those rods could shock as well.

Rex had been one of the finest jinn warriors of his day—the best, some said. Powerful. Huge. Feared. But he hadn't been that person in aeons. He was human now, and his powers and strength were zilch compared to a jinn and especially compared to that hulking creature banging on the thick timber gate.

"When I say go, you start climbing the fence, you hear me? Get to the top, and then you run. Use whatever power you can, hurt whoever you need to hurt, and get back to the portal." Em didn't respond. Rex grabbed her shoulders. His hands were shaking. "Swear it, Emma. You get the hell out of here."

Her large brown eyes looked even larger ringed by the black paint. She blinked. Maybe she was in shock. What was he talking about, *maybe?* She had to be. Hell, even he felt a sense of the surreal. Weak human in a huge arena, surrounded by a bloodthirsty crowd, with a fucking troll. He shook her. "Swear it."

His heart pounded. They'd had so little time together. He'd lived for thousands of years, countless lives in one body after another, and he'd had a good run. He wasn't ready to go, but he'd be damned if he'd let one hair on Emma's head be harmed. He'd fucked up as usual, but she would *not* pay for his mistake.

Em's expression slowly transformed into . . . a smile? Rex did a double take. She reached up and cupped his face in her small, black-gloved hands. "I love you, Rex."

"I love you, too," he said absently, wanting to get back to that promise, wanting to know she'd run. He began to tell her so, but she cut off his words.

"I've got this."

"Wha—?"

The timber gate groaned as it began to crank open. The crowd went wild. Shit. He swung his gaze back to Emma.

"Remember what I said," she said, cutting him off again. "I know what to do. I figured it out. I'm scared to death. I didn't mean to get caught, that wasn't the plan, but . . . I'm not giving up." She turned to look at Brim. He was shaking his head, struggling with the jinn and getting shocked repeatedly. "Just . . . keep it distracted for a minute, and don't get hurt. Brim and I will do the rest." The gate went up. The troll burst through. "Trust me!" Emma gave him a blinding smile and ran toward Baasîl's box.

The confidence, the calm belief, in her expression—it stunned and humbled him.

The troll was in front of him. Dirt flew up as it slid to a stop and swung its heavy club. *Shit!* He dodged right. His hair moved in the breeze created by the club as it whispered inches from his head. He rolled sideways, popped to his feet, and dashed to the other end of the arena, arms pumping, eyes wildly searching for Emma.

She was in front of the box. Two of the jinn holding Brim blew backward. She'd used her power. Brim flung his body, trying to shake off the other two. He rammed the rods into the bench. One snapped off at the collar. The other hit Baasîl in the head, sending his top hat flying.

Rex couldn't see more. The troll swung at him again. He dove to his left and hit the ground as the club slammed down next to him so hard, it vibrated the ground. He scrambled up and ran.

The roar of the crowd filled the space. The thumps of their boots on the wooden benches sounded in time to the frantic beat of his heart. "Emma!" He found her again, this time a blur as she sped past the troll's right side. He ran for her. From his peripheral vision, he saw commotion as Brim, free of the box, plowed through the crowd, trying to find a way down to the holding gate where the troll had been released.

The troll was after Emma. She screamed and rolled beneath its massive feet as it swung its club. Rex grabbed her and threw her behind him.

Brim bolted through the holding gate, the two broken rods still clinging to his collar. He'd made it.

Emma ran right. Brim ran left.

They darted by the troll, one after the other, confusing it. Finally, it shook its head, turned, and zeroed in on Rex.

"Distract it, Rex!" Emma shouted.

"Why am I always the bait?" he muttered, and then shouted, "Come and get me, you big bastard! Take your best shot!"

EMMA WATCHED REX wave his arms, jog in place, and roll his shoulders while talking smack to the troll. It charged. Rex screamed.

Now, Brim!

Brim's muscular hindquarters bunched and he took off like a rocket, sweeping around the oval arena toward Rex. Just as he was upon him, he veered sharply, spraying Rex with dirt and then charging the troll headlong as it raced down the centerline. Brim leapt. His massive jaws latched onto the troll's bare shoulder. His body flipped over, twisting in midair. But he held on, the troll's flesh twisting in his mouth and tearing.

It worked. The momentum tipped the troll backward, knocking it off balance. It backpedaled, dropping to its rear, its lethal club coming to rest in the dirt as its hand reached out to stop itself from falling completely on its back.

Brim released the troll and ran behind Emma. Her heart beat so fast, it made her dizzy. Fear numbed her entire body. This was it. She had to do this. Now or never and all that. If they were going to get out of this alive—all of them—she had to act, and act now.

She ran and leapt just as the troll leaned forward to push itself to its feet. Her body slammed against its shoulder. Her breath whooshed from her lungs, but she kept to the task and wrapped her arms around its thick tusks, facing it. The stench of its breath was beyond gross and triggered her gag reflex. Her eyes stung. Yet there was something intelligent inside that thick skull. She had glimpsed it when it had lunged at her in the menagerie.

She had to make eye contact.

This was her power. This was her gift. Her skin tingled like it was asleep. She caught its gaze, met it eye to eye. Emma gave herself over to her power. With everything she had, she forced her way inside and sank into the troll's mind.

A huge, beefy hand slapped onto the back of her head and squeezed as it prepared to yank her off.

There. There you are. The hand stopped squeezing but didn't let go. *And here I am. You're going to be just fine . . .*

Emma realized, as she'd pretty much suspected all along, that besides being able to communicate, she could influence. She could force her will upon a creature, which was why she'd always been so careful with Brim. She never wanted to do that, never wanted their relationship to be one of master and slave.

But this creature . . . this one was different. This one was hard, the connection weak. *But I'm strong,* she reminded herself. She was stronger than the troll, not physically but mentally. And that's where it counted.

Pain spread through her head. But she kept on, knowing the beast wanted a way out, was desperate to escape. It needed to know she was on its side, that freedom was at hand. She heard Rex shout. Heard Brim's ferocious growl. And then she drifted, remembering her lessons in the backyard with Rex—always on concentration, always on control, always on tapping into the core of one's power. And Rex, the way he'd wave his hand and always say, "These are not the droids you're looking for."

She laughed inside.

She knew what to do.

By the time the giant hand released her skull, Emma was coated in a cold sweat. Her skin was sticky, the face paint like glue on her skin. She slid off the smelly creature, and her legs collapsed beneath her. Rex caught her and dragged her away as the troll slowly got to its feet, bent over, picked up its massive club, and then lifted its head.

Time slowed. The crowd went quiet.

The troll stood straight and proud, its eyes raised to the crowd. It drew in a deep breath, its chest expanding.

And then it let out the loudest, scariest, angriest roar Emma had ever heard.

Silence descended. The crowd seemed to sense things had changed, sensed something different was about to take place. The troll turned its head, glanced over its shoulder at Emma. Poor thing. So angry, so scared, craving the mountains and its home, its family. She nodded. With a quickness not expected from such a hulking beast, it swung its head back around and zeroed in on Baasîl's box.

Emma watched in satisfaction as Baasîl's gray skin went a few shades lighter.

And then it was on. The troll charged. The hunt began. The crowd freaked and stampeded for the exits.

Her legs were still weak, her body still shaking, but she stepped out of Rex's hold. She didn't look back. Didn't want to. Didn't need to. Instead, Emma walked toward the arena gate, calm and focused. Tired and sad.

Baasîl was on his own. The troll, a female, would do what she wanted to the one who had trapped and caged her. Emma had been surprised about the gender, but not the emotions, not the desire to go home. She hadn't given an order to kill. But that's what the outcome would be. It was the troll's choice, but Emma knew the role she played, and she knew she'd have to live with it. And after the troll had its revenge, it would flee, escaping out the gaping mouth of Telmath and into the Charbydon wilds. Flee rather than fight. Harm no one else, just . . . run—that's what Emma had imprinted on its mind.

Tears stung her eyes as she walked over the soft earth to the sounds of screams. Rex and Brim caught up with her, and together they went through the gate and into the back area of the tent.

"We're releasing them," she told Rex as panicked carnival workers ran past them.

"Emma. We can't. Turning them out in the city . . . They're wild animals. They'll kill innocent people."

She looked into his eyes, so like her father's, and felt like she'd aged by years. "I know. I'll take care of it. I can influence them, Rex. They'll listen to me. They want to go home. They'll run, nothing more. The ones who live off-world can follow us to the portal or choose to make a life in the wild. There are sixteen animals in the menagerie and two in cages back here." Her voice was shaky, her body numb. She drew in a deep, steadying breath and waited to see if he'd back her up. And somehow, his answer meant more to her than anything.

Rex parked his hands on his hips. He looked ridiculous in his tuxedo leotard and face paint. Her smile grew from the inside out because she knew that look and knew his answer.

"I swear, it's never a dull moment with you Madigan women," he said, shaking his head and letting out a dramatic sigh. "Okay, kid. Let's do this."

"DAUGHTER OF THE MIDWAY, THE MERMAID, AND THE OPEN, LONELY SEA"

Seanan McGuire

If there's one thing seventeen years of traveling with the Miller Family Carnival has taught me, it's that harvesttime is carnival time.

Spring is good, if what you want is young lovers cluttering the Ferris wheel like clinging burrs, moon-eyed and drunk on the wonder of learning that lips can be used for kissing. Summer brings in the families, screaming children with fingers that smell like cotton candy and mischief, wistful parents who remember their own turns around the Ferris wheel. Springs and summers are profitable. We're hopping like scalded cats all through spring and summer. The midway lights never go out, and my throat feels like twenty miles of bad road by the time we get to August from all the cheering and cajoling and calling for the townies to step right up and see the wonders of the world.

Springs and summers pay for new equipment, for repairs to

the old equipment, for fresh ponies in the paddock and good bread on the table. Winters are for resting. That's when we retreat to the family's permanent home outside of Phoenix, Arizona, and take stock against the year to come. But autumns . . .

Autumns are harvesttime, and harvesttime is carnival time.

Even the trees know it, and they dress themselves up in reds and yellows and kiss-a-carnie gold. Especially in the South, where the pulse of the seasons runs right under the skin of the world. Alabama met us at the border with a celebration, and the mood spread through the carnival like a rumor. Everything was going to be good here. The ticket sales would be fantastic, the marks would be easy, and the people would be easy to please.

But first, we have to get them to come. There's where I come in: me, and the rest of the scouts. I ride into Huntsville on the roof of Duncan's pickup truck, sitting with my legs dangling and my face turned toward the road behind us. It falls away like a secret no one cared to keep. My heels drum against the glass with every bump and pothole, setting up an uneven tattoo that says *Carnival's-coming, carnival's-coming, carnival-is-almost-here.*

It's a perfect day.

I should know by now that perfect days can't last.

The pickup rattles to a stop in front of a convenience store. The storefront is plastered with flyers and faded advertisements so thick that no trace of the original paint remains. I slide into the bed of the pickup, retrieving my shoes from where I dropped them among the piled-up posters that will tell the town that we're coming. They're old sneakers, a size too large for me, loose on my feet with the laces untied. I don't tie them.

Shoes are a necessary evil, reserved for the company of townies, after seventeen years spent running barefoot along the midway.

Duncan walks around the truck and holds out his hands without a word. I pick up the nearest stack of posters and hand them to him. "Do you want to wait here, or do you want to come inside and meet the locals?" he asks.

He's been asking me that since I was old enough to come on town runs, and I always give the same answer: "I don't know that I care much about the locals, but I'd love something to drink." Duncan laughs, bundles the stack of posters up under his right arm, and sweeps me down from the bed of the pickup with his left arm. He holds me so that I'm still facing behind myself, still watching where I've been, and he lets my denim-clad behind serve as my herald to the world as he walks toward the store.

A bell chimes when the door is opened, just before the rush of too-cold air-conditioning hits us. My skin lumps itself into fat knots of gooseflesh, making the scales around my collarbone burn. I squirm against Duncan's arm, hoping he'll get the hint and put me down. Being carried in is part of the tradition, but I'd rather walk than freeze.

Duncan ignores me—Duncan always ignores me—as he focuses on the store's unseen inhabitants. "Good afternoon, sirs and ma'am," he says. He's using his friendly midwestern accent, the one that can pull in townies from miles away if they let him keep talking for a few minutes. That's why he's head scout and I just carry posters. "I'm Duncan Miller, and this is my cousin Ada."

"H'lo," I say, waving vaguely at the air behind me.

"We're with the Miller Family Carnival, and we were just wondering if it would be all right for us to drop off a few posters for you to hang outside your lovely establishment." There's a pause while he flashes a smile at the sirs and ma'am. I don't need to see it. I've seen this routine before. "We'd also be happy to hang them ourselves, if that would be easier for you."

"The carnival's coming to town?" It's an older man's voice, with a disbelieving tone. I close my eyes, trying to picture him. He'll be a thin man, weathered and drawn, without nearly enough hair to cover his head. He'll smoke—not inside, of course—and the tips of his fingers will be stained yellow.

Guessing people's faces from their voices is a parlor trick, and it's one I'm good at, probably because I've had so much practice. I squirm again, trying to get Duncan to put me down and let me see whether I'm right.

"Yes, sir, it is," says Duncan.

"But the carnival *never* comes to Huntsville," says a woman. She sounds younger than the man. I picture her as larger, too, not fat, but soft and rounded like Eglantine, who teaches math to us carnie kids and trains the dancing girls in the hoochie tent. "Not for going on twenty years."

"Well, ma'am, the carnival is coming now," says Duncan. He finally yields to my squirming, bending down to set my feet on the floor. "I'm delighted to hear it's been so long since you've had the opportunity to enjoy the wonders of a proper midway. Why, I'll expect to see each and every citizen of Huntsville pass through our gilded gates."

"I can't say you'll see everyone, but a carnival will be a nice change of pace around here," says the second man. He sounds big.

Fixing my talking-to-townies smile firmly in place, I turn and see the people behind the counter. The first man is old, and thin enough to pass for a scarecrow, in the right clothes. He has a full head of hair, but it's too thick, and the color isn't right: he's wearing a toupee. The second man is both younger and larger, with arms almost as big around as Duncan's and a gut like one of the silent pot-bellied twins who run the pony ride.

Only the woman doesn't match her voice. She's too small, with that crumpled-up look people get when they lose more weight than they should. Her eyes are cloudy with some old sorrow, and I know just by looking at her that whatever hurt her is more than even a Ferris wheel ride in the moonlight can heal.

The woman blinks when she sees me, clouded eyes going wide and a little bit clearer as she raises a hand to cover her mouth. The older of the two men hits her in the arm.

"M-my," says the woman, almost sounding like she's hiccupping in the middle of the word. "Aren't you a pretty thing. What did you say your name was again, sugar?"

"Ada Miller," I say, still smiling. "We surely would appreciate seeing you all at the carnival. We have a midway that's second to none in this half of the country, and the best sideshows you'll see anywhere."

"You the ones who have that mermaid?" asks the younger man.

Everything seems to stop. It feels like the whole store is holding its breath along with me. Then Duncan smiles and says, "The Alabama Mermaid? Three shows a night. Be sure to buy your tickets early or you might not get in. Thanks for hanging those posters, now." He drops the posters on the counter and turns, smile dying the second the townies can't see his face.

He doesn't need to tell me why. I turn quickly, and together we walk through the arctic chill to the door and out into the hot autumn afternoon, where the truck is waiting. I start automatically for the back. He grabs my arm.

"Not this time, Ada." The friendly midwestern accent is gone, replaced by his normal New Jersey sharpness. There's no need for pretend among family. "We need to get back to the lot."

I blink at him. "But the posters—"

"Plenty of people can pass out posters," says Duncan. "Now, get in."

I get.

THE VIEW FROM the cab of the truck is disorienting, all forward and no back. I try watching the road behind us in the rearview mirror, but that just gets me a headache and a vague impression of where we've been. By the time we turn off the main road and into the field we've rented for the next three weeks, all I want to do is go back to my own trailer, chew some candied ginger, and sleep.

"Ada."

I freeze with my hand halfway to the door handle and look back at Duncan. He's looking at me solemnly, brow furrowed. He looks worried. Not just worried: worried about *me*.

"What?"

"Don't run off. We need to talk to your mother."

I blanch.

"Are you sure?" I try to make the question sound casual. I fail. It's midafternoon. Mama will be out in her tank, enjoying her few days of sunlight before the carnival starts up and we have to erect a tent around her, stopping prying eyes in favor of paying customers. She never gets more than half a week in the sun, and she *hates* to be disturbed when she's sunbathing, even by me. *Especially* by me.

Duncan sighs. "Unfortunately, yes. Come on. We need to talk to Uncle Chester, and then we need to go see your ma."

I can't think of any arguments that he would listen to. "All right," I say, and slip out of the truck, my head still pounding like a drum. We walk into the camp together. I take his arm. He doesn't stop me.

The camp will be a carnival in a few more days. But like a caterpillar needs to spend time as a cocoon before it can be a moth, a caravan needs to spend time as a camp before it can be a carnival. Camp time is when we throw down roots, transitory as they are, building foundations and frames to hang dreams and nightmares from. The Ferris wheel is half-constructed, a skeletal assemblage of uncovered bars that rises against the sky like a strange new kind of spider's web. The midway is taking shape, wooden stalls and games of chance blossoming up from the mud. The bone yard sits just outside the circle of rides and games of chance, our trailers still looking like a part of the landscape. We'll move the yard further away when the trailers start to seem small and shabby, allowing the townies to believe that we never sleep, that we live on ticket stubs and midway dreams.

The air smells like sawdust and sweat. This is home.

Everywhere we walk we're met with silent waves and companionable nods from the family. Everyone at the carnival is kin, by marriage, blood, or adoption, and we look out for one another. Mama was adopted. I was born on the midway. "Better than a Kewpie doll" is what Uncle Chester always said when I asked him, and that was good enough for me.

It confuses the townies when we say we're all family, because we come from so many places, and we look nothing alike. Duncan is broad and dark-skinned, with hair that's well on its way to being completely gray, even though he's not much older than I am. I'm fish-belly pale and slim as a slip, with long dark hair that curls like wood shavings and eyes the color of deep water. We're family all the same.

Uncle Chester is standing by a plywood structure that will be the Haunted House, in the fullness of time and another few dozen coats of paint. He's a tall, thin man with hair the lacquered black of the cars on the kiddie coaster. When I was little, I used to pretend he was my father. He frowns when he sees us coming. "You hang five hundred posters as fast as all that, Duncan?"

"Not quite, Uncle. We may have a problem."

"Someone ask about our permits? They're all square."

"No." Duncan looks toward me, then back to Uncle Chester. "One of the men at the first store we stopped at asked whether we were the ones had the Alabama Mermaid. And I think his friend recognized our Ada."

That's the last straw. I step away from Duncan, crossing my

arms. "Someone want to tell me what you're talking about?" They turn to look at me, expressions saying what their voices won't: they've been so wrapped in worrying about me that they've nearly forgotten I was there. "Well?"

Uncle Chester sighs. "I suppose we ought to go and see your mama." He turns and barks an order at the cousins setting up the Haunted House. Then he starts across the field, leaving us to chase after him.

"I hate you all," I mutter darkly.

Duncan laughs—but there's no joy in the sound, and that's the most frightening thing of all. Together, we follow Uncle Chester.

MAMA IS STRETCHED out on the rock at the center of her tank, naked as a jaybird and face turned toward the sun. Her eyes are closed, and they stay closed as we climb the ladder to the platform fitted against the tank's edge. I spent countless nights curled up on that platform when I was a little girl, too afraid to be away from my mother for a whole night.

I stopped coming when she stopped singing me to sleep. There didn't seem much point, after that.

Uncle Chester crouches, placing a hand against the surface of the water. "I'd like to talk to you, Martha, if you don't mind."

His voice is mild, but its effect on Mama is electric. She rolls off her rock, becoming a blurry streak of motion in the tank. Uncle Chester straightens just before her hands burst from the water next to the platform. She slaps them down against the wood, and the Alabama Mermaid, pride of the Miller Family Carnival, pulls herself up next to me.

No one could look at her while she's this close and see a human woman in a carnie costume. Her tail's too real, for one thing, and her bones and the skin stretched across them are subtly *wrong*, shouting her alien heritage to anyone who cares to look. She'll be plastered down with pancake for the show, until she doesn't gleam amphibian-wet in the light, until the minds of the townies no longer instinctively try to make them turn their eyes away. It's hard to look straight at mermaids. There's too much about them that shouldn't be.

She smells like fresh fish and salt water, and it's all I can do not to recoil from the fear that she'll touch me.

"Hello, Uncle!" she says. She looks inhuman, but she sounds pure Alabama native, born and raised within the shadow of Birmingham. The water hasn't taken that from her. Not yet, anyway. "Cousins," she adds, with a nod to me and Duncan. I swallow the lump in my throat. So this isn't going to be one of the days when she knows me. I don't know whether I'm grateful or not. "To what do I owe the pleasure?"

"Do you know where we are, Marti?" asks Uncle Chester.

Mama frowns. "Well," she says, after a long pause to consider, "I can't rightly say I do. Are we in Indiana again? I liked Indiana."

"Indiana was six months ago," says Uncle Chester. He takes one of her hands in his own. The webbing connecting her fingers looks like a veil over his rougher, work-chapped skin. "Think, Marti. Where does the sky look like this? Where is the ground the color of drying blood?"

Her frown deepens. "But we can't be in Alabama, Uncle." There's a note of petulance in her voice. "Alabama is where we started. We can't be back where we started. I've been here too long."

"I know." He pats her hand. "Marti, do you remember what happened the last time we were in Alabama? It was a long time ago. Almost twenty years. Remember?"

"No," she says guilelessly, and pulls her hand away. "I'm cold, Uncle. I'm cold." Then she's gone, slipping back into the water. She doesn't surface again, but retreats to the far corner of the pool, a dark, sullen splotch against the blue.

I don't want to. I have to. "I can go in after her, if you want," I offer uneasily.

Uncle Chester looks up, narrowing his eyes. "How are your scales?"

"They haven't spread these last few months. I've been keeping dry, showers only, and eating less meat. Seems to be working well enough." They itch constantly. Sometimes they break off in the night, leaving my bed full of splinters formed from my own body. But they aren't *spreading*.

"Then no, I don't want you to go in after her. If your scales aren't spreading, we're going to keep it that way." Uncle Chester and Duncan exchange a look so laden with meaning that I can't even start picking it apart. "Go back to the bone yard. You look peaked. I'll have the cousins come and fetch you for supper."

"But—"

"You're excused from setting up for the rest of the day. Rest, Ada. You need it."

I take a breath to argue. Then I swallow it, nodding. "Yes, Uncle." Forcing my shoulders to slump, I turn and descend the ladder. I keep my head low as I walk away, until the edge of the camp hides me from their view. Then I turn and run through the maze of half-built rides and piles of plywood until I find another path into the field.

Low to the ground, I creep toward the tank. The sound of voices drifts down and across the water: "We could move." That's Duncan. "Pull up stakes and go."

"We can't afford that and you know it. The spring's take repairs the rides, the summer's take pays the wages, and the fall's take sees us through the winter. We're not living hand to mouth yet, but we will be if we get a reputation for running out on shows we've already committed to." Uncle Chester now. "We're going to have to see this through. And damn you, Martha, for making us do it."

I stay where I am until I see them climb down the ladder and walk back toward the skeleton that will become a carnival. Then, silently, I turn and creep back to my trailer, leaving the field, and the tank, and my mother behind.

I'M THE ONLY girl in the bone yard with her own trailer: most of us have to share with at least one other person, and the cousins who don't want to bunk with their parents wind up stacked like cordwood in trailers that were never meant for more than two. Uncle Chester says I have "environmental needs," and since his word is law, I get a little privacy to go with my jury-rigged collection of dehumidifiers and open jars of silica gel. No matter where we go, from Seattle to Georgia, the inside of my trailer is dry as the Arizona desert.

I throw myself down on the bed, trying to shut out the pounding in my head as I breathe in the dust-dry air. It hurts my lungs, but in a good way: in a *human* way.

Maybe if they'd thought to give Mama a few dehumidifiers, she'd still know who I was.

She had legs when I was a little girl; she wore flowing skirts that didn't pinch the fins growing down the sides of her thighs, and she hated shoes, just like I do, because her toes were webbed, just like mine. Fine scales grew in the hollows of her collarbone and on her lower belly, and in all the soft places where her joints bent.

"Don't you worry, Ada-love," she used to say as she tucked me into bed, all cotton sheets and mismatched blankets. "The sea wants me awful bad, but it won't have me while you're still here needing a mama." Then she'd go to her own bed, a scavenged hot tub filled with salt water, and take one more step away from me.

The first time I woke up to find her all the way under the water, I screamed my throat raw. I was only eleven. Uncle Chester nearly broke the trailer door down getting inside, and when he saw my mother at the bottom of the tub, he reached in with his shirt still on. She was limp when he hauled her to the surface, propping her head against the little shelf she used as a pillow.

And then she opened her eyes, and blinked at him, and asked, in a tone so reasonable it hurt, "What's that child shrieking about? Can't a body get a moment's peace in this place?"

Uncle Chester took me for a walk that day, after he had her settled. We sat on the fence outside the pony ride and he told me everything he knew about mermaids, everything he'd learned and guessed and worked out for himself. "When your mama came to live with us, she was six months pregnant and she looked almost human, as long as you didn't mind the webs between her fingers. She could hold her breath a long time. She could swim like a fish. But she was a human lady, or close enough to pass for one. Do you understand what I'm telling you?"

"You're saying she's changed."

The look on his face then . . . I think that was the moment he knew he'd lost her. I didn't realize until years later that it was also the moment when he knew he was going to lose me too. "Ada, I think your mama is going to need to move out of the trailer soon. She's not walking as well as she used to. Has she been complaining in the mornings?"

I didn't say anything. I didn't need to. Everyone had seen the way her knees had started giving out on her, dropping her into the midway dust without a bit of warning. She laughed it off every time, but still. Her balance was going, and there was something . . . something *wrong* about the way her legs moved, like her bones were going soft, and she was holding them straight only through force of will.

Uncle Chester sighed. "Don't you worry, Ada. We'll take care of her, and we'll take care of you. This carnival is your home. We'll always, *always* take care of you. You understand me? Always."

I said I believed him, because what else was I supposed to do? Mama was my future, written in blood and bone and scale and salt. The carnival was my home. The carnival will always be my home.

I fall asleep still holding fast to that thought, my face pressed into the pillow: the carnival will always be my home.

No matter what.

SOMEONE IS KNOCKING on my trailer door. I peel my face off the sweat-stained towel, wipe the grit from my air-dried eyes, and call, "Who is it?"

"It's your uncle. You good for company?"

I want to tell Uncle Chester no; I want to say I'm naked, that my head still hurts, that he needs to go away and not come back until I'm ready for him. But I also want to know what's going on. I sit up and say, "Come in."

Uncle Chester opens the trailer door and steps inside, looking out of place here, confined inside four walls. He's supposed to be outside on the midway, making the carnival come together, moving us toward opening. "How are you feeling?"

"Better." My head doesn't hurt anymore. That's close enough to "better" that I'm not quite lying. "Uncle Chester, what's going on? Why do those people know who Mama is, and why's that enough to worry everyone?"

"Ada . . . it may be that we never told you the full story of how your mother came to travel with us. I'm sorry about that, but we felt it was better if you didn't have to grow up knowing." He sits on the edge of my bed. I pull my feet up to make room for him. "Didn't you ever wonder why we didn't come to Alabama, with your mother being the Alabama Mermaid and the biggest draw in our sideshow? We should have been here regular as clockwork, but we stayed away. For eighteen years, we stayed away."

"No." I'm almost ashamed to admit it. I tilt my chin up and say, "I didn't even realize Alabama was a place until the year you turned us back at the Tennessee border. I thought it was made-up, like Atlantis, or England."

"Ah." Uncle Chester shakes his head. "Well, that's my fault. I should have found a way to insist you pay more attention in your studies."

"I paid as much attention as the state said I had to." Like all the carnival kids, I've been homeschooled since I was six, and every year I take and pass another standardized test full of things I'll never need to know. Not one of those tests has asked me how to assemble a Ferris wheel, or rig a game, or talk a mark out of his money.

Or say good-bye to a mother in the process of turning into something alien.

"Don't talk back," says Uncle Chester, but there's no heat in it; he's just going through the motions. "Ada, your mother was adopted, to start with. The family that took her in found her in a place called Okaloosa Island when she was a baby. It's near the very bottom of the state, where Alabama meets Florida on the Gulf of Mexico."

"Lots of people are adopted."

"Are lots of people found lying on beaches, wrapped in kelp, not even a week into the world? She was just a baby. They didn't know who her people were or where she'd come from. So they picked her up and took her home, to raise as their own." Uncle Chester shakes his head. "Townies." There's a world of scorn in that word, and it's an emotion I can understand. Carnival folk are great scavengers, and we'd never leave a baby to starve on the beach, but

we wouldn't *take* it. We'd look for its people. We'd find where it belonged.

Nothing thrives where it isn't meant to be. That's why we're so
careful with our classes, no matter how useless they are. Fail the
tests and the government takes you away from the carnival, to suffocate in airless rooms that never move. Being found by the water
didn't make Mama a sea-baby, but they should have been more
careful. They shouldn't have *taken* her.

"They did as right by her as they could; I don't want you to
think otherwise," says Uncle Chester. "She was happy, and she was
dry, mostly. She *hated* to be wet when I met her. Took showers instead of baths, wouldn't go outside when it was raining. Said the
water made her head fuzzy. That was at the start of the summer."
His gaze is far away. He isn't with me. Oh, he's still here, but it's a
here that happened eighteen years ago, before I even existed. "She
asked if we'd come back when the leaves turned, give them a proper
autumn carnival. Maybe it was wrong of me—you shouldn't
change the schedule to suit your own whims; I knew that then, and
I know it even better now—but you didn't see her. She was perfect.
Smart as a con and pretty as a midway morning. I said I'd see her
in August."

"And you did," I say. I don't want to hear the rest of this story.
It doesn't belong here, in my small dry room where mermaids are
myths and mothers, not bright-eyed teenage girls who ask friendly
carnies if they'll be coming back through town. "You came back,
and she came away with you, and everything was happy ever after."

Uncle Chester eyes me sternly. "Ada Miller. Does this look like
'happy ever after' to you?"

I don't have an answer for that.

"You're right about one thing: we did come back. I was new to
running this show, and everyone was a little slow to listen, but my
daddy taught me well, and my brothers vouched for me before they

split off with their own shows, and eventually, everyone listened. We turned around, and we came rolling back into Huntsville, looking for profits, looking for marks . . . and looking for that teen-age girl who'd smiled at me so bright when she was standing in the shadows of the midway." He sighs again. For the first time in my life, I realize that Uncle Chester is getting old. "I found her. She came to the carnival the first night we were open, and her stomach was already starting to swell up under the dress she wore, and the scales . . . the first time I saw her, I thought she was wearing body glitter. They'd been so small, and so easy to overlook. Not that time. They were the size of my pinkie nail, and they were all along her collarbone. 'I can't stay out of the water anymore, Mr. Miller, and I don't know who I am when I go under,' that's what she said. She asked if we'd take her with us. She didn't want her baby born here."

"But what about—"

"We've never talked about your father, Ada, and I know you've wanted to. I know you've guessed at who it might be."

I blush, feeling my cheeks turn hot and red. "I thought it might be one of the cousins," I say.

"I wish it were. But your mama was pregnant when she came to us, and whoever got her that way . . ." He takes a breath before he says, as slow and measured as a man pulling nails out of a board, "The Marti I met on the midway would have done al-most anything to stay out of the water, and the Marti who was waiting for me when I brought the carnival back around had gone to the water of her own free will. That tells me she had some things she wanted to forget, and she'd already figured out what the rest of us had yet to learn: to a mermaid, every body of water is the River Lethe. All she had to do was go under and she'd forget whatever happened to her. Only, once she started drowning, she couldn't stop. You pulled her out of it for a few years. She tried so hard for you. In the end, I suppose she was too tired to keep swimming."

He stops speaking. I don't say anything. I'm trying to wrap my mind around the size of what he's said, and I can't, I can't. I can't be here, thinking these things; I can't be the reason Mama chose to go into the water and forget the girl she'd been, the one who was sweet enough to pull the carnival off schedule and back to Huntsville. I *can't.*

Uncle Chester puts an arm around my shoulders. "Stop it," he says sternly. "I can see what you're thinking, and you need to stop right now. Whatever happened, it wasn't your fault. We just have to deal with what we have to deal with now."

"And what's that?" I ask bitterly.

"I think you know what that is. Someone recognized you; someone was asking after your mama." Uncle Chester shakes his head. "We have to tread careful, that's all. We don't want someone getting clever and deciding they have a right to you just because they want you."

"Why can't we leave?"

He looks at me calmly, and I know he knows I eavesdropped on them, just as surely as I know he'll never call me on it. I'm expected to do things like that. If I can't sneak around on my family, how am I supposed to sneak around on a bunch of strangers? Still, even as I'm expected to do my share of spying, he's expected to pretend I'd never stoop so low. "We can't afford it," he says, and there's something bone-dry and adult about those words. They're bleaker than they were when he said the same thing to Duncan. There it was a secret; here it's a confession. "We're at the end of the season, and we still have some bills to cover. The big coaster needs repairs, and the Haunted House has to be completely rebuilt before spring. Your mama's tank . . . the cost of the water alone is something that has to be thought of whenever we set a route. We're here because we can't afford to cross the South without stopping, and we can't afford to pull up stakes and head out. Not without making some gate. If it were almost any other reason, we'd already be rumors and dust, and damn what it would do to our reputation."

Numbers don't lie. People lie—townies, especially, to us, and us, especially, to townies—but numbers are the faith by which a carnival lives and dies. I swallow and force myself to nod. "I understand, Uncle," I say. "I'll be careful."

"Good girl." He leans forward and kisses the crown of my head, the way he's been doing since I was just a ticket stub of a child. "You've always been a good girl."

Then he stands and leaves me alone in the hot dry air of my trailer. I watch him go, and wonder if being good isn't its own punishment as much as it's supposed to be its own reward.

When I sleep, I dream of mermaids.

I wake up screaming.

I DON'T HAVE time to dwell over the next three days; they pass in a dizzy whirl of preparations, posters, and a thousand small, half-forgotten tasks that seem to build up in corners, waiting to spring. The rides are assembled and tested; the sideshows are set up, and the attractions are brought, grumbling, to take their places. Mama has the best tent, of course. She's not the show's only genuine "biological impossibility"—the modern-day way of saying "freak" without offending anybody—but she's definitely our high-ticket item, or has been, these last few years. I have to wonder how much longer that's going to last, with her slipping a little further away from human every season.

Duncan turns on the Ferris wheel while I'm screwing the safety bars into place, and he laughs at me when I shout at him. Classes are canceled for all the cousins young enough to be in

schooling, and we swarm like monkeys across the forming landscape of the midway. There's always so much to do, and we race the
bell to opening day.

When it comes, it's perfect. No place in the world does autumn like the American South, and nothing suits the autumn like
a carnival. Even the air tastes like harvest. The sun is neither too
hot nor too cold, and the humidity is low enough that I can smear
body glitter on my arms and legs and go out in a tank top and
shorts, pretending my scales are just a part of the show I'm putting
on for the townies.

And oh, the townies. They come by the dozens; they come by
the hundreds, flocking to see what wonders we have to offer. I
spend the morning shilling for the midway games, sometimes
alone, carrying teddy bears three times my size and laughing about
how easy they were to win, and sometimes with Duncan, letting
him "prove his skill" over and over. Everyone knows the booths are
rigged. Everyone plays all the same—and a certain number of people *do* get prizes, even if almost none of them actually *win* anything. We want Huntsville to remember us fondly, after all. Towns
that remember us fondly tell their friends to watch for our banners, and that can make the difference between a lean year and one
where we're rolling in the clover.

When the sun dips low on the horizon, the tenor of the carnival changes. The families pack it in, heading home with sunburns
and sticky fingers and heads full of memories. Some of the younger
cousins wait by the gate for the sole purpose of waving and cajoling
them to come back before we leave. It's a fun duty, as long as you
can endure a few nasty comments from the townie kids. The cousins aren't allowed to throw rocks at them. I've always considered
that unfair.

With the children gone, the midway belongs to the teenagers
and the sideshows belong to the adults, all of them looking for an

adventure. That's part of what makes autumn so perfect for carnivals: just the right balance between darkness and daylight.

Uncle Chester sees me heading for the Ferris wheel and waves me over, a mercenary glint in his eyes. "You up for barking?" he asks.

I'm a good barker. One of the show's best, especially when it comes to the "biological impossibilities." Maybe it's my resemblance to Mama, or maybe it's that I enjoy yelling at townies until they pony up for another ticket. "I'd need to change," I say.

"That's fine. I've got Eglantine and her girls warming up the crowd, but that just gets the people *to* the tents. I'm counting on your fine turn of phrase to get the people *in* the tents."

I smile. "Happy to."

"Good girl. Just let me call one of the cousins to walk you to your trailer."

"I don't need that," I say. "This is home, remember?" I turn and run out of the neon brilliance of the carnival, heading into the bone yard before he can tell me to stop. My trailer isn't far, and it won't take me long to change—all I'll need is a sequined jacket, some better shorts, maybe a hat—

I'm so busy thinking about the possibilities that I don't realize someone is stepping out of the shadows before they're grabbing me, arms locking around my shoulders in something that feels obscenely like affection. I take a breath to scream for help. A cloth is forced over my nose and mouth, and it's too late, the inhale has begun and I can't stop it in time.

The last thing I see before I lose consciousness is the light from the midway, reflecting off the window of my trailer like the ghost of some impossibly distant harbor.

And then even that is gone.

* * *

WHEN I WAKE up, the room is wrong.

Everything else is wrong, too—the air is too wet, the bed I'm on is too soft, and unlike the contortionists, I don't usually fall asleep with my wrists and ankles tied. But it's the room that's the worst. The walls are wood paneled, the sort of thing you see in townie houses. The ceiling is the same, and the light is too bright, the sort of electric glare you only get when you're hooked to the city power grid instead of running off an honest gennie.

My breathing must have changed. The woman from the convenience store is suddenly leaning over me. The sorrow in her eyes is gone, replaced by a bright glare that almost hurts to see. "Hello, sweetheart," she says, and touches my cheek. I jerk away from her hand as best as I can. The ropes they've used to tie me down haven't left much room.

If my movement bothers her, she doesn't show it. She just smiles, looking away from me as she calls, "She's awake." Then she focuses back on my face. She looks hungry. I don't want to be the thing that fills her up. "I'm sorry about before. We had to get you away from those people, and we didn't think you'd come willingly. They've had too long to twist your mind around."

"It only took a season with our Marti." The voice is bitter, and I don't need to look to know that it belongs to the old man from the convenience store, the one with the bad toupee and the bone-thin arms. "Look at me, girl. You've been kept away too long."

"'Those people' are my family," I say, turning to face him. "Untie me. I want to go home."

"A carnival's no place for a young girl, and you've got no business running around like a barefoot slut in the company of carnies," says the man, with perfect calm. This is the truth as he knows it. There is no room for anything else in his world. He leans forward, studying me. "You look too much like your mother" is his final verdict. "We'll have to keep an eye on you."

"Who *are* you?" I demand.

His hand lashes toward my face. I expect a blow, but it turns into a caress at the last minute, fingers light against my cheek. I shudder. "I'm your grandfather," he says. "Mind me, now, and everything will be all right. Patricia?"

"Yes, sir?" asks the woman.

"See she doesn't go anywhere. She needs to learn to hold her tongue when she's speaking with her elders." He pulls his hand away from my face and turns, leaving the room.

As soon as the door closes, I start to demand, "What is *wrong* with you people? I am not—"

The woman—Patricia—doesn't pull her blow the way the man did. Her palm strikes my cheek, rocking my head to the side. "Don't talk back," she says. There's no anger in her voice. I almost wish there was. Anger, I could understand. "We tried to save your poor lost mama's soul, and we failed her. We'll save you. We won't fail again."

Do mermaids even have souls? "I don't need saving," I say.

Patricia's smile is hard, a knife for me to impale myself against. "That's what all the lost ones say." She stands, following the man out of the room. She turns the lights out before she exits, and leaves me in the sudden and absolute dark.

No one does dark like city people. They have too much light, and they have walls that are thicker than walls need to be. It's like they cultivate the darkness even as they try to beat it back. I close my eyes and wait, holding my breath to make it easier to listen for the sound of receding footsteps. Once I'm sure that I'm alone, I start to pull against the rope that holds me to the bed.

That sort of thing only works in the movies. After what feels like an hour, I'm bleeding and sore, and the ropes are still holding me fast. Alone and afraid, I start to cry.

I'm still crying when I fall asleep.

* * *

DAWN WAKES ME, coming through windows I didn't know were there. I open my eyes and the old man is waiting for me, standing framed against the window.

"Marti was a gift from God," he says, no hesitation, no preamble. "She was a test and a challenge, and we failed her. We will not fail you."

"Let me go," I say. "This isn't legal. You can't just kidnap me."

"We're your kin. We can do whatever we like with you."

I want to protest, to tell him Mama was found, and that means they're no more my blood kin than the carnival is. Less, even, since I grew up with the carnival. I know those people. I love them. I don't know this old man at all.

But his eyes are the color of deep water, and my mother chose the water over remembering why she ran away, and I don't say anything at all.

He seems to take that as agreement, because he smiles, and nods, and says, "I knew you'd be a better girl than she was."

"Where are we?" It's barely a whisper. It's all I can manage.

"We're home. That's all you need to know."

He steps away from the window, walking toward the bed, and behind him I see the sun glinting off a sheet of water that seems to stretch on forever. It reminds me of the few glimpses I've had of the ocean, when the carnival was close and I felt daring. My heart lurches, longing and terror tangling around me in a net I can't shake off. I tear my eyes from the water, and there he is, my grandfather, standing close and looking at me.

"Are you my father?" The question is out before I can call it back.

His expression hardens. "No," he says, biting the word in half between his teeth. "That would be a sin. You'll meet your papa later, when you learn how to mind your tongue."

The other man in the store, the one who asked about Mama first. It has to be. I want to laugh. I want to cry. Of all the places we could have gone, we had to pick the shop owned by the people who'd driven my mother out of Alabama. "Please," I say. "Please, I want to go home."

"This *is* your home, Ada," he says. "The faster you come to realize that, the faster we can all make our peace with this."

He doesn't wait for me to say anything.

He just leaves.

THE SOUND OF voices raised in anger wakes me from another unintentional nap. I try to sit up, and the ropes pull me short, keeping me in place. Someone shouts. Someone else shouts back. There are words in that second cry: "They found us!"

And someone—Duncan, I think—is calling my name.

I yank against the ropes. There's no give to them. I don't have any other ideas, and so I take a breath, and yell, "Back here! I'm back here! Help! *Help!*"

The door bangs open and Patricia rushes in, a knife in her hand and the man who's probably my father close behind her. "Shut your mouth," she snarls, and grabs my wrist.

This is it: this has to be the end.

But the knife bites into the rope and not my flesh, and the man is ripping the ropes away from my ankles. I'm too weak to walk, and I don't have the chance to try: he grabs me and slings me over his shoulder, running alongside Patricia for the door.

He carries me down a hall and out another door onto what I presume is the back lawn. The sun is too bright after being inside so long, but I force my eyes to stay open. I'm looking behind myself, my head bouncing hard against his back as he runs, and I can see Duncan's pickup in front of the house, parked at a diagonal, alongside a dozen other cars from the carnival. They found me, they *found* me, and all I have to do is get away.

All I have to do.

"Come on, Christopher, run!" shouts Patricia, and the man—Christopher, my father—changes direction, moving toward the sound of water. I hear a car door slam ahead of us, and suddenly it all comes clear. They knew they might be followed; they expected to run with me. So they hid a car down by the lake, where the old man wouldn't see it, intending to carry me off and disappear.

If they reach the car, I am never going home.

We're running alongside the water now; I can smell it, can see it glittering in the sunlight. I have been good for my whole life. I have stayed dry.

Maybe that will be enough.

Christopher isn't worried about me escaping; he's bigger than I am, and I've been tied to a bed for the last day. I twist around and bite him on the ear, bringing my teeth together until cartilage crunches and hot blood fills my mouth. He bellows, the guttural cry of a wounded bull, and I fall to the ground as he loses his grip on me. The impact bruises my tailbone.

There isn't time to worry about that. I'm already up and on my feet, running as hard as I can for the mirrored surface of the lake. It's so close. I can smell the water. A voice shouts in the distance, and I twist around to see Duncan running toward us, Uncle Chester and a half dozen others close behind him. But Patricia and Christopher are with me, between me and any escape, and there isn't time, there isn't *time*.

Please, let me have stayed dry for long enough.

I jump, and the arms of the water open wide and take me home.

* * *

I DON'T KNOW how long I'm there, in the deep blue wonder of the lake. I swim deep and far, until time is something that happens to other people. Everything is twilight-dark, like the midway when the lights go down. My feet ache, and I twist until I can grab them and rub the hurt away. My clothes make it hard to swim right, and so I shrug them off and leave them floating among the waterweeds. They deck the bottom of the lake like banners deck a carnival midway, fluttering in the wind that moves within the water.

It's beautiful down here.

Fish dart past me, and crawdads with their ruddy shells. I grab them and shove them into my mouth, greedy greedy greedy, and nothing has ever tasted so good, nothing has ever been so *right*. I should have done this years ago. But I stayed away from the water. I stayed away—

Why?

I don't remember why I stayed away from the water. I stop swimming and let myself drift, trying to think. My thoughts are slippery like fish, and they squirm away from me.

Something round falls past me, sending a plume of mud rising from the bottom of the lake. I look up. There's a boat in the water, and someone on the boat is dropping things. I dive, retrieving the object. It's a baseball with a weighted bottom. The kind we use in the midway games.

Midway games . . .

I clutch the baseball to my chest and rise, my head breaking the surface beside the boat. A man is sitting there, looking down at me, waiting. His hair is black as the bottom of the lake. Mutely, I offer him the baseball.

"Thank you." He takes it. Then he takes my hand. The webs between my fingers are pale against his skin. "Do you remember who I am?"

"No."

He nods. His eyes are sad. "That's all right. I'm your Uncle Chester. Do you remember *your* name?"

"I . . ." I stop, and frown. Finally, I venture, "Ada?"

"Good girl." He reaches down, and because I trust him somehow, I reach up, and he pulls me into the boat. The sunlight glitters off my scales. It's beautiful. I giggle. He looks sadder. "Ada, I have a question for you."

"What, Uncle Chester?"

"Those people who took you . . . they won't hurt you anymore. They won't be hurting anyone anymore, and I'm sorry. I'm so sorry that I didn't keep them from hurting you."

I smile at him, uncomprehending. Maybe he'll start making sense soon. Even if he doesn't, the sun is shining, and it's nice to be here in the warm autumn daylight.

"Ada. Focus, now."

I blink, and frown. "On what? You haven't asked a question yet."

"I'm sorry." He shakes his head. "I forgot that you couldn't . . . I'm sorry. Do you want to go home?"

The baseball is rolling around the bottom of the boat. They'll be missing it back on the midway. They need the baseballs if they want to play the game, even if I'm not sure what the game is, or why anyone would want to play it. I nod solemnly. "It's autumn. Autumn's carnival time." The words feel right.

Uncle Chester finally smiles, although it doesn't take the sad away.

"Good girl," he repeats. Then he starts to row, heading for the shore.

I wonder what a midway is.

I wonder if I'll like it there.

I don't look back.

ABOUT THE AUTHORS

RACHEL CAINE is the *New York Times*, *USA Today*, and #1 internationally bestselling author of more than forty novels, including the Morganville Vampires, Weather Warden, Outcast Season, and Revivalist series. She has also been featured in many anthologies, including *Many Bloody Returns*, *Hex Appeal*, and *Shards and Ashes*. Visit her online at www.RachelCaine.com and @RachelCaine.

DELILAH S. DAWSON is the author of *Wicked As They Come* and *Wicked As She Wants*, the first two Blud novels in her steampunk paranormal romance series with Pocket Books, and two e-novellas set in the enchanting land of Sang, *The Mysterious Madam Morpho* and *The Peculiar Pets of Miss Pleasance*. She is at work on a young adult series for Simon Pulse. Delilah lives with her family in Atlanta. Visit her at www.delilahsdawson.com and @DelilahSDawson.

JENNIFER ESTEP is a *New York Times* bestselling author prowling the streets of her imagination in search of her next fantasy idea. *Spider's Bite, Web of Lies, Venom, Tangled Threads, Spider's Revenge, Thread of Death, By a Thread, Widow's Web, Deadly Sting,* and *Heart of Venom* are the other works in her red-hot Elemental Assassin urban fantasy series for Pocket Books. Jennifer also writes the Mythos Academy young adult urban fantasy series and is the author of the Bigtime paranormal romance series. Visit her at www.JenniferEstep.com and @Jennifer_Estep.

KELLY GAY is the author of the Pocket Books urban fantasy series featuring Charlie Madigan, which includes *The Better Part of Darkness, The Darkest Edge of Dawn, The Hour of Dust and Ashes,* and *Shadows Before the Sun.* She is a two-time RITA Award finalist, a 2010 finalist for Best First Book from the Southern Independent Booksellers Alliance, and a recipient of a North Carolina Arts Council fellowship grant in literature. She also writes as Kelly Keaton and can be found online at: www.KellyGay.com and @KellyHGay.

KEVIN HEARNE is the *New York Times* bestselling author of the Iron Druid Chronicles. He's a middle-aged nerd who still enjoys his comic books and old-school heavy metal. He cooks tasty omelets, hugs trees, and paints miniature army dudes. He lives with his wife, daughter, and doggies in a wee cottage. Online at www.KevinHearne.com and @KevinHearne.

MARK HENRY gleefully twists urban fantasy into extremes of comedy, filth, and horror. He also writes young adult horror and fantasy (as Daniel Marks), spends way too much time glued to the internet, and collects books obsessively (occasionally reading them). He's been a psychotherapist for children and adolescents, a Halloween-store manager, and a cafeteria janitor (gag), and has survived earthquakes, volcanoes, and typhoons to get where he is today, which is to say, in his messy office surrounded by half-empty coffee cups. He lives in the Pacific Northwest with his wife, Caroline, and three furry monsters with no regard for quality carpeting. None. Urban Fantasy for the Twisted: www.markhenry.us and @Mark_Henry.

HILLARY JACQUES is an up-late, Alaska-based author of speculative fiction. She has a love of words, travel, small-plate dining, and action movies. Sometimes her husband and son allow her to play grown-up. She has worked jobs as diverse as carnival vendor and federal contractor. She is drawn to risk management occupations because she wants to make the world a safer place. Also, because she gets paid to figure out how things can be blown up. Her urban fantasy Night Runner series is published under the pen name Regan Summers. Find her online at hillaryjacques.blogspot.com and @HillaryJacques.

JACKIE KESSLER writes about demons, angels, and the hapless humans caught between them; superheroes and the supervillains who pound those heroes into pudding; ghosts; and, in her pseudo-secret identity as YA author Jackie Morse Kessler, witches and the occasional Rider of the Apocalypse. She also had a stint in the Buffyverse, writing a short comic for Dark Horse. She lives near Albany, New York, with her Loving Husband, Precious Little Tax Deductions, and a sweetly psychotic cat. For more about Jackie, including the full bibliography of the Hell on Earth series, visit her at www.jackiekessler.com and @JackieKessler.

SEANAN McGUIRE comes from good carnival stock and had her first Ferris wheel–related injury when she was seven years old. Both she and the Ferris wheel recovered nicely and are currently in good health. She attended UC Berkeley, where she majored in folklore and mythology. These two things go a long way toward explaining why she now writes urban fantasy.

Seanan is the *New York Times* bestselling author of two ongoing urban fantasy series, the InCryptid and the October Daye series, and she also writes under the name Mira Grant. She is a founding member of the Hugo Award–winning SF Squeecast, and her short fiction has appeared all over the place, sometimes including on the floor of her bedroom. She won the John W. Campbell Award for Best New Writer in 2010 and was the first woman to be nominated for four Hugo Awards in a single year.

It is widely rumored that Seanan doesn't sleep. The rumors are pretty much true. She lives in a crumbling farmhouse, which she shares with her collections of books, horror movies, and creepy dolls, as well as her three ridiculously large blue cats. Seanan is happiest when at a carnival or in a cornfield, and she collects machetes. This tells you everything you need to know. Her online homes are www.SeananMcGuire.com and @SeananMcGuire.

Born and raised in southern Delaware, KELLY MEDING survived five years in the hustle and bustle of Northern Virginia, only to retreat back to the peace and sanity of the Eastern Shore. An avid reader and film buff, she discovered Freddy Krueger at a very young age and has since had a lifelong obsession with horror, science fiction, and fantasy, for which she blames her interest in vampires, psychic powers, superheroes, and all things paranormal.

Three Days to Dead, the first book in her Dreg City urban fantasy series, follows Evangeline Stone, a paranormal hunter who is resurrected into the body of a stranger and has only three days to solve her own murder and stop a war between the city's goblins and vampires. Additional books in the series include *As Lie the Dead*, *Another Kind of Dead*, and *Wrong Side of Dead*.

Beginning with *Trance*, Kelly's MetaWars series tells the story of the grown-up children of the world's slaughtered superheroes who receive their superpowers back after a mysterious fifteen-year absence, and who now face not only a fearful public but also a vengeful villain who wants all of them dead. Other books in the series include *Changeling*, *Tempest*, and *Chimera*. See her online at www.kellymeding.com and @KellyMeding.

ALLISON PANG is the author of the Abby Sinclair urban fantasy series from Pocket Books as well as the online graphic novel *Fox & Willow*. She spends her days in northern Virginia working as a cube grunt and her nights waiting on her kids and cats, punctuated by an occasional husbandly serenade. Sometimes she even manages to write. Mostly she just makes it up as she goes. She loves Hello Kitty, sparkly shoes, and gorgeous violinists. www.heartofthedreaming.com and @Allison_Pang.

NICOLE PEELER received an undergraduate degree in English literature from Boston University and a PhD in English literature from the University of Edinburgh, in Scotland. She's lived abroad in both Spain and the UK, and all over the United States. Currently she resides outside Pittsburgh, teaching in Seton Hill University's

MFA in Writing Popular Fiction program. When she's not in the classroom infecting young minds with her madness, she's writing the Jane True series for Orbit Books and manga for Yen Press, and taking pleasure in what means most to her: family, friends, food, and travel. www.NicolePeeler.com and @NicolePeeler.

ROB THURMAN lives in Indiana, land of cows, corn, and ravenous wild turkeys—the rural velociraptor at large. Rob is the author of the darkly gritty Cal Leandros urban fantasy series: *Nightlife, Moonshine, Madhouse, Deathwish, Roadkill, Blackout, Doubletake,* and *Slashback*; the Trickster novels *Trick of the Light* and *The Grimrose Path*; and the thriller-suspense novels *Chimera, Basilisk,* and *All Seeing Eye.*

Besides wild, ravenous turkeys, Rob has two rescue dogs (If you don't have a dog, how do you live?). Both were adopted from the pound (one on his last day on death row). They were fully grown, already house-trained, and grateful as hell. Think about it the next time you're looking for a Rover or a Fluffy. For updates, teasers, deleted scenes, social networking (the time-suck of an author's life), and various other extras, visit the author at www.RobThurman.net and @Rob_Thurman.

USA Today bestselling author JAYE WELLS writes urban fantasy novels with grave stakes and wicked humor. Raised in bookstores, she loved reading from a very young age. That gateway drug eventually led to a full-blown writing addiction. When she's not chasing the word dragon, she loves to travel, drink good bourbon, and do things that scare her so she can put them in her books. Jaye lives in Texas with her husband and son. For more about her books, go to www.jayewells.com and @JayeWells.